Reaching out she touched his shoulder. "Please, dance with me."

"I don't want a damned dance." The harshness in his voice would have sent any other young miss scurrying back to the safety of the ballroom. But not Mary. She was the most courageous creature he knew.

"What do you want?"

"To forget." He thrust a hand into her hair, cradled his palm against her cheek, moved her farther into the shadows.

"Mary," he whispered like a soft benediction. He tilted her face up and covered her mouth with his. He wasn't gentle. He was not only starving, but greedy.

She didn't protest, skimmed her hands up his arms, entangled her fingers in his hair, pressed herself closer and became as bold as he. He almost smiled.

Had she wondered, as he had, what it might be like between them?

SHE TEMPTS THE DUKE

LORRAINE HEATH

AVON

An Imprint of HarperCollins*Publishers*

This is a work of fiction. Names, characters, places, and incidents are products of the author's imagination or are used fictitiously and are not to be construed as real. Any resemblance to actual events, locales, organizations, or persons, living or dead, is entirely coincidental.

AVON BOOKS
An Imprint of HarperCollins*Publishers*
10 East 53rd Street
New York, New York 10022-5299

Copyright © 2012 by Jan Nowasky
Excerpt from *A Rogue by Any Other Name* copyright © 2012 by Sarah Trabucchi
ISBN 978-0-06-202246-2
www.avonromance.com

First Avon Books mass market printing: February 2012

Avon Trademark Reg. U.S. Pat. Off. and in Other Countries, Marca Registrada, Hecho en U.S.A.
HarperCollins® is a registered trademark of HarperCollins Publishers.

Printed in the U.S.A.

10 9 8 7 6 5 4 3 2 1

For Nancy
Who taught me the importance and
joy of making the time to dance on the beach.
You are an amazing, incredible woman, and I am so
grateful to have you in my life.

SHE TEMPTS THE
DUKE

Prologue

The Tower, Pembrook Castle, Yorkshire
Winter, 1844

Tonight was the night they would die.

At fourteen, Sebastian Easton, the eighth Duke of Keswick, wished he could be brave about it, could face death with the stoicism and courage his father would have expected and demanded of him, but he was so scared, his mouth so dry, he couldn't even work up enough spittle to fling as an insult at whoever came for him.

Within the ancient tower, no fireplace provided a homey atmosphere, but even if one had been built into the stone wall, he doubted that his uncle—Lord David Easton—would have graced them with a fire. He'd provided no blankets to ward off the bitter wind that whistled between the bars at the window. They had nothing except the clothes they'd been wearing when they were escorted to the tower for "their own protection," as soon as all the mourners had left following their father's internment in the family mausoleum that morning.

He supposed his uncle was hoping they'd catch their death, and thus spare him the bother of killing them. But as Sebastian gazed out the tiny window, he could see no moon, only stars. It was an excellent night for making three troublesome lads disappear.

"I'm hungry," Rafe muttered. "I don't see why we can't eat the mutton stew."

"Because it could be poisoned," Tristan retorted, and Sebastian heard the longing in his voice. Each of them was hungry. And although too proud to admit it—terrified.

"But why would Cook poison us? She likes me. She sneaks me extra biscuits."

"Not Cook, you dolt," Tristan snapped. "Uncle."

Their squabbling carried on, but low enough that it no longer disturbed Sebastian as he peered into what had to be the blackest night he'd ever seen. No torches flickered to indicate any guards or servants patrolling. No one was about—so certain was his uncle that they were secure here. The clocks in the manor had no doubt long ago tolled the midnight hour. He and his brothers should be asleep, but he had no intention of going quietly. He had already tested the bars. They weren't likely to give. Only a sparrow could slip between them. Their options for escape were dwindling. He never thought to be grateful that their mother had died in childbirth, but at least she wouldn't have to endure the agony of losing her children. Although perhaps Lord David would have done her in as well, to spare her the sorrow.

"But I'm freezing." Rafe's voice suddenly rose with

frustration as though he needed to make his brothers understand how miserable he truly was, as though they weren't all suffering the same discomforts. It wasn't his fault he wasn't made of sturdier stuff. He was only ten, and as the youngest he'd been coddled.

"If you don't stop whining, I'll give you something to truly whine about—a bloody nose," Tristan threatened.

"Leave him be, Tristan," Sebastian ordered. He was a mere twenty-two minutes older than his twin, but with those twenty-two minutes had come power, rank, and responsibility. He was worried he'd be unable to live up to all three, that he'd disappoint his father from the grave.

"But his whining grates."

"You both need to be quiet, so I can think."

He heard a shuffling, and then Tristan was standing beside him. They had no candles, no lanterns, no lamps. But he didn't need light to see Tristan clearly in his mind. He looked exactly like Sebastian. Tall for his age, with unruly black hair that constantly fell into his pale blue eyes. Ghost eyes, the gypsies called them. Easton eyes, his father had assured them. Like his own. And their damned uncle's.

Lord David had brought their father—his head bashed in—back to Pembrook, their ancestral home, after the riding accident. He claimed their father had tumbled off his horse. But he was an exceedingly excellent rider. He'd have never become unseated. Not without someone arranging the unseating, although Sebastian thought it more likely that he'd dismounted to attend to something, and then someone had come up behind him and whacked him. Hard. And he was fairly certain who that someone had been.

"So what's your grand scheme for getting us out of

here?" Tristan asked quietly. "I won't tell. Even if he puts me on the rack in the dungeon."

The dungeon housed all manner of torture devices, remnants from when the first Duke of Keswick had served Henry VIII and done some of his more unpleasant bidding. It seemed a penchant for bloodthirstiness ran in the family. He couldn't shake off the sense that his uncle wanted what his father had possessed—and that meant three more murders.

"Do you even have a plan?" Tristan asked.

"You and I will jump whoever comes through the door next. You go low, cut him off at the knees. I'll go high." Take the greater risk for if that someone had a weapon, instinct would have him striking out at what he'd be able to see more clearly: the rabid boy aiming to smack him in the nose.

"Then what?"

"We saddle up our horses and make a dash for it."

"I'm for staying and dealing with Uncle now. We kill him. Right quick. We're done."

"Are you so daft, Tristan, that you can't figure it out? The fact that we're here means we have no allies."

"We must have some. You're the rightful heir."

"But who? Who do we trust? No, our best course of action for now is to run, then split up. We'll return when we're men. Reclaim what is ours."

"What proof will we have that we are who we say we are?"

"How many twin sons with our shade of eyes do you think there are?" And he wore his father's ring on a chain about his neck. His finger was not yet large enough to provide it with a secure home. But one day . . .

"I don't agr—" Tristan began.

"Shh!"

Sebastian heard a distant scuffing, scraping. It was getting louder, nearer.

"Someone's coming." Even in the dark, he unerringly found his brother's slender shoulder, gave it a squeeze. They wouldn't have strength on their side. Their best weapons would be surprise and agility. "Don't hesitate. Be quick and sure. Make it count."

He heard Tristan swallow, felt his twin's body move with his forceful nod.

"Rafe, to the far corner," Sebastian ordered.

"Why?"

"No questions. Do it, Brother," he demanded harshly. Rafe was too young to be of any great assistance; besides it was Sebastian's duty to protect him.

He scampered quickly to the door, was aware of Tristan following in his wake. The only furniture to be avoided was the small table and two stools in the center of the room. Someplace was needed for the signing of confessions, he thought wryly.

Holding his breath, he pressed himself flat against the wall, felt the stone biting into him. He heard the key go into the lock, scrape as it turned. The door opened, light spilled in. He rushed forward—

The girl leaped on him, securing her legs around his waist, tightening her arms around his neck. Her tears cooled against his cheek. "You're alive," she croaked. "I was so scared I'd be too late!"

Holding her close, he could feel her trembling. A lantern on the floor in the hallway cast a pale glow into the room. She must have brought it and abandoned it there as she dug the key into the door. "Shh, Mary," he urged tenderly, "keep your voice down. Whatever are you doing here?"

Lady Mary Wynne-Jones, daughter to their neighbor the Earl of Winslow, hiccupped, sniffled, and buried her face harder against his shoulder. "I was looking for you. Heard him . . . heard him say to kill you."

"Heard whom?"

"Your uncle."

"Damned blighter," Tristan growled. "I knew it!"

"Quiet," Sebastian ordered. As quickly, but gently, as possible, he extricated Mary from her perch. She was all legs and arms, light as a feather. When she was finally standing again, he took hold of her shoulders and stared into her green eyes. Two years younger than Sebastian, she was a wild one and often snuck away from her father's estate to visit with him. Without a chaperone. They would pretend to be adventurers and would explore various ruins. The nearby broken-down abbey was their favorite haunt. Last week she boldly kissed him there. He knew if his father found out that he kissed her back, he would be in trouble. He wasn't supposed to kiss a lord's daughter unless he intended to marry her. His father had told him that often enough.

But Mary wasn't just a lord's daughter. She was his best mate. He'd taught her to move about stealthily. At many things, she was as skilled as a boy. He loved that about her. She wasn't afraid of anything. Or almost anything. He could see now that she was as pale as a ghost, her myriad freckles standing out in stark relief. "Who did he tell?"

"I didn't see," she said on a rush. "I dashed up to your room and when you weren't there, I thought to look here."

"Is your father with you?"

She shook her head forcefully. "I rode over alone. Knew you'd be sad about your own father dying. I wanted to be with you—like you were with me when my mother went to heaven." She'd been ten when her mother died of the fever. That night he'd ridden over, climbed the tree outside her bedroom window, and slipped into her bedchamber, into her bed. And held her while she cried and grieved. "I was sneaking about searching for you. That's when I heard what I did."

"We've got to hurry then. Tristan, stay close to Rafe."

"I don't need watching," Rafe objected.

"Shut your mouth," Tristan snarled. "It's not a game. Uncle means to kill us."

"Why?"

"Because we're all that stand between him and everything. Now come on."

Sebastian grabbed Mary's hand and stepped out of the room. Reaching down, she picked up the lantern and they rushed down the steps. He heard his brothers following behind them. At the bottom, the guard was sprawled on the floor, a large branch abandoned beside him.

"I crept up behind him and smashed him in the head," Mary said.

"Well done, Mary."

She beamed, her clover-green eyes sparkling for only a moment before the worry settled back in. They didn't dare tarry here. Still gripping her hand, he raced outside. Her legs were long enough to keep up with him. She was as graceful as a filly and almost as fast. They had been friends for as long as Sebastian could remember. He'd never seen anyone with hair as vibrant a red as hers. It was braided now and tapping rhythmically against her back as they ran for the stables.

Once there, he and his brothers each saddled a horse.

Mary's horse was tethered nearby. He boosted her onto it, mounted his own.

"I'll catch up to you, Tristan. I'm seeing Mary safely home first."

"No. We stay together as long as we can."

"Right then. Let's ride like the wind."

Mary's lantern guided them, causing the shadows to ebb and flow with their progress. They couldn't travel too fast; they didn't want their horses tumbling. But still there was an urgency that snaked along Sebastian's skin. They were halfway across their property when he had an undeniable urge to stop.

"Hold up one minute," he shouted.

Everyone did as he ordered. He was, after all, the duke. He dismounted and moved to where Mary's lantern shed a bit of light. "Mary, can I have your hair ribbon?"

She handed it over without question. That was so like her. They trusted each other implicitly. Pulling out the handkerchief that his father assured him a gentleman always carried, he knelt down.

"Sebastian, what the hell are you doing?" Tristan asked. "We don't have time for nonsense. We've got to go."

But he couldn't leave without taking a bit of home with him. He clawed, scraped, and scooped up a handful of the rich soil over which seven previous dukes, several kings, and queens had galloped their horses. He enfolded it in the linen, secured it with Mary's ribbon, and stuffed it into his pocket. He remounted and they were off once again.

The next time they brought their horses to a halt, they were outside her father's stables. Sebastian vaulted off his horse and approached Mary's.

"Come inside. My father can help you," Mary insisted.

"It'll be too dangerous for you and your family." *And probably for us as well.*

"I'll go with you then."

"No, you can't go where we're going."

"Where are you going?"

"If you don't know, you can't say." *And no one can torture it out of you.* Reaching up he wrapped his hands around her narrow waist and brought her down to the ground.

She clutched his arms. "Don't leave me, Sebastian. Take me with you."

"I'm Keswick now. And I can't take you with me, but I promise you that I shall return. Ten years, on this night, at the abbey ruins." Bending down he gave her a kiss, brushing his lips so quickly and lightly over hers that it resembled little more than touching a butterfly's wings as it took flight. "Thank you, Mary. I'll never forget what you did for my brothers and me."

"You must be careful."

"Always," he said with a confidence that belied his youth—and his fear. He had no idea what the future would hold.

"Send me word when you're safe," she said, and he realized she didn't understand the true peril that lurked.

"No matter what happens, Mary, never tell anyone what you heard or what you did. It has to remain a secret, for all our sakes."

"I promise."

He felt like there was more he should say but he wasn't quite certain what it was. Climbing back into the saddle, he urged his horse into a gallop, his brothers' horses thundering alongside him, all of them leaving Mary behind.

As they rode into the night, into the darkness, into the unknown, he vowed that he would one day return to Pembrook to claim all that belonged to him. Nothing mattered more than that.

It was a vow that would shape the man he was to become.

Chapter 1

London
July, 1856

If curiosity killed the cat, then Lady Mary Wynne-Jones expected that she'd be dead before the night was done. After all, it was curiosity that had lured her to Lady Lucretia Easton's ball. Mary knew very little of the woman except that she had married Lord David Easton in the spring. Hence the niggling seed that had sprouted Mary's curiosity and resulted in her presently occupying a corner in the ballroom with her cousin Alicia and two other young ladies. It was the perfect spot for observing the comings and goings—to see and be seen.

Lord and Lady Wickam!

Mary barely paid attention as the arriving guests were announced. She was far more interested in her host and hostess, in deciphering what they were up to, how they were received by Society. She'd not seen Lord David in years. Shortly after his nephews disappeared, he'd abandoned Pembrook. She supposed he had taken up residence at one of the other estates. Although perhaps he lived in London year-round. This residence had certainly not been neglected. It glittered and sparkled, as though well cared for.

Tonight the many guests glittered and sparkled as well. One would not expect the second son of a duke to garner such interest, but then Lord David had a wretched past that he touted for all it was worth. His older brother's devastating accident. His three nephews' unexplained disappearance. Did they run off? Were they abducted for ransom, only to have been killed? Or were they kidnapped for some nefarious purpose? Put on a ship perhaps? Sold into slavery somewhere? No one knew.

They had become the stuff of legends—the lost lords of Pembrook.

"Have you ever known a more dull or tedious ball?" Lady Alicia bemoaned in her usual dramatic fashion as though she'd just declared that the world as they knew it would soon come to a dreadful end.

Mary gave her cousin a wry smile. Her hair was a burnished copper, more tame than Mary's fiery red. Her eyes, however, were the same green. But then their mothers were sisters, and it seemed no female on that side of the family had escaped green eyes. "I can't imagine that Lord David is known for being entertaining. After all, how much fun can a man with his misfortunes be?"

Her sarcasm earned a sharp look from her cousin, but was hardly noticed by the other two ladies who had joined them a few moments earlier. They were too busy searching the crowd for masculine prey.

"He's never entertained before," Lady Hermione said distractedly, patting the few blond curls that dangled from her upswept hair and lay lightly against her neck. This was her second Season and she was well acquainted with much that went on, while Mary and her cousin were at a disadvantage, for this summer was their first in London since they'd reached an age to be included in such festivities.

"But then he's never been married before," Lady Victoria mused, her arched brow as black as a raven's wing. "I heard from my mother who heard it from her cousin that Lady Lucretia married him because he expects to be duke before Season's end, and she rather fancies the title of duchess. The possibility has garnered everyone's attention. No one wants to be out of favor with a duke. Hence, the absurd number of guests."

Mary's father had told her that Lord David had petitioned the Court of Chancery, pressing his claim to the title since his nephews had yet to be found. It had been a little over a year since the youngest had reached his majority. The failure of even one to appear and claim the title could only mean one thing: they were all well and truly dead.

It was an argument Mary could hardly fault, no matter how much it pained her to accept the harsh reality. During all the passing years, she'd received not a single word from any of them. Although it was quite possible that if she had, her father might have destroyed it.

She'd broken her promise to Sebastian. That night she'd run straightaway to her father and explained what she witnessed and how she helped the boys escape. She'd expected him to take the matter in hand and confront his neighbor. Instead, she'd been disappointed to learn that her father feared even his own shadow. He sent her to a convent where she could contemplate the merits of causing mischief. He didn't believe that in this day and time, someone would seek to gain a title by illicit means. "It simply isn't done," her father declared.

When she was finally allowed to return to Willow Hall this spring, she had gone to the old abbey ruins and, with the winds howling, wept. She knew why Sebastian chose it as the spot where they would reunite. It was a special, magical place. She had boldly kissed him there, then worried that her father would discover what she had done and banish her from her home for her brazen behavior. She'd been all of twelve, but she knew she'd never forget the press of his lips against hers—how sweet and terrifying it had been.

"A sad thing, his nephews being devoured by wolves," Lady Alicia said. Their partial remains found near the abbey ruins was one of the rumors regarding their demise that floated about, and Alicia always chose the dramatic over the ordinary. That story of their ghastly deaths became the seed for cautionary tales—to keep wayward lads from desiring midnight adventures. Another report asserted that they died of fever. But in both cases no bodies were ever produced. From time to time over the years, someone alleged a sighting—in London, at the seaside, in a forest—but no proof was forthcoming. Their true fate remained a mystery.

Mary was certain, however, that they had indeed perished somewhere along the way during the long years of their absence. Otherwise, they would have returned as promised. Sebastian would have come to her. Nothing would have stopped him from keeping his vow. Nothing except death. She'd lost track of how many nights she mourned their passing, only to awaken the next morning convinced that somewhere they still lived. Any number of reasons could have delayed their arrival. But with each passing year, it seemed less likely that they would return, that any of them had survived to manhood.

Out of the corner of her eye, she spotted Lord David heading down a distant hallway. The toad cut a fine figure, dressed in his finery, and that grated terribly on her nerves. He should be bloated and hideous. Hunchbacked even. Like Richard III who, in order to gain the throne, had locked his nephews in the Tower of London. The two were not so very different.

It had taken everything within her not to cast up her accounts when earlier in the evening, he smiled at her in passing. His eyes possessed a cunning that only she seemed capable of recognizing. Everyone else fawned over him, enamored of his charm. At least he possessed the good sense not to take her gloved hand and press a kiss to it, as he'd done to her aunt upon their arrival. If he had, Mary surely would have had no control over her foot and he'd have found it connecting with his shin.

Lord and Lady Westcliffe!

Mary wondered if perhaps she and Alicia should take their leave. She was no longer certain what she'd thought to accomplish by coming here. So far, all she'd managed was to upset her digestion whenever she thought of how Lord David had come to have this residence and that very soon, if his petition was granted, he would acquire so much more. He would acquire everything.

She couldn't let that happen. She would write a letter to the Court of Chancery and explain what he'd done, what she heard, what had happened that night when the lads had disappeared. Would her words be believed or would they be considered simply another fanciful tale to add to the many that surrounded the mystery of the Pembrook lords?

Her musings were interrupted when two gentlemen came to claim dances with Ladies Hermione and Victoria. Once the couples had wandered onto the dance floor, Alicia said, "I can't believe you'll be married at the end of the month."

Nor could Mary. During the first ball she had caught the fancy of Viscount Fitzwilliam. A devoted courtship involving an abundance of flowers, promenades in the park, and long afternoons in the parlor had followed. They shared the same interests in music, literature, and art. Conversation was always pleasant, and she wasn't certain why she sometimes felt that it should hold a bit more fire. Apparently she'd left her hellion days behind.

"I feel a tad guilty about it. It was supposed to be *your* Season," Mary reminded her cousin. Her own father had denied her a Season, left her languishing at the convent. It was only when her aunt—Alicia's mother—had taken matters in hand and insisted that she "be released from exile" and share the Season with Alicia that Mary had been given her first taste of the glitz and glamour that could be London. She fell in love with it.

Mr. Charles Godwin!

"It's not yet over. I could still find my true love," Alicia told her with an air of confidence that indicated she truly hadn't given up hope.

Mary felt another prickle of guilt because she wasn't certain she could claim that Fitzwilliam was her *true* love. Certainly she held a fondness for him. His manners and dress were impeccable. She suspected that if Sebastian had lived, he'd have very much resembled him: respectful, charming, occasionally witty. She also rather liked his parents—the Marquess and Marchioness of Glenchester. They appeared to think well of her. They even approved of her time in the convent—thought it had taught her mercy and grace. What it had taught her was to never trust her father with a secret.

"Any gentleman would be fortunate to have you," Mary assured Alicia.

"You're much too generous with your praise. And speaking of fortunate men, there's yours now."

Turning her attention in the direction Alicia indicated, Mary watched her betrothed make his way toward her. Viscount Fitzwilliam was a few years her senior, which gave him an air of maturity and sophistication that some of the younger lords lacked. Tall and slender, fair of complexion and quick to smile, he graced her with one of his winning smiles now. Her father heartily approved of the match, even if the estate Fitzwilliam would eventually inherit was in Cornwall, far from her home in Yorkshire.

Lord and Lady Raybourne!

Lord Fitzwilliam stopped before her, his brown-eyed gaze wandering over her, filling with appreciation. "Don't you look lovely, Lady Mary."

While she had been here most of the evening, he arrived only a short while ago and she'd noticed one person after another capturing his attention as he made his way around the ballroom. She smiled softly. "Thank you, my lord."

He turned his head slightly. "And you as well, Lady Alicia."

"You're too kind, my lord."

"Hardly, I merely speak the truth." He gave his attention back to Mary. "Did you save the requisite dance for me?"

The seventh. He was a suspicious sort, but it only endeared him to her all the more. Seven was his lucky number. He had danced the seventh dance with her during the first ball of the Season when he had become—as he was fond of reminding her—entranced by her beauty and spirit.

"I have indeed."

"Splendid. If you'll excuse us, Lady Alicia?"

"Of course, my lord."

Mary disliked leaving her cousin standing alone, wasn't certain why gentlemen weren't flocking to her side. Fitzwilliam placed his hand on the small of Mary's back and guided her toward the dance floor. "Will you dance with her next?" she asked him.

"Who?"

"Lady Alicia, my cousin."

"If it would please you."

"It would immensely."

"Perhaps it would even make you a bit jealous?" he asked, a teasing glint in his brown eyes.

"It would, but mostly it would make me happy. I don't understand why more gentlemen aren't giving her attention."

"Because she pales when compared with you."

A blush warmed her cheeks. She felt a bit selfish for hoping the ease with which he gave compliments would continue after they were married. The lilting chords of a waltz wafted through the room as he took her into his arms. His touch was both gentle and kind. It held no promise of passion or adventure, but then she'd left those childish things behind. Many considered her on the shelf, yet here she was with an admirer when she'd never thought to have one after her years of isolation in the nunnery.

It had not helped that she lived her younger days in fear that Lord David would come for her as he'd come for his nephews. She knew his secrets, his sins. She knew she was prone to rash decisions, not always giving proper thought to things, but if she hadn't trusted her instincts that night—

His Grace, the Duke of Keswick!

The odd, unexpected words startled her.

"Good God!" Fitzwilliam exclaimed, slowing their momentum. "Is that what this affair is about? Has his petition already been granted? Trust Lord David to surprise us all and make quite the show of it."

She couldn't stand the thought of what Fitzwilliam was intimating. If Lord David now held the titles, then the brothers had been declared dead. She craned her neck—

Lord Tristan Easton!

Her knees weakened.

Lord Rafe Easton!

Her world narrowed, blackened at the edges, threatened to consume her. With her heart thundering, she spun around to gaze at the stairs that led down to the ballroom. The music was drifting into silence. Couples stopped dancing. Low murmurings began, only to increase in volume as people rudely whispered and pointed. Several ladies gasped. Out of the corner of her eye, she saw one swoon into her husband's arms.

Three towering men with unfashionably long hair as black as midnight stood on the landing. Their well-tailored clothing did little to disguise the savagery in their faces as their icy blue gazes roamed over the crowd, alighting briefly on one person after another before quickly moving on. With an obvious disdain, they implied that all were beneath them. One held a pistol toward the steward—no doubt the very reason that the man had announced the name that his employer soon hoped to possess.

She realized Rafe was the one wielding the weapon. While he was tall, he had not achieved his brothers' height. On the far side stood Tristan. She never had any trouble distinguishing him from his twin, because his cocky smile—in evidence now—was slightly crooked, always tipped up a bit more on the right.

Sebastian's always went up higher on the left. Or at least it used to. Presently he was not smiling. Based on the hideous scars marring that side of his face, she wasn't certain he could smile. A black patch covered his eye. Dear God in heaven, whatever had happened to him?

Mary took a step forward, only to have Fitzwilliam place a restraining hand on her arm. "Easy there, dear girl," he whispered. "You don't know what dangers await."

She suspected a good many. The lords of Pembrook had arisen from the dead.

And she could not help but believe that tonight's boring ball was about to become the most memorable of the Season.

Chapter 2

"**I** do believe we've managed to gain their attention," Tristan said with the confidence of a man who not only commanded men, but the sea.

In spite of all he'd suffered, it was also quite apparent he'd not lost his sense of humor. Sebastian couldn't say the same for himself. But then he'd lost a good deal more at the battle of Balaclava in the Crimea. His good looks. His eye. And portions of himself that were not so easily identifiable.

The physicians said he should have died from his wounds. But he was a man possessed by the need for retribution. So he'd refused to allow his heart to stop beating. Clutching the threadbare handkerchief that contained the soil he'd scooped up before leaving, filling his nostrils with its rich fragrance, he endured the pain and the agony. He survived, because to do less was unthinkable.

He *was* the Duke of Keswick. The rightful heir to

Pembrook and five other estates, as well as three other titles. And by God, he was here to claim what was due him.

His uncle—everyone who had abandoned three lads—was on the verge of discovering that they had each become a man to be reckoned with. Even Sebastian had been astonished to discover the men his brothers had become. They rivaled him in determination and purpose. No spoiled gentlemen were they. In no way were they typical of second and third sons who gladly welcomed an allowance and sought only pleasure. He could not have been prouder or more at ease to have them at his side, watching his back, prepared to battle at his front.

He gave his gaze freedom to roam over the crowd, searching for his vile uncle. Sebastian's father had introduced him to numerous lords when they hosted country parties, but he'd been more interested in running off to play Waterloo with their sons. Now these sons were grown and certainly a good many of them were here, but identifying them was not an easy task when he'd not seen them in years.

"See here, now," an older gentleman admonished, stepping forward. "You do not come into a man's home, disrupting an affair, and waving a pistol about."

Two more could have been waved about. He and his brothers were all armed, but only Rafe had drawn his pistol when the steward—a man they did not know—had refused to announce Sebastian as he'd asked because they had no invitation. It seemed Rafe had developed a knack for impatience over the years.

"It is *my* home," Sebastian proclaimed, "and I shall come into it any way I damned well please."

The gentleman appeared taken aback, and Sebastian regretted the harsh tone, but he couldn't apologize without coming across as weak, and his most challenging moments still awaited him. Where the deuce was his uncle? The coward had no doubt slipped out through a back door, was at this very moment possibly scurrying away like the vermin he was.

A young woman, short of stature but with determination in the mulish set of her mouth, climbed the steps, halting halfway up. Her gown was a violet satin. A choker of pearls wound about her throat. Diamond and pearl combs adorned her blond hair. Her figure was ample, and he suspected she feasted on far too much chocolate. He saw doubt flicker in her eyes before she jerked up her chin. "I am Lady Lucretia Easton, wife to Lord David, soon to be the Duchess of Keswick—"

"No, madam, I regret to inform you that you are not destined to be a duchess. And if my uncle married you under those pretenses, may he go to the devil."

Her mouth fell open, her eyes widened, and she blinked repeatedly. He was surprised no one came to her rescue. Perhaps they were equally stunned, or more likely they simply wished to see how things would play out. He suspected he was providing far more entertainment than one might find on Drury Lane, and that was unfortunate, but his success hinged on making his case before witnesses.

She finally pursed her lips and narrowed her eyes as though she thought by doing so that she could cause him to wilt. But wilting had never appealed to him. "I don't know who you are, sir, but—"

"I am the Duke of Keswick."

"That's not possible."

"I assure you, madam, it is."

"You speak falsehoods." She caught the eye of a footman and clapped her hands twice. "Remove this pretender and his rapscallion friends immediately."

"He speaks true! He is the Duke of Keswick!" a feminine voice rang out, and suddenly a tall slender woman was wending her way through the massive crowd. She reached the stairs and tripped lightly up the steps, her pink satin slippers peering out from beneath her pale pink ball gown. She stopped a short distance from him and grabbed the railing as though she needed to support herself, because she was in danger of swooning now that she was near enough to get a good look at what remained of him.

He knew what she saw. What they all saw. Mutilated flesh, thick scars that trailed down his cheek, over his jaw, along his neck, until they disappeared beneath his collar.

And just as she saw him more clearly, so he saw her.

Her hair was a familiar crimson. A memory washed over him, of riding over the land, chasing after a girl who could never elude him because her hair prevented her from blending in with the countryside. Her presence had given all that surrounded them a vibrancy that matched her spirit, a richness that rivaled the sun.

But this woman standing before him could not be who he thought. Where the deuce were her freckles? The girl he'd known had been covered in a constellation that he mapped out whenever she was still enough for him to study her. He knew them as well as he knew the stars in the night sky. And she'd been as flat as a plank of wood. This woman had curves that invited a man to touch and linger. Her throat and shoulders were bared, and he imagined the silky smoothness of them. He spied one freckle just above the swell of a breast and he wondered how the sun had come to kiss her there. His mouth went dry. She could not possibly be—

"Mary?" he croaked.

She smiled in answer, just a soft tilting up of her lips. Familiarity fed a ridiculous notion to speak with her first, to ask how she was, then go in search of his uncle.

But then he saw the pity in her lovely green eyes, the tears welling. His gut clenched. He had both dreaded and anticipated this moment of seeing her again. And a pain far worse than anything he'd endured on the battlefield pierced his heart.

He knew what he'd become. Had smashed the mirror that had first revealed it to him. He would have spared her the horror of it, but to expose his uncle he had to expose himself. Just this once, and then he would be done with it.

"Don't," he commanded, barely moving his lips, the force of the word not carrying beyond her ears.

Blinking back her tears, setting her jaw in a familiar determined manner, she gave a quick nod and squared those distracting bared shoulders. "Your uncle knew only that you disappeared. No one knew where you'd gone, what your fates had been. Speculation abounded that you'd died. Wolves, illness, murder. So many stories. No one knew which was true. But after all this time, the certainty was that you were dead."

It was Tristan who laughed darkly, without humor. "Well, then it seems that word of our demise was a bit premature, doesn't it?"

Mary nodded. "For which we're all grateful."

Sebastian doubted that his uncle would be as pleased. He slid his gaze over to the party's hostess. She, too, was gripping the banister now, reminding him of a baby bird that had suddenly found itself shoved out of the nest before it was ready to test its wings. He couldn't risk taking pity on her, of showing even a hint of weakness. She was the devil's plaything, and while she might be innocent, she could still prove very dangerous. "Where is he, madam? Where is your husband?"

She appeared dazed, her brow deeply furrowed. "Playing cards most likely."

"Send someone to fetch him."

From a well of indignation deep inside her, she regained her equilibrium, drew herself up to her full height, and matched him stare for stare. "See here! I am not to be ordered about in my own house."

"It is mine," he ground out, descending two steps. She released an ear-splitting screech and, with hands fluttering, raced down the stairs. "Lord David! Lord David!"

Sebastian went down two more steps, heard the echo of his brothers' boots hitting the marble after his. "I am the true Duke of Keswick. My brothers and I are reclaiming what was stolen from us."

"You look like your father," a gentleman announced.

Sebastian almost laughed. "I no longer do, but Tristan does. Remarkably so. As my twin, he will serve as proof enough that we are who we claim to be. And I wear our father's signet ring."

He thought the ballroom had been quiet, but if at all possible a heavier silence descended, with the solemnity of a funeral. He had not expected jubilant rejoicing but he'd hoped for a bit more acceptance. He could feel the stares, sense the speculation. He did not like airing dirty laundry before strangers, had considered confronting his uncle in the privacy of his library, but the man had earned a public flogging. This was as close to one as Sebastian could deliver.

"What the devil is going on here?"

And at long last, there he was: the usurper. Blustering and lumbering his way through the crowd. By Sebastian's estimation at least three hundred people were in attendance. When his uncle reached the stairs and looked up, he came to a staggering stop. Sebastian knew he shouldn't have been, but he was surprised by the man's appearance. He didn't know why he had expected him to remain the same when no one else had. His uncle had never been particularly tall, but he was stockier than he'd been in his youth. Obviously he enjoyed the fruits he'd stolen. Rings adorned thick well-manicured fingers. His hair was awash in white. His nose was pointing too high in the air, a man who thought he was owed things he was not.

"Greetings, Uncle."

Lord David shook his head in obvious disbelief before glancing around with wide eyes, perhaps searching for a hole in the floor through which he could conveniently drop. "My nephews are dead."

Sebastian did laugh then, although it more closely resembled a bark. He couldn't remember the last time he'd truly laughed, but he knew it had been before his father died. "Believing your own lies?"

"I don't know who you are—"

Sebastian was down the stairs so quickly that his uncle barely had time to take two steps back before Sebastian's hand was wrapped firmly around his throat. He heard gasps, a muffled cry, a few clearing throats, and harrumphs, but no one came forward to challenge him. He could only imagine the pending threat that his misshapen face conveyed to anyone who might consider interfering. It would not be tolerated. Not by him, and not by his brothers. He suspected they were silently issuing warnings with their stances. By God, but it seemed each of them had learned to convey menace without bothering with the nuisance of words. A talent that came in handy when confronting one's enemies— and there could be no doubt that Lord David Easton was enemy to one and all.

When Sebastian was a lad, he'd thought his uncle to be a towering man, fearsome and invincible, but now Sebastian loomed over him. And he'd not lived a life of ease. His muscles were firm, his body hardened by the challenges of war. He could take a man down with a sword, rifle, or pistol. He could destroy a man with his bare hands if need be. The temptation to do so with this bit of excrement was almost overwhelming.

"You know damned well who I am," Sebastian said evenly, although his voice was seething with a fury that threatened to bubble past the surface. He'd known it would be difficult to hold his emotions in check, to act a gentleman rather than a barbarian, but he was rapidly reaching the end of his tether. He should have had a life of few worries, attending schools, being educated in the ways of a future duke.

Instead he'd had hardship, blood, and horror. His brothers had experienced much of the same. He'd been born to protect them, to care for them, and all he'd managed was to lead them through the gates into hell. He'd let them down. His father would have been sorely disappointed in him, but no more so than he was in himself.

"We can go before the Court of Chancery if you wish, but one way or another I will hold the titles that my father passed down to me. You can skulk away quietly or you can fight me on it. But let me warn you that I was a captain in Her Majesty's army. When I have an objective, nothing will sway me from reaching it. Tristan has sailed the seas. You're nothing to him. While Rafe . . . well, let's just say that he knows a dark side to London that terrifies even me."

His uncle dug his fingers into Sebastian's wrist and gagged. His eyes bugged.

"You have one day to pack up your things and leave. We were given much less time to run from Pembrook with our lives. Take one item that does not belong to you, and Tristan will deal with you the way he saw thieves dealt with in the Far East. He'll slice off your hands."

"And be glad to do it," Tristan announced laconically, as though the task would involve little more effort than swatting a fly.

His uncle's eyes rolled upward. Another gag. A huff. A gurgle.

Sebastian knew he should release his hold, but he seemed incapable of letting go. This man had been responsible for the last twelve years of misery. In their absence he'd lived the life of luxury that they should have. From them, he'd stolen. In all likelihood he'd killed. He didn't deserve to draw in breath. He didn't deserve—

On his shoulder, Sebastian felt a touch as light as a butterfly's passing, but it communicated an urgency, caught his attention as shouts and orders would not have.

"You're killing him," Mary said quietly. "After all you've endured, surely you don't want to find yourself led to the gallows now."

No, but suddenly what he was doing didn't bring enough satisfaction with it. He'd dreamed of this moment, anticipated it, and yet it was sadly lacking. His uncle was not a worthy adversary. He was little more than pond scum. Sebastian flung back his uncle, watched his arms windmill madly before he landed with a hard thud on the floor, sprawled out like an over-turned tortoise. "Sunrise, day after tomorrow, I expect you to be gone, Uncle. Then I never want to set eyes on you again. The same holds true for my brothers. Our compassion has reached the limits of its tether. Challenge us on this and you shall see hell unleashed."

Glancing around, he saw expressions of horror, confusion, disbelief. And the pity again—when his gaze fell on Mary. The pity made him feel like a vile beast, because he was no longer certain that it was his marred features she took pity on. He feared it was his actions, his words. He'd hardly behaved as a gentleman. He should have called his uncle out, he supposed, no matter how it might have been frowned upon. Although judging by the reaction of the guests, his attempt at ret-ribution was being met with equal disfavor. Not that he gave a bloody damn.

His uncle deserved to rot in the nearest cesspool.

Sebastian did little more than give a brisk nod toward Mary before marching up the steps. He strode from the residence hoping he had made it perfectly clear that the Duke of Keswick was at long last home.

Unfortunately the harder task still lay before him: convincing himself.

Chapter 3

What followed was total and complete madness.

As soon as the brothers disappeared through the doorway a crescendo of objections, protestations, speculations, and assurances rose to a deafening knell. It was all a person could do to think, much less converse.

Mary stood clutching the banister, because it was the only way to prevent herself from barreling up the stairs after them. What a disaster that would be. Her reputation would no doubt be questioned, possibly destroyed. A lady didn't go gallivanting after a retreating gentleman, especially one who had behaved as anything but a gentleman, and yet she had so many questions. Where had they been all these years? What had delayed their return until now? What had happened to them while they were away?

They had grown to manhood, obviously, but it had not been a pleasant journey. With wintry eyes that had sent a chill through her bones, they had each looked so harsh, unforgiving. Not that she blamed them. They'd suffered the worst sort of betrayal. Their own blood had wished them harm, had sought to murder them.

"I thought they were dead," Lord David was blubbering now as one of the lords questioned him regarding how all this could have happened. "I've not had a word from them in all these years. I've served as steward to the duke's holdings, because my brother would have wanted it. Their distrust and accusations are uncalled for."

No, they're not, she had an urge to shout. *You locked them in the tower. Why do that if your purpose was not to kill them?*

Lord David was sweating profusely, fighting for breath, the whites of his eyes clearly visible as he searched frantically around him at those who had once expected him to rise in their ranks.

"I'm telling you," he ranted on as though questions had been asked when in truth people were only staring at him. "I'd have not petitioned to gain the title if I'd known they were alive. I did all in my power to find them. They did not wish to be found. Even you all thought they were dead. You've heard the rumors. Wolves, disease, murder. How was I to know the truth? Did you know? Did any of you know?"

Then his wild gaze fell on Mary, and she saw hatred there, directed at her as though he suspected, as though he knew what she'd done. A shiver of dread coursed through her, but she angled her chin defiantly and met his gaze with a challenging one of her own.

Then he was shoving people aside as though they were all beneath him and did not warrant his regard. "The revelry is over! Go home! Leave me be!"

He broke through the crowd and barreled down the

hallway, his wife of a few months traipsing after him, wringing her gloved hands, squeaking like a cornered dormouse. She stopped, turned to her guests, moved her lips, flapped her arms, and released a distressing moan before turning to chase after her husband once again. Mary's heart went out to her. She'd certainly not warranted this upheaval to her life.

She was startled when someone gripped her arm. "What is he to you?" Fitzwilliam asked.

"Pardon?"

"The man claiming to be the Duke of Keswick. You looked . . . enthralled."

"Joyous," she admitted, clutching his hand. "They're alive. Until this moment, I feared they were truly dead. And it is more than a claim. It is the truth. They are who they say they are. We all grew up together, until they disappeared, but I would recognize them anywhere."

At least when they were together. She wasn't quite certain that she could make the same claim if she saw them separately. They possessed little refinement. There was nothing genteel about them. Their character exuded a roughness, their presence spoke of hardships endured, possibly not all conquered. She had long dreamed of seeing them again, but what she had imagined was not what appeared before her.

People were shoving past them, making their way up the stairs as the drama seemed to have ended. For now, anyway. She ignored the whisperings and murmurings, giving her attention to the man before her even though she dearly wanted to know what people were saying, what they were thinking. "You do believe them, don't you?"

He suddenly appeared uncomfortable. "It matters

little what I believe. My title is simply a courtesy. It carries no weight."

"Among your friends it does." And she knew that some of his friends held their true titles. They could be powerful allies, should the brothers need them.

"Come along," Fitzwilliam said. "It would be best if we left as quickly as possible. I don't trust the ruffians not to return and inflict chaos. I'd heard of bloodlust, but dear Lord until tonight, I'd never seen it."

"They're not ruffians and they have a right to be angry. Lord David wished them harm. He was the reason they ran away." She squeezed his hand, wondering how to make him understand, only she glanced around and saw that people were slowing their step, lingering to hear their conversation. She'd not have the recently returned lords serve as fodder for gossip. Although that ship had sailed, she'd not add to its cargo. So instead she said, "I came with Alicia and Aunt Sophie."

"You shall all travel in my carriage."

"We have our own."

"I don't like the way that man looked at you. He could be lurking about. Considering tonight's turn of events, it would be unconscionable for me to allow three ladies to travel without a male escort to see after them."

They had the driver and footman but she supposed he didn't consider servants protection enough. Nor could she deny that she rather enjoyed his concern. "We shall need to find my cousin and aunt," she told him.

"I shall see to it posthaste," he assured her. "Do not leave this spot."

"I wouldn't dream of it."

She watched with fondness as he marched off to find

them. He would excel as a husband, always seeing after her needs and wants. Caring for her, protecting her. She could not ask for a more attentive man in her life.

She pressed herself up against the banister to allow more room for others to leave. There was such a din, everyone talking at once. The ladies' eyes were bright, and while they tried not to show it, it was apparent they were all tantalized by the delicious events that had interrupted the dancing. And she suspected, by the three brothers who had made their appearance tonight.

Slowing her step as she passed by, Lady Hermione touched Mary's arm briefly. "Do you know if they have wives?"

Mary knew precisely to whom she referred. The question bothered her when she knew it shouldn't. She shook her head. "I don't know."

"But you do know them."

She wasn't sure. She knew the boys they'd been, but the men who had been here tonight—

"I know they are who they say they were: the lords of Pembrook."

Lady Hermione's eyes sparkled. "Handsome devils. Well, except for the duke, of course. What do you suppose happened there?"

Mary shook her head. "I really—"

"Hermione!" her father called out. "Come along."

Lady Hermione gave Mary's arm a quick squeeze. "We shall have tea tomorrow. We simply must talk. The remainder of the Season has the potential to be most interesting."

Before Mary could respond, the lady was dashing up the stairs. They'd never had tea together before. Based upon the way other ladies were scowling at her, she wondered if she was suddenly seen as notorious, wondered what people were speculating. She refrained from explaining that they'd been neighbors, that she'd helped them escape.

"He locked them in the tower!" she wanted to shout.

Instead, she simply endured the pointed glances and nodded politely as two more invitations to tea were surreptitiously given to her. Suddenly, thank the Lord, her cousin was grabbing her arm and propelling her up the stairs, her aunt and Fitzwilliam following.

"We have so much to talk about," Lady Alicia said.

"I know no more than you at this point," Mary said as they reached the top of the stairs.

With the crush of bodies, they didn't get another chance to speak until they were all safely housed within Fitzwilliam's carriage.

"Well, I daresay," her aunt Sophie began, "that was a rather interesting turn of events. Although I'm not certain I approve of the handling of the matter. Such a public display of family feuding is ill-mannered. The situation warranted discretion and much more decorum."

"Come, Mama," Alicia said. "You can't deny that it was fascinating to watch and quite dramatic. The lords have such presence. They will be the talk of the town tomorrow."

"They're the talk of it tonight," Aunt Sophie muttered.

"They had a purpose in their method, Lady Sophie," Fitzwilliam said. "To humiliate Lord David—"

"He deserved humiliation, my lord," Mary blurted before she could stop herself. "And I suspect they handled the matter as they did so they would have many witnesses to their claim. I daresay he's fortunate that they didn't involve Scotland Yard."

"He is ruined," her aunt lamented. "As is his poor wife. After only three months of marriage."

"Yes, I do feel for her," Mary said. "How horrible it must be to discover the man you married is not the man you thought he was."

"And in his disgrace, he has disgraced her. Not certain I would forgive him for that," her aunt continued.

"He shouldn't be forgiven at all by anyone," Mary assured her.

Her aunt gasped. "I've never known you to be so unkind."

"He sought to have them killed."

"Truly?" Lady Alicia said with unwarranted excitement in her voice, as though she had simply arrived at an unexpected twist in a novel.

"How would you know that?" Fitzwilliam asked.

"I overheard him give the order."

"To whom did he give it?"

"I didn't see. I was passing the room and overheard the words. I was all of twelve and frightened out of my wits. I dared not tarry. I immediately went in search of Sebastian."

"Oh my word!" Alicia cried. "You never told me about that. I can't believe you'd withhold such a delicious secret from me."

"I promised Sebastian I wouldn't tell anyone." She'd broken the promise once. It had cost her dearly.

"You were a child," Fitzwilliam said. "You must have misunderstood."

"No, I'm certain, I didn't."

"Mary, darling, it's preposterous to think that Lord David would resort to murder in order to claim a title. He would have to kill three lads."

Mary tried not to be hurt by his words. He was the

man she was going to marry. Surely he of all people should believe her. "Richard III killed two."

"No one has proof of that. Besides that was four centuries ago. I'd like to think we're a bit more civilized. And he wanted a kingdom not a dukedom."

"It is one of the most powerful dukedoms in Great Britain."

"It was. But since the seventh duke passed away, it's lost a good deal of its influence. It can only be as powerful as the man at the helm, and there's been no one there."

"That will change now. With Sebastian back."

"I wouldn't be so sure. He seemed rather barbaric to me."

She couldn't deny the words, so she simply gazed out the window. All grew unbearably quiet as though everyone needed to absorb the events of the evening.

She welcomed the silence in order to embrace the joy that spiraled through her. They were back. At long last.

Sitting in the library, Mary watched as her father stared into the fire, an empty glass in his hand. He'd downed the whiskey in one long gulp after she'd told him what had transpired at the ball. He'd always been a bit of a hermit, preferring the company of his liquor to that of people. He didn't attend the social events. Sometimes he went to his clubs. He'd only come to London to keep a close watch over her. He finally looked at her. "You are not to interfere in their business. You are betrothed to a respectable lord, whose family lineage is impeccable. You leave these Pembrook lords and their uncle to sort out their own squabbles now. I want you nowhere near them."

"But they are our neighbors."

"Not here in London, they're not. And not in Cornwall, they won't be."

"But if I told the other lords what I heard—"

"You have no proof Lord David would have killed them. Perhaps they'd misbehaved and a few hours in the tower was to be their punishment."

"As the nunnery was punishment for me?"

He paled, licked his lips, took another swallow of his liquor. "You must do nothing to endanger your betrothal to Fitzwilliam. You have no brother to look after you when I am gone. I cannot rely on my nephew who is to inherit to be generous with you. He will have five sisters to marry off."

She had only a passing acquaintance with her father's family. They did not like the northern climes, and preferred to stay in the south. She did hope her cousin would appreciate what he was to inherit. She knew her father was concerned for her future, was providing her with a substantial dowry. She did not want to consider how it might have influenced Fitzwilliam.

"Surely all his sisters will be married by the time you are again with Mama," Mary said.

"The eldest girl is only nine. My brother started his family late in life." Then he died of typhoid. Her father gave her a small smile. "Perhaps you're right. I worry overmuch, but I do not want you to lose this opportunity to marry well. Now off to bed with you."

Nearly an hour later, Mary sat on the window seat in her bedchamber and looked out on the night. She considered disobeying her father, getting dressed, going out, and trying to find Sebastian and his brothers. She wondered where they were residing. She wondered why he'd not sought her out to let her know that he was safe. She supposed that he wanted to keep his arrival secret so he could make a grand entrance, but he should have told her. He should not have left her worrying about him.

So many times over the years, she'd thought of running away from the convent. But she had no funds at her disposal. And what skills did she have with which to earn a living?

She may have languished there forever if her aunt hadn't taken it upon herself to come for Mary and give her a Season.

Then another miracle.

During her first ball she'd met Lord Fitzwilliam and shortly thereafter he'd proposed. At the end of the month, she'd be free of her father and his manipulations. When Fitzwilliam looked at her, he saw someone who was strong, and capable. He saw someone who could provide him with a pleasant home life. He was not the most sought-after lord. In truth, she didn't think he was sought-after at all. Which made them different sides of the same coin, for no one was banging on her father's door, asking for her hand. Fitzwilliam had become her knight.

In the quiet recesses of the night, when slumber lulled her, she would sometimes dream of Sebastian. She would sometimes wonder: what if he returned?

And now he had. She had spent a good deal of time envisioning him growing into manhood. But the gentleman on the stairs more closely resembled something from her nightmares, not her dreams.

"We shall no doubt be all the gossip tomorrow," Tristan lamented, sprawled in a chair in the living area that was part of the private suite of rooms on the top floor of Rafe's gaming establishment. All three of the brothers had adjourned here after returning from their uncle's. They were comfortable accommodations and Rafe had the finest of liquors at his disposal.

Sitting in a nearby chair, sipping his brandy, Sebastian stared at the writhing flames. He couldn't get the image of Mary out of his mind. He'd thought of her from time to time over the years of course, but he'd always envisioned her as she'd been the last time he saw her: a young girl. Braided hair, gangly limbs, and a smile that filled most of her face. Freckles. So damned many freckles that he'd often teased her about them, even as he'd adored the way that they made her look like a little imp.

He thought of the way she'd not hesitated to speak up for him. She had always championed him, and in equal measure, challenged him. She was the reason he had climbed to the top of an ancient oak tree, only to take a tumble and break his arm. She was the reason he had learned to scale the castle walls. She was the reason that he and his brothers were alive to gather here now.

"I wonder why I do not feel more satisfied," Rafe commented. He was only twenty-two but he'd done very well for himself in a short amount of time. When Sebastian had left him at the workhouse, begging to go with him, he'd feared the sheltered life they'd led would leave his brother vulnerable. Perhaps in the beginning it had. Rafe was quite tight-lipped about how he had come to own a den of vice. Tristan certainly couldn't accuse him of whining now.

"Because the bastard still breathes," Tristan said.

Of course Tristan was equally reserved when it came to discussing his life. Along the docks, Sebastian had managed to find a captain willing to pay for a cabin boy. The money had allowed him to purchase his first commission in a regiment. But he couldn't help but wonder at what cost to Tristan. He'd seen his back. A cat-o-nine had done some nasty work. Tristan had always been more suited to being the one in charge rather than the one doing the work. It was little wonder he'd finally acquired his own ship. Carrying goods had made him a wealthy man. Sebastian didn't want to consider that perhaps not all of it had been legally obtained.

"Mary grew into quite a beauty while we were away," Tristan said now, sounding as surprised as Sebastian had been at first. Not so much that she had transformed into a butterfly but that she'd grown up at all. He realized that she was long past an age for marriage: four and twenty. Did she have a husband then? Where the devil had he been? *Who* the devil was he? Why hadn't he been at her side?

"Perhaps we should have warned her of our plans," Tristan continued. "She seemed quite unprepared for it."

"Which no doubt saved her reputation," Sebastian surmised. He downed his brandy and refilled his glass, refusing to acknowledge that it was because he'd still seen her as a child, had wanted to protect her, had not even considered how the shock of seeing them might affect her. In his mind, she had always remained as unchanged as Pembrook. Although time had its way with the estate as well, but the changes there were subtle. None of Mary's changes had been subtle. It seemed inappropriate to consider all the dips and swells that her gown had revealed. The unblemished bare skin of her shoulders that some man would have the great fortune to touch.

How silky she would feel. How warm.

He imagined now what he hadn't at Easton House:

removing the pins from her hair and watching it tumble around her. How far would it reach? Was it as thick as it appeared? Would a man's fingers become lost in it? As easily as a man might become lost in her?

Her eyes. Even her eyes had changed. Not the shade of course. They were still as green as the fertile land. But they no longer held a mischievousness. If eyes possessed the ability to laugh, hers would have done so when she was a child. Not so tonight. Although, unfortunately, tonight, there was very little to laugh about. But still, her eyes held too much knowledge. Wisdom perhaps. What had she seen in all the years he'd been away?

How was it that he had managed to understand that *he* had grown to adulthood but had never considered her doing the same? Perhaps because he had stepped into a man's boots the day his father died. She'd always been someone with whom he'd enjoyed exploring the world. Only now he thought of exploring her.

Damnation, but these thoughts regarding Mary were unsettling, not to be tolerated. Her role in his life was that of friend, not lover.

"Any notion with whom she was dancing when we made our grand entrance?" Tristan asked, breaking into his thoughts, and Sebastian couldn't help but wonder about the path that his brother's musings might be traveling. Surely not the same direction as his.

"You noticed her dancing?" he asked. He could well imagine how graceful she would be as she was glided across the floor in another man's arms.

"How could you not?" Tristan challenged.

"I was occupied with other matters—convincing the steward that he was to announce us with our titles took a bit more cajoling than I'd anticipated." The steward was not someone who had worked in their father's household, so he'd not recognized them nor even been aware of their existence apparently.

Tristan suddenly appeared uncomfortable, taking great interest in the brandy that lingered in his glass. "Come to think of it, I believe she was on your blind side at the time. And we've strayed from addressing my concerns. We may have hurt her by keeping our presence here a secret from her. Without her—"

"I know what we owe her," he snapped, not certain why he was so blasted irritated with Tristan's inquiries, or the fact that she had matured into womanhood with astounding perfection. Perhaps because seeing her was a blatant reminder of years lost that up until now he'd not had to truly face.

"She's spoken for," Rafe said casually. When both brothers looked at him, he merely shrugged. "You two are carrying on like a dog with a bone. I see no point in arguing about what we should have done when the moment is passed. Whether you find her a beauty, whether we owe her is moot. She's betrothed to Viscount Fitzwilliam. The gent with whom she was dancing. I saw the announcement in the *Times*."

Rafe had noticed her dancing as well? Perhaps Sebastian was going completely blind.

"She's a bit on the shelf to be only betrothed," Tristan said, his words echoing the thoughts Sebastian had been veering toward.

"I can't imagine our Mary settling for just anyone," Rafe surmised. "So I suspect it took a bit longer to find a gent worthy of her."

Our Mary. She didn't belong to all of them. She belonged only to—

The truth slammed into him. She didn't belong to *any* of them.

"Perhaps," Tristan said. "But still. A viscount? What do you know of him?"

"He's unimportant. Mary is not our concern," Sebastian snapped impatiently. He didn't want to ponder her being with another man. He'd never laid claim to her. Had never even considered it. They'd been children when he was forced to run off. As a woman, she might no longer have anything in common with him. Might be entirely unsuitable to serve as his duchess. Without conscious thought, he ran his hand over his jaw. Stopped. The scars taunted him. It was quite possible no woman would consider serving as his duchess. That path was truly for traveling another day.

"Establishing ourselves," he told his brothers, "ensuring that our claim to Pembrook is not questioned—that is where our energies must go. Did you not see the doubts in that room? We are far from done."

"Mary might be useful to us," Rafe said. "She remained in that world that cast us out."

"You would use her?" Tristan asked.

"I would use anyone to get what I want."

The cold words sent an icy shiver through Sebastian. Who was this unrelentingly harsh man whom he called "brother"? On the one hand a bond existed between them that could not be broken. On the other was the truth of the matter: he knew very little about him, yet he could not claim him to be a stranger because he trusted him completely. But still there was so much he didn't know, wasn't certain he wanted to know.

Silence eased in around them as though they each needed to ponder the ramifications of their actions tonight. Sebastian had expected a few of the lords to object quite vocally, but they hadn't. Too dignified perhaps. Or perhaps they cared for his uncle as little as he did. Or perhaps they were just waiting to see how things sorted themselves out.

"What is your next step?" Tristan finally asked.

"To take up residence at Easton House as soon as the imposer has scurried away. You are both welcome to reside there."

"I will remain here," Rafe said without hesitation. "It is where I am most at home."

"You have comfortable accommodations here," Sebastian said. "Of that there is no question. But now that you are once again recognized as a lord, you might consider selling this place. Its ownership is hardly befitting a gentleman."

"I never claimed to be a gentleman."

"But you are," Sebastian insisted.

Rafe shot to his feet. "Trust me, brother, I have done things that no gentleman would do. Polite Society would find me . . . not quite so polite. My wealth, my more questionable resources are at your disposal. I have already sent two men to keep watch over Easton House and its current resident. I will do all in my power to ensure you hold your title, but my place is here."

He made to leave and Sebastian stood. "Rafe."

His brother stopped but did not turn around.

"I could not take you with me. Not twelve years ago. I can take you with me now."

"It's too late." Rafe's voice carried no emotion, yet the words slammed into Sebastian with the force of cannon fodder. "Perhaps you can regain what you lost, but I cannot. Nor do I have any desire to. Make yourself at home."

He strode from the room, never glancing back. Sebastian took a step forward. He would catch up to him; he would make him understand—

"Leave him be," Tristan ordered.

Sebastian didn't want the wounds that marred his relationship with Rafe to fester, but he suspected his obstinate brother was in no mood to listen. So instead, he studied his twin, still lounging in the chair. It was difficult to look at him and see what a handsome devil he himself had once been. With great reluctance, he wandered back to the fireplace and pressed his arm against the mantel. "Do you know what happened to him?"

"He talks to me as little as he talks to you."

"I thought they would keep him clothed, fed, and housed within the workhouse."

"Whatever he went through it is not your fault. All the fault rests with Uncle. Which is the reason that I do wish you'd bloody well let me kill him."

"So you could hang?" Mary had issued a similar warning, but somehow accompanied by her sweet voice it had held more power. He wondered if she realized how close he'd been to not releasing his uncle. He wondered if she'd be disappointed to meet the darkness he harbored inside him.

"I have a fast ship. And the sea suits me," Tristan said.

Sebastian pressed his thumb to his brow, rubbed just above the despicable patch, and stared into the fire. "Will you join me at Easton House?"

"I don't think so, no. I've been on my own far too long. I prefer it, Keswick."

Sebastian jerked up his head and met his brother's unflinching gaze. From the moment his uncle's henchman had escorted him to the tower, he'd not been addressed by his title. He'd whispered it to himself every night before he went to sleep—a quiet reminder, a solemn vow. He did not want to forget who he was, what he was, what was owed him. Everything he'd done from the moment Mary slipped the key into the lock to free him had but one purpose in mind—to see that he regained what belonged to him, and in so doing provide a place for his brothers.

His throat tightened. He'd paid a dear price to once again be duke. But then so had they.

They did not need him now. It left him feeling unworthy, as though he had failed them. Like him, they should have been gentlemen. They should have lived leisurely lives. They should have been like the gents in Rafe's club who had little more required of them than indulging in their vices. They should not have born scars—both visible and hidden.

He watched as Tristan slowly rose and approached him. "Make no mistake, Brother. The desire to see you standing rightfully in Father's place burned within me with a vengeance. I would endure it all a thousand times, with no regrets, to ensure that you are once again duke."

Sebastian released a bitter laugh. "I am humbled, Tristan. By your devotion and Rafe's. I have been blessed with brothers who would do anything to see me hold my title. Our father was cursed with one who would do all in his power to see that he did not."

"You still believe he killed him?"

"Without doubt." He shook his head, regretting the truth that lay before them. "But to prove it will be nigh on impossible. Justice cannot be left to others to consider. I have spent years plotting how best to serve as judge, jury, and executioner. Tonight I feel as though we at least killed his place within Society."

"We may have achieved that, but there is more we can do. We do not need proof to make his life miserable."

"That should happen soon enough once he moves out of Easton House. I doubt he has anywhere to light."

Tristan grinned. He'd always been quick to smile, but this one was more wolf than cub. "Then we should put him out of his misery and kill him straightaway."

"I've killed. It is not a pleasant undertaking."

"As have I, although I am not at all adverse to sending to the devil those who deserve it."

Sebastian studied him. It had been only a fortnight since he and his brothers had managed to reunite. He had left each of them with the command to meet at the abbey ruins near Pembrook in ten years on the date that they escaped the tower. But war and wounds had delayed Sebastian. The sea had thrown obstacles Tristan's way and he, too, had failed to show at the appointed time.

Rafe had hired a man to live near the ruins until the brothers arrived. Not once had it ever occurred to him that they were dead. After months spent recovering from his devastating wounds, Sebastian finally made his way to the abbey. The man had provided him with the address to The Rakehell Club and a message from Rafe. Here he would be safe.

But rather than head to London straightaway, he'd spent a fortnight securing the estate. Then he'd come to London. He and his brothers had planned their return to London Society. They'd wanted a dramatic entry. He thought they'd achieved that end with a remarkable bit of success.

But the final curtain had yet to draw closed, and several acts still remained unperformed.

"I don't want any more blood on my hands," Sebastian said now.

"They'd be on mine."

He didn't much like the speed with which Tristan responded. "You've become quite bloodthirsty."

"I've learned to survive, no matter the cost." He shrugged. "I've also learned to take comfort where I can find it. Rafe has a charming girl working here who is very talented at giving comfort. So if you'll excuse me, I believe I shall seek her out. I'm certain she has a friend if you're interested."

"Not tonight."

Tonight he had far too much on his mind. After his brother left the room, he dropped into the chair and filled his glass with more brandy. He took a long swallow and leaned back. From his pocket, he removed the threadbare bundle. The yellow ribbon had faded with time, but it still managed to hold secure that which he treasured most.

He brought it near his nose and inhaled deeply. The rich scent of the soil tantalized him, spurred him on, made him yearn for home. He would return there soon—once his place in Society was firmly established.

I am the Duke of Keswick, he told the fire. It merely snapped and popped, as though it didn't believe his words any more than he did.

Chapter 4

*F*ool! *So close. You shouldn't have waited so long.*

"What choice did I have? I had to fend off suspicions."

But twelve years? Fool.

Lord David Easton paced with agitation. So close. So close. So close.

Twelve years ago, he sent his man to the tower to dispense with his troublesome nephews. He was going to claim a hunting accident. It was a poor explanation. He'd known it at the time, but creativity had never been his strong suit.

Only the lads had somehow managed to escape. Search parties had no success in finding them. The boys had skillfully eluded Lord David until even he began to believe the rumors that they were dead.

He shouldn't have waited to press his claim to the titles, but he hadn't wanted to be suspected of foul play. Not that it would have done him any good. A half-blind man could see the twins' remarkable resemblance to their father.

Only one of them does. The other is half-blind, which fosters a weakness, would make him easier prey.

"After tonight's fiasco, you can't think I can get away with killing them."

You must. Lucretia will leave you if you once again become nothing—just as the lads' mother tossed you over for their father, for Randall. She was yours. But it took only one smile from Randall for her to turn her favors toward him. She said she loved him, but all she wanted was the title. It's all any woman wants.

"But three murders—"

Accidents. Just as one befell their father. They are cursed.

"No one will believe it."

They believed your father died of illness. You proved to him how clever you were.

Lord David stopped his pacing and stared into the fire. "You are not as clever as your brother," his father told him over and over as he was growing up.

"I am clever." His laughter echoed around him. "Even my father had to admit how clever I was in the end, when the poison had done its work and all thought he'd fallen ill." But when he died, Randall became duke and stole David's love.

He had to pay for his betrayal, for his thievery.

"I never should have listened to you," he whispered to the shadows that had long been his companions.

And Eve never should have taken a bite from the apple. You have tasted vengeance. Surely you would not pass up a feast.

He licked his lips, already savoring the sweetness of it.

Chapter 5

The morning following the most interesting ball of the Season, Mary was sitting in the morning room reading *Jane Eyre* when the butler walked in and bowed slightly.

"M'lady, you have a guest."

Inwardly she groaned. Lady Hermione had certainly wasted no time in seeking her out for gossip. "Inform her that I'm not at home."

"Not 'her,' m'lady, but the Duke of Keswick."

Her heart thundered as she rose quickly to her feet, patted her hair, smoothed her skirt. "Show him in."

"He is in the library with your father. I'm to take you there."

"Why did you not say? He's here to see my father then. Not me." And why? Why would he seek out her father? Why had he not come specifically to see her? Why did it pain her so that he hadn't? Because they were friends, that was all. It was no more than that.

"My apologies, m'lady. I know only that I was sent to fetch you as the duke wishes to speak with you."

"Yes, I'm sorry. I don't mean to be so irascible." And why the deuce was she apologizing to a servant? Because she was flustered by Sebastian's arrival.

Not waiting for the butler to escort her—she was after all quite familiar with the location of her father's library—she hurried from the room and down the hallway. She wasn't certain why she felt such a need to rush or who it was that she thought might need protecting—Sebastian or her father.

As soon as she was near the library, the footman opened the door and bowed slightly as she glided past. Her father's study was small. A wall of shelves, a few chairs scattered about, and his massive desk. When she was a child, she would sit on his lap while he read reports from his estate manager.

Now he stood by the fireplace, an empty tumbler in hand. She suspected he dearly wanted to refill it but Sebastian was gazing out the window near the table that housed all manner of spirits. His dark blue jacket was finely cut, outlined the broad expanse of his shoulders. Even at this distance, she could see that there was strength in his back. Tall and erect, he stood with a military bearing. Or perhaps it was simply a mark of self-discipline, although he'd come close to losing it last night. She didn't want to consider that had she not stepped in, he might have never released his uncle. The fury distorting his features—while she understood it—had also been remarkably unsettling.

At the sound of her clicking heels, he turned in such a way that he could see her clearly but the disfigured portion of his face was not visible to her, and she realized that he'd deliberately chosen his position near the windows with that purpose in mind. Out of the corner of her eye, she caught her father's shudder because he was able to view what she could not. He'd never possessed much in the way of a cast-iron stomach, but still his reaction irritated her. Based upon the small bit of information Sebastian revealed last night, he'd been a soldier. As such he was deserving of their consideration and gratitude. Coming to a stop only a few feet from her childhood friend, she curtsied. "Your Grace."

"Come, Mary. Surely such formalities are not needed between us."

His voice was rough, as though his throat had been scraped raw. She noticed it last night, but for some reason it seemed more so now. She couldn't help but believe that a different life would have given a different timbre to his voice.

"It's lovely to see you . . . Keswick."

He released a low bark of laughter. "You are the first outside of family to address me by my title."

She scowled at her father, who had the good grace to blush before shifting his gaze longingly at the decanters. She turned her attention back to their guest. "Rather appropriate, don't you agree, that it should be I?"

"Quite. I was hoping you might take a turn about the garden with me."

"That's hardly appropriate," her father said. "She's betrothed, man."

"Yes, so I heard," Sebastian said, never taking his gaze from her. "While I've not had the honor of meeting him, I do know Fitzwilliam is a most fortunate man."

She felt the heat burning her cheeks. "You're very kind."

Sadness touched his remaining eye. "No, Mary, I fear I'm not."

"Being in service to the Queen changed you I suppose."

"A good many things changed me."

She nodded, suddenly at a loss for words, wishing her father wasn't close enough to hear what they might say. "I must retrieve my wrap . . . and my lady's maid. She may serve as our chaperone. If you'll be so good as to excuse me for a few moments?"

"Naturally."

"I'll meet you in the garden."

He gave a quick nod.

"You don't mind do you, Father?" She thought he intended to object again but then his gaze swung to Keswick, and he did little more than mutter, "No, of course not."

She couldn't deny that Keswick could be quite intimidating. She suspected her father would be shaking in his boots if he'd witnessed the incident at last night's ball.

She strolled from the room, hoping she gave no indication that her nerves were tingling. As soon as she was through the doorway and heard the quiet snick as the footman closed the door, she scampered down the hallway. She had a thousand questions for him, hoped he would provide a thousand answers, but she thought it unlikely. He was very different from the lad with whom she'd ridden across fields. But surely a small piece of him still existed somewhere.

In her room, she rang for her maid, then snatched up her shawl and draped it over her shoulders. She went to her vanity and dabbed perfume behind her ears. A silly thing to do, and yet she couldn't help herself. She wanted him to look at her as though she were a woman, not a child. Not that she had any interest in him other than friendship, but if he didn't see her as equal in maturity it was unlikely that he would share all he'd endured these many years. Once no secrets had existed between them. Now she feared there were a good many.

As Sebastian waited in the garden, he couldn't help but think he'd made an awful mistake in coming here. Lord Winslow had looked at him as though he'd seen a ghost. Surely he'd been told of Keswick's reentry into Society, so it must not have been his arrival so much as his marred features that had taken the earl by surprise. In truth, he wanted to simply escape to Pembrook and live out his life in solitude, but as he'd made a public appearance he'd decided to get another matter taken care of while he was in London. He would find a wife. Because God help him, he needed an heir. Which meant he'd have to keep himself on public display until the task was done. He did not expect her to love him. He didn't think it would be possible when he couldn't even love himself. But once she had seen to giving him an heir, he would grant her freedom. It would be her reward for enduring his presence in her bed.

He was a skilled lover. Or at least he had been before he'd awoken to discover that ignoring the call for retreat and further engaging the enemy in order to save a wounded man was a fool's mission. The soldier had been beyond saving. Sometimes Sebastian wondered if it would have altered his decision had he known how gravely wounded the fellow was. Probably not. In the heat of battle, all men believed themselves invincible. Why else would they charge with such enthusiasm into hell?

He heard the soft footsteps and turned ever so slightly to greet Mary. She smiled at him, and his chest

constricted. Yes, it was a mistake to come here. To have
the opportunity to memorize every line and curve of
her face, to search for the remembered freckles that had
faded, to be disappointed that they were not to be found.
To inhale the flowery fragrance—orchids, perhaps—
that seemed stronger outside than it had in the study.
Strange, he would have thought just the opposite.

He had deliberately placed himself so that when she
joined him she'd have no alternative except to stand to
the right of him. He did not wish to offend her delicate
sensibilities by what remained of the left side of his face.
Although the girl he'd known probably would have not
been sickened by such a ghastly image, she was a lady
now. And that made all the difference.

They began walking with the maid following dis-
cretely behind. He did not offer Mary his arm. Rather
he planted his hands behind his back. Little point in
touching what he could never hold.

"How long have you been in London?" Mary finally
asked.

"A little more than a fortnight."

"You did not think that I might wish to know you
were alive?"

He heard the sharpness of her tone, the hurt. They had
been friends once, and he cursed Tristan for being correct. They should have told her. "We thought it best to
keep our presence here a secret until the right moment."

"I would have held your secret."

"But contacting you may have put us at risk for discovery. Rafe has been in London for some time, but
he used a different surname and ran into no one who
might identify him. Considering his age when we left,
he was fairly safe from being properly identified."

"But you and Tristan—twins."

"Yes, we are a bit more noticeable." Or at least they once were. He supposed it would take a keen eye indeed to notice their similarities these days, but it was a risk they'd not been willing to take.

Her bow-shaped mouth curled up slightly. "You were certainly noticed last night. I'm not sure I ever realized you had such a flare for the dramatic."

"I would have thought you of all people would not have been surprised. Was I not Lancelot to your Guinevere? As I recall, I fought the enemy off quite daringly with my wooden sword."

"That was so long ago that I'd almost forgotten." Her smile withered. "Why did you not have him arrested for what he did to you?"

"What exactly did he do, Mary? He locked us in a tower. He could argue that we'd misbehaved and were merely being brought to task."

"I could tell the courts or the house of lords or whoever I needed that I heard your uncle order someone to kill you," she said.

"You were a child. Years have passed. He could argue that your memory was faulty. It would become a battle of words, Mary. I would not subject you to such unpleasantness."

"But it is not right, what he did."

"I'm well aware of that. My brothers and I will deal with him."

"What have you in mind?"

"Your gardens are lovely."

"Sebastian!" She stopped walking and he watched the familiar mulish expression cross over her features. "Why will you not reveal your plans?"

"I will not have you put in harm's way when there is no need."

"I want revenge as much as you."

"It is not revenge. It is retribution." And he doubted anyone could want it as much as he. "To be quite honest I've not finished mapping out my plans, and I did not come here to discuss my uncle." He longed for one conversation that did not revolve around the man.

"What of his wife?" she asked.

"What of her?"

"My heart goes out to her. You might have been a bit kinder to her."

"Twelve years, Mary. There is no kindness left in me."

She glanced away and he wondered if she feared what she might see in him if she looked too closely. He had taken to avoiding mirrors whenever possible. It wasn't so much the scars that bothered him any longer but rather what he saw in his eye. If eyes were truly the window to the soul . . . he did not fancy what he saw within his.

"When confronting your uncle last night, you said that you were a soldier," she said after several moments of reflection.

"Yes. I did not mean to stay away so long, but there never seemed a good time to sell my commission. Then we declared war on Russia, and to have left then would have shown me to be a coward."

"I suspect you were anything except a coward. Shall we sit?"

She indicated a wrought iron bench. He would have preferred walking, but he nodded and followed her over. In her youth, she'd been a bundle of mischievousness—which was part of the reason she'd uncovered his uncle's plot. And now she sat on the side of the bench that would give her the clearest view of his mottled flesh.

She was no fool, so it had to be a conscious decision on her part.

"Scoot over," he said. "I fancy sitting in that spot."

He was not facing her directly, knew she had a limited view of him, but she studied him with an intensity that made him think she could see all of him, clear through to the center of his darkened soul. "Were you wounded in battle?"

He gave one brisk nod. To his horror, she rose and walked toward him. He should have stepped away, but the challenge in her eyes held him immobile.

"You don't have to hide from me," she said, her voice a whisper on the waning breeze. She placed one of her delicate hands on his shoulder, and ever so slowly as though he were a skittish stallion, she glided her fingers up until they rested against his jaw. He could feel the pressure but not the softness of her skin. He wanted to shove his fingers into her hair, tear it down, watch it unravel over her shoulders. The need to wrap his arm around her waist, draw her up against him, press her close until her every curve had made an indentation against his body, and blanket his mouth over hers astounded him. He wanted to get lost in the sensuality of a kiss. He wanted the heat of her flesh to brand him. Even as he had these tumultuous thoughts, he was repulsed by the savagery of his desire. Dear God, this was Mary. She deserved more than uncontrollable lust from him, but he'd not been with a woman since before he was wounded. He longed for the gentle touch, the silky skin moving sensuously over his. He longed to be held, and to hold, to skim his fingers—

Then he saw the tears welling in her eyes. They achieved what his own thoughts couldn't, dampening his desire with unerring swiftness.

"Do not weep," he ordered through clenched teeth.

"It must have hurt terribly."

Unbearably. If not for his need to reclaim Pembrook, he'd have succumbed to the allure of death. But he'd not admit that, not reveal that weakness, not even to her. "Others were worse off."

"Your eye—"

"It's gone." Left on a godforsaken battlefield. Although he had not memory of it or the specific pain that might have been associated with it. The agony had encompassed all of him. It had been months before he'd been able to identify where specific points of pain originated.

Blinking, she glanced away. "Does it hurt now?"

"Sometimes it aches, but it is a minor inconvenience."

She released a small laugh, filled with sadness and perhaps a touch of admiration. "Spoken like a true soldier."

"It is what I am. A soldier. I don't yet know how to be a duke."

She returned to the bench, sitting where she hadn't before, giving him the luxury of joining her. Once he was seated, she said, "I believe you will make an excellent duke."

Better than his uncle at least. "You shall make an excellent viscountess."

She glanced at her fingers, steepled them, wove them together. "I shall certainly try. Although I'm not certain you know me well enough to make a claim about my suitability."

He realized she was still upset that he'd not visited before now, that he'd left her to discover along with everyone else that he and his brothers had returned. He regretted it, the impulsiveness of it, his inability to trust her now when she had saved him before. He regretted that he'd hurt her, but at the time it seemed the wisest course of action. He couldn't risk losing Pembrook or his titles. Reclaiming them had filled his life with purpose. "Have you changed so much?" he asked.

She twisted around to face him. "Have you?"

Far more than he cared to admit, far more than he wished her to know. In spite of all he'd achieved, he suddenly felt unworthy. Not that she sat in judgment of him, but perhaps she should.

"Regrettably, I have. But then I suppose the years take their toll on everyone. I'd certainly not expected to find you grown up."

"What had you expected?"

He wanted to laugh like a maniac at how naïve he'd been. "I'm not sure. To step back into the way things were, I suppose. Even knowing it was gone."

"Have you been to Pembrook?"

He saw the sorrow in her eyes, as though she wished she had the power to spare him what he had seen. "Yes. It was like walking through a house of ghosts. Father never closed it up, never draped cloths over the furniture, the statues, the paintings. It was always kept ready. Now it is covered in dust and the hills are barren of sheep."

She placed her hand over his bare fist, pressing into his thigh. "Before I came to London I rode to the highest hill on your father's land, where I could see Pembrook. It seemed so dark and foreboding. I couldn't bring myself to go any nearer. Not until you returned. Now here you are and I am the one who will not be in Yorkshire."

He couldn't imagine it. A heaviness settled in his gut. All these years, his thoughts had centered around Pembrook, yet it had never occurred to him that he would not hear her laughter echoing over the dales or catch glimpses of the sun reflecting off her hair.

He could think of nothing to say except that Fitzwilliam was a fortunate man, and he'd already told her that. What the deuce was wrong with him? Why was he suddenly without words, without thought?

"I've strayed from my purpose in coming here." The words sounded as though they came from a great distance, were not spoken by him.

"I thought you came to visit," she said softly.

"No, I . . . I came to thank you for your assistance all those years ago." He removed a small wrapped package from his jacket pocket and extended it toward her.

He saw the hurt wash over her expression. Was he doomed to always wound her—keeping secrets, withholding his trust, talking only of superficial things, offering gifts for dangers confronted?

"You do not owe me. My actions that night were done with no expectation of reward."

He didn't know how to respond to her heartfelt declaration. He should have waited until Tristan returned from the docks so he could accompany him when delivering the gift. He doubted his brother would be tongue-tied. He'd make light of it. But Sebastian had not wanted to wait. The truth was he'd wanted a few moments with Mary alone, although for the life of him, he didn't understand why the yearning had been so strong. Perhaps because she'd been a friend more to him than to the others. Now that she was grown, he didn't appreciate that they'd noticed the beauty she'd become, or that they'd noticed her before he had.

"It is only a small token of our appreciation," he finally said.

"So, it's from all of you then?" Now she appeared disappointed.

He didn't understand her mercurial moods. He'd known women over the years—many women—but he'd been only interested in determining how best to quickly divest them of their clothes. He'd certainly had no interest in figuring out anything beyond that. He felt as though he were lost at sea, drowning in tidal waves of uncertainty. What did she want him to say? He would say it if it would please her, would bring the smile back to her face.

"Yes. From all of us. I selected it."

He must have gotten it right because the disappointment retreated. Thank God. That was troublesome. That he cared about disappointing her. When they were children, he had simply accepted that she'd always be there. He'd never weighed his words or his actions. Now he measured each one and found them sadly lacking.

His inadequate conversational skills didn't bode well for his success in finding a woman to marry him. If he wished to place blame elsewhere, he could blame it on his throbbing face or the lingering results from the trauma of his wounds, but he feared the fault rested with something more, some deficiency in him that was doomed to unravel the friendship they'd possessed as children.

She lowered her gaze, hesitated. "A lady should not accept gifts from a gentleman."

"It is from three friends. And we are hardly gentlemen."

She lifted her gaze to his. The clover green in her eyes reminded him of the verdant hills of home. He could look forever, and never tire of them. On the top of one rounded cheek, he spotted a bold freckle. He wanted to remove his glove and trace his finger over it. But he feared his errant hand wouldn't stop there. He would want to touch the whole of her cheek, trail his thumb over her plump lips, especially the lower one that appeared as welcoming as a pillow. He'd had little enough softness in his life, and the temptation to revel in it here was almost beyond enduring. He'd been on the verge of explaining that based on the idle banter Rafe had overheard at his club from those who were at the ball before seeking more wicked pleasures, the brothers were seen as little more than barbarians. But his thoughts toward her exemplified his point. If not for the maid standing nearby, he wasn't certain he'd have been able to restrain himself. She was such a temptation—sweet, innocent, a beauty beyond measure.

And she belonged to another man, but that truth seemed to hold him in place rather than cause him to depart as it should.

"So many of your freckles disappeared," he said quietly, knowing he was veering from one tawdry subject into another—one that had the potential to be far more dangerous.

"With you gone, I had little occasion to play in the sun. And then, of course, a lady should never be without her bonnet or parasol."

"I rather liked the freckles."

She smiled, a ravishing smile that transformed her lovely features into an exquisiteness that was breathtaking. "I abhorred them. And you *are* a gentleman. You may have come across as somewhat brutal last night, but I believe the situation regarding your uncle warranted it."

Her words sent his thoughts careening back onto the

path they never should have left. If only his menacing, harsh outlook were limited to last night, but a part of him embraced the brutality as a means of protecting himself. He wasn't proud of it, but he knew he needed it to survive, to do what had to be done in order to reclaim Pembrook. "Because you're our friend." He nudged the box against her hand.

He could not have been more pleased when she took it, removed the paper, opened it, and gasped. It was a simple necklace that sported nothing more than a small oval emerald that matched the shade of her eyes.

"Oh, it's so lovely." Smiling brightly, she held out the box. "Will you place it on me?"

He would have to remove his gloves in order to grasp and work the delicate clasp. He was shaken by the immediacy with which his fingers trembled. The thought of them being so near to her skin, of his knuckles touching the silkiness at the nape of her neck—

He shot to his feet while he was still able to stand without his lower body revealing the errant direction of his thoughts. This was Mary. God, she deserved more than a rutting bull or a man with lascivious thoughts who would like nothing better than to take her behind the rose bushes for a leisurely sojourn into pleasure. She was a lady. Betrothed. Hardly deserving of the beast he'd become. "I'm sure that is a task more suited to your maid. It was a pleasure to see you again, Mary. I wish you well in your marriage."

Before she could respond, before he could fully recognize the emotions that might have played over her face, he spun on his heel and slammed into the maid whom he hadn't seen. Standing on his blind side, dammit. "Out of my way, woman!"

He stormed from the garden as though the very

hounds of hell were nipping at his heels. How could so simple a request have unmanned him to such a degree?

He was the Duke of Keswick for God's sake. But at that moment he wished he was back on a battlefield. It was so much easier to fight an enemy that was not himself.

What the deuce had just happened?

Mary rose to her feet, stared after Sebastian's stiff retreating back, and plopped back down in confusion. Had she offended him in some manner? His reaction was the strangest thing. He had been staring at her with such intensity that she'd barely been able to draw in a breath. For the briefest of moments, she thought he was on the verge of leaning in to kiss her. For the briefest of moments, she had wanted him to.

What a disaster that would have been! Dear, kind Fitzwilliam had been forgotten. Only Sebastian had filled her senses. The size of him, the breadth of his shoulders, the expanse of his chest. The fragrance beneath the cloves that was the true essence of him. He'd always smelled like the heady soil of Pembrook: earthy and rich. For a moment it was almost as though they were there, as though the pain and separation of the intervening years had never happened.

But they had, and he took great care not to subject her to his scars. Did he really think her so shallow?

The thought filled her with disappointment, caused an ache to settle in her chest. He knew as little of her as she knew of him. Once again she found herself wondering why her request to place the lovely gift about her throat upset him so.

"Would you like me to assist you in putting it on, m'lady?" Colleen asked.

She smiled at her maid. "No, I believe I shall save it to wear at the next ball."

"The pink gown with the green velvet trim?"

"Yes."

"It will look lovely."

"I quite agree. You may go inside. I believe I shall sit here for a while and enjoy the gardens while I may."

"The residence will not be the same without you here."

"I shall try to visit. Often. Go on now."

"Yes, m'lady."

Feeling like an ungrateful wench, Mary watched her go before turning her attention to the assortment of flowers that were blooming in riotous colors. She should find the energy to gather some for her room, but all she seemed capable of doing was thinking about Sebastian. She grazed her finger over the small emerald. She had once felt so comfortable with him. She could have told him anything. She could have bared her soul to him with no regrets. But the man who had visited with her in the garden now—she did not know him. She didn't know the journeys he had traveled, what challenges may have shaped him. She possessed a romanticized bent that would see them sitting before a roaring fire, sharing every aspect of the past twelve years. But it was only fantasy.

Their time apart had truly separated them. Now they seemed to be little more than strangers fumbling into an acquaintanceship. They traversed separate paths, the distance between them ever widening. It saddened her to consider they might never truly converge.

During one horrendous night they'd shared experiences that had created an unbreakable bond between them. They would forever be connected. But a connection did not ensure a snug fit. At that moment, she wasn't even certain that she liked the man he had become. He was irascible and harsh. She had yet to see a smile, and the laughter he released was more bark than joy. She had always expected the lad he'd been to return unscathed. She feared that nothing of the boy she'd known had returned at all, because she still missed him, still longed to see him again.

Chapter 6

L ord Tristan Easton liked the way his name now rolled off the tongue. Although Captain Easton was equally as gratifying. He'd been down to the docks to check on his ship and crew and all seemed well there. He hired a couple of extra thugs to keep watch. He did wish that Sebastian hadn't blurted out that he'd been to sea. He doubted that the Swine—the name with which he'd christened his uncle the first time a cat-o-nine had cut into his back—would have the wherewithal or intelligence to consider that Tristan had a ship and to come looking for it, but he wasn't above being prepared.

Now he strode into Rafe's office and quirked up a corner of his mouth at the sight of his brother at his desk, looming over a mountain of ledgers. Rafe had been such a sniveling puppy as a boy—he favored their mother to such a degree that their father had spoiled him as he hadn't his heir or his spare—that Tristan had never garnered much respect for him. But he couldn't deny that somewhere along the way Rafe had acquired an impressive backbone.

He finally looked up, and it irritated Tristan to have his brother's impatient glare land on him. It was strange because in their youth he was the one who never had the patience to deal with the younger boy.

"Has Sebastian returned from visiting Mary?" Tristan asked.

"Yes."

His brother had also become a man of few words. Even when he was into his cups, he didn't talk. He was successful, Tristan would give him that, but he was an awfully gloomy sort. But then to various degrees, he supposed they all were.

"Do you know where I might find him? I stopped by his room. He wasn't there."

"He wanted a woman. I sent him to Flo."

Flo, a buxom blond with legs that went on forever. "Excellent choice."

With a scowl, Rafe returned his attention to his ledgers. He was damned protective of his girls, but then he seemed to be damned protective of everything.

Tristan wandered into the room. On his previous visits here, he'd been more focused on his brother than the things that surrounded him. Now he couldn't help but believe that they were somewhat telling. In a corner stood an immense globe on a wooden pedestal. He went over to it and gave it a spin, caught glimpses of every sea he'd ever sailed.

From one side of the corner spread a wall of shelves lined with books dotted with an assortment of globes that revealed continents, islands, and oceans. Various sizes, shaded differently. He wondered if his brother had collected them as a means to follow his brothers' travels, even though he knew not where they were. Or did the globes serve more as a testament that he'd been left behind? Tristan scoffed at his analytical mind that wanted to examine and understand all things. Perhaps his brother simply fancied globes.

"Don't you find it odd?" he asked, looking over his shoulder.

"What?" Rafe didn't even bother to glance up.

"That he goes to visit with Mary and returns in need of a woman."

With a deep put-upon sigh, Rafe tossed his ink pen aside, leaned back in his chair, and gave his brother a withering glare. "You are obviously under the mistaken impression that I both have time for and relish your intrusion."

Tristan was not to be put off. He strode over to the chair in front of the desk and sank into it with practiced ease. He took some pleasure in the tightening of his brother's jaw. It was almost like when they were lads and he'd irritate him on purpose just to get him riled, hoping their father would scold Rafe, but it was always Tristan who was at the receiving end of the sharp tongue or the birch switch. "There was once a woman who I wanted to bed with a fierceness that nearly unmanned me, but she was the daughter of the tribal chief on the island where we weighed anchor. I could not have her but I nearly drowned in feminine bodies while I was there."

"So you're explaining to me that you're a cad with neither morals nor conscience?"

"Considering the type of establishment you run, I would not be so quick to cast aspersions upon my character." He quickly held up his hand as he saw the temper flare in Rafe's eyes. "Forgive me. I am not judging you. My point was that if he lusted after Mary, he might return here to slake that lust."

"Why should I make this my concern?"

"Did you fail to notice that he is hardly a handsome fellow these days? To face the situation squarely, we must admit that it will be a challenge for him to secure a wife."

"So you wish to play matchmaker?"

A chill went through Tristan. Was that where he was going with this? Matrimonial bonds were exactly that. Bonds. Chains. Captivity. Did he wish that on his brother?

"I wouldn't go that far. But it would be satisfying to see matters between them return to what they once were. He and Mary were always spending time together, traipsing through the forests. She has grown into a beauty, while he—"

"Is a beast?"

Sebastian's voice barked behind him. It was a testament to Tristan's stalwart disposition that he did not so much as flinch, that he gave no indication he was startled. Instead he merely glowered at Rafe. "Thank you, Brother, for the warning."

A corner of Rafe's mouth quirked up, a glimmer of mischief touched his eyes for the span of a heartbeat, and in that time Tristan saw a shadow of the boy his brother had once been. "I told you that you were under the mistaken impression that I had time for this nonsense."

Tristan threw an arm back over the chair and twisted around to meet Sebastian's unnerving stare. It was somehow worse that he could deliver such a powerful message with only one frosty eye. "How was Mary?"

"Well."

"And Flo?"

If at all possible Sebastian's glare became even more menacing. "I am going to Easton House to watch Uncle as he packs to leave. I thought I would see if you both wished to come with me."

"I have more pressing matters that require my attention," Rafe said.

"More pressing than reclaiming what is ours?" Tristan asked, studying his brother as though he didn't know him. He supposed he really didn't.

"I did my part by accompanying you both to the damned ball. I don't need to see the packing."

"Rafe is right," Sebastian said. "He was with us when it counted most. What I intend to do now is little more than relish the outcome."

Tristan rose to his feet. "Then by all means, let's go relish."

With mischief in their eyes and secretive smiles, Ladies Hermione and Victoria arrived at precisely half past two. While Mary attended balls, parties, and soirees, she had never had an official coming out. She had simply begun to appear at events, tagging along after her aunt and cousin. She was tolerated with mild curiosity. Her betrothal to Fitzwilliam had raised her stature somewhat, but with no brother to inherit her father's title, she was hardly sought after for gossip or connections. But whatever her lack in standing, the ladies sitting in her drawing room could hardly be bothered with it. They were on the hunt for much larger game.

"So they are friends of yours . . . these lords from last night?" Lady Hermione asked pointedly. Both she and Victoria were sitting on the edge of their chairs, as though Mary's answer would determine their futures.

"Our country estates rest beside each other's, so we grew up riding our horses over the same hills, exploring the same forests." Her answer did not seem to impress the ladies. In fact, they seemed rather baffled by it, and she realized they had probably grown up caring for their porcelain dolls. Mary had much preferred the outdoor pursuits, especially when she could entice Sebastian away from his studies. Often Tristan or Rafe would join them, but they would soon grow bored with their adventures while Mary and Sebastian could always find something of interest.

"It was rather naughty of them to run away," Lady Victoria said, her squeaky voice propelling Mary back to the present.

"Their uncle wished them harm."

"My papa says we can't know that for sure."

Mary stared at her, hardly able to believe that after what they had witnessed last night, anyone would have doubts. But then what had they witnessed? Three younger men treating their uncle shabbily while he proclaimed to have their best interests at heart. Sebastian was correct. Even if she told them what she'd overheard they might not believe her. It could very well do more harm than good, so she held her tongue when she wished dearly to use it with ferocity.

"Their reason for leaving is hardly important," Lady Hermione said, further confounding Mary. "The point is that they are unlike any gentlemen we've ever met. Frightfully fascinating in a rough sort of way. And devilishly handsome with a touch of wickedness about them. While the duke was carrying on with his uncle I managed to capture Lord Tristan's gaze last night, and I swear he looked at me as though he could envision me without my unmentionables."

She wanted to say that flirting with young ladies was probably the last thing on any of the gentlemen's minds as they had stood on the stairs reclaiming their birthright. But these silly girls were so sheltered and innocent that Mary felt ancient sitting here with them. They viewed the lords as little more than the latest in entertainment.

"Have they means?" Lady Victoria asked.

Perhaps a bit more than entertainment. Possibly husbands apparently. "I'm not familiar with their individual fortunes, but Keswick has inherited a dukedom. At one time Pembrook was instrumental in the wool industry. I suspect it will be again."

"Their clothes were finely tailored, well-fit, and the latest fashion. Shoes were polished. Hair was a bit long but I rather liked it."

Mary was once again left speechless. These ladies seemed to only care about trivial matters. She supposed it was a result of their sheltered lives. They'd prepared for marriage, and suddenly a trio of fascinating men had stepped onto the marriage block.

Lady Hermione took a sip of her tea as though only out of politeness, then set aside her cup and saucer. "Here is the reason for our visit. We would like to call upon the duke and we were hoping that you could provide us with a proper introduction."

"I have no intention of providing guided tours to his residence."

"Of course not, but surely you will visit your old chums, and if we traveled with you . . . well, it could be quite pleasant for everyone."

"Is your mother aware that you have this plan?"

Lady Hermione was taken aback by the pointed question. "Absolutely not."

"To be quite honest," Lady Victoria said, "we were

warned to steer clear of them. Papa views them as trouble."

"Which makes them all the more appealing," Lady Hermione said. "If you will not escort us to their residence, will you at least encourage them to attend my ball late next week? You would be doing me an incredible favor. It would make my ball talked about almost as much as Lord David's."

"I heard his wife returned home to her mother this morning," Lady Victoria said. "Ghastly state of affairs for her."

"I would not want to be in her slippers," Lady Hermione concurred. "But then I never understood her marrying him to begin with."

"The possibility of title, wealth, and power," Lady Victoria said. "It is the same reason that some lady will agree to marry the present hideous Duke of Keswick."

"He's not hideous," Mary snapped.

Lady Victoria's blue eyes widened as though she'd encountered someone who belonged in a mental asylum. "My dear, did you not catch a glimpse of his face?"

"A man is more than his features."

"True, but one must consider that those features will greet one each morning at the breakfast table. I'm quite sure it would upset my digestion."

Mary shot to her feet. "I believe you ladies have overstayed your welcome. I shall have the butler see you out."

Both ladies rose. "But you will provide an introduction," Lady Hermione said, her voice wavering between a statement and a question.

"After all the unkind words that have been said here regarding the duke, why would you desire an introduction?"

"Not one to the duke, dear girl. Lords Tristan and Rafe Easton."

Mary shook her head. "I believe they would take as unkindly to your sentiments regarding their brother as I."

"Do you fancy him for yourself? The duke?"

Mary could only stare at her in disbelief. "I'm betrothed to Lord Fitzwilliam. My regard toward him remains ever constant." She was determined to dispel any such nonsense regarding her affections for Sebastian. Fitzwilliam deserved, and would have, her loyalty.

Lady Hermione turned to Lady Victoria. "Wait for me in the entry hallway."

"But—"

"Please."

Once Lady Victoria left, Lady Hermione gave all her attention to Mary. "She said unkind words, and I should not be made to suffer simply because we traveled here in the same carriage. I was quite taken with Lord Tristan and I would dearly love to ensure that he is taken with me. If you believe at all in love, please see to this favor for me."

"You haven't even spoken to him. How can you love him?"

She placed her gloved hand over her breast. "The heart needs not an exchange of words. It simply knows."

With a sigh, Mary felt all the fight go out of her. "I cannot guarantee success, but I shall speak with the duke if our paths should cross."

"I can ask for no more than that. Thank you."

She walked out and Mary sank back into the chair. She wondered if Sebastian was aware that confronting his uncle might be the easiest of all his tasks. Being accepted by the nobility might prove to be much more of a challenge.

Chapter 7

Lurking in the shadows of the park across the street from the London residence, Sebastian watched the flurry of activity. He and Tristan had come and gone several times since yesterday afternoon, but now they waited because the sun would soon make its appearance and the deadline he'd given his uncle would be upon them. He didn't intend to allow the man to remain in residence one moment longer than he'd already declared. It seemed Lord David understood the weight of the threat. Two coaches and a wagon were loaded to overflowing, the horses impatiently pawing at the cobblestone, their whickers echoing through the fog. His uncle had amassed an inordinate amount of possessions in the intervening years.

"I suppose truthfully," Tristan murmured, "if he used Keswick funds to purchase all that garbage that it's yours."

"He's welcome to it. I have no intention of splitting hairs as long as he takes nothing that belonged to Father. For now I simply want him out."

"And then?"

"Destroy him. His credit, his credibility. I want him begging on the streets."

"I still don't fancy the notion of him drawing in air."

"Killing him would shorten his suffering. I wish to prolong it."

"There is satisfaction in that, I suppose. What are your plans regarding yourself?"

"Unfortunately, I shall have to remain here for a time to secure my place and to find a wife."

He was well aware it wouldn't be an easy task, but it needed to be done. He didn't delude himself into believing it would be a love match. He wasn't certain that he had the ability to love. Not any longer. The years since he left he'd not felt anything toward any woman—other than lust. That he seemed to have in abundance, even where Mary was concerned. Although it had certainly been lacking when Rafe had sent the woman to him.

Flo. He remembered her name only because Tristan had mentioned her several times since, trying to determine his satisfaction with her efforts. Why Tristan should care was beyond Sebastian's reasoning. He'd forgotten the woman's name two seconds after she'd given it to him. Which had made it rather awkward ten minutes later when it became obvious that whatever his needs, she couldn't satisfy them. She'd then sent a raven-haired beauty to him, but he'd had no interest in her either. And he'd greeted the red-haired wench who followed with an immediate request that she depart. If he hadn't had such a strong reaction to Mary's nearness, he'd have thought the war had taken more than his sight on one side. But he had reacted. For the first time in a terribly long time. He had reacted with a fierceness that verged on barbaric.

"I realize that we have a good bit of time to make up for, but aren't you rushing it a little there, when it comes to securing a wife?" Tristan asked. "Good Lord, we're only six and twenty. I don't plan to marry until I'm at least forty—if then."

Six and twenty? How could he possibly be that young? He felt as though he were on the far side of thirty. "I want to be on display as short a time as possible."

"And do you have a lady in mind?"

"If I did, I would already be on my way back to Pembrook."

"Perhaps you seek to achieve too much too quickly."

"Good God, Tristan, I've had twelve years to ponder it all. To scheme, to plan, to dream. Surely you have done the same."

His brother kept his gaze fastened on the activity across the street. "While I'll admit that I quite enjoyed being unfettered, returning to Society is all I thought of. I quite fancied being a lord again, and having any woman I want at my beck and call."

"Have *you* someone in mind?"

"Hardly, but my time at sea gave me a knack for discovering buried treasures. Although I must admit that I take equal pleasure in the search as much as in the discovery." He nodded toward the residence. "It appears the imposer is set to take his leave."

Sebastian shifted his gaze to the departing carriages. They didn't carry the ducal crest. It seemed his uncle had taken his threats seriously. He was to take nothing that didn't belong to him. The horses and wheels clattered over the cobblestone drive, echoing through the fog as the first rays of sunlight began to ease their way into the city. He listened until the sounds were absorbed by distance, then he gave a nod to the man on horseback waiting even further back in the shadows. The man took off in a trot in the direction that Lord David had gone.

"When you discover where he seeks refuge?" Tristan asked.

"Then I shall know where to confront him when I'm ready and better savor his decline." He would begin by ensuring all funds to him were cut off.

"How long shall we wait before entering the residence here?"

"I wish to relish the moment."

"He's not coming."

Rafe. He kept impossible hours. Working through the night, sleeping through the day. Still, while he'd known that his brother had important matters with which to deal the day before, Sebastian had hoped he would find the time, make the effort, to be with them this morning as they finally realized the fruition of their efforts. "I fear he despises me."

"He was ten. Too young to truly comprehend what was happening or the danger that dogged our heels. He saw us both riding away, and didn't understand that we, too, would part company. He thought we were up to our usual tricks—us, the twins, against him."

"He told you all this?"

"Of course not, but it doesn't take a genius to deduce it all."

"You've become quite the observer of men."

Tristan grinned. "And women. Although I must confess that I much prefer observing the fairer sex. Men are far too easy to understand. But women . . . I rather enjoy the challenge they offer."

Sebastian chuckled. He laughed so seldom these days that the scratchy noise sounded foreign to his ears. "Do you take anything seriously?"

"Contrary to how it may appear, I take *everything* damned seriously." He nodded toward the residence. "Have you done enough relishing?"

He glanced around, felt a tightening in his chest at the sight that had been denied him because that portion of the street was not within his limited line of vision. "One moment more," he said quietly, but unable to withhold the jubilation that soared through him.

Tristan glanced back over his shoulder. "Well, I'll be damned. Good thing I didn't make a wager on this outcome."

For up the street strode Rafe. While he always dressed properly when wandering about his establishment, his clothing this morning was a cut above. Black jacket, pristine white shirt and cravat, gray waistcoat, and fawn trousers. He used a walking stick to pace his steps. His beaver hat sat at a rakish angle. He could have been any lord out for a morning walk. In fact, he was.

"Did I miss Uncle's parting?" he asked as he came to a halt near them.

"Unfortunately yes," Sebastian said.

"Not unfortunate. He's gone. That's all that matters."

"It matters that the three of us are here," Sebastian assured him. "I'm grateful you were able to join us."

Rafe shrugged, as though it were of no consequence. "I finished with my ledgers earlier than I anticipated and had a bit of extra time. Shall we cross the street so you may take up residence?"

"By all means. Let us reclaim Easton House as ours."

Their footsteps resounded and the fog swirled as though anxious to get out of their way. Sebastian could only imagine how they must have looked to anyone glancing out a window. Three men—he in the middle, his brothers flanking him and following one step behind—their walking sticks hitting the ground in perfect synchronicity. They passed through the gateway, the wrought iron gate having been left ajar in his uncle's haste to leave. He wondered what sort of welcome the servants would give him. He'd seen no one he knew the night of the ball. If his uncle had replaced them all, he might very well be doing the same. He wanted no one about whose loyalties could be questioned.

He and his brothers marched up the drive, climbed the steps. They'd just reached the top, when the massive oak door swung open, and the butler stepped out. His was a familiar face. His hair had begun turning white, but he still had a proud, erect carriage. He bowed slightly. "Your Grace."

"Thomas."

A sparkle lit his brown eyes. "You remembered, sir."

"How could I forget? You slipped me lemon drops when my father wasn't looking."

"I thought you did that only for me," Tristan said.

"For all of you, sirs. Welcome back to Easton House. Anticipating your return, I have taken the liberty of assembling the staff. There are some who will no doubt not meet with your approval, but I believe you will find most are willing and anxious to see to your needs."

"I appreciate it. Let's see to business." As he stepped through the doorway into the marbled foyer, his nostrils twitched as he caught the rancid stench of his uncle. Then he heard a gasp, a breath catch, and a tiny squeak. Three of the maids had lowered their gazes, and he wondered why he could so easily forget that his face was a shock to most who first saw him.

"I am the Duke of Keswick," he announced. "My brothers, Lord Tristan Easton and Lord Rafe Easton." Each nodded when introduced. "We are here reclaiming what is ours. If you doubt our claim, I will help you find employment elsewhere for I will tolerate no disloyalty to myself or my brothers. It would behoove you to be honest with us now if you cannot serve us as we require, for you will discover that forgiveness is not our strong suit."

No one moved. No one spoke.

"Excellent then. I want everything in this residence washed, aired out, and polished until all looks new and I will be unable to find even a hair from the previous resident. Do I make myself clear?"

Heads bobbed. "Then see that it is done." He turned to Thomas. "You and I shall meet in the library in an hour to discuss the particulars of this household."

"Very good, Your Grace."

With his brothers beside him, he began his tour. The familiarity of the surroundings was settling into his bones and beginning to feel welcoming. The one thing he noticed were the occasional empty spaces on the wall. Portraits of his father were not to be seen. He remembered as young lads that he and Tristan had stood for a portrait—one facing one way, one the other. Later they'd all had a portrait done with their parents. Those were also missing.

"Where do you suppose the paintings are?" he asked. He didn't need to elaborate.

"In the attic, hopefully," Tristan said, "although I'd not put it past Uncle to have burned them."

"I'm quite surprised he lived here," Rafe said. "I

would have thought Father's ghost would have haunted him."

"Only a man with the ability to feel guilt can be haunted by his actions," Sebastian said. He spoke from experience, but he was not going to share that with his brothers.

They reached the library. A footman opened the door for them. For some reason this room was more difficult to face than the others. Perhaps because it had been their father's domain. Their mother had a smaller library, more of a sitting room, with vibrant colors and books that appealed to her. But this room possessed a darkness, a boldness. Leather books lined mahogany shelves. Hunter green chairs were arranged in intimate sitting areas. Within reach of each was a table of crystal decanters. Their father had entertained here.

Sebastian didn't want to consider that their uncle may have as well. He strode across the room to the large table near his father's massive desk. He retrieved three glasses and filled each with whiskey. After each of his brothers took a glass, Sebastian lifted his. "To Father and reclaiming what belonged to him."

"And what now belongs to you," Tristan said.

"To all of us," Sebastian corrected. "It may be entailed, but make no mistake, I consider it ours."

A resounding clink filled the corner as the brothers touched their glasses together. He didn't know why he didn't feel as though he was yet home.

But he downed the whiskey, relished it burning, and swore that he would never again abandon his legacy or his brothers.

He heard a door opening and glanced over as Thomas strode in carrying a silver salver. "A missive was just delivered for you, Your Grace."

Sebastian took it, dismissed the butler, and set aside his glass to open it. He read the elegant script with a measure of dread.

"What is it?" Tristan asked.

"We've been invited to a small dinner party at Lady Ivers's this evening."

"Lady Ivers? Isn't she Mary's aunt?"

"Yes."

"Then I don't see how we can decline."

Chapter 8

The carriages they'd seen arriving should have served as a clue. Still, Sebastian was taken aback when he and his brothers were escorted into the parlor to see such a mass of humanity.

"Good God," Tristan murmured. "There must be at least fifty people here. I would hate to see what she considers a *large* dinner party."

Sebastian supposed he should have anticipated that all conversation would cease and all eyes would turn toward the door when the lords of Pembrook entered. Damnation but he thought facing the Cossacks might have been a sight easier.

A woman of average height and build with hair that the passage of time had faded to a faint red bustled over. As she neared her green eyes sparkled, and it was that green that would have given her identity away if Mary hadn't been following closely on her heels to give credence to his suspicions.

"Your Grace! My lords! I am so pleased you were able to join us this evening." She held out her hand.

Taking it, Sebastian bowed over it. "Lady Ivers, it is indeed a pleasure to be invited."

She winked at him. "Do not think I did not catch the exact meaning of your words. Yet I assure you that it shall be a pleasure to *attend* as well."

"Your guests don't seem to be quite as pleased as you with our arrival."

"On the contrary, they are simply agape that *I* managed to be the first to lure you gentlemen to such an affair. Allow me the honor of introducing my daughter, Lady Alicia."

The lady was slightly taller than her mother, considerably more slender. Her hair was a less vibrant red than Mary's, and he wondered if he would be comparing all women he met to Mary. It was a ridiculous notion. It was only that he knew her so well—

Only he didn't. Not really. He knew little of what her life had been like while he'd been away.

The girl curtsied. "Your Grace. My lords."

"Lady Alicia."

"She is quite accomplished on the pianoforte and will entertain us following dinner. And of course, you are acquainted with my dear niece Lady Mary," the countess said.

He thought neither of the other two ladies held a candle to her in beauty, although they came close. "Yes. It is good to see you again, Lady Mary."

"And you, Your Grace, my lords."

"Allow me to introduce Viscount Fitzwilliam," Lady Ivers continued.

Sebastian had a strong need to groan. The night would no doubt be filled with tedious introductions.

"You are a fortunate man, my lord, to have won Lady Mary over."

"I'd have not asked for her hand in marriage if I'd thought otherwise."

Right then. So we're not going to get along famously. He was actually glad. He hadn't wanted to like the man, and he wasn't certain why. It went without saying that he wanted Mary to be happy. He just wasn't certain this was the man with whom he wanted her to be happy. He couldn't explain his strange thoughts.

"Your Grace," Lady Ivers began, "you will discover that I am most unconventional and known for being a bit eccentric. I have dispensed with formal seating this evening. If you will be so kind as to escort me into dinner when the time comes . . ."

Her pointed stare indicated that no was not an option as a response.

"I would be honored."

"Splendid. Lord Rafe, my daughter shall be on your arm and, Lord Tristan, if you will be so kind as to escort Lady Mary. You don't mind do you, Fitzwilliam?"

The viscount opened his mouth.

"Good. I thought not. Come along then, Fitzwilliam. I want to ensure that you are acquainted with the lady you'll escort into dinner. Gentlemen, I shall see you shortly."

She bustled off. Fitzwilliam bent down and whispered something to Mary. She nodded, said something in a low voice. The intimacy of their belonging together struck Sebastian like a blow to the chest. Which was ludicrous. He had no claim on her. He'd rarely thought of her over the years. Pembrook was always uppermost in his mind. As Fitzwilliam strode away, she turned back to them. "I do hope you're not put

off by my aunt's manipulations. She can be quite . . .
enthusiastic."

"I would better describe her as a tempest at sea,"
Tristan said.

Lady Alicia smiled. "I hope to have at least half her
energy when I'm her age."

"I haven't half her energy now," Mary said. "We are
truly pleased that you accepted Aunt Sophie's invitation. We thought this small affair might be a less overwhelming introduction back into Society. If you'll come
along, Lady Alicia and I will introduce you around."

It was a ten-minute maze of nodding, bowing, and
taking gloved hands. It was only as the bell was rung
for dinner that it occurred to Sebastian that he should
have been paying more attention to the young ladies
to whom he was introduced, to determine if one might
make a suitable wife. Then he realized that if he'd already forgotten their names that they probably weren't
for him. Shouldn't he at least be attracted to them
enough to want to remember their names?

Thank goodness he was rescued by his formidable
hostess and escorted her into dinner. He had been
dreading the seating but with her at the foot of the
table and he to her right, only she, the wall, Tristan,
and Mary—both of whom sat across from him—had to
endure his scars. Lady Alicia was to his right. In spite
of the number of people in attendance, Lady Ivers had
managed to arrange the seating so dinner was more intimate. After he quickly downed two glasses of wine, he
also found it more relaxed.

Fitzwilliam was on the other side of Mary, so while
he'd not accompanied her into dinner, he was no doubt
somewhat mollified to find himself sitting beside his betrothed. The poor chit he'd escorted into dinner was

ignored as the viscount sought to engage Mary in conversation. Once he had her attention, Tristan began cleverly luring her back to him. Sebastian suspected she'd have a stiff neck before the night was done.

However, he couldn't deny he appreciated the view he had of her. From beneath her lashes, she met his gaze and damned if it wasn't as though she'd reached across the table and touched him. He lifted his wineglass in a silent salute, which she returned with a soft smile. His gaze followed the slope of her throat to her bared décolletage. Her skin was a creamy white that drew the eye, but then everything about her commanded attention.

She turned away as Fitzwilliam diverted her once again. He wondered if the viscount was an exceptional conversationalist or if he was as boring as his clothing. Black and white. Not a single thread of color.

"Amazing, isn't she?" Lady Ivers said so quietly that no one else heard, and the heat burned his cheeks at being caught staring at Mary. "One can hardly countenance that she had no formal preparation for her own Season. But then what do nuns know of etiquette outside of the church?"

All Sebastian's personal discomforts in this situation vanished, and he studied the countess as though she'd just spoken in a foreign language. "Nuns?"

"Quite." She blinked, offered a slight smile, then appeared flummoxed. "Oh, my word." Her voice went even lower. "Did I let the cat out of the bag? I would have thought she told you, but then I suppose in reflection that it is not something about which one boasts—even to an old friend. But yes, her father sent her to a nunnery when she was little more than twelve. In spite of my earnest objections. She was already ensconced behind those walls by the time I found out. One of those orders that doesn't allow visitors. I wanted to bring her to our home, but my husband insisted it was not my concern. The nerve. My sister's daughter not my concern. I can tell you it was some months before he again found his bed warm."

If Sebastian weren't still shocked and seething by this revelation he might have smiled at her acerbic tone.

"Can you imagine a girl of her spirit being confined to such a restrained world?" she asked.

Asking why the Earl of Winslow would do such a thing to his only daughter was on the tip of his tongue but he feared he knew. Surely not, but he couldn't quiet his suspicions. The man was fortunate that Sebastian hadn't known of this when he'd visited. He could hardly imagine a crueler fate for the girl who had once raced wildly over the moors with him.

"I finally had enough of it. Put my foot down this year I tell you. Told Winslow to his face that if I was bringing my daughter to London for the Season that I was good and well bringing my dear sister's daughter with me. Her dear mother would have wanted her to have a proper suitor."

"And is he? A proper suitor. Fitzwilliam."

She drew herself up as though she were responsible for the arrangement. "Oh, quite. He is the heir to Glenchester."

He tried to place the name—

"Marquess," she said as though she could see that he struggled.

"It seems I am far less prepared than Lady Mary for a night such as this."

"Don't concern yourself. You'll get the hang of everything quickly enough. I suspect your father taught you a great deal that you've merely locked away."

He remembered the few times she and her family had visited. "Your husband. He's not here tonight," Sebastian said. "Are condolences in order?"

"Oh, my dear, that would be quite premature. Unfortunately, some wretched problem with his tenants called him away to the estate for a few days. Quite honestly he prefers the country."

"I can relate to his preference."

She smiled. "I suspect most men do, but they must tolerate what women prefer from time to time. Makes for a more pleasant marriage."

Her words had him glancing back over to Mary, and wondering what her husband would tolerate from her. Would he give her the freedom she needed? And if he didn't what recourse did Sebastian have to ensure she was happy? None at all, he supposed.

Her light laughter floated toward him, the sound as pleasing as crystal glasses tapped gently with a silver fork. Tristan had said something to elicit her response. It seemed his brother was quite the flirtatious devil.

He wished when he returned to Pembrook that she would be there. Where the deuce was Fitzwilliam's estate anyway? He knew so little of the man, knew so little of most of these people. But then they knew nothing of him.

"Did you enjoy your time in the army, Your Grace?" Lady Alicia asked.

He felt Mary's gaze light on him like a caress, could sense her holding her breath, anticipating his answer, and he wondered if she was as aware of him as he of her. Even when he didn't hear the words, he heard her voice. The succulent aromas of the feast wafted around him, and yet he was acutely conscious of the scent of orchids—when not a single blossom graced the room.

The scent was hers, all hers. Of that he was certain. Lady Alicia and her mother carried the fragrance of roses. "It provided interesting . . . experiences," he finally answered curtly, far too curtly.

The girl blushed such a violent hue of red that he wished he could take back the tone if not the words. He simply hated being dissected as though he were the latest species of insect discovered.

"Did you serve in the Crimea, Your Grace?" Fitzwilliam asked, emphasizing the address as though it were undeserved, a challenge in his voice that indicated he might doubt Sebastian's claims.

He had no intention of revealing that he'd lied about his age. One need be only sixteen to serve, but he'd felt a desire to lose himself in military life. He'd forged a letter from a fictitious father and never revealed that he was of the aristocracy. He'd been treated as a common man and that had given him a perspective many of his peers would never experience. He began his career as an ensign, serving as a captain's assistant. "I did. Balaclava. Tennyson immortalized the battle."

"*The Charge of the Light Brigade,*" Lady Alicia said in wonder. "You were there?"

"Unfortunately."

"Nasty business that," Fitzwilliam said.

"All war is nasty business, my lord."

Tension radiated between them.

"I believe all our soldiers are to be commended for their duty to our country," Mary said.

Sebastian lifted his glass. "I shall drink to that."

"I think we all should," Tristan said. "Hear! Hear! To our soldiers who keep the devil from our shores."

Everyone at the table joined in the toast, even Fitzwilliam. Sebastian wasn't certain why a gauntlet had been thrown down but he was fairly certain one had been.

Pray I don't pick it up, Fitzwilliam, he thought. Based on the smiles he'd witnessed, Mary fancied the fellow. Considering her feelings and his desire to make amends to her, he would leave the gauntlet where it lay. For now.

In the piano room, as Lady Alicia's fingers tripped merrily over the keyboard, Mary cast a surreptitious glance over to where Sebastian stood with his brothers. Her aunt had hoped to enfold them into the aristocracy, but they continued to remain apart. She didn't think they were uncomfortable with their surroundings. They simply didn't see themselves as belonging within it.

She could understand the feeling. When she'd first come to London, she'd felt as though everyone watched and remarked on her every move. Without a proper introduction into Society, she'd been an object of curiosity. She knew she'd managed to win many over, but some still weren't quite sure what to make of her.

She glanced around. Fitzwilliam had slipped out, no doubt to puff on a cheroot with one of his friends. She was surprised he left her. He'd been hovering all night as though he expected her to do something inappropriate. Silly man. She'd do nothing to bring embarrassment to her aunt when she had been so kind.

She knew he wouldn't be pleased with what she was about to do, but she couldn't leave the brothers so isolated. She skirted around the edge of the room until she was standing beside Sebastian. She caught a whiff of his strong, masculine scent. So much earthier than Fitzwilliam's, as though a bit of Pembrook flowed through his veins. A silly thought, but she had always associated him with the land, the wildness of nature. Fitzwilliam was the city. Gaslights and piano recitals.

"There are some empty chairs on the other side of the room," she said quietly.

"I'm at ease here."

"If this is you at ease, I would hardly care to see you when you are not."

It brought her pleasure to catch the slightest twitch of his mouth. "I see the years didn't diminish your feistiness."

It had somewhat but with him she could be herself as she couldn't with others. She was no longer Lady Mary, but simply Mary. If she didn't behave quite properly he was more likely than others to forgive her.

"I'm a bit more circumspect with others," she confessed. With Fitzwilliam especially, she realized, and was suddenly struck with the thought that it should not be so.

She wondered if Sebastian would be offended if she pointed out that he was keeping himself apart from everyone else. Years ago, she'd never given any thought at all to anything she said to him. Whether he laughed, scolded, or argued—she'd always felt free to speak her mind. She'd felt the tension at the table and knew that Sebastian did take offense at words spoken.

"You didn't tell me you were sent to a nunnery," he said, his voice low enough that only she could hear him.

Her smile withered. "Bless Aunt Sophie. I assume she's the one who told you as it's not common knowledge around here."

"She thought I knew, that you would have told me. Why didn't you?"

"What could you do about it except perhaps feel guilty?"

"We're the reason you were sent."

He hadn't posed a question. His words held conviction. She shouldn't have been surprised that he managed to decipher why her life had taken such an unpleasant turn. He'd always had a talent for figuring out puzzles. Still she did not want him to bear the burden for her foolishness. "Not really, no. It was my fault. You cautioned me to tell no one. When have I ever heeded someone else's counsel?"

Her question enticed him into twitching his lips. Before he could interrogate her, she continued. "I went to Father, believing he could put matters to right, would confront Lord David on your behalf. Instead, I discovered he believes the answers to life's difficulties rest at the bottom of a whiskey bottle."

She saw understanding and sadness in his pale blue gaze. And regret.

"I'm sorry, Mary. Was your time with the nuns difficult?"

"As getting blood from a turnip. Does that make you feel better?"

"No, it makes me want to pummel your father into the ground."

"Which is why I saw no reason in telling you. It's in the past. Aunt Sophie declared I would have a Season and took me through my paces. Hired tutors to teach me etiquette and dancing, so here I am."

She tilted her head so she could see him clearly, wished she hadn't. He watched her with an intensity that was unsettling.

"Then I owe your aunt a debt of gratitude," he said. "It's easier facing London, knowing you are here."

She could have sworn a blush crept up beneath his bronzed skin before he looked away. "Even if I convinced my aunt to lure you out of hiding?" she teased.

"Even then."

"I'm glad you came," she said. Before he could respond, she wandered away. She wondered why issuing a compliment embarrassed him. She didn't want to contemplate how harsh his life might have been that a kind gesture—a sensitive one—was cause for embarrassment. But more she walked away before she was sorely tempted to invite him to take a turn about the garden with her, so they could truly talk, could once again become comfortable with each other. Although she was fairly certain that would only lead to disaster.

Stopping beside her aunt, she squeezed her hand. "Thank you for inviting them."

"It is not as though the dinner party was not already planned, although I daresay your father will not be pleased when he discovers that I included them."

Mary knew that Ladies Hermione and Victoria would not be pleased that they'd not been invited, but she suspected their enthusiasm for the lords would overwhelm them.

"He informed me this afternoon," her aunt continued, "that I am to keep a close watch over you and ensure that you do not speak with them overmuch."

"He fears Fitzwilliam will not tolerate my renewing an old friendship."

"He is no doubt correct on that score."

Their conversation was interrupted as the final chords resounded and Alicia stood. Polite applause quickly followed.

Alicia curtsied. "Thank you so much. Now if the young people will join me in the parlor for some games."

Charades no doubt. Mary absolutely abhorred the game. She'd avoid it if she could. Unfortunately, Fitzwilliam adored it. He returned from the terrace, smelling pleasantly of tobacco and offered her his arm.

"One moment," she said to him, and walked over to where Sebastian and his brothers remained standing. She smiled at them. "The invitation to the parlor was meant for you as well. You are, after all, young people."

"Funny, I don't feel young," Rafe said.

She understood his emotion. He was two years her junior, but she didn't feel young either. "But you are. Come along. It'll be fun."

"We should probably thank your aunt for her hospitality and take our leave," Sebastian said.

"Not yet. My cousin will be so disappointed." She would be disappointed. And Mary wasn't certain why she herself so desperately wished them to stay. "Just a while longer."

"I suppose no harm can come of it," Tristan said.

"None whatsoever," she assured him.

Chapter 9

Mary suddenly found herself wishing for charades, no matter that she was horrible at it. She'd never quite seen the humor in the game Alicia chose: "Questions." They all sat in a circle. Sixteen people. She hadn't meant to place herself between Fitzwilliam and Sebastian. It had simply happened that as they'd taken their chairs so they had ended up in the same area. Each of them held a card with a unique number on it. In the center of the circle was a stack of cards.

The game was simple. Someone posed a question, turned over a card, and the person with the corresponding number had to claim the question.

"I'll begin," Alicia said. "Who is the silliest person in the room?" She turned over a card bearing the number three and glanced around. No one responded, and Mary had her first sense that this game was not going to go well at all.

Alicia frowned. "Who has the number three?"

"I do," Tristan said.

She scoffed. "You're supposed to put your card down and say, 'I am the silliest person in the room.'"

"But I'm not."

"Doesn't matter. You see, that's what makes it funny. The question doesn't apply to the person who answers, and therefore, it makes us laugh. Now you ask a question and draw a card."

"Any question?" he asked with a devilish glint in his eye.

"Any question."

Tristan lowered his gaze into a sultry invitation that Mary could not help but believe had lured many a woman into his bed. "Who does not wear undergarments beneath her skirts?"

One lady gasped, a couple tittered, and Alicia smiled broadly. "That's the spirit."

He reached out and turned over a card. Five.

"That would be me," Fitzwilliam said, clearly irritated as he tossed his card on the table.

Tristan grinned. "I should have known you'd fancy wearing a skirt now and then, Fitzwilliam. Do you don a corset as well?"

"Watch your manners, lad," Fitzwilliam growled.

Mary placed her hand over his. "It's all in jest."

"Of course it is," Alicia reiterated. "Don't take offense, Fitzwilliam. It'll ruin the fun. Now ask your question."

He took a moment to regain his calm. "Who smells like roses?"

"Boring," Tristan muttered.

Beside Mary, Fitzwilliam stiffened. Before she could wonder overly long as to why Fitzwilliam had chosen her cousin's fragrance and not hers of orchids, she quickly reached out and flipped over a card. "Six."

"I smell like roses," Lady Kathryn answered. Only she didn't. She smelled of vanilla. "Who snuck out of the music room earlier for a secret tryst in the garden?"

She turned over a card. "Twelve."

Alicia laughed and revealed her card. "That was me! Quite the trick, wasn't it, to do so while I was playing the pianoforte?"

Mary laughed. "Your mother always claimed you were good at handling more than one task at a time."

Beside her, Fitzwilliam relaxed. "A very useful talent to have indeed."

"You make me blush, my lord. Now, who is the handsomest devil in London?" Alicia asked and flipped over the number ten.

Sebastian went so still that Mary wasn't certain he breathed. Dear God, no. She wanted to snatch the number from his clenched fist.

"The hour is late," he said, bringing himself to his feet. "If you'll be so good as to excuse me, it's time I took my leave."

Alicia appeared stunned. "But we've not finished the game."

How could her cousin not realize who held the number ten? "Alicia—"

"My brother is quite right," Rafe said. "If you'll excuse me, I, too, must depart."

He didn't wait for a response, but followed his brother out. Not certain what to do, Mary rose. She couldn't let them leave. Not like this. "Excuse me."

As she was walking out, she heard Tristan say, "Lady Alicia, perhaps you would be kind enough to oblige me and allow me to teach you a game I learned in the Orient. It involves a blindfold and . . ."

Mary didn't care what else it involved, although she

suspected it would be scandalous. She hurried into the hallway, only to find it empty save for a footman standing at attention. "The Duke of Keswick."

He stared at her dumbly. She touched the left side of her face. "Scars. Where did he go?"

"Through the front door, m'lady."

She dashed out, saw him standing in the drive, and raced down the steps. "Sebastian!"

He turned. The gaslights were kind, only revealing his unmarred side. She was struck with the realization that he had been the handsomest man in the parlor. Although he and Tristan were twins, something in Sebastian's features was nobler. Had always been so, but was more pronounced now.

She brought herself to a staggering halt before she rammed into him. "Don't leave. Not like this. It's only a silly game. It doesn't mean anything."

"I'm too old for games, Mary."

"You're what? All of six and twenty?"

"I have been on the earth for that many years, but within a few days of leaving Pembrook I grew into manhood. Add twelve years to that, and I would say that I'm well into my thirties. I have no time for nor any interest in parlor games."

"Come back inside. We'll find a quiet corner, sit, and talk."

He laughed darkly. "And how do you think your betrothed will welcome that notion?"

Not well, not well at all, and her father would be even more furious. "You're my friend. You will always be my friend. I wanted you to feel as though you belonged here."

"I don't. Not yet. But I will in time." He touched her cheek, and she felt the sweep of his thumb over the spot where she knew a freckle resided. His fingers were rough, callused. She wondered when he'd removed his gloves, was ashamed to admit that she was glad he had. They'd held hands as children and thought nothing of it. "Thank you for tonight, Mary. Thank your aunt as well."

Before she could say anything, he was walking toward a carriage that was barreling up the drive. As it slowed, he climbed inside with a grace she'd seldom seen in other men. Of course most of them had the good sense to wait until the vehicle came to a halt. She took a step forward, not certain what she planned to do. A hand came to rest on her shoulder.

"Give him leave to go," Fitzwilliam said.

She rubbed her brow. "It was such a ridiculous game."

"Not as ridiculous as the one his brother wished to play. I swear to you, Mary, that when I take my place in the House of Lords, I shall see to it that a law is passed that will allow only charades to be played in parlors."

She couldn't help it. She laughed lightly and leaned against him. He wound his arm around her shoulders and pressed a kiss to her temple. "You can't protect them anymore, dear girl. They need to make it on their own now."

As he guided her back into the house, she knew he was right. Still it was so very hard to stand by and watch while they floundered.

Mary was sitting up in bed, brushing her hair, when the clock chimes rang through the hallway announcing the arrival of midnight. A servant would soon be about to quiet them until late morning. Mary wasn't certain why her aunt insisted that they be allowed to clang until the end of day. Her father insisted on silence much sooner.

A knock sounded on the door. "Yes?"

Alicia peered in. "Are you terribly angry with me?"

"Not too terribly." She shook her head at her cousin's crestfallen expression. "No, not at all, really. It wasn't your fault."

Alicia darted across the bedchamber, jumped into bed with her, and snuggled beneath the covers. "I'm so glad you agreed to stay the night. And I'm so sorry about the silly game. It never occurred to me that Keswick would be holding the card. It was a rather stupid thing to say. I wanted to be clever, like Lord Tristan."

"I don't know if he's so much clever as he is wicked."

Alicia grinned, her eyes sparkling with mischief. "He is, isn't he? He wanted us to play a game with a blindfold. We would have to caress someone's face and guess who it was, but Fitzwilliam said we'd had enough of games. Then he went in search of you, but I think he must have found Mother first because she came in and said it was time for refreshments."

Alicia sounded so terribly disappointed. "Then Lord Tristan took his leave. The evening wasn't nearly as much fun after that." She grabbed a pillow and held it to her chest as though it were a lover. "I thought the dinner at least went splendidly well. The Pembrook lords are not quite so frightening when they aren't brandishing pistols about. Although Lord Rafe confessed to me during dinner that he had one on his person. And a knife."

Mary was not surprised. They left Pembrook in fear of their lives. How difficult it would be now to trust anyone.

"Were you and Keswick making eyes at each other during dinner?" Alicia asked.

Mary's heart galloped. She had little enough reputation as it was, with everyone speculating as to why her father had never given her a proper Season. She certainly didn't want Fitzwilliam to doubt her. "What? No. Why would you think that?"

"You kept looking in his direction."

"He sat across from me."

"So did I yet you hardly looked at me at all."

Mary plucked at the bristles on her brush. "I just wanted to make certain that he was comfortable with all that was happening around him."

"I don't think Lord Fitzwilliam likes Keswick."

"I daresay you're right on that count. But it's only because he doesn't know him. Once they get to know each other better I think they'll become chums."

"I'm not so certain. I think he noticed you watching Keswick as well."

"I gave him no reason to doubt my affections." Although she couldn't deny that he'd been far more relaxed and pleasant after the brothers had all taken their leave.

"I'm quite fascinated by them. They appear to be gentlemen and yet one is left with the distinct impression that they are not. I daresay they look to be quite skilled at ruining a lady's reputation."

Ah, yes, quite skilled. Mary thought they could do it with little more than a look.

Sebastian sat beside the fire in his library, savoring the flavor of whiskey on his tongue, and attempting to push back the memory of Mary's soft skin beneath his fingers. He'd been a fool to touch her.

The door opened, but he didn't look away from the fire at the echo of Tristan's resounding footsteps. As soon as Sebastian had arrived home, he sent his carriage back to Lady Ivers's residence so Tristan would have transportation.

His brother settled into the chair across from him, reached for a glass, and filled it with whiskey. "You should have simply tossed down the card, made light of it."

"Do you not think it would have embarrassed the girl?"

"No more so than she was already. It was a game, Sebastian. It meant nothing."

He knew that, but he was not yet to the point where he could laugh about his disfigurement. He didn't know if he ever would be.

"What did you think of Fitzwilliam?" he asked, to direct the conversation away from his poor handling of the situation.

"Don't like him."

Sebastian studied his brother who was studying his glass of whiskey as though he could read the future in it. "Why not?"

Tristan lifted his gaze over the rim of the glass. "Do I require a reason?"

"Opinions are usually based on some foundation."

"My gut."

"Surely there was more than that."

"I don't need more. I trust my instincts."

"Do you think he will make Mary happy?"

"I think you would make her happier." He tossed back his whiskey as Sebastian grunted.

"We hardly know each other any longer."

"Yet you seemed incapable of taking your gaze from her." He held up a hand. "Not that I blame you. She is quite fetching."

"She's more than that. She's beautiful."

"You noticed."

"I'm only half-blind."

"There you are," Tristan said with a grin. "Exactly what you should have said during that wretched game. 'I'm only half-handsome.' People might have laughed."

Sebastian scowled. "I don't enjoy people laughing at me."

"Which is why we must laugh at ourselves first. But then you were always the more serious."

"I had heavier burdens to bear."

"That you did." With a sigh, he rose. "I'm off to Rafe's for a bit of sport. Care to join me?"

"No."

Tristan glanced around. "The place doesn't smell as much like Uncle tonight."

No, it didn't. "The servants worked hard to achieve that end. Perhaps they disliked his stench as much as we do."

"I rather think it's more that you terrify them. Which is not always a bad thing." Before Sebastian could comment, Tristan said, "Was your man able to follow him?"

"Yes. He moved into a room at a boarding house on the outskirts of London."

"Didn't go far then. I'd advise you to sleep with one eye open."

Sebastian saw that his brother regretted the words as soon as they were spoken. He held up a hand to forestall any forthcoming apologies. "You have no need to watch your words around me."

"You should have gone to the sea and I to the army."

"Our fates might not have changed. I've seen seamen aplenty with only one eye. Besides I have a tendency toward seasickness."

Tristan stared at him. "You're jesting."

"Afraid not. I spent most of my journey back from the Crimea with my head hung over a bucket."

Tristan craned back his head and released a bold laugh. His legs were braced far apart as though even now he stood on the deck of a bucking ship. When only the crackling of the fire in the hearth again filled the room he said, "Good night, Brother."

He strode purposely from the room, leaving Sebastian to his demons.

Chapter 10

During the week since his return to Easton House, Sebastian had been busy sorting through the mess of records and documents that his uncle had left behind. The man was a slovenly slob when it came to keeping a tight accounting of all five estates that had been under his care. He had managers and solicitors handling various aspects, but little had been arranged in any sort of order.

Sitting at his desk in the library, he glanced over at Tristan, casually sprawled on the sofa—obviously life at sea was not as regimented as the army—leisurely reading an assortment of documents they'd discovered in a drawer. They looked to be little more than reports from various overseers, but it was imperative that Sebastian learn as much of the important matters in as short a span of time as possible. If not for his devious uncle, he would have been at his father's side, learning all that he needed to know to manage his estates. As it was, he had to ferret out information. He was simply grateful that his brother had decided to join him in residence and assist with the monstrous task. It made sense that he be as familiar as possible with everything associated with the titles and estates. He was, after all, the spare.

And if Sebastian had no luck securing a wife, it would be Tristan or *his* son who would eventually inherit and hold the titles. Sebastian intended to ensure that his heir presumptive was educated in all things. If it came to that.

"You should consider joining me at Rafe's tonight," Tristan said distractedly. "His gaming tables are excellent."

"Which I suppose means that no one catches you cheating."

Tristan grinned. Even as a lad he'd had a penchant for seeking shortcuts. "A man caught cheating on the seas is tossed to the sharks . . . or feels the bite of a cat-o-nine."

It was the opening Sebastian had been waiting for. He leaned back and kept his voice as casual as possible. "Is that what happened to you? You were found guilty of cheating?"

He'd only caught a glimpse of his brother's back once—when he'd walked into his room at Rafe's without knocking. But it had been enough to send guilt and fury spiraling through him. His brother's back had been torn apart—more than once based upon the thickness of the scars. Tristan had merely shrugged into his shirt and ordered him to never walk in unannounced again.

Tristan tossed aside the missive he'd been reading. "Boring rubbish, this. I don't know why we're bothering with it."

"Because we don't know what may be of value. And you avoided answering my question."

Tristan shoved himself to his feet, walked to the window, and gazed out on the magnificent gardens. Sebastian couldn't fault his uncle for the manner in which he'd taken care of the London residence. Everything was in good repair. An abundance of fine liquor was easily at hand. The horses were of strong stock. The carriages were well-sprung. Nothing was in want of attention. Except the books. They left him feeling as though he were overlooking something vital.

"I wasn't accustomed to being ordered about," Tristan finally said quietly. "I enjoyed a good brawl. A lot of anger churned within me, and there are few places to unleash it on a ship."

"I'm sorry for the hardship."

Tristan faced him. "Did you find orders easy to take?"

He shook his head. "Saved every ha'penny I earned so I could purchase my way up the ranks to be the one who gave them rather than the one taking them. I never was completely without orders being thrown at me, but in time they became fewer in number and I was issuing most of them."

"Well, there you are then. We are better suited to being gentlemen of leisure." He spread his arms wide. "So here we are."

"Why do I have the impression you are chomping at the bit to be elsewhere?"

"Because there's no blasted wind here. I enjoy standing on the deck with the wind billowing the sails. Out there is freedom. Here I am left with the constant sense that I'm on the verge of being caught."

"By Uncle?" Had there been threats? Had he spied

someone lurking in the shadows? Sebastian was at a disadvantage because he could only ever clearly see the shadows to his right.

Tristan scoffed. "God, no. I'd welcome him attempting to do me harm. They couldn't hang me for self-defense." He shook his head. "I'm not quite sure what it is that bothers me. The thought of domesticity perhaps. Of being reined in."

"A woman then. Has someone caught your fancy?"

He laughed. "They all catch my fancy."

Sebastian was well aware that Tristan caught theirs. During his time at Rafe's, he'd seen the women draped over Tristan as though he stole the bones from their bodies with a mere glance. Even at Lady Ivers's dinner party, the young ladies were eyeing Tristan as though he were their favorite chocolate. He wasn't envious, but he did miss the enthusiasm with which women had once come to his bed.

The door opening caught his attention. His butler strode in, carrying a salver. Sebastian came to his feet, wondering who might be calling.

"A missive has arrived, Your Grace."

Sebastian took the envelope, turned it over. The waxed seal carried no crest, but outlined a single rose. Perfume wafted up to tease his nostrils. Orchids. It had been more than a week since he'd relished Mary's sweet fragrance, but he would recognize it anywhere.

"You're done here, Thomas. I'll ring for you if I need to send a response."

"Very good, sir."

He waited until the butler had left before returning to his chair. He'd never had any correspondence while he was away. He'd envied the men who had received missives from home. He slid the tip of the letter opener into place and relished the ripping sound. He removed the folded paper and opened it.

It's imperative that we meet at Rotten Row at four. I shall be riding a chestnut gelding.

Always your friend,

Mary

As though he needed to know the shade of her horse in order to find her. Her hair would give her location away. Even tucked up beneath a hat, it would serve as a divining rod for him.

"I can't determine if you're delighted or bothered by what you're reading," Tristan murmured.

"It's from Mary. She wishes to meet me at Hyde Park. She says it's important."

"Rather cryptic. Any notion regarding what might be important?"

"No, but I doubt it bodes well." He trailed his finger over the delicate script. He wondered if this meeting would go any better than the previous ones. He did hope they weren't forever destined to have abrupt partings.

"Maybe she's simply inventing some excuse to see you again," Tristan said. "You two seldom went a day without visiting each other, and here it's been several."

"We were children, caught up in play."

"'Tis true she's no longer a child, but that doesn't mean you can't get caught up in play."

Sebastian scowled at Tristan. "She is a lady for God's sake. Do not imply otherwise."

"Have you no interest in her at all?"

"As a friend, of course. As more than that . . . I do not think we'd suit." He looked away when Tristan arched an eyebrow. "Besides, she's betrothed."

"Betrothals can be broken."

"Not without consequences."

"So you've considered it?"

"No." Blast his brother for even putting the notion in his head.

"I think he selected her for her dowry. Her father was quite generous with it. Fitzwilliam's family's coffers are not quite as flush as they lead people to believe."

"How do you know this?"

Tristan grinned. "Not all *ladies* are indeed ladies. And as much as I like Rafe's girls, I don't fancy paying for my pleasures. We are a curiosity. As such many bedchamber doors—or in my case often windows—are opened to us."

"We're striving to regain our place and your actions could very well undo it."

"I'm insulted, Sebastian. I'm very careful, and I would never take advantage of an innocent. But I swear to you, Brother, there are a good many uninnocent wenches who long to embrace the danger I can provide. You could have some fun yourself."

"We have enough scandal associated with our name. I see no reason to sully it further."

"And I see no reason not to take advantage of our notoriety. But we've wandered off topic. You had an interest in Fitzwilliam."

"Not in the man, per se, but in his . . ." How could he explain? "Is he good for Mary? Her aunt assures me he is of good stock, but is that enough?"

"Perhaps that is a question you should ask her when you see her."

Perhaps he would.

As Mary trotted her horse along Rotten Row, she knew she would have been wise to have come to the park in the landau so her aunt and cousin could accom-

pany her, but she and Sebastian had often ridden together as children. She thought that familiarity should
serve her well now. She'd not seen him since the night
of the dinner party, and while she didn't owe him any
consideration, she did feel a sense of obligation toward
him. Not pity. He would detest that emotion. She'd seen
that well enough after her tears had surfaced at the ball
when he made his appearance. Charity, perhaps. Although even that he would no doubt disdain.

The lords of Pembrook were the topic of conversation at every dinner, and last night's ball as well. The
older ladies plotted how to keep them away from their
daughters. The daughters gathered in dark corners and
whispered about occasional sightings. Someone had
seen Lord Tristan striding into a tailor's on Regent
Street. Someone else reported seeing him at the haber-
dashery. Lord Rafe seemed to be as much of a recluse
as the duke for no one spied him. They understood Keswick's hesitancy to be seen, but still they discussed how
best to lure the lords from their lair. It was Rafe and
Tristan that they seemed most intent upon capturing.

Often Mary was sought out for advice. As though she
knew the intimate details about the brothers. But they
were not the lads she'd known, and she could provide
very little in the way of assurances that they would soon
be making the rounds. While she doubted they would
ever admit it, she suspected they weren't quite comfortable with their return to Society. They had never traversed the maze of etiquette or—more importantly—the
elusive rituals not taught to children. One's reputation
was improved or tarnished based upon to whom one
was seen speaking. How one danced, how one laughed,
how one dressed—all were studied and commented on.
Did a lady stand beside a frond, behind it, or in front

of it? Did one look as though she desperately wished to dance or did she act as though she could hardly be bothered? Trivial behaviors that could mean so much. Her own experiences had taught her that it could all be quite intimidating, and she suspected that even men as world-weary as the lords of Pembrook would find it so.

Still when Lady Hermione had cornered her at last night's ball and asked once more for the favor of Mary encouraging the brothers to attend her ball, she decided no harm would come of asking.

She spotted Sebastian in the distance, his black horse loping along. From here, although she couldn't see his scars, it was easy enough to identify him. He sat a horse magnificently and rode with confidence. Even if she'd not known who he was, she'd have identified him as a lord. His erect carriage spoke of self-assurance, a man who knew his place, one not to be trifled with. Even as a lad, he'd ridden with the same grace. She found comfort in knowing not everything had changed.

Unerringly he guided his horse toward her, as though he'd spied her the moment he entered the park, had known exactly where she was to be found. She brought her own horse to a halt as he drew his near. Reins in hand, he did little more than touch his fingers to the brim of his hat, and she assumed he felt more at ease with his face remaining in shadow. Just as he had during each encounter, he ensured that his handsome side was directed toward her.

"Lady Mary."

"Your Grace." She longed to see his mouth twitch with humor or to hear his laughter echoing over the green of the park.

"You indicated an urgency to our meeting."

Blushing, she tilted her head down slightly and peered

up at him, giving him an impish smile. "I may have overstated matters, but I feared if I merely requested you join me that you would find an excuse not to."

He narrowed his eye, tightened his jaw, and she thought if she had no history with him that she might have been intimidated. "So your missive was a ruse?"

"It was for your own good. You can't possibly think that attending my aunt's dinner party was enough to earn your place in Society. You need to be seen about. Shall we walk?"

"I prefer to ride."

She squelched her disappointment. Walking provided an ease in talking that riding didn't, but it also would shelter her reputation. "Then ride we shall."

She urged her horse forward. Rather than simply turn his about, he guided it around hers until the unmarred side of his face was again within her view. It irritated her that he would think her so shallow. "I'm not put off by your scars."

"Still, no need to inflict them on you when there is an alternative."

"You can be quite obstinate."

"I learned it from you."

Laughing, she peered over at him. "I do believe, Your Grace, that *you* taught me about obstinacy. I was quite biddable as a child."

"Never. Not from the moment we crossed paths were you ever biddable."

Even though the words indicated easy banter, his tone didn't, as though he were forcing himself into a role that didn't quite fit.

"You mustn't let your discomfort during the parlor game keep you from attending other affairs," she said quietly.

"It hasn't. I've been quite busy putting matters to rights."

"Such as?" she challenged.

She could see the determined set of his jaw. He didn't want to explain his actions, but their long-ago friendship prevented him from telling her to mind her own business. He owed her, and while he might instruct everyone else to go to the devil he wouldn't toss the order out to her.

"If you must know, my uncle was known to purchase items on credit," he said succinctly.

"Most of the aristocracy does." Her father paid his creditors once a year.

"Yes, well, I don't hold with the practice. I've informed them that they'll receive no further funds from the house of Keswick for anything he purchases."

"Does he have his own means?"

"I think it unlikely. He presently resides in an area that is one step above squalor." He glanced over at her. "I suppose you think me without mercy."

"No, of course not. I think you have every right to be even more harsh where he's concerned. But I have wondered . . ." She let her voice trail off. Bringing forth the words was not easy.

"What, Mary? What have you wondered?"

She forced herself to meet his gaze. "What if I misheard? What if he was talking of killing chickens for the following day's dinner or . . . I don't know. Why did he wait so long to make a claim for the title?"

"To avoid suspicion of foul play." He studied her. "What exactly did you hear that night?"

It all seemed so distant. A foggy memory now, faded with time, and yet the words came to her as though she heard them only moments before.

"Someone said, 'The lads, m'lord, now that they are in the tower . . . what would you have me do with them?' And then I heard your uncle say, 'Why, kill them, of course.' He laughed then. Could he have been joking? My father does not believe he was serious. I could hardly countenance the words I heard. I do wish I knew to whom he spoke."

"It sounds as though it was one of the men who escorted us to the tower. I've not seen any of them since our return. I should look at the record of servants hired and let go. See if I can determine what became of them."

"How many were there?"

"Four. We went so docilely. I think we were still reeling from our father's death. It was not until the door in the tower clanged closed and I heard the key grinding in the lock that I realized something was amiss. I'm not certain how I could have been so unaware."

She looked out over the greenery of the park. So lush and peaceful. It was difficult to believe that such evil lurked in the world.

"Why would you suspect your uncle of wishing you harm?"

"I should have suspected. Not until we were in the tower did I even consider that he might have killed Father."

She stared at him in open-mouthed amazement. "You don't believe your father had a riding accident?"

He gave her a pointed look. "You bashed in the head of a guard and you were a mere slip of a girl."

"He didn't die. I snuck back to Pembrook the next day to make sure he was all right. I saw him walking about."

Sebastian glared at her. "Do you know how reckless that was?"

"I had to learn the truth. I couldn't live with myself if he'd died."

"Unlike my uncle who seems to live with himself very well."

"Have you proof he killed your father?"

"No, only suspicions."

"You may never have proof, Sebastian."

"I'm well aware of that, but I shall not rest until he is made to account for his actions."

Mary realized she'd strayed from her purpose in having him meet her here. She could feel gazes coming to light on her, imagined that speculation was brewing. A time existed when she'd have not cared, but now her reputation extended to Fitzwilliam and she'd not have him regret asking for her hand in marriage. She would do nothing to bring him shame. Yet here she was, flirting at the edge of it. Word would no doubt reach him that she'd been spied in the park riding with Keswick. She'd tarried long enough.

"The Countess of Weatherly is hosting a ball this evening," Mary told him. "I know you received an invitation." Lady Hermione had decided to send a servant around with it, in spite of her mother's objections. "It would behoove you and your brothers to make an appearance. Even if only for a short time."

"Still watching out for us, Mary?"

"Someone must or you could make quite a mess of it. Your uncle had twelve years to develop friendships and trust among those who matter. It is not enough to exile him from your home. Some are less than impressed with your claim."

"I have no need to impress anyone. The law is on my side."

"But Society is not." She hated the harshness of her

words, wished she'd been able to find a softer way to deliver them. "I assume you and your brothers, at some point, will want to marry. Will want children. If Society does not accept you, it matters not that you hold a title. Your family will suffer the scandal and gossip."

"I am quite busy putting other matters to rights."

"Yes, as you said earlier but you cannot use that excuse to ignore this aspect of your title. It will serve you greatly to be well-thought of."

She detected a subtle stiffening in his posture. "Are you implying that I'm presently not?"

"No one knows you, Sebastian. They speculate. They gossip. They arrive at their own conclusions. And I must reluctantly confess that most are not flattering. Unfortunately I've not been in London long enough to acquire enough currency so that my words in support of you carry much weight."

If at all possible he became tenser. "And what of your betrothed? Do his words carry weight?"

"Not as much as they will when he inherits his father's title."

He hesitated then said, "Fitzwilliam. Is he a good man, then?"

She scowled teasingly at him. "You think I am such a silly ninny as to select a bad man?"

She detected a bit of light in the blue of his eye, almost as though he'd stumbled upon something humorous and wasn't quite sure what to make of it. "I suppose it was a rather pointless question. I always did enjoy bantering with you."

She had enjoyed doing so many things with him. "I feared you'd forget all about me."

"With hair as red as yours? How could anyone forget about you?"

She was surprised by the disappointment his words brought. She wanted it to be more than her hair that was memorable. She wanted him to remember every aspect of her, but more importantly she wanted him to remember how well they had gotten along, how strong their bond had been, how they had once laughed, how they'd dared to share a forbidden kiss. She wanted him to admit that he'd missed her as much as she had him. And she realized her thoughts had turned onto a dangerous path. When had she become such a self-centered chit who wanted to be the focus of his world when she could no longer be in the center of his world? "I fear I've lingered here too long. Please consider the Weatherly ball. I'll save you a dance."

She wasn't certain why she'd said the last. He'd given no indication that such an offer would sway him, and now she was rather embarrassed that she'd made it. Besides she was betrothed and it was completely inappropriate for her to casually toss out any sort of flirtatious banter. Before he could catch sight of the blush warming her cheeks, she urged her horse into a trot.

She hadn't issued the invitation for her personal gain. She'd done it because everything she'd told him was true: he needed to secure his place among the peerage in a more civilized manner. Still a small part of her couldn't help but hope that he would accept her offer for a dance.

Chapter 11

It was a mistake to come to the damned ball, Sebastian realized almost immediately. No steward announced the arrivals, and yet a silence permeated the crowd when he and his brothers stepped through the open doorway into the gilded ballroom. Mothers scurried to their daughters; fathers took steps forward as though to form some sort of protective wall around them.

The host and hostess, Lord and Lady Weatherly, approached cautiously. Slightly behind them, a blond-haired beauty glowed with anticipation, her gaze directed at Tristan. Sebastian despised himself for considering that at one time he would have garnered as much attention. More in fact. Besides astonishingly good looks, he possessed a title. He would have been the sought-after brother rather than the one who wished he were on the sea instead of here. But he had come to understand that Mary had spoken true: their entrance back into Society required they make yet another appearance. Even Rafe, for all his protests to the contrary, had recognized the importance of their being here.

They were dressed to the nines, in matching black swallow-tailed coats, white shirts, and black cravats. The only thing that varied was their waistcoat: his, gray; Tristan's a royal blue, and Rafe's a hunter green. His valet had trimmed his hair, but it was still longer than was fashionable. It seemed his brothers had also taken measures to tidy up a bit more, but not completely. They were part of this Society and yet each felt a need to not be totally absorbed by it. They'd been too long on their own.

"Your Grace," Lord Weatherly said stiffly. "My lords. Welcome to Camden house."

"We were honored to receive the invitation," Sebastian assured him.

Lady Weatherly snapped her head around to the blond, whom he assumed had to be her daughter. The girl blushed, then curtsied. "It was our pleasure to send it. Forgive my boldness, Lord Tristan, but I did keep a spot on my dance card reserved for you in anticipation of your attending."

"I quite prefer my women bold," Tristan said, a devastatingly wicked smile accompanying his words. Lord Weatherly tightened his jaw, his lady gasped.

"I am Lady Hermione," their daughter said.

"I look forward to whispering your name later."

The girl looked to be upon the verge of swooning. Her father looked on the verge of delivering a blow to Tristan's face. Or at least attempting to. Sebastian doubted he'd make contact before Tristan introduced the man's skull to the floor.

"My lord—" Weatherly began.

"Only during the dance, of course," Tristan said, smoothly cutting the man off. "Which is when, my lady?"

"Two dances hence."

"I shall wait with baited breath."

With a quick curtsy, she scurried away, her hands fluttering so madly that she had no need of a fan.

"Relax, Weatherly," Sebastian said. "She's far too young for my brother, and we have scandal aplenty in our family without creating more."

"Innocent flirtation, Weatherly," Tristan said in an additional effort to reassure the man.

"If you wish introductions . . ." the lady began, then halted as her husband's jaw turned as hard as granite.

Sebastian suspected she'd rather not make them anyway. "I'm certain we shall get along on our own. I've already spotted a few familiar faces." He didn't know who the devil the people were but he remembered seeing them the night he and his brothers burst into his uncle's ball. And of course there were those he'd met at Lady Ivers's dinner. The woman had indeed done him a great service.

He didn't think Lady Weatherly could have looked more relieved if he'd stated that they were taking their leave. With a bow to their hosts, he strode past them in to the main portion of the salon. He located an unhampered area that gave way to shadow. A perfect spot for watching.

"Well, it seems we are once again garnering attention," Tristan mused laconically.

"We are hardly known and, therefore, we are a curiosity," Sebastian said. He scanned the crowd, noticed a man walking toward him. Unlike everyone else in the room, he seemed neither curious nor intrigued, but he wore confidence with the ease that most men wore their jacket. His black hair was perfectly styled. As he neared, his emerald eyes caught Sebastian's attention. He'd seen them before.

The man stopped before him. "Keswick. My lords."

Sebastian shook his head. "I'm sorry, man. You look familiar but—"

"Ainsley. Our paths crossed at Eton some years back."

"I was there for only a year. I can hardly countenance that you remembered me."

"I must confess that I doubt I'd have known who you were if someone hadn't pointed you out to me. I understand you fought in the Crimea."

"I did indeed."

"My brother returned home last fall to recover from injuries. Bloody awful thing. I'm glad you're home, man."

"Thank you, Ainsley." He wondered if Ainsley had heard everything. Surely he had, but apparently he was not one to speculate or gossip.

"If you gentlemen will excuse me now, I must take my leave."

"The evening is young," Rafe said.

"I seldom attend these affairs, but I have made it a policy that when I do, I call it an evening as soon as I've enjoyed one dance. Less chance to give the mothers ideas or hope. Gentlemen." He made his way out of the ballroom without making any further stops.

"Ainsley?" Tristan murmured.

"An extremely wealthy and powerful duke," Rafe said.

"I suppose you know them all," Tristan said.

"A good many of them. Some belong to my club.

Ainsley doesn't. His speaking with you should give you a certain amount of cache."

"And has delayed my searching out the lovely Lady Hermione," Tristan said. "If you'll excuse me, I believe it's almost time for our dance."

"Do take care with her, Tristan," Sebastian ordered. "She is a lady and not a doxy."

"I'm not as uncivilized as you might think. I know we're being judged by our actions tonight."

"I meant no insult."

"None taken."

But Sebastian could see the lie in his eyes. Damnation. As Tristan walked away, Sebastian knew the last thing he needed was to cause a riff between himself and the one person who seemed to truly understand the importance of all they were doing. No, that wasn't exactly true. Mary seemed to have a sense of it as well.

"I believe I shall seek out the card room," Rafe said.

"We need to talk."

Rafe had taken only a partial step when he glanced back at his brother.

"I'd like to know what happened while I was away," Sebastian said. "Perhaps after this affair, you would stop by Easton House for a bit of whiskey and conversation." Rafe had not returned to the house since the morning Sebastian had taken up residence.

"No good would come of the tale, and I suspect you'd find my company unpalatable. I shall stay long enough to make a favorable impression by losing a modest sum."

"You can guarantee your loss?"

"I can guarantee any outcome I desire. But men will look more favorably on us if we're not taking from their coffers. Once I've seen to it, then I shall be on my way."

Sebastian didn't object when Rafe strode toward the hallway. Then he spied the real reason he'd come tonight. Mary. He'd wanted to see her once more dressed in a ball gown. He wanted to watch her dance, to see the glow in her eyes as she enjoyed the occasion. As always the shade of her hair drew him. Even with it piled up and held in place with pearl combs, revealing the long slope of her neck. Graceful, like a swan. But then everything about her was graceful. She was no longer the hoyden who had torn over fields with him, who had dared him to climb trees, or goaded him to crawl into a badger's den. Thank God the badger had not been in residence at the time.

She had tempted him with childish things. He feared she could tempt him with a great deal more now. Things he shouldn't want from her. Things he didn't deserve from her. She deserved the elegance of this life. The balls and soirees. Ladies frequently stopped her progress through the ballroom for a brief chat. She was sought-after, adored, loved. He caught the occasional gentleman admiring her. How could they not? Her pale pink gown with its deep emerald trim bared her shoulders and the ample swells of her breasts to a man's discerning eye, cinched in tightly at her small waist. Her white kid gloves stretched past her elbows. He had a flash of memory that involved ungainly long limbs. She had grown into them, transformed them into elegance and grace.

Three other ladies joined the last group of gossip-mongers who held Mary's attention. He had no doubt that it was the talk of scandal that tripped off their tongues. One pointed her fan toward the crush of dancing couples just as Tristan and Lady Hermione came into view. He couldn't deny that his brother certainly knew how to take advantage of a dance floor. But it was also evident that he was daring enough to hold the lady a little too near. Although she certainly didn't seem to object as she gazed up at him, her smile bright enough to illuminate the room should all the candles suddenly be doused.

Careful there, Tristan, he mused. *You'll find yourself with a pistol at your back and a clergyman at your front if you don't watch yourself.*

These were not Rafe's girls who expected nothing from a gent except a quick tumble. No, these ladies expected—and deserved—everything.

Another fan, pointed in his direction, caught his eye and he focused his attention back on the group of ladies. The holder of the fan quickly opened it and hid her face behind it, as though embarrassed that she'd been caught displaying rude behavior. Or perhaps his solitary gaze simply disarmed her. Much more comfortable to gossip when the object in question wasn't paying attention. He recognized none of the ladies from the dinner party. Dear Lord but there were an abundance of people to meet.

Mary swung her gaze over and smiled. He wanted to think the upturn of her mouth was pleasure at seeing him, but he thought it more likely that she was responding to some bit of trifle spoken by one of the ladies. She turned away for just a moment, touching a hand here, an arm there, and then was strolling toward him.

He could only pray that she was not coming to claim her dance.

To Mary the scars marring Sebastian's face were nothing beyond an insignia of courage. But he obviously considered them otherwise because just as he had during their previous encounters, he hid his left side in shadows. Yet he couldn't hide the true breadth of his shoulders or the strong cut of his jaw. He couldn't hide his entitlement or his impatience with the entire affair. He was here out of obligation, duty. A need to make a statement.

The Duke of Keswick had reclaimed what had been stolen, but she couldn't help but feel as though he had not yet acquired it all. His titles, yes. His lands, his estates, his London residence. But there was so much more, something that wasn't quite so easily defined. She feared that was still being denied him. Hence her suggestion he attend tonight's affair. But it did him little good to skulk in corners and frighten young maidens.

"I never thought you to be a wallflower," she said after she came to a stop at his side.

"I'm simply getting a lay of the land."

"Your intensity is quite intimidating. Young ladies are conflicted as to whether they should ask for an introduction. They fear your bite. I assured them you will only bark."

"You shouldn't be so confident of that."

She heard no teasing in his voice. When he had run for his life, she feared he'd lost his heart and soul along the way. She supposed he had every reason to be bitter, but it hardly made him a candidate for good company. "You might try to cease your scowling. Even the lords are wary."

"Yet, here you are, facing the ogre."

"You're hardly an ogre. A bit reticent, but then under the circumstances, quite understandable. Is there someone to whom you wish an introduction?"

"Tonight I am merely observing."

"That won't go over well. Perhaps you'll feel more at ease once we dance."

"I have no desire to dance."

She didn't want to acknowledge the sting that his rejection wrought, or how much she had been looking forward to an excuse to be near him. As children they had danced enthusiastically at the village fair, but that had entailed little more than holding hands, running around, and kicking up their heels. She wondered if he even remembered. "A pity. I saved a waltz for you."

"Offer it to Tristan. He seems to have found his calling."

She glanced toward the dance floor, and saw that he had claimed a dance with her cousin, Lady Alicia. She was glad he realized that he should spread himself around. "My cousin often laments how boring these affairs are. I suspect that will not be the case tonight. You do think he'll take care with her heart, don't you? She looks rather enamored."

"I wish I could offer reassurance, but I'm not completely confident in my brother's character."

She turned back to him, only to find his gaze riveted on her, leaving her with the sense that while she had enjoyed the dancers, he had enjoyed her. A strange notion. He made no unwarranted overtures, provided no flirtatious banter, but still his intensity made her thoughts wander along forbidden trails. What if he'd never left? What if twelve years ago fate had not conspired to create divergent paths that had forced them to take such astonishingly different journeys? The paths had converged now, but it was not a gentle meeting of wooded byways. Rather it was as though sun-dappled meadow and stormy rock-hewn mountain had crashed together. A strange analogy to run through her head, but she was left with the opinion that life would never be easy for him. Something else lost.

"Are they as much strangers as the rest of us?" she asked quietly.

"In some ways yes." And then, as though uncomfortable with his admittance, he said solemnly, "You wore the necklace."

She touched the delicate oval jewel. She had purposely chosen this gown to accentuate the stone, knowing that it also brought out the green of her eyes. "Yes, it's so lovely. I must apologize for not thanking you and your brothers for the kindness earlier."

His laughter was low, dark, did not arrive with an accompanying smile. "We would not be here to present gifts if not for your courage."

"I suspect you would have found a way to thwart your uncle's plans."

"We shall never know. Thanks to you."

He was discarding his own cleverness in favor of hers. But she'd acted without any thought or plans. Still, she supposed she couldn't argue with the results. Here they were.

"Darling."

At the familiar refined voice she spun around and smiled, silently chastising herself for the speculation she saw in Fitzwilliam's eyes. She'd spent far too long speaking alone with Sebastian. It was hardly appropriate behavior for a woman who was betrothed. Hardly appropriate for any unmarried woman. She had no wish for him to doubt her loyalties. "Fitzwilliam."

"I've come to claim my dance."

"I'm sorry. I was distracted. I don't know what I'd do if you didn't keep up with them." He didn't smile at her teasing tone. She supposed she couldn't blame him. She turned slightly and gave Sebastian a pointed look. Surely he realized that he needed to acknowledge Fitzwilliam.

"Fitzwilliam," he finally said.

"Your Grace. I daresay, I was enjoying my time in the card room until your brother relieved me of my blunt for the evening. He seems to have quite the luck with cards."

"Every man has something at which he excels."

The tension radiating between the two was thick enough to slice with a knife. Surely Sebastian couldn't resent every man who had never been dispossessed of his fortune and place in Society. And Fitzwilliam. Was he jealous? She didn't know whether to be flattered or irritated.

"He more than excels," Fitzwilliam said.

"If you're accusing him of something spit it out with straight words."

The tension ratcheted up several notches. She placed her hand on Fitzwilliam's arm to remind him she was there. His muscles were as hard as stone. He didn't like Sebastian. That much was obvious. But he was smart enough to remember the swiftness with which Sebastian had moved that first night when he'd taken offense at his uncle's words.

"Merely a compliment," Fitzwilliam said and she felt his muscles relaxing.

"I shall pass it on to my brother."

"By all means, please do. Now if you'll be so good as to excuse us, my favorite part of the evening is upon me."

Sebastian turned to her. "It was good to see you again, Lady Mary."

"My pleasure, Your Grace. I hope you will reconsider dancing. The ladies always outnumber the gentlemen. I do believe you'll find yourself never lacking for a partner."

Before Sebastian could respond, Fitzwilliam was leading her away. "Were you trying to entice him into a dance?"

She heard the displeasure in his voice. She supposed she couldn't blame him, even though betrothed ladies—indeed married ones—danced with many partners. "I was trying to entice him away from keeping the potted plants company. He's not comfortable here."

"I do not see that it is your concern. It's as though you've adopted a stray. First securing him an invitation to your aunt's dinner and then to this affair."

"Lady Hermione extended the invitation for tonight."

"You deny that you had anything at all to do with his presence? That your meeting in the park was merely coincidence and not an attempt to lure him here?"

He'd heard? Of course he had. There was not an action taken in all of London that was not commented on—repeatedly. "I was there as a favor to Lady Hermione."

"She wanted him here?"

"She wanted Lord Tristan here. But I knew he would only come if Keswick came."

"You also no doubt have more sway over the duke than over his brother."

"We were childhood friends. You know that. You also know that it is imperative he be seen at these functions in order to be accepted."

"I still fail to see why you should care."

"Because of our friendship. I would share the same concerns for any friend. Lady or gent."

Taking her in his arms, holding her gaze, he swept

her over the dance floor. "Never forget that you belong to me."

Her eyes widened at that. "You've never been quite so possessive."

"My apologies. I have a bit of a jealous streak, especially where you are concerned. I fear it does not flatter me."

"And a competitive one. I suspect you didn't fancy losing your money in the game room."

"My only consolation is that I was not the only one. These brothers are hardly typical lords."

"But then they've hardly had a typical upbringing or experiences."

"Your heart is too soft, Mary. Take care or you might find it bruised."

His warning came just a tad too late, because her heart was already aching for Sebastian and wondering how she could make him more comfortable with his surroundings. Life had thrown many an obstacle his way. It seemed it was not yet done.

Chapter 12

~∽❧❧∽~

Sebastian reluctantly admitted that he wished Mary weren't smiling quite so brightly as Fitzwilliam expertly twirled her over the dance floor. What a selfish bastard he was. Her relationship with Fitzwilliam was not a threat to their long-standing friendship.

"Lovely, isn't she?"

Sebastian heard the soft voice on his left, and damned the woman for coming up on his blind side. How long had she been standing there observing him? It was difficult to hold back his irritation when he swung his head around to get a good view of whomever the deuce she was. Then regretted his irritation. "Lady Ivers." He took her gloved hand, bowed over it, and kissed the tips of her fingers.

The countess blushed. "Why do you waste your charms on an old woman such as me? Why are you not out on the dance floor?"

"You are not so old."

"Balderdash." She turned her attention back to the crowded ballroom. While he wanted to do the same, if he did he would lose sight of her. "You avoided my question."

"I have not danced in a good many years."

"It is not something one forgets. They make an interesting couple, do they not? My niece and Fitzwilliam?"

He thought hers was a telling choice of words. "Do you not approve?"

"I do *not* disapprove. Yet I watched the two of you during dinner the other night. There is something between you."

"Friendship," he said much too quickly.

"It makes for a good foundation for a marriage."

"She is betrothed."

"Indeed she is, and her father likes him. But I am not so sure that he is not looking beyond seeing that she is secure. His nephew will inherit, you know, when Winslow is gone. He is not quite confident in his nephew's strength of character or generosity. Winslow worries that he is not much longer for this world. His brother was only thirty-eight when he passed. His father forty. I hate to say it, but resilient hearts do not run in that family. Still, my sister saw something in him to love. I told Winslow he need not marry Mary off in haste. She will always have a place in my home, but I think he wants to see her settled. Fitzwilliam is of good stock. She will be happy. I'm certain of it. If she is not, her husband will have to deal with me."

Damned if he didn't like the woman. "Mary is fortunate to have you as her champion."

"I am fortunate to have her as my niece." She patted his arm. "Don't let the lionesses dissuade you from enjoying this affair. The one thing I am completely confident about is that a gentleman who has worn the uniform is always an accomplished dancer."

Not when his sight was restricted.

"Give it a go, Your Grace."

For a moment there, he feared she was hinting that he should ask her for a dance, but with another pat on his arm, she strolled away. He could quite imagine that in her day she had turned many a head. Just as Mary did.

He looked back toward the dance floor and gritted his teeth. She was in Tristan's arms, moving gracefully in rhythm with the music. Tristan was cutting quite the swath through the ladies. He knew it shouldn't grate that his brother was dancing with Mary. Tristan knew her more than he knew any of the others. It was expected. But still he didn't like the way Tristan watched her through hooded eyes. But then Tristan caught his gaze and issued a silent challenge: *Cut in. I dare you.*

Damn him!

Lady Ivers was correct. Soldiers were known to cut quite a figure when they danced. Sebastian had always considered it a silly bit of nonsense. A soldier's place was on the battlefield, but he was expected to reflect his glory in the ballrooms. He'd danced with his fair share of the ladies. Had even enjoyed it, but holding Mary in his arms would no doubt be an experience that rivaled all others. Would waltzing be so difficult if he did no grand sweeping? He could claim a small bit of the dance floor.

Her aunt had tossed down the gauntlet. Crafty old biddy. He caught sight of her watching him, daring him even. One dance. Surely he could survive that.

After all, he'd survived the carnage of war.

*   *   *

After her dance with Tristan, Mary retired to a corner and spoke with Lady Alicia. And spoke with her, and spoke with her, and spoke with her. It seemed she'd found her place and intended to remain there. While Sebastian knew awkwardness would no doubt arrive with him, he squared his shoulders and marched forward as though an enemy awaited. He supposed sooner or later he would be forced to speak with Lady Alicia. Might as well make it quick.

Before he'd reached Mary, she turned and smiled at him, and he suspected Lady Alicia had said something to make her aware of his coming over.

"Your Grace," Mary said.

"Lady Mary." He bowed slightly. "Lady Alicia."

"Your Grace," she replied with a slight tremble in her voice, and he realized a faint blush crept up her face. "My sincerest apologies for the debacle of the other night. I assure you—"

"Leave it go, Alicia," Mary murmured. "Keswick has already forgotten about it, I'm sure."

"I don't see how he could."

"It is forgotten," he assured her.

"I was such a ninny."

"It is. Forgotten," he said as firmly as he could.

"I truly meant no harm."

Dear God, was he going to have to ask the chit to dance in order to convince her that the lies he spoke were truth? "No harm was done."

"Still, it was unconscionable—"

"Alicia—" Mary began, a plea in her voice.

"—to make you feel uncomfortable in our home and I—"

"Perhaps you will honor me with a dance later," he forced out.

Her eyes widened but at least her mouth remained closed. Thank God. She blinked, looked at Mary, looked back at him. "Yes, certainly." She began to scour her dance card.

Mary caught his eye and smiled softly, apparently pleased with the way he'd handled the awkward situation. He thought her smile alone was worth the agony he would endure as he dreaded the upcoming turn about the floor with her cousin, especially as it was not her cousin with whom he wished to dance. He held Mary's gaze and thought there were no more expressive eyes in all of Great Britain. She drew him in, made him think all things were possible. That he could indeed traverse the maze of a dance floor—if she were in his arms. Suddenly he wanted her there with a fierceness that he'd only experienced in battle, when he'd charged the enemy, when defeat was not even a consideration. He considered how it would be to have her so near, to hold her briefly, knowing he could not hold her forever. He would find a piece of heaven in his hell, and he would suffer for it later when it was gone, but for those few moments—

"A quadrille?" Lady Alicia chirped, interrupting his wayward thoughts. "Would a quadrille suit?"

"Yes."

"Lovely." She wrote on her dance card with endearing concentration, then peered up at him. "Shall I write it on your card?"

Gentlemen generally carried a card in their jackets to keep up with their dance partners. He hadn't expected to dance so he hadn't bothered with one. "I'll remember."

"I shall look forward to it with great anticipation."

"As will I." When had he become such an accomplished liar? He turned to Mary. "I was hoping you would honor me with a dance as well."

"I would be delighted, and as it so happens I am currently free."

He held out his arm, and she placed her hand on it. As they walked onto the dance floor, he constantly scanned the twirling couples. His confidence began to grow. He simply needed to remain aware of who was about and where they moved.

Then she was in his arms and his surroundings became the last thing on his mind. He wasn't certain he'd realized exactly how small her waist was until his hand settled in against it. Because of her height, he could easily gaze into her eyes. They sparkled now and her lips tilted up in pleasure. He saw very little evidence of the hoyden she'd once been. She was reserved, polite, a lady any gentleman would be proud to have as his wife.

"You were very kind to her," she said softly.

"Should I have been a beast?"

"I don't think you're capable of that."

"Do you ever feel as though we don't truly know each other?"

"Quite often, and yet there are times when I feel as though there is nothing about you that I don't know. I wasn't certain you'd ask me to dance."

"Your aunt insisted."

Her smile broadened. "You don't have to always be completely honest with your answers. Now my heart is crushed."

"It was never my intent to hurt you, Mary."

Her eyes glimmered. "I was teasing. You mustn't always be so serious, Sebastian."

"I fear I know nothing else."

"You might try smiling at least."

"I did. Once. After I was wounded. It's a hideous sight. I smashed the mirror that revealed it to me. You want me to be civilized. I'm not certain I'm capable of it."

Her own smile withered, and she squeezed his hand that held hers. "Our dance is a start. Simply enjoy it."

Her smile returned. She was right. He wanted this moment. He should savor it. Without conversation to distract him, he found himself becoming lost in her.

That damned freckle on the upper swell of her left breast kept drawing his attention. If he'd just ask her how she came to have it, he'd no doubt lose all interest in it. But how did one word such an inquiry? *I daresay I was noticing your breast . . .*

In truth he was noticing everything about her. No lady in this room compared with her—

He rammed into someone, stumbled, stepped on Mary's hem, heard material rip, followed by her gasp.

"Watch where you're go—" A voice he recognized began, then stopped.

He spun around and found himself staring at Fitzwilliam.

"Apologies, Your Grace," he said. "It is I who should have been watching."

The implication was clear. Sebastian was lacking. At that moment he wanted to plant his fist in the man's face. If he hadn't felt Mary's hand come to rest on his arm, he might have done something he'd later regret.

Glancing down, he saw her clutching the fabric at her waist. "I need to see to getting this taken care of. Would you be so kind as to escort me off the floor?"

Kind? Nothing about him was kind. Still he did as she asked.

"It looks beyond repair," he told her.

"It's not nearly as bad as it appears. They'll have a seamstress in the retiring room who'll put things to rights quick enough. Ladies are always stepping on their hems."

"I knew dancing would be a dreadful notion. I'm sorry I subjected you to it."

They were away from the dancers now, near the doorway that would take her to the stairs.

"Don't be silly. I enjoyed it. I hope to have a chance to dance with you again."

Never. Never again. But he merely nodded and strode away, leaving her to tend to her torn gown.

Fortunately there was no line to the seamstress and the woman was quick of fingers. It wasn't long before Mary was back in the ballroom. She spied her quarry standing with a group of gentlemen. She plastered a smile on her face and glided over with all the grace and poise she could muster.

"Gentlemen, forgive my intrusion," she said, smiling even more brightly, batting her eyelashes as though a cinder had flown into her eyes. "My lord Fitzwilliam, may I have a word?"

"Shortly. As soon as I'm finished—"

"This is important. I fear it can't wait."

"A man is a fool," Lord Chesney said, "to spend his time prattling with men when he can be in the company of a beautiful woman."

"You're quite right, of course," Fitzwilliam said, before offering Mary his arm.

She waited until they were in an alcove, hidden from prying eyes, before she let her anger seethe to the surface. "You did it on purpose."

"What's that, sweeting?"

His pretended innocence only served to anger her further. "Bumped into Keswick."

"What an absurd notion. He crossed into *my* path. Yet as a gentleman of the first order, I took the blame in order to spare him the humiliation."

"You spared him nothing."

"Do not take that tone with me. You are to be my wife."

"That does not make me your property."

"According to the law it does." He slammed his eyes closed, took a breath, then opened them. "Good God, what are we doing here, Mary? We had a bit of a snuffle on the dance floor. Hardly worth scathing words and anger. Barging into him would have also served to embarrass you. I'd have not done it." He touched her cheek. "You are too precious to me."

This was the closest he'd come to declaring he might have strong feelings for her. That he cared, she had no doubt. But he'd never given voice to the strength of his affections. It was her understanding that few men did. For them, actions spoke louder and Fitzwilliam had never given her any cause to doubt his fondness for her.

Yes, in all likelihood the incident was Sebastian's fault. His gaze had been riveted on her with such intensity that she'd scarcely been able to breathe. For a few moments it had seemed as though they were the only two in the ballroom, in the entire world. She'd become lost in the wonder of him. His strength, his masculinity were so apparent that he made other men seem lacking.

In retrospect, the sudden end to their dance had come at a most fortuitous moment, before she'd made an utter fool of herself and asked him to escort her onto the terrace so they might have a moment of privacy. She wasn't certain what she intended to happen during it, but it could not have boded well.

"My apologies for the accusations," she said contritely.

"None needed. Now let's return to the festivities before our absence is noted. I'd not have your reputation tarnished before we are wed."

"Nor afterward either, I should think." She gave him a teasing smile, which he returned with one that held the promise of passion.

"I must confess that I am very much looking forward to having you alone," he said with a seductive whisper.

She couldn't mistake his meaning. She'd hardly given any thought to the intimacies of marriage. She felt her skin grow warm with a flush. She was certain she would find pleasure in his bed. But she suddenly found herself wondering if it would be enough.

He did not belong here, Sebastian reflected. He would never belong here. In the glittering ballrooms where ladies and gents flirted, waltzed, laughed without care. Their easy banter sliced deep for nothing in his life had been easy. He was only twenty-six and yet he felt to be a man twice his age.

After the debacle on the dance floor, he found Lady Alicia and explained that regretfully he would have to forego their dance. She merely blushed, stammered her understanding, and hurried away. She'd no doubt witnessed the ungainliness he'd exhibited with her cousin and was relieved to be spared a similar fate. Then he conversed with a few lords about trivial matters: weather, agriculture, bills before Parliament. He made his way to the card room and discovered that Rafe was nowhere to be seen. He'd obviously taken his leave. He was no more comfortable in these surroundings than Sebastian. He did wish his brother had sought him out to see if he might be of a mind to depart with him.

Not that he would have. It would have been cowardly to leave so soon after arriving. But taking a turn about the garden—that spoke only of a man who required a bit of fresh air. Based on the scent assailing his nostrils the garden was awash in roses. Based on the quiet murmurings that reached him, the garden was dotted with secretive trysts. He wondered if one of them involved Tristan. He'd lost sight of his brother in the ballroom. He did hope he wasn't doing something reckless that would find him with a wife in hand before Season's end.

It irritated the devil out of him that he didn't know his brothers well, wasn't certain of the kind of men they were. They were loyal to him, but that had been ingrained in them from birth by their father. Sebastian was the heir and they owed their fealty to him. But other than that, he knew them hardly at all. He despised his uncle for stealing that knowledge from him as well. He and his brothers were joined by blood, but beyond that, they shared few of the same experiences. None of them seemed wont to speak of the years they were apart, which lent a well of loneliness to their being together.

But he had Pembrook to sustain him. Based on tonight's fiasco, he had decided he would return there. To hell with London. Tristan seemed more at home here. He could see after the London residence and keep an eye on matters. Watch for any nefarious plans their uncle might be plotting. As for the wife—he wasn't in the mood to hunt for one. He would hire a matchmaker perhaps or—

"Sebastian?"

He paused at the soft voice. He was far into the garden now, should no doubt continue on. But he turned ever so slightly and watched as Mary strolled gracefully toward him. She was limned by the glow from the gaslights that lined the pebbled path. Even shadows could not disguise her beauty.

"You're not enjoying the ball," she said quietly, and he heard her disappointment, which only served to make him feel like an ogre who had let her down.

"Do gentlemen usually?"

"I'm sure some of them don't, but they're generally better skilled at hiding it. Alicia informed me that you recanted on your invitation to dance with her."

"I thought it best under the circumstances to spare her the embarrassment of having a torn gown."

"Mine was fixed easily enough."

"Still, it should not have happened at all."

Silence eased in around them and brought with it a comfortableness that had often accompanied the pair in their youth.

"Do you enjoy the balls?" He didn't know why he asked. Perhaps because he knew as little of her as he knew of his brothers, and it seemed a shame after all they'd shared as children.

"More than I should, I suppose. I love the glitz and glamor of them. I enjoy seeing the ladies in their ball gowns, draped in jewels, and exuding excitement as they anticipate the night. The gentlemen are always so dashingly handsome in their swallow-tailed jackets. The music fills me." She laughed. "I could go on."

In the distance, he could hear the faint strains of the music that filled her. Her father had denied her this because of him. "By all means do."

He meant it. She could discuss the manner in which

grass grew and he thought he would be fascinated. He'd not been with a woman—truly been with a woman—since shortly before the battle in which he'd nearly died. He preferred women who gave of their bodies willingly, not for gain. Mary would be such a woman, and her willingness would be gilded with enthusiasm that came from deep within her. She'd never been one for half measures. While he'd amassed years of not knowing the details of her life, he was fairly confident he still knew the particulars of her character. She was strong, bold, and had a penchant for caring deeply for those who needed it. She would fight to save a wounded sparrow with the same determination she'd fought to save three abandoned lads.

"I would only bore you," she told him. "Besides, that was not my purpose in seeking you out."

He wasn't certain why his gut clenched or why he was so sure he was not going to like what followed, but still he heard himself ask, "And what would that be?"

"I wanted to apologize for what happened earlier on the dance floor."

"You're clearly not to blame. You nearly lost a toe in the process." He caught a flash of her smile in the flickering gas lamps. He wished he had the ability to keep her smiling. But it was neither his responsibility nor his place. "Fitzwilliam, blast him, was correct. I wasn't watching where I was going. I knew I had to be ever vigilant." *But I'd become lost in you, and for a moment had felt close to being whole.*

Not that he could tell her that. Not that he should even admit it to himself. Yet he had. Her sweet fragrance, the green of her eyes, the delicate touch of her hand folding over his.

"I would ask you to forgive my boldness, that it is a

friendship forged as children that prompts me now, but I was hoping we might finish our dance. Here in the garden. Where we're less likely to bump into anything other than roses."

"Thorns can hurt, Mary."

"I'm willing to risk it."

Terribly bad idea, sweetheart. To hold you in my arms again, to have your clothes occasionally brushing against mine, to have your scent so much nearer.

His thoughts traveled along paths they shouldn't traverse. She was betrothed. She belonged to another.

"No." He bit out the word.

"That's your pride answering, Your Grace."

"Leave it be, Mary."

She moved a step nearer, and it took everything within him not to take a step back. She brought with her the sweet fragrance of orchids. And a glimmer of tears. And a stubbornness in the set of her jaw that he'd never been able to defeat. She'd always possessed the power to conquer him, to make him ignore his better judgment.

Reaching out she touched his shoulder. He could feel the gentleness, the slight trembling of her fingers. "Please, dance with me."

"I don't want a damned dance." The harshness in his voice would have sent any other young miss scurrying back to the safety of the ballroom. But not Mary. He'd never been able to intimidate or frighten her. She was the most courageous creature he knew.

"What do you want?" she asked with equal parts tenderness and challenge.

How often had he done things only to prove something to her? Let her see now the sort of man he was. What the years had transformed him into.

"To forget." He thrust a hand into her hair, cradled his palm against her cheek, moved her farther into the shadows.

"Mary," he whispered like a soft benediction and hoped to God that she didn't connect the two sentences and think it was she he wished to forget. Never her. She was the only thing worth remembering. No, he wanted to forget his disfiguring scars, his sightless left side, the stares he garnered, and the doubts and guilt that plagued him. But never her.

He tilted up her face and covered her mouth with his. He wasn't gentle. He wanted to replace horrendous memories with something worth remembering. He was not only starving, but greedy. He would hate himself in the morning. Hell, he'd hate himself as soon as his mouth left hers because the blackguard he'd become was taking advantage of her charitable nature.

She didn't protest, but her tongue was hesitant against his. He suspected she'd never had her mouth ravished to such a degree. The thought had him gentling the plunder, had him relishing the taste and feel of her. She'd sipped champagne and the rich flavor of it teased him now just as her orchid scent filled his nostrils.

She skimmed her hands up his arms, entangled her fingers in his hair, pressed herself closer, and became as bold as he. He almost smiled. She'd always matched his adventurous spirit with one that rivaled his. He wondered now if it was the competitor in her nature that had her stepping forward instead of back. Or was there more?

Had she wondered, as he had, what it might be like between them?

God, but she was delicious. He locked his other arm around her, assisted her in her quest to get nearer, pressing her close. His palm cradled her chin, the side of her throat, and he could feel the hard, rapid pounding of her heart. He became lost in the wonder of her. He'd wanted this when he sat on the bench with her that long-ago afternoon, when he'd given her the necklace. He'd wanted to know her flavor. Now he knew he would never forget it, even though he would never taste it again.

This was a forbidden moment between them. She was betrothed. She deserved better than he could provide. He could give her all the comforts of life, but he lacked the ability to comfort her heart and soul. He recognized this shortcoming in himself. He wasn't particularly proud of it, but he didn't delude himself into thinking that he would ever be able to give a woman more than a contented marriage. And Mary deserved far better than that.

She deserved love and adoration. She deserved a whole man who could not only take her to unheralded heights of pleasure but could lift her up from depths of despair. Life was not always pleasant. She needed a true partner who would give his all to her.

His all belonged to Pembrook.

Her soft moan echoed between them, and it fired his blood. A tempest raged through him. He could take her deeper into the shadows, lay her on the grass, ease up the hem of her gown—

He growled with the desperation that gnawed at him to do just that. This was Mary. Mary who had saved them. He owed her everything.

Breaking off the kiss, breathing heavily, he gazed down on her upturned face. From somewhere, light chased away the shadow and he could see her heavy-lidded gaze, her slightly parted lips. Her confusion.

"Forgive me, Mary. I . . ." What words could he give her? What possible explanation for his actions would suffice?

"You won't dance with me in the garden, yet you'll kiss me?"

"I've obviously become a barbarian. I have no excuse. And if we're seen, you'll have no reputation."

Before she could respond, he spun on his heel and stormed back toward the garden path, but rather than turn toward the manor, he picked up his pace and headed even farther into the darker confines provided by roses and trellises. He had to leave now. He would exit through a back gate, leave his carriage for Tristan. He could walk back to his residence. It would do him good, cool his ardor.

He heard a sound. Dried leaves crushed beneath the weight of a foot.

He knew better than to turn to his left, to lose his advantage by a momentary blindness when meeting a foe, but he'd thought it was Mary chasing after him as she had when they were children. Only as he felt the knife slicing into his side did he recognize the true cost of his folly. Before he could even see the enemy he launched a powerful swing with his right arm. He took satisfaction in the sound of cracking bone, the grunt, the seething curse. He expected his attacker to attack again, but instead his pounding feet echoed and faded away.

Sebastian's knees hit the ground with a jarring thud that caused everything to shake. The world spun crazily around him and then turned black.

Chapter 13

Who would have ever thought that Tristan would find women who flung themselves at him so utterly boring? He'd had a life of challenges, had longed for the life of ease that came from being born the son of a duke, but now that he held it, he wondered why he'd ever wanted it.

He intrigued the ladies. They all desired introductions and a dance. But they didn't fascinate him in the least. They were all the same. Smiling, batting their lashes, peering from behind their ivory fans. He knew what their questions would be before they were asked. He knew what they would say before they spoke. Everything was practiced, rehearsed. Even the woman who had swooned in his arms had been performing. A grand performance to be sure, but a bit of acting nonetheless.

It was a mistake to have come here. He intended to find Sebastian and inform him that he was taking his leave. He'd seen his brother escape through the double doors that led into the garden, but had yet to see him return. Perhaps he'd arranged a tryst. If so, regrettably it would be interrupted.

He scoffed. Why should he care if he spoiled his brother's pleasures? He should simply leave, but something nagged at him. He needed to find Sebastian before he departed this affair. It was a sense he had. With Sebastian, he'd always known when something wasn't quite right. Perhaps because they had shared the womb. It bothered him that he'd never felt the same connection with Rafe. With Rafe, there was no mooring, nothing that anchored them. Tristan had known when Sebastian had been gravely wounded. Although he'd been at sea, he'd still known. A coldness as frigid as death had settled into him. He'd never prayed for himself, but he'd prayed for his brother that day.

Even knowing what he would inherit if his brother died, he'd never wished for his death. Which made it more difficult for him to reconcile his uncle's motives. Brothers should place blood above possessions, above titles, above land.

He walked onto the terrace and was heading for the steps that led into the garden when he saw Mary hastily dashing up them.

"Lady Mary."

She stumbled to a stop, jerked her gaze to the garden, the ballroom, and finally settled it back on him. "My lord."

"Is something amiss?"

"Everything is fine. Thank you."

A woman who had not mastered the art of lying. What a welcome diversion. Taking her arm, he led her toward a more secluded, shadowy area. "Are you certain?" he asked.

"Of course."

"I don't suppose you've seen Sebastian?"

Nodding, she glanced down. "Our paths crossed in the garden."

He slipped his finger beneath her chin, tilted up her head, and stroked his thumb over her lower lip. "Based on your swollen lips, I would say he kissed you."

She began rubbing her hand over her mouth. "Oh, dear God, you can tell?"

He hitched up a corner of his mouth. "No. It was a guess. Your lips aren't swollen."

She slapped at him. "You cad!"

If not for the seriousness of the matter, he'd have dropped his head back and roared out his laughter. "But he did kiss you."

Nodding, she averted her gaze. "Please keep this between us."

"Did you kiss him back?" he prodded.

"I did not dissuade him." She returned her gaze to his, such earnestness in her expression. "I should tell Fitzwilliam."

"Good God, don't even entertain such a foolish notion. If it was no more than a kiss—"

"It wasn't. One moment we were talking and the next . . . we weren't."

He wanted to shout Hallelujah! His brother wasn't perfect. Instead, he said, "Do you know where he went? Afterward?"

"Further into the garden. I started to follow, but I thought it would be best if I didn't. He seemed angry."

Frustrated, more like, if a kiss was all he claimed. "I'm sure he did. But not with you, sweet lady. I don't imagine he liked losing control."

"He changed, Tristan."

"We all did, love."

She smiled. "You didn't."

If only that were true. He was simply better at masking it. Reaching out he tucked some stray strands of hair back behind her pearl combs. "Go on inside before you're missed. I'll find Sebastian, and then we shall probably take our leave, quietly and without fanfare."

"Is it truly not obvious that I was kissed?" she asked, and he could see the worry in her eyes. Those in Society focused on such trivial matters. He'd have been the same had his life not taken such a drastic turn. Would he have liked that man any better than he liked the one he was now?

"No one will know," he assured her.

"I never thought of you as the kind twin."

"Because I'm not. Now off with you. You don't want to be seen with me in the shadows." Then because she seemed reluctant to leave, he leapt over the railing with the ease of a man who had climbed sail rigging during the height of a tempest at sea and lived to tell the tale of it. Glancing back, he saw that she'd moved on. He breathed a bit easier. He didn't want to be the one responsible for ruining her good name. They owed her, should ensure that she was happy. He wondered if she would be so with Fitzwilliam. He seemed rather like a stick-in-the-mud. But then Tristan was discovering that most of the men he'd met tonight were boring beyond measure. They lived sheltered lives lacking in adventure.

The same certainly couldn't be said of him and his brothers. He knew Rafe had gone on his merry way. Sebastian may have as well.

He passed one couple and another strolling back toward the house—a guilty air about them. In the shadows off the path, he heard a giggle and a soft repri-

mand for quiet. Ah, the dangers. He imagined hearts
were racing at the thought of being caught. He couldn't
imagine that had not fate intervened the most exciting
part of his life might have been enticing a lady into an
illicit kiss.

The dangers he had faced made all this subterfuge in
the garden seem trivial, and certainly held no appeal.

He slowed his step when he noticed a gentleman
on the path hesitate before continuing toward him.
"Fitzwilliam."

"My lord."

He wondered what he was doing out here alone,
wondered if he'd happened across Sebastian and Mary
earlier. Surely not, for if he had he'd have confronted
them.

"I don't suppose you've seen my brother out here,"
Tristan asked laconically.

"Which one? The one who cheats at cards or the one
who airs his dirty laundry in public?"

"Take care with your accusations, my lord," Tristan
said with a voice that mimicked the calm before a storm.

"Are you threatening me?"

"For a moment there I feared you weren't a percep-
tive fellow. So relieved you proved me wrong."

"You and your brothers do not belong here. You are
barbarians."

"On the contrary, my lord. I asked a simple question. You are the one who responded by disparaging the
character of my brothers."

"I haven't seen them. Now if you'll excuse me?"

He walked past without waiting for an answer.
Tristan patted himself on the back for not tripping him.
Arrogant cad.

Tristan strode into the darker confines of the garden.

He despised the notion that other lords were not giving Sebastian the respect with which he was due. He fought in a bloody war, for God's sake. Was still fighting to reclaim his birthright. As far as Tristan was concerned it wasn't enough to cut off their uncle's financial resources. They needed proof of his intended actions where they were concerned. Even Mary's words wouldn't be strong enough to dispel his claims that they'd merely run away, as young lads were wont to do. And if he had killed their father as they suspected—

Someone rammed into him, causing him to stagger back. Tristan had his own knife in hand before he fell beneath the weight.

"Tristan?" his brother croaked.

Tristan was too familiar with the warm stickiness soaking his clothes not to know what it was. "What the devil, Sebastian?"

"Mary. Have to make sure she's all right."

Sebastian was clutching at Tristan's arm, striving to right himself.

"She's unharmed. I just saw her on the terrace only a few moments ago," he reassured his brother.

Sebastian sank back down. "Then just get me the hell out of here."

Chapter 14

"**Y**ou were most fortunate, Your Grace," the physician said, as he finished wrapping a bandage around Sebastian's midsection. "The knife didn't slice into any organs."

If the pain in his side was that of a fortunate man, then Sebastian would hate to experience the pain of an unfortunate one.

"Not a professional assassin then," Rafe said. He was leaning against one of the posters at the foot of the bed, his arms crossed over his chest. Once Tristan had gotten Sebastian home, he'd sent word to Rafe who had come posthaste, physician in tow. William Graves seemed not much older than them, but he knew well the business of healing.

"Or a soldier," Tristan said, holding the drapery slightly aside and peering into the night. "Otherwise he'd have known where to strike."

"I turned. I could have thrown him off."

"Either would have stayed to finish the job," Tristan said. "You said he ran off."

"Maybe he heard someone else coming."

"Wouldn't have mattered if he were an assassin," Rafe insisted. "He'd have done what he was paid to do."

"Know a lot about assassins do you?" Sebastian asked.

To Sebastian's consternation, Rafe held his gaze somewhat defiantly, then shifted his attention over to Tristan. "You don't have to keep watch. I have a couple of my men patrolling."

Tristan released his hold on the draperies. "So he'll live?"

Graves completed his task and stepped away. "Most certainly."

"Pity. I rather fancied the notion of becoming duke."

The physician halted in the closing of his bag to stare at Tristan. Sebastian settled back against the pillows. "My brother has a strange sense of humor."

Graves gave a brisk nod. "I shall return on the morrow to change your bandages and assess the healing."

"I'll escort you out," Rafe said and proceeded to lead the doctor from Sebastian's bedchamber.

Tristan ambled over and dropped into a burgundy velvet chair near the bed. "Our little brother seems to have quite the knowledge regarding unsavory matters."

Sebastian didn't want to ponder how he had come to have that knowledge. Rafe returned and took up his position at the foot of the bed, leaning against the post, arms once again crossed—as though he had no desire to make himself comfortable here. Or perhaps he simply didn't *feel* comfortable here.

His reappearance, however, seemed to be a signal to Tristan to continue striving to uncover the events of the night. "So you didn't see the fellow who attacked you?"

Sebastian shook his head. "He came from my left side."

"I crossed paths with Fitzwilliam as I was looking for you. Perhaps he scared him off."

"Fitzwilliam couldn't scare off a rabbit."

A corner of Tristan's mouth hitched up. "You don't like him. Why is that?"

Shrugging, Sebastian regretted the movement as soon as he did it. His side burned as though someone had built a fire beneath the skin, but he'd endured much worse. The physician had given him laudanum before beginning his work. It left him feeling as though he traveled through a fog, striving to snatch hold of his thoughts, only to find them disappearing on gossamer wisps.

"Does it have anything to do with Mary?" Tristan asked.

Mary. She was with him. She left. His heart picked up tempo. Then he remembered that Tristan had seen her, that she was all right. But his heart refused to slow. If anything had happened to her—

"I know you kissed her," Tristan said.

His arms falling to his side, Rafe straightened as though the news had come as a blow to his midsection. "Why the devil would you do that?"

"Why does any man kiss a woman, Brother?" Tristan asked, his voice laced with humor.

"But Mary. For God's sake, we don't want to ruin her, not after what she did for us."

"I have no plans to ruin her," Sebastian ground out. "It was simply a . . . a distraction."

"Distract yourself with one of my doxies. Not with Mary."

"I don't need you telling me how to behave. I've apologized to her. It won't happen again."

"Why not?" Tristan asked. "If you want her, take her."

"She wants Fitzwilliam. If she didn't, she'd have never agreed to marry him."

"When she accepted his offer of marriage, she thought you were dead. She invites you to dinners and balls. For what purpose?"

"She invites *us*. She does it to aid us in our efforts to reclaim what is ours. It is her nature to help where she can. Now leave it be." Sebastian pressed a hand to his head in a vain attempt to stop the room from spinning. He couldn't deny that Mary was a beautiful woman or that she stirred him, but she deserved a man who was not as broken as he—a man who could love her, and he no longer had the capability of loving anyone. Marriage to him would be a miserable existence. "I believe we've strayed from our purpose here. I suppose we can assume Uncle was at the root of this situation tonight."

"He's a fool if he thinks killing all three of us will go unnoticed," Tristan said.

"Perhaps he believes it enough to kill one and the other two will run—as we did when we were lads," Rafe offered.

"Then he failed to notice that we are no longer lads. More's the pity. We know where he is. I say we confront him," Tristan said.

"Would be better to first discover what resources are at his disposal. His wife might know," Rafe replied.

"We could ask Mary to speak with her," Tristan mused.

"We're not going to involve Mary," Sebastian told him.

"She's already involved."

"Not in this." He made to get up, to give more power to his words, but the pain rifled through him and he collapsed back down. Breathing heavily, gritting his teeth, he hated opening his eye to discover Tristan leaning over him. He'd suffered worse. He wasn't going to be unmanned by so trifling a wound.

"You need to rest," Tristan said. "Rafe and I will ask around. See what we can discover."

"Not Mary."

Tristan studied him a moment before finally nodding. "No, we won't involve Mary."

Knowing she would be safe from scandal and danger, Sebastian allowed himself to sink into the oblivion of the laudanum.

Bloody, bloody, bloody fool! How could you be so stupid?

Lord David stared at his reflection in the mirror. The gash on his cheek burned where his brother's signet ring had sliced deeply into his flesh. He pounded the basin with his tightened fist.

It must look like an accident.

"I know that!"

He hadn't meant to attack his nephew, but when the opportunity had arose—

Why waste it? he'd thought. He hadn't even known his nephews would be at the Weatherlys'. He'd been sneaking through the gardens to see if he could catch a glimpse of Lucretia at the ball. She so enjoyed dancing. He couldn't envision that she would not attend. And damned how he missed her.

But then his cursed nephew had distracted him from his purpose.

He couldn't stay here. Knew they had him followed, knew where he was. Cunning lads, but he was more so.

Where will you go? How will you get there? No vendor or shop owner will extend you credit. They saw to that.

He'd tried to buy a bit of jewelry for Lucretia earlier in the week, only to be denied. He sent the basin hurtling through the room and took satisfaction as it crashed against the wall, breaking into a thousand shards. His landlady had warned him that if he broke another she'd not replace it. Who did she think she was to talk to him like that? To make threats.

He was a lord!

One day he would be duke. Then Lucretia would return to him. He would have everything then, everything he should have always had.

He would show his brother the price to be paid for stealing from him the only woman he'd ever loved. Even Lucretia could not compare to her beauty.

You should have killed him last, made him suffer more.

But then, opportunity that could not be ignored had presented itself. And it would again.

Chapter 15

❦

The afternoon following the Weatherly ball, as
Mary studied her reflection in the mirror, she
could hardly believe that the lovely lady standing in the
gown of white satin and Honiton lace was truly her.
The workmanship on the dress that so very closely resembled the gown that Queen Victoria had worn on her
wedding day was truly exquisite. Imitating the Queen's
attire was all the rage of late, but still Mary had never
expected to wear something as incredibly heavenly as
the gown that now adorned her.

"It's so beautiful," Alicia said. "I can't wait until I
have occasion to wear something similar for a wedding."

"Next Season, my dear," Aunt Sophie assured her.
"This Season is Mary's, and I could not be happier that
it has turned out so well. You are most fortunate to
have caught Lord Fitzwilliam."

"Yes," Mary said, and bit her lip to stop it from tingling at the memory of Sebastian's kiss, a kiss for which

he had apologized. She wished he hadn't done that. She wished he had simply walked away with no words spoken . . . after kissing her one more time.

She wasn't certain how the first had even happened. One moment she was touching his shoulder, and the next his mouth was devouring hers. Passion had slammed into her, causing her to encourage him further. Her moans and sighs had been wanton. She'd been wanton.

They'd kissed once before when she was all of twelve and he was fourteen. But the forbidden touching of their lips then had not hinted at the heat that could erupt between them now. She didn't know whether to be terrified or fascinated.

He was not the boy she'd loved as a child. He was a dark, brooding man, with fury boiling below the surface. Who knew when it might erupt and what casualties it would leave in its wake? Already it had left her behind. He'd stormed from the garden without even a backward glance. If he'd only looked back . . . she might have followed. She might have clambered into his coach and gone somewhere far away, where they could be alone—to truly talk, to explore their feelings, to stop being so blasted polite around each other.

"Do you think Keswick would have pressed his suit if he'd arrived in London earlier in the Season, before you were spoken for?" Alicia asked.

Mary twisted around. "Why would you—"

"Please stand still, m'lady," the seamstress said, as she worked to mark the hem.

"Yes, quite, I'm sorry," Mary muttered before facing forward again and meeting her cousin's gaze in the mirror. "Why would you think that?"

"I simply noticed that Keswick seems to watch you with what appears to be longing."

"You're mistaken. He looks upon me as no more than a friend."

"Nothing more?"

Why the deuce was her cousin pursuing this? Had she happened upon them in the garden for God's sake? "I'm quite content with my selection in husbands."

"Oh, my dear girl, tell me that's not so," her aunt said, her voice indicating her distress.

"Would you rather I not be content?"

"Content will hardly bring a fire to your bed."

Sebastian, however, based on his kiss would bring a fire to the bed that would ignite it and send it into flames. She didn't want to consider how his kiss had left her burning for more, how she had tossed and turned in her bed all night, tangled in covers until she thought she would suffocate, needing surcease. Whenever she closed her eyes, she imagined him prowling toward her, crawling onto her bed, covering her—

She swallowed hard. "I'm sure Fitzwilliam will do nicely in that regard."

Her aunt moved to stand in front of her, blocking her view of the mirror. She was a small woman, but could be quite formidable when she set her mind to it. "My dear, are you having second thoughts regarding this marriage?"

Second. Third. Fourth. Ever since Sebastian had kissed her, doubts had plagued her. She no longer knew her own mind. She, who never questioned her actions, was now questioning a good many things. Why had he kissed her? What had he hoped to accomplish? Was it simply for sport? To satisfy curiosity? He wanted to forget. Exactly what did he wish to forget? The long years he was away? The war? Her? Had he taken her in his arms because she was convenient? Would any woman have sufficed for his purposes? That thought brought with it a devastating disappointment. Perhaps she should confront him. Or would it be better to ignore him?

"Mary?" her aunt prodded.

She'd almost forgotten the question. Was she having doubts? "No, of course not."

Fitzwilliam did not burn with passion. Rather his moods more closely resembled the constant ticking of a clock. No surprises. Nothing unexpected. Just the reassuring constancy that each tick would be followed by another. A month ago, she'd found it reassuring. Now she found it boring. How unfair to him. He'd not changed since he asked for her hand. She knew exactly what she was getting when she accepted his proposal. But she had changed. Somehow, within only a couple of weeks, she'd become someone completely different, wanted something completely different. Too late, too late. Besides perhaps it was only a passing fancy, and in another two weeks she would once again yearn for what she'd longed for a month ago. *You'd damned well better long for it.*

"It really doesn't matter, Mama," Alicia said. "The betrothal has been announced. It can't be broken. Lord Fitzwilliam would sue for damages, and Uncle would not be pleased about that at all. It would be scandalous."

"Better scandal now than to marry a man you doubt and have years of regret," her aunt announced, her gaze boring into Mary until it made her uncomfortable.

"I don't doubt Fitzwilliam," Mary assured her. But she doubted herself. Why had she not stepped away from the kiss instead of into it? She couldn't deny that for years she'd thought of Sebastian, had dreamed of him, had fantasized about him as a young girl might, but the reality of him as a man was far removed from her imaginings.

Her aunt harrumphed.

"I don't!" Mary insisted. "And Alicia is right. All has been arranged for the wedding. I'm sure all ladies wonder as the time draws near if they travel the right path."

"I certainly didn't," her aunt said.

"Because you and Papa eloped," Alicia said. "To Gretna Green. There was hardly time for any misgivings. It was so romantic. I would so dearly love to be swept away." She sighed dreamily.

Mary wondered when she herself had given up on the notion of being romanced, of being swept away. Was she settling for Fitzwilliam? She didn't think so. Yes, he was the only one to have asked but that didn't signify that she'd have not selected him if a hundred gentlemen had asked. He'd captured her attention from the start. She enjoyed his company. He was charming, elegant. Not brash. His temper was even. He did not easily take offense. Marriage to him would be calm and placid. No upheavals, no tempers flaring, no anger.

A bell tinkling above the door caught her attention. Another lady coming in for a fitting no doubt. This seamstress was one of the more sought-after in London.

"There you are!" Lady Hermione announced. "When I saw your carriage in the street, I told Lady Victoria that we must stop and have a look-see for surely you would be here."

In the mirror's reflection, she saw Ladies Hermione and Victoria gliding into the room, an excitement in their step as though they both had delicious gossip to share.

"You're not to spread rumors about the design of

Mary's gown," Alicia said. "We want it to remain a secret—"

"Oh, dear girl, we couldn't care less about a gown. We want to know the truth about what *really* happened in the garden last night with Keswick. So many delicious rumors are running rife through London this morning that it's difficult to sort the wheat from the chaff. So, Lady Mary, what the deuce happened in the garden?" Her gaze honed in on Mary with such force that had it not been for the danger of pins pricking her, she would have sunk into the nearest chair.

Her knees had grown so weak that it was a wonder she was able to remain standing. Who had seen them in the garden? What precisely had they seen? More importantly—

"Does Fitzwilliam know?" she asked, pushing the words through her knotted throat.

"I should think so. No matter where Lady Victoria and I have gone today, it's been on the tip of everyone's tongues. Such delicious gossip. I daresay I'm frightfully surprised to find you here having a fitting done, considering all that transpired in the shadows. Now, come, you must give us specifics for surely—"

"We only kissed," Mary blurted out, in an effort to stop this madness. "Keswick and I."

Her aunt gasped and pressed a hand to her chest as though she needed to contain her heart beneath her ribs. The three younger ladies stared at her open-mouthed. Even the seamstress seemed unable to move from the shock of her words.

"He apologized afterward," she hastened to explain. "It didn't signify. Was only a moment of insanity." She was babbling. It was important that she speak with Fitzwilliam, explain everything, but that would indicate that she understood what had happened, when she really didn't.

"Welllll," Lady Victoria said, dragging the word out as though she were savoring a delicious bit of chocolate. "That was most unexpected."

Mary jerked her attention to Lady Hermione. "You said everyone knew, everyone was talking about Keswick and what happened in the garden."

"Yes, well, apparently a good deal more happened than we were led to believe."

Mary was torn between begging the ladies not to say anything and holding her head high, never straying from her story that it was all in innocence. But the kiss had rocked her to the core. How could she not blush with even the thought of it?

"So come, Lady Mary, now you must give us the juicy details of what transpired between *you* and Keswick," Lady Hermione said.

"You didn't know about the kiss?"

"No. How did it come about? Details. We must have the details."

"I don't understand. If you weren't aware of the kiss, what did you think happened? What have people been saying about us?" Could it be anything worse than what she'd already confessed?

"Not you. Only Keswick."

"What is your gossip?"

"Not nearly as interesting as yours, it seems."

"For God's sake, girl," her aunt snapped. "Stop torturing Mary. What the devil did you *think* happened in the garden?"

"Someone tried to kill Keswick."

* * *

Sebastian had just slid out of bed and was struggling to straighten to his full height, when the door to his bedchamber was flung open and Mary burst through like an avenging angel, her aunt and cousin in her wake.

Thank God he was wearing trousers. Unfortunately he wore no shirt, and he was still hunched over like some creature that should be skittering about Hugo's Notre Dame. Fighting the pain, he forced himself to stand tall, then realized the folly in that when Lady Ivers gasped and took a step back, while Lady Alicia paled. The sunlight streaming in through the window washed over his scars, *all* his scars. The damned eye-patch was resting on the table by the bed. He should have been reaching for it instead of striving to stand with some dignity.

"What the devil are you doing here?" he barked, before gritting his teeth and shuffling like an old man to the table to snatch up the patch. It was an awkward thing to strive to put it on when every movement strained his stitches, ignited fire in his side. Where the hell was his valet?

Thomas worked his way between the ladies hovering in the doorway. "Your Grace—"

But then even he came to a stop at the hideous sight before him. Unlike his valet, the butler had never seen the scars that Sebastian's clothes hid.

"We'd heard you were attacked," Mary said, before striding across the room with purpose as though shot from a cannon.

Her aunt called after her, but she simply marched on. He was tempted to back away, but forced himself to stand his ground. Something in her determination unsettled him. It was dangerous for her to be here. Dangerous for them both.

She stopped so near, her orchid scent wafted around him. Reaching up, she adjusted the patch before skimming her hand lightly over his cheek, his jaw, his shoulder, bringing it to rest where his heart thudded so hard that it was in danger of cracking a rib.

"They hurt you so badly," she whispered.

He was close to becoming unmanned. He would if he saw a single tear, but what he saw was far worse. Anger in her lovely green eyes. Perhaps even hatred. She pressed her lips tightly together, lowered her hand to just below his ribs. Her touch contained such tenderness that it made him want to weep, made him want to wrap his arm around her, draw her in against his good side, hold her near. Never let her go.

But he couldn't risk even a moment of softness, couldn't risk revealing a hint of weakness. He could not take what he could never keep. She was not his. It was a litany he'd repeated in his laudanum-induced haze when the pain kept him conscious. She was not his.

"You're bleeding," she said.

Tearing his gaze from her, he looked down and saw the bright red marring the bandage wrapped around his waist.

"He did this to you, didn't he? Your uncle."

"I do not think he would be this brazen."

She lifted her gaze to his, held it, and for a heartbeat he was back at Pembrook, young and innocent, believing that the world would one day be handed to him on a silver platter. Life would be fox hunts and pheasant shooting. Not rifles aimed at men. Life would be riding horses for sport not survival. Pleasures would involve beautiful women who wanted to be with him, instead of women who gasped and feared approaching him, as though his scars were contagious, as though they would somehow find a way to make the ladies ugly as well.

He had kissed Mary in the darkness when all that he was had been hidden from her. Now the harsh sunlight was revealing the marbling of puckered flesh that marred so much of him. Yet she didn't step back, she didn't turn away. He wondered if he lowered his mouth to hers now without the kindness of shadows, if she would close her eyes on a sigh or grimace as the creature he was grew too near.

"What have we here?" Tristan asked, his deep voice breaking the spell, sending Sebastian's thoughts careening back to the reality of where they were, what they were. "My brother with three lovely ladies in his bedchamber? I could very well become jealous."

"We're not *in* his bedchamber," Lady Alicia protested.

"Close enough, dear lady," Tristan said as he strode into the room, his speculative gleam running over both Sebastian and Mary.

Mary stepped away, her hand leaving Sebastian's skin, taking the warmth with her, sending a chill through him.

"Your brother is bleeding. If you'll bring bandages, I'll see to it." Mary began tugging off her gloves and only then did Sebastian realize that she'd been wearing them the entire time. Her touch had been so gentle, so warm that he could have sworn it was skin upon skin.

"My valet can see to it," Sebastian said. "Thomas, escort the ladies to their carriage."

Mary spun around and glared at him. "I'm not leaving until I know what happened last night."

Stubborn wench! "How did you even hear of it?" They hadn't told anyone, had planned to keep it quiet.

No sense in having rumors bandied about until they knew the truth of what had transpired.

"Unfortunately, it's all over London," Tristan said before Mary could answer. "That's why I'm here. I thought you should know."

"Yes, I heard of it at the dressmaker's," Mary confirmed.

"The dressmaker's?" Sebastian repeated.

"Mary was being fitted for her wedding gown," Lady Alicia explained.

He hadn't been questioning why she was at the dressmaker's, only that the gossip was being spouted in the corner of small shops. But now to know what she was doing, to be reminded that she would be married soon—

"We may have a problem there," she said quietly.

"I should say," her aunt suddenly announced. "Apparently you kissed her in the garden, Your Grace, and that bit of news shall no doubt be known throughout all of London by nightfall."

Mary slammed her eyes closed and her cheeks burned red. "Oh, I have mucked things up."

"Well," Tristan drawled, "life in London just got more interesting. And here I was thinking of setting sail, but how I can leave this behind?"

"The rumors are that you were attacked by a soldier from your regiment who says men died because you were a coward."

Standing in front of the cheval glass, Sebastian could see his brother's reflection as he lounged in a nearby chair. Even when Tristan was sprawled over furniture there was an alertness to him that suggested he could enter into the thick of a battle before he drew his next breath.

Sebastian was hoping for at least a day's reprieve from the business of securing his title. He wanted to take a large dose of laudanum and return to his bed. His side ached unbearably. His valet had changed the bandages and was now helping him to dress so he could visit with his guests in the parlor.

"Why are there rumors at all when we said nothing, and no one saw us?" he asked.

"I suspect Uncle had a hand in that. He's striving to discredit you. He wants the lords to back the petition he's preparing that urges the queen to grant the title to him because you are undeserving."

"If being deserving were a criteria, a good many lords would find themselves without titles." With a grimace, he moved as best he could to assist his valet in putting on his jacket. It was a dark blue, very conservative. Still he looked to be a man who was not at his best.

"You think Uncle is responsible for the attack?" Sebastian asked.

"Were you a coward on the battlefield?"

"Do you have to ask?"

Tristan arched a brow. "Others will. While I can't see you being a coward, I must admit that I don't know you as well as I might have otherwise."

"No, I was not a coward."

"Then yes. I think Uncle is responsible, and having failed, he is striving to make the best of a poor situation, perhaps to reflect suspicions from him. He either hired an incompetent or did it himself. Could it have been him, do you think?"

Sebastian cursed. "I did not see him at all. I struck him, but I couldn't judge his height."

"I'd wager it was him."

"Even if he were to have success convincing Queen

Victoria that the title should not be mine, you are next in line. Discrediting me does not make him the next logical choice."

"I suspect he plans to cross that bridge when he gets to it. Quite honestly, I doubt Victoria would be pleased to have as one of her noblemen a man who was once a pirate. And Rafe is also of questionable character. I suspect Uncle sees you as the only one who needs to fall. The rest of us will follow."

Sebastian dismissed his valet. Once he'd left the room, he turned to face his brother. "How involved were you in pirating?"

Tristan laughed darkly. "You are either a pirate or you are not. There are not degrees. Just as a lady's reputation is neither slightly ruined nor terribly ruined. It is simply ruined. The question is: what are you going to do about it?"

He knew Tristan was referring to Mary and the kiss in the garden. He could overlook it when it was a secret, but now if others knew . . .

Measures would have to be taken to protect her.

The only sounds in the parlor were the clinking of teacups on saucers and the ticking of the clock on the black marble mantel. A young female servant had brought in the tea, and Aunt Sophie had seen to preparing and serving it. She'd not spoken a single word since they left the duke's bedchamber. Mary assumed she was at a loss for words regarding her niece's uncharacteristic brazen behavior.

Mary knew that a proper lady did not barge her way into a gentleman's bedchamber unannounced and uninvited—or even invited for that matter. But the butler had been unwilling to provide any information regarding the duke's condition. And a lady certainly didn't approach a man who wore no clothing save his trousers. *And* she never, ever touched her fingers to his bare chest. Even though she wore kidskin gloves, she still managed to feel the fire radiating from his flesh warming hers, the rapid thudding of his heart against her palm, the subtle vibrations coming from his throat whenever he spoke.

For the first time no shadows had played over his features. He'd been too stunned to turn the marred side of his face away from her. Not that she would have let him. In the confines of his bedchamber, she'd imprisoned him in that corner and had been truly able to see all the damage that had been done to him on a faraway battlefield. She'd wanted to press her lips to every scar in order to ease the hurt. If they'd not had an audience, she wasn't certain even he would have had the power to stop her, although she could well imagine the one word he would have spoken in a raw voice: *Don't.*

He'd have not welcomed her pity, sympathy, or empathy. He'd have assumed she detected weakness when all she saw was strength. She wasn't certain she'd truly realized how much courage it took each time he made an appearance in Society. Now she understood that his scars went far deeper than the surface.

Her reputation would soon be as scarred as his flesh, and yet his wounds reflected a noble tapestry because he had suffered them in defense of country.

"Something seems different here," Alicia finally said, drawing Mary from her musings. "It's changed since the ball, and I can't quite put my finger on what it is."

"The rightful duke is at long last in residence," Mary said.

"You were quite bold in your actions regarding him

in the bedchamber," her aunt said, clear censure in her voice.

"He was in need of assistance." He would hate her saying that. He was so proud, so determined to make his own way.

"It was not your place to provide it."

"I could not stand by and watch as he struggled to regain his dignity."

Her aunt shook her head. "He'd have never lost it if you'd not charged into his bedchamber without thought or proper regard." She heaved a heavy sigh. "Unfortunately, your boldness apparently did not begin there. By nightfall, I fear everyone will know about your scandalous kiss in the garden, and your father shall be put out with me for not keeping a closer watch over you."

"Perhaps Ladies Hermione and Victoria will keep that news to themselves," Alicia said.

"Yes, I'm quite sure that's a possibility," her aunt snapped, "and I shall awake twenty years younger in the morning."

Mary hid her amusement. Under the circumstances, her world on the verge of calamity, she knew she shouldn't find a moment of relief in her aunt's acerbic tone, but she did. As long as she could still smile, perhaps all was not lost.

The brothers walked into the room, Sebastian moving more gingerly than Tristan. She didn't know why so many others always had such a difficult time telling one from the other. Even though that was no longer an issue, the brothers had never looked exactly the same to her. Sebastian had always been the more serious, now even more so.

"Ladies, my apologies for not being able to welcome you properly earlier," he said.

"Our apologies for barging in on your privacy," her aunt replied.

"I believe I was the only one who actually barged," Mary pointed out, and she could have sworn that a corner of Sebastian's mouth twitched. She wondered what it would entail to make him smile fully once more.

"Yes, well, I see no point in splitting hairs," Aunt Sophie said. "We are gratified that you seem to have escaped death's clutches."

"As am I."

Sebastian took a chair far from Mary, while Tristan selected one nearer. His gaze seemed to challenge his brother, and she wondered what that was about. As lads they'd always seemed to know each other's thoughts, but she suspected that the years apart may have changed their relationship somewhat. She despised their uncle for all the tragedy he'd visited upon them, for everything he'd stolen—so much that could not be easily identified.

"So what exactly happened last night?" Mary asked. "Where were you attacked?"

"In the garden. After—" He slid his gaze to her aunt before returning it to Mary. "—we parted. I was heading for the mews, intending to walk home. I heard a sound, turned, and became acquainted with someone's knife."

Both her aunt and cousin gasped in horror. Mary, however, noted that he told the tale with no emotion, as though it had happened to someone else. She wanted to know if he'd been angry or frightened or if he'd thought he might die. Where would his last thoughts travel? To regrets, to his youth when he was happy, to men he'd fought beside, to women he'd known? To her? She considered that her last thought might be of him. How unfair to Fitzwilliam.

"Fortunately, Tristan found me," he continued. "We thought to leave without anyone being the wiser but it seems rumors are running rampant nonetheless."

"You hold your uncle responsible?" Mary asked.

"We're not yet ready to cast accusations."

She was impressed with his restraint. Who else except his uncle would wish him harm?

"Lady Mary," Tristan began, "did you happen across anyone in the garden last night?"

It was too late to save her now so she might as well acknowledge the truth. "His Grace."

Tristan gave her a wolfish grin that she suspected would win over many a lady. "Besides my brother."

"Not really. No. I heard whisperings in the shadows and couples were strolling about of course, but from a distance, I couldn't identify them. And my thoughts were occupied elsewhere."

"Yes, I'm sure." Tension tightened her shoulders with the implications of his words. He turned his attention to Alicia, and Mary thought her cousin might be on the verge of swooning. She seemed to be having difficulty drawing in a breath. "Did either of you ladies take a stroll in the garden?"

"Absolutely not," her aunt said. "I speak for both of us. We did not leave the ballroom."

"Yes, I can imagine Lady Alicia was far too busy dancing."

"Not so busy as you might think." Blushing, she lowered her gaze to the tepid tea in her cup.

Mary shifted her attention to Sebastian to determine what he might think of this little exchange, and nearly dropped her own teacup when she saw how intently he was studying her. She considered setting the cup aside but her hands had begun to tremble and she didn't want to have a rattling saucer give away how disconcerted she was by his study of her. She wondered if he was upset that she'd unintentionally let the cat out of the bag about him kissing her. He'd obviously regretted pressing his lips to hers or he'd have not stormed off. If she'd not taken the coward's route and scurried back to the ballroom, she might have seen who attacked him.

"I don't suppose we'll ever discover who attacked Keswick," Tristan said.

"Unless he returned to the ballroom bloody. I did manage to land a blow."

"I can't imagine that it was a lord who attacked you," Aunt Sophie said. "Lords do not attack other lords. It was no doubt some ruffian. Although what he was doing there is beyond me. Perhaps he meant to rob you."

"Perhaps."

But Mary heard the doubt in his voice. He suspected his uncle of foul play. Not that she blamed him, because she did as well.

"We're much relieved to see you were not too terribly hurt," her aunt said, setting her teacup aside and rising. "We should be leaving now."

"I would like a moment with Mary," Sebastian said.

Her aunt sat. "Of course."

"Alone."

"Hardly appropriate."

"I'm in no condition to take advantage."

"Still—"

"Aunt, my reputation is no doubt in tatters by now anyway. What harm can come of letting us have a few moments of privacy? The door may remain open. You can stand in the entryway and peer in."

"If Fitzwilliam were to discover—"

"I'm not going to tell him." Besides, once he heard about the kiss, it would all be over anyway.

"Very well." She rose again. "Alicia, with me."

Both ladies began to walk out. Tristan shoved himself out of the chair.

"I'll keep the ladies out of mischief."

Mary smiled at that. She suspected it had been a good many years since her aunt had caused any mischief and Alicia was too mindful of her reputation to do anything untoward. Pity Mary could not claim the same. After everyone disappeared through the doorway, she said, "You've grown paler."

"I'm not quite up to receiving guests."

"I'm sorry for the imposition, but when I heard that someone tried to kill you . . . I just needed to see for myself how badly you were injured."

"You saw a good deal more than that."

"Yes, I'm sorry about that as well." Only she wasn't, not really. Now that she knew the true extent of his injuries they would haunt her. She should have insisted that he seek out her father for his aid that long-ago night. Sebastian had been a boy and the path he'd chosen for himself and his brothers had not been easy. "I appreciate your chastising me in privacy."

Groaning, he rubbed his jaw. "It was not my intent to chastise you at all. I merely . . . how did your aunt hear about the kiss and why is all of London going to know about it as well?"

She'd rather be chastised about her behavior in the bedchamber than reveal what a silly nitwit she'd been. She plucked at a thread on her skirt, realized that the way her luck was going, she would no doubt unravel all the threads with a mere tug and her dress would fall off.

It simply appeared to be a day where if something could go wrong it would.

"Mary?" he prodded gently.

She took comfort in that gentleness, in that hint of the boy he'd been, the friendship they'd shared. "When Lady Hermione came into the dressmaker's with the news that everyone was talking about what happened in the garden, I was vain enough to believe they were talking about me."

"You're hardly vain."

"You're kind. But I blurted that it was only a kiss between us and it meant nothing. So now they know we kissed and they are not ones to hold such juicy gossip."

"And mere rumors of a kiss without a single witness are enough to ruin your reputation?"

How could she forget that he'd not been in Society for years, that he didn't know how swiftly the gossip-mongers worked, and how precious a lady's reputation was? When they were children, he'd thought nothing of lifting her skirt to see how badly she was scraped when she took a tumble. The adult world was so very different. She might be as uninformed as he if her aunt hadn't schooled her.

"In all likelihood. Fitzwilliam will not be pleased when he hears."

Sebastian furrowed his brow. "So you didn't mention it to Fitzwilliam afterward?"

"Absolutely not." She shook her head. "Or I wouldn't have. I didn't see him afterward."

He grew incredibly still, so still that she wasn't certain he continued to breathe. "Is something wrong?"

"Tristan crossed paths with him in the garden."

"Oh dear Lord, do you think he saw us?" It would explain his not returning to the ballroom, not seeking her out for the last dance. She'd been so obsessed with what had occurred between her and Sebastian that she'd given little thought to the fact that she'd not seen Fitzwilliam again. In truth, she'd been relieved because she feared he'd take one look at her and know what had transpired. In spite of Tristan's assurances that she didn't *look* as though she'd been kissed, she'd certainly *felt* as though she had been well and thoroughly seduced.

"If he had, would he have not said?"

"Of course. He would have confronted you—us. His pride would not have allowed him to overlook such a transgression without seeking some sort of satisfaction. Not a duel, of course, but a round in the boxing ring perhaps. So he did not bear witness to our inappropriate behavior. Of that I'm sure. Still, I must tell him. I can't let him hear it from the gossips."

"He won't be pleased."

"No, he won't." Neither would her father.

"Mary, I'm sorry for whatever trouble I've brought you."

"It's my fault. I should have never followed you into the garden." She rose. "Please don't get up."

He ignored her, grimacing as he struggled to his feet. It took everything within her not to rush over and assist him.

"I do hope you will rest," she told him, "and ensure your wound does not become infected."

"I've had quite a bit of experience dealing with wounds. I assure you, I will be well in no time at all. Mary, I owe you—my brothers owe you—and yet it seems we have brought you little more than trouble. I regret any embarrassment you might suffer because of my bad judgment in the garden."

Bad judgment. What did she expect him to say? That the kiss devastated him? That it left him yearning for another? That it made him realize she was no longer a child? Could a kiss possess that much power?

"I shall be fine," she lied. "After all, it was only a kiss."

Chapter 16

Only a kiss. She had used the phrase before when referring to what had passed between them and added the little caveat that it meant nothing. Nothing.

As his carriage rolled through the London streets, Sebastian wondered what he had expected. That she would confess to being devastated by it, yearned for another? That the kiss he'd delivered in the garden was far more powerful than the bold brush of his lips over hers that he'd delivered at the abbey ruins all those many years ago?

"You're brooding," Tristan said.

He looked up at his brother sprawled on the bench across from him. "I've been brooding for twelve years."

"No, this is different. I suspect it has something to do with the words that passed between you and Mary before she took her leave."

He wondered what it would be like to not have such a profound connection with another person. Lonely, he decided. Much more lonely than he was now. And at the same time, it would be a bit of a relief to know that one's moods and the reasons behind them could not be so easily deciphered.

"I'm simply exhausted."

"Then we should return to the residence. Calling on Fitzwilliam could be for naught. I don't recall seeing any blood on him."

"But you also admitted to being in the shadows and not having a clear view of him."

"What would be his motive?"

"Perhaps he saw me kiss Mary."

"Killing a man for kissing your betrothed seems a bit drastic."

I would, he thought, surprised by the vehemence behind the words. An image of Mary lifting her face for a kiss suddenly loomed in his mind—only it was Fitzwilliam, not Sebastian, lowering his mouth to hers. His stomach knotted so tightly, he feared he might tear loose one of the stitches in his side. What the deuce was wrong with him? It had meant nothing to her. She'd said as much. It had meant even less to him.

A distraction. That was all it had been. A momentary escape from the blight that the night had become. Attending the ball had done little more than reveal the harsh reality of his shortcomings and he'd sought to regain something of what he'd lost. Passion was a powerful distraction.

With Mary it had been incredibly so. He had used her, and for that he should be flogged, but damnation if he didn't want to use her again. Her lips were as plump as a freshly plucked strawberry. He wanted to settle his in against them and once more become lost in the pleasure of her.

"You're not going to kill him are you?"

He jerked his attention to Tristan. "What are you on about?"

"You look to be a man on the verge of committing murder."

"My thoughts turn to dark places. It seems to be the way of it of late. I think it more likely that he will murder me—if he's heard the gossip regarding Mary and me."

"If he hasn't, are you going to tell him?"

He shook his head. "On the off chance that the rumors concerning Mary are not being spread."

"Oh, I'm sure they're being spread. Lady Hermione does not seem to be acquainted with the notion of silence. I've never known a woman to talk incessantly about absolutely nothing of importance. I almost kissed her on the dance floor in an effort to cease her babbling."

"If you had, you'd have had her in your life permanently."

"Precisely why I did not. I would never know a moment's peace."

The carriage drew to a stop in front of Fitzwilliam's modest residence. The footman opened the door and Sebastian stepped out, followed by Tristan.

"So this is where Mary will live when in London," Tristan said.

Sebastian refrained from commenting that she deserved something grander. Instead he simply charged up the steps and banged the knocker against the door. The butler answered, and to his credit, at the sight of Sebastian he did little more than arch an eyebrow.

"The Duke of Keswick to see Lord Fitzwilliam."

"His lordship is not in residence."

"To me or to anyone?"

"He is not in residence, meaning, Your Grace, that he is not here."

"Do you know where he is?"

"His lordship is not in the habit of informing me of his intentions other than that he is going out."

Of course he wasn't. It had been a pointless question.

"When will he be returning?"

"I can't say."

"You can't say or you won't say?"

"I do not know when he will return."

Sebastian spun on his heel and began trudging down the steps.

"What are your plans now?" Tristan asked.

"Return to my residence to rest."

He'd overtaxed himself, dammit. And this had been a futile exercise. He'd just felt a need to take some action. He could only hope that by now Mary's fragrance had deserted his residence. Otherwise he would have little luck not thinking about her for the remainder of the day.

When Mary first entered her father's library where she'd been summoned, she was so incredibly grateful that Fitzwilliam sported neither bruise nor cut nor swelling about his face that she nearly rushed forward to embrace him, to hold him tightly. She was even willing to squeal near his ear. She hated to admit that she had not quite believed he hadn't harmed Sebastian.

It was ludicrous in retrospect now. She knew that. She'd simply forgotten when confronted with the possibility that he could have done harm. He was not a vengeful man. Jealous certainly. He'd confessed that, but every lady desired a man with a bit of green in him.

It was a sign of how much she meant to him. That he cared.

Although right now she feared he cared about all the wrong things. He stood solemnly before her, his hands clasped behind his back. Staring up at him, she felt rather like a naughty girl who had been caught with her hand in the biscuit tin.

Looking none too happy, her father sat in a far corner downing whiskey as though he feared the pleasure would soon be denied him.

"Mary," Fitzwilliam began.

"My lord." She smiled at him. He tightened his jaw. That didn't bode well. Only one day had passed since the debacle at the seamstress's. Surely he'd not yet heard. She'd been in her room penning a letter to him—an explanation. Coward. She should have gone straightway to his residence yesterday to explain it all to his face but a small part of her, a tiny little part of her had hoped that her aunt would indeed awaken twenty years younger this morning, and that Ladies Hermione and Victoria would keep to themselves what she had blurted out.

"I tolerated your speaking with Keswick during Lady Alicia's recital because I knew he was a friend and you'd not seen him in a good many years. When I heard that you met with him in Hyde Park—alone—I overlooked the transgression."

"It was hardly a transgression. I merely wished to convey to him the importance of attending a ball. We were in full view the entire time."

"I'm aware of that. As those who reported seeing you made it clear that you were riding and that nothing untoward occurred. Still, you were there with him. Then at the ball, you spoke with him alone, near the fronds, without chaperone."

"We had a hundred chaperones in that ballroom."

He arched a pale brow. "And in the garden? How many were there?"

Feeling as though he had tricked her, trapped her, and willingly sought to humiliate her, she wilted against the seat.

"Yes, it has reached me that you and he had a tryst in the garden."

"Good God, Mary!" her father exclaimed.

"It was hardly a tryst."

"You deny kissing him?" Fitzwilliam asked.

"Mary?" her father barked.

She studied the pointed toes of her shoes. She wondered how she might go about kicking herself.

"So there is truth to these rumors," Fitzwilliam said.

"After the mishap on the dance floor—" She gave him a pointed look. "—I wanted to ensure that he understood that it could happen to anyone, as you reassured me it was not done on purpose."

Fitzwilliam knelt before her and took her hands. She couldn't recall him ever being so near, not even when he'd proposed. They'd been sipping tea and he hadn't even bothered to set his teacup aside. He'd simply taken a sip and then said, "I say, dear girl, I was wondering if you might consider marrying me."

It wasn't romantic or passionate, but still it had touched her heart. He was so endearingly reserved. Unfortunately with recent events, she had hurt him. She could see that as she gazed into his brown eyes.

"I suppose if you are guilty of anything, Mary, it is a charitable heart. But Keswick is not yours to worry over."

"But he is my friend, Fitzwilliam."

"He *was* your friend, when you were children. If

he was your friend now, do you think he would do all these things that tarnish your reputation and mine?"

"It just happened. The kiss. I'm not even sure what prompted it. One moment we were talking and the next we were kissing. I'm sorry. I never meant to give you cause to doubt me."

"Hence the reason I shall overlook it. This once. We shall attend the next ball together so that all of London shall see that you are mine. You are mine, are you not?"

Feeling the tears sting her eyes, she nodded. "Yes, without question." Only she'd been asking so many blasted questions lately.

"Splendid. But you must promise me that you will not speak with him again."

Startled, she stared at him. "You mean ever? Are you suggesting I give him a cut direct? Ignore him?"

"It is either him or me, Mary. If you write to him and explain the boundaries, then he should be gentleman enough not to put you in a situation where you must choose."

"I've had twelve years of not seeing him, not speaking to him. You can't deny me—" The pleasure, she'd almost said. Only it wasn't a pleasure exactly. It was more of a challenge, more of a rightness. They'd shared so much in their youth. To never be able to share anything ever again was maudlin.

"What if I promise to never be alone with him? To only speak with him when you are there? Surely that should suffice."

He brought her hands to his lips, pressed them there, squeezed his eyes shut. "I can tell that you are going to be a difficult wife."

"I won't. I promise."

He opened his eyes, smiled. "Difficult because when

you ask for something I find it very hard to deny you. I will be content if you are never alone with him and if you only speak with him in my presence. Or your father's."

Relief swamped her, and she smiled. "Thank you, my lord. I thought you would be done with me if you heard the rumor."

"Two weeks from our wedding? It will take a good deal more than gossip to keep me from the church. But I should very much like not to hear anymore."

"Perhaps I should lock her in her room until it is time to head to St. George's," her father suggested.

"She's not a child, Winslow," Fitzwilliam said. "I trust her word."

She wanted to hug him near for that bit of trust. She vowed then and there that she would never disappoint him again. She would be an exemplary wife and give him no further cause to doubt her.

Releasing her hands, he stood. "One more thing. The necklace with the green stone you wore the other night—you're not to wear it again. As a matter of fact I think it would be best if you return it to Keswick."

She stared at him in muted surprise. "How did you know?"

"I asked your father about it. He asked your maid. I will not have my wife accepting gifts from other gentlemen."

"I'm not yet your wife."

"If you wish to be you will return it. Consider the action a token of good faith. I've been injured here, Mary. Am I really asking too much?"

Slowly, she shook her head. She'd even told Sebastian that she shouldn't have accepted the gift. "No. I shall see to its return posthaste. Although you should know it wasn't a gift from Keswick. It was from all three brothers."

"A gift from *three* men? I can only imagine how that might be spun by the gossips. Even more reason to return it."

Pleasing a gentleman was such a sticky web. He bid her and her father good-bye, then strode from the room, leaving her to wonder if she would indeed be happy married to him.

"You need this marriage, Mary," her father said pointedly. "I need it. To know you are secure. If I fail you, I have failed in everything."

"You've failed in nothing, Father."

"I failed to produce an heir to watch over you when I am gone."

She supposed the fault there rested as much with her mother as with him.

"You say that as though you are planning to leave me at any moment," she told him.

"Life is precarious, Daughter. I would have thought the Pembrook lads would have taught you that."

"Had you heard that someone tried to kill Sebastian?"

He nodded. "Terrible thing that. They say it was a soldier who believed him to be a coward."

"Do you believe that?"

Slowly, he shook his head. "But you would be wise to keep your thoughts to yourself. Do not seek to help the Pembrook lords further. It can only lead to your downfall. Your loyalty now is to Fitzwilliam. It must be to him."

"Yes, Father." He didn't realize what he asked of her. What Fitzwilliam asked. To abandon her friends. She knew the brothers would not find fault with her. Had

Sebastian not encouraged her to keep out of harm's way? Still it did not stop her from feeling like a traitor as she walked from the room.

My dearest Sebastian,

It is with a large measure of regret that I must return this lovely gift that you and your brothers bestowed upon me. I must also regretfully request that should our paths cross, you not speak to me. My betrothed believes that if I act in a manner above reproach that we may weather this storm of gossip that has made the Season most difficult for us all. Please know that I will always hold all of you in my heart.

Yours,
Mary

Lying in bed, Sebastian picked up the necklace that had slithered out when he'd unfolded the missive that his butler had brought to him earlier. He wondered why she'd had to return it. Who had made her? Was it because of the gossip about town: that they'd shared an illicit kiss in the garden?

Although it certainly hadn't felt illicit. It had felt bloody marvelous.

Unlike his side that was burning hotter than hell.

The fever had arrived sometime the night before. He should have expected it, he supposed. He hadn't stayed in bed as the physician had advised. Not until today when he'd had no energy to get up. He should call on Mary to ensure all was well with her. He should visit Fitzwilliam and explain that he was no threat. He wanted only what was best for Mary.

Yes. Get up. Set matters to right, he ordered himself. That's what he needed to do.

Instead, he succumbed to the lure of cool oblivion.

Chapter 17

The afternoon after the day that Mary had returned the necklace to Sebastian, she sat in the garden pretending to read. From time to time she even turned a page, just in case her father was watching her from his library window. She had not expected, but she had rather hoped, that Sebastian would return the necklace to her so she might have a chance to explain—

Only she wasn't supposed to speak to him, so how would she—

But if he came here, etiquette required she be a polite hostess—

Only her father could send him away before she saw him—

And if he told Fitzwilliam—

She damned well wanted to pull out her hair.

The girl who had ridden over to Pembrook would not have allowed others to dictate her actions. When had that changed? Was it part of being a lady? Or a coward?

Did she so desperately desire marriage that she would not be true to herself? Or was it Fitzwilliam she so desperately desired?

And if she desired him, why was it that whenever they were together, she never once wondered what it might be like to have him press his lips against hers? Why could she not forget what it had felt like to have Sebastian's on hers? Why the devil did she want him to kiss her again? Only softer this time, not quite so brutish—although it had certainly been exciting. Still, why did she think softer would bring back the boy he'd been?

That lad was long lost.

She doubted they would ever be friends as they'd once been. A friend did not look at one as though he was contemplating devouring her. But then he always looked as though he had no patience for anything. He wanted what he wanted and he wanted it now. She supposed she couldn't blame him. He'd had twelve years of waiting. But his impatience would likely result in a harsh life for his wife. Always trying to anticipate his moods, his needs could very well drive her to madness.

Fitzwilliam was much easier to decipher. He was proper. His moods controlled. Even when he'd been angry with her, his words had lacked heat. He'd merely scolded, then insisted on proper behavior. Her embarrassment had come because she should have never engaged in any improper behavior that would require his correcting her. He had every right to be upset with her.

She disappointed herself.

She was not a child, free to run hither and yon, and do as she pleased. She had responsibilities now. Was required to act in a certain manner, to complement her husband and his station in life. Fitzwilliam was a viscount, one day to be a marquess. She understood why he didn't want her speaking with men alone. That he had overlooked her previous lacks in judgment boded well for a future marriage of equanimity. He would not bully. He would not be unkind. They would not have upheavals or storms or adventures.

She sighed. She could very well be bored out of her mind.

She squeezed her eyes shut. She should not be entertaining these thoughts. They'd have never intruded if Sebastian hadn't returned. Although she certainly couldn't regret that he had. Because it meant he still lived. And she cared too much for her childhood friend to wish him ill.

"M'lady?"

She opened her eyes to find the butler hovering, a silver salver in his hand. She took the cards that rested on it. It seemed Ladies Hermione and Victoria were in wont of the latest gossip regarding the lords of Pembrook. How disappointed they would be to discover she could no longer serve as a source for their amusements.

"I shall entertain them here," she said. "Have someone bring tea and cakes."

"Yes, m'lady."

She closed her book, set it on the table, and rose to await their arrival. Two more weeks and she would be receiving guests at Fitzwilliam's. Well, perhaps a bit longer than that as they would be taking a month in Italy after they were married. She was quite looking forward to it as she'd never left England's shores.

Spotting the ladies scurrying up the walk, she forced herself to smile. Hermione reached her first, and to Mary's surprise, placed her hands on her shoulders, drew her near, and touched her cheek lightly against

Mary's. "My dear girl, how horrible for you. I do wish you'd told us everything."

What the devil was she talking about?

Hermione pulled back, but did not release her hold, her brow furrowed so deeply that Mary feared she might forever wear the frown. "I must confess, regrettably, that Victoria and I did not keep your confidence regarding the kiss—"

"I never expected that you would. Terribly juicy bit of gossip, I'm sure."

"—but had we known that he had forced you, that you had to fight your way free of him—"

Shock rippled through Mary. "What? No, what are you talking about?"

"That Keswick behaved as a complete blackguard and gave you no choice in the matter."

"Who told you such nonsense?"

"It's all over London. He and his brothers are to be refused admittance into any proper residence. And it's not fair. It's simply not fair."

"I couldn't agree more. It shan't be tolerated." Lies! Lies running amuck over London. How had they even started?

"Thank the Lord that you see the truth of the matter. So you will speak out in favor of Lord Tristan so that at least he can be welcomed into homes?"

"Lord Tristan?" Mary felt as though she were trapped in a whirlwind of words that were slamming together in no logical manner.

"Yes. He should not be made to suffer—*I* should not be made to suffer—because his brother is a savage."

"But Keswick is not a savage. He did not force me. Where did these awful rumors start?"

Hermione finally released Mary's shoulders, stepped

back, and gave a light tug on her gloves. "Where all rumors start. With the truth."

"The truth is that we shared a kiss in the garden. A kiss that we both—or at least I—welcomed."

Lady Hermione arched a fair, delicate brow. "You invited him to take liberties?"

"I did not invite him, and no liberties—" Her words would be misinterpreted, twisted about. "He kissed me. It was no more than that. Lips exploring—" Again she stopped. Anything she could think to say in way of explanation would only worsen matters.

"They say he ripped your bodice in his eagerness. The seamstress admitted to repairing your gown."

Mary could only stare in stunned disbelief. This madness resembled a parlor game she'd once played where one person whispered to another and around the circle it went until when the whispered words finally made their way to the originator, they barely resembled the original phrase. It had been a fun game at the time. Everyone laughed. She certainly wasn't laughing now. "Who is *they* who are spouting these ridiculous claims?"

"Well, everyone, of course."

"I returned to the ballroom after the kiss."

"I didn't see you, but I heard you left rather quickly."

"Your hair was askew," Lady Victoria added. "I saw Lord Tristan straighten it. On the terrace."

She had spent so many years with no one paying any attention to her at all, no one noticing that she had come of age for a Season but failed to appear in London, and suddenly it was as though everyone had their spyglass pointed her way. "This whole matter is ludicrous."

What must Sebastian be thinking? Had he heard these rumors? Had Fitzwilliam? What a colossal mess!

"Your tea, m'lady."

She glanced over at the female servant holding a tray that contained the china and small cakes. So civilized, so proper. She could not possibly sit down and sip tea as though nothing were amiss. "Return it to the kitchen."

The girl curtsied and hurried away as though she recognized a storm brewing within her mistress. Hermione apparently was not so intuitive.

"But I would like to have a bit of tea while we talk further. If you would provide us with the details of that night perhaps we can set matters to right so Lord Tristan may again be welcomed into homes."

Lord Tristan again? How could Lady Hermione not understand that Lord Tristan was the very least of Mary's worries at the moment? "He was never welcomed. Not even into yours. Your parents didn't want him there. How can you be so dense, so focused on only your own wants?"

Lady Hermione drew herself up. "No need to get nasty here."

"If you will please excuse me, I must pay a call on Lord Fitzwilliam. He will be terribly upset by these rumors." What if he challenged Sebastian to a duel? Sebastian with his military training would make short work of him. No, with his hindered vision it was very likely that he could no longer properly sight a target. Fitzwilliam could come to incredible harm.

"Fitzwilliam didn't seem terribly upset when he spoke to Father about them," Lady Victoria said.

"Why would he discuss them with your father?"

"He said the gentlemen needed to ensure that Keswick was not allowed near any of the women. He said his cowardly behavior on the battlefield apparently extended to his treatment of ladies. They want him out of London."

It made no sense. No sense at all. Why would Fitzwilliam speak ill of Sebastian? With questions tumbling through her mind, she began marching toward the house.

"What are you going to do?" Lady Hermione called out.

But she didn't answer them. She just left them to stare after her.

She thought of speaking with her father but he would only advise her to leave the matter be. That was not an option. So she changed into her calling dress and had a carriage readied. As it rumbled through the streets, rain began to fall. It matched her mood. Whatever was wrong with people? Why had they not celebrated the lords' return? Why did they view them as questionable? Why did they believe rumors that Sebastian was a coward on the battlefield? Why did they believe that he would force himself on her?

Did they think she would be cowed by such behavior that she wouldn't report it? She'd have scratched, kicked, and fought. She'd have never succumbed willingly to something she didn't want.

The carriage came to a halt. The door opened and the footman, holding an umbrella, handed her down. But even his long legs had a time of it keeping up with hers as she hurried to the massive doors at Fitzwilliam's residence. She didn't care that rain droplets rolled down her face when she stepped into the foyer.

"Where's your master?" she demanded as the butler appeared.

"I shall announce your arrival."

"Just tell me where he is. Do it or relieving you of your duties will be my first act after becoming mistress of this household."

"The library, m'lady."

She marched down the hallway with her hands fisted and her shoes beating out a steady cadence that resembled that of militia drummer. She was ready to do battle if need be, but she hoped, dear God, but she did hope that she would discover she was wrong in her suspicions.

With a bow, a footman opened the door at her approach. She charged into the room and staggered to a stop. Fitzwilliam was lounging in a chair by the fire, snifter in hand, swirling the amber liquid within it, apparently lost in thought. He seemed so vulnerable for a moment there, and she imagined they would have many nights of sitting together before a fire. They would read together, and talk quietly, and hopefully laugh about some silly nonsense.

Glancing over, he furrowed his brow and slowly came to his feet as though she'd awoken him or perhaps he simply couldn't believe the sight of the hoyden standing before him, dripping on his parquet floor. "Lady Mary, whatever's wrong? What are you doing here?"

Bravely, she took several steps forward along with a deep breath. "Did you start the rumors that Keswick had forced his person on me in the garden?"

Irritation chased away the furrows, but he steadfastly held her gaze. "No."

One word delivered like the shot from a pistol. She'd offended him, and as much as she'd regretted it, she'd had to ask. That knowledge bothered her, sent a fissure of unease through her, but she wasn't certain why. She'd have to examine it later.

"It must have been his uncle then, striving to discredit him, to make his entry back into Society that much more difficult. I'm certain he spawned this ludicrous story of Keswick's cowardice on the battlefield."

"Why is this a concern to you?"

"Because he's my friend."

He set aside his snifter and approached. "So anxious were you to question me that you couldn't even arrive with an umbrella?"

She watched a raindrop fall from her hat to the floor. "I was upset, not thinking."

"You do not believe him capable of moral shortcomings and yet you question mine?"

Not only offended, but hurt him as well. "I'm sorry. I know you're a good man."

"Apparently you don't."

"I do. I'd have not accepted your offer of marriage if I doubted the sort of man you are. I thought perhaps you'd done it in a misguided well-meaning attempt to protect my honor."

"I assure you that I'm not in the habit of being misguided in any of my actions."

"Of course you're not. I hope you will find it in your heart to forgive my impertinence."

"I wish I could say that I would forgive you anything, but I must confess to growing wearisome of constantly finding Keswick in our lives. He will not be there once we are married, I should hope. I'll have your word on that."

What was he saying? That she would never see him again?

"I don't suppose you would do what you could to help quash these rumors that he took unfair advantage of me," she said quietly.

He turned away. "If I did that, it would be to imply that you kissed him willingly. Do you understand how that would make me appear? Cuckolded before we're even wed. I believe silence is the better part of valor here. The rumors will die out of their own accord if tinder is not constantly thrown on them."

He was correct, of course. If the rumors garnered no reaction, people would soon lose interest in them. But what damage to Sebastian's reputation might be done in the meantime?

Fitzwilliam faced her. "I can't help but admire your loyalty to the man. I simply wished it extended to me."

She suddenly felt as though she didn't deserve this man. "It does. I'll be such a devoted wife you'll never have cause to doubt me."

"I'm counting on that. So shall we put this behind us?"

Not quite yet. "Lady Hermione told me that she overheard you encouraging her father to convince others not to allow Keswick into proper homes."

"He asked for my opinion and I gave it to him. They've caused nothing but trouble since they arrived. I told him they will not be welcomed in mine. What he chooses to do is his business."

"It's so unfair."

"Perhaps in time when they've learned to behave with a bit more decorum, when they realize the value of conformity, people will be more at ease with them."

They would never conform. Of that she was certain. Perhaps she'd been hasty in trying to lure them into Society. Fitzwilliam was correct: they needed to make their own way in their own time.

Reaching out, he touched her damp hair. "You were very naughty to come here without a chaperone."

She wondered if he might take advantage, might in fact use the opportunity to kiss her. She couldn't imagine that Sebastian would let such a moment pass if he found himself alone in the presence of a woman he intended to marry. She didn't like thinking of him as being barbaric. He was simply blatantly sensual, even if he didn't see himself as such.

Fitzwilliam skimmed his knuckles along her cheek, gave her a look of fondness. "We have a dinner tonight at Lord and Lady Moreland's. Allow me to escort you to your carriage so that you may return home and begin preparing for it. I shall bring my carriage around at half past seven."

The moment shouldn't have ended with her being disappointed that he'd not sought to take advantage. Her reputation was on perilous enough ground as it was. She had no need to have him further doubt her ability to act as a lady.

He extended his arm and she slipped hers through the crook of his elbow. She walked so close that her skirt brushed against his trousers but the nearness didn't seem at all scandalous. Shouldn't she want to lean into him, press her entire side against his?

Why was she questioning so much of late? He was good for her. They were well suited.

A footman with an umbrella followed them out to the carriage and Fitzwilliam handed her up. "I shall see you soon. Remember your promise to me. No Keswick. Men's reputations are hardly as important as ladies'. It's the reason so many of us excel at being rakes: no one really cares what we do. This nasty business about the kiss will die soon, especially after we are wed."

She nodded. "Again, I'm sorry that I thought you sought to do him harm."

He tucked her beneath her chin as though she were a child. "I would not be marrying you if you were any different."

Slamming the door closed, he instructed the driver to return her home. The carriage bolted up the drive. Glancing back out the window, she saw Fitzwilliam still standing there, watching her. He worried over her.

But who worried over Sebastian? If he heard the rumors, if he thought she were responsible for spreading them—

She could barely tolerate the possibility.

As soon as the carriage turned onto the street and she was certain she was no longer visible to Fitzwilliam, she leaned her head out of the window and ignored the rain pelting her. "Chambers, take me to Easton House."

"Yes, m'lady!"

Settling back against the bench, she removed a handkerchief from her reticule and dabbed at her face. She knew that Fitzwilliam wouldn't approve. She simply had to ensure that he never found out.

She could do that easily enough with discretion. She stuck her head back out the window. "Chambers, use the mews not the front entrance."

If he answered, she didn't hear it because thunder rumbled. She slipped back inside and hoped it had not been a sign of disapproval from on high. No one would look for her at the servants' entrance. She would meet quickly with Sebastian, explain that she was not responsible for the ugly rumors and if they all just ignored them they would fade away. She needed no more than five minutes. Then she would return home.

Simple enough. While she was there she would explain in person about the return of the necklace and how they must avoid each other. Surely he understood her betrothed's jealousy for he would no doubt feel the same toward the woman he intended to marry. He'd not tolerate her seeking solitary moments with another man. Nor should he.

Then an awful thought occurred to her. What if he wouldn't see her? What if her letter and the awful rumors circulating had torn asunder the last threads of their fragile friendship? By the time the carriage drew to a halt, she'd worked herself up into a worrisome lather. If he weren't angry with her, if he understood, he'd have at least sent her a missive indicating such.

Instead, she'd had only silence from him since having her own message delivered. The footman opened the door and handed her down. Just as he had at Fitzwilliam's so he had a devil of a time keeping pace with her as she raced up the path. It suddenly seemed imperative that she see Sebastian, that she make things right between them. Yes, her loyalty was to Fitzwilliam but she couldn't ignore Sebastian.

The rain slashed at her sideways, each frigid drop as painful as she suspected Sebastian's icy words to her might be. The puddles splashed, soaking her hems. She reached the back door and pounded on it. A footman opened it, and she burst through as though she'd been invited.

The servants' eyes widened but no one stopped her progress until the butler caught up to her in the foyer. She was a soggy mess and her hair was falling, but she didn't care. "Please let His Grace know that Lady Mary Wynne-Jones has come to call."

"I'm sorry, m'lady, but he is not receiving."

She thrust up her chin and spoke with the full weight of her father's rank. "He will receive me."

He gave a slight bow of acquiescence. "I shall let him . know you're here."

She expected him to go down a hallway. Instead, he started up the stairs. She wondered if Sebastian were readying himself for the Moreland dinner. It seemed rather early and she'd not considered that he would attend. It would be quite awkward unless he understood everything. Her coming here had been a wise decision on her part, essential in fact, to ensuring that she did not anger Fitzwilliam unduly tonight.

She glanced around, caught sight of a mirror, and moved toward it. As soon as her reflection greeted her, she gasped. She was a fright. Her hat was wilted, her hair drooping from the weight of the wet strands. She looked like a cat that someone had attempted to drown.

Sebastian would no doubt laugh just as he had when they were children and she'd tumbled into the river. He'd rescued her then. How fortunate she'd been that he was near, because she hadn't a clue how to swim. But he'd taught her. While she'd worn nothing except her undergarments. It hadn't seemed wrong at all. She'd forgotten about that. Now of course it was unconscionable.

At the sound of heavy footsteps, she gazed upward, surprised to discover that it wasn't Sebastian making his way down. "Lord Tristan."

He smiled slightly. "Lady Mary."

"Forgive the formality. It seems pretentious after everything we shared. I was simply caught unawares by your presence. I'm here to speak with Sebastian."

"Yes, so Thomas informed me. Unfortunately Sebastian is not up to receiving callers."

"Callers? Or me?" Without waiting for his reply, she started up the stairs.

He caught up with her easily enough, grabbed her arm, and halted her progress. "Mary, wait."

"I know he's upset about the gossip, but I must explain." Wrenching free, she carried on. This time he didn't try to stop her, but she was aware of the echo of his footsteps following in the wake of hers.

At the top of the stairs, she took the familiar path that had added to her downfall once before, but this time there were no witnesses other than Tristan, who would certainly hold his tongue. She would have her say and leave. No one would be the wiser. The door was open so she simply swept into the room and stumbled to an ungainly stop.

Sebastian was in the bed, breathing heavily, bathed in dampness as though he had been the one running through the rain instead of her. He was wearing a nightshirt, but it was unbuttoned and soaked, plastered to his skin. She took tentative steps forward until she was near enough to press a hand to his brow. Fevered. Worse than fevered. She'd never felt skin so hot. "He's burning up."

"His wound is festering. I've sent for the physician."

She caught scent of the rancid odor now. Then she noticed something clasped in his hand, the gold filigree chain dangling onto the bed. Her necklace. Cautiously she touched his fist.

"I've not been able to get him to release it," Tristan said.

It was silly to think that her returning it had caused the decline. "How could this have happened? He visited with us."

"I think he got out of bed too soon, exerted himself too much."

Because of her. Because of suspicions. Because of his uncle.

"You can't stay, Mary."

She nodded absently. She knew that.

"I'll send word once the physician has seen him. Let you know how he fares."

Once again she nodded, just before sitting on the edge of the bed, reaching into the bowl of water and lifting out the cloth nestled in it. She wrung it out.

"Mary, you can't stay," he repeated.

"Yes, I know." She pressed the cloth to Sebastian's brow. She had a dinner party to attend. Fitzwilliam was going to arrive at her residence at half past seven. She needed to be ready. She patted the cloth along Sebastian's neck over the scars. She'd promised Fitzwilliam that she wouldn't approach Sebastian, that she would never again be alone with him.

Only she wasn't alone. Tristan was here.

"Mary—"

"If I remain wet, I'll catch my death. Will you please see if a servant has a dress I might borrow and find one willing to assist me as I change?"

"You don't always have to save us, Mary."

But this time, she wondered if she might be saving herself as well.

Chapter 18

He'd abandoned Pembrook. He'd left Rafe at the workhouse. An orphan. They would put him to work but they'd feed and clothe him. He'd sold Tristan to a ship's captain. He could excuse his actions then because he'd been a boy. Now he was a man and he would not abandon a fellow soldier on the field of battle. He would never again abandon anyone.

The battle raged. The heat consumed. It shouldn't have been so hot. The Crimea was cold, ghastly cold and miserable. But in the thick of battle he sweated. He had to get to his fallen comrade. He ducked low. Shells landed, exploded. Cannons boomed. Men cried out. Horses screamed. Blood splurged over him, burned. Something sharp pierced his side—

His torturous yell brought him from the depths of hell.

"Shh. Shh."

Breathing heavily he found himself gazing into familiar green eyes. He wanted to touch the softness of her cheek. Surely it would be cool. Would cool his fever. But when he reached for her, his arms wouldn't obey the command. He realized he was bound. He tugged. "No!"

"Shh," she urged again. "Your wound. It needs to be treated. It won't be pleasant, Sebastian."

"Release me." His voice sounded as though it had been scraped raw.

"We can't have you thrashing about, Brother."

Tristan. Dammit. He'd expect this of Rafe, but not Tristan. Rafe would no doubt relish the agony his helplessness brought.

"The doctor's going to give you ether," Mary said quietly. "You should sleep through the worst of it."

He rolled his head from side to side. "No, don't send me back there." Not to the nightmares, not to the regrets.

"I'll hold your hand. I won't let go."

"No." Something obstructed his vision of her, clamped down over his face.

"Breathe, Your Grace," someone ordered. "Breathe deeply."

He didn't want to sleep. He hated to sleep. When he slept he dreamed. All his regrets, all the nightmares welled up—

He fought to keep his eye open, to remain with her, to not succumb . . .

Mary feared that the physician had given Sebastian too much ether. After he'd cleaned the wound, removed the putrid flesh—a ghastly endeavor—he'd aroused Sebastian only enough to ensure he was still alive and then plied him with laudanum before leaving.

"Best to let him sleep through the worst of it."

From time to time he would moan or groan. He often said no. Sometimes he cried out with the word.

"What do you suppose he's fighting?" she asked, gently patting a cool cloth over his neck and chest.

Tristan leaned back in a chair on the other side of the bed, his stockinged feet crossed on its edge. "What we all fight. Demons."

She supposed she'd have hers to battle in the days to come. Honor had forced her to write a letter to Fitzwilliam. Preservation had forced her to lie. She'd told him that a migraine had sent her to bed and that she'd be unable to attend the dinner. She doubted that her father would check on her. He would no doubt spend the evening at a gentleman's club.

If her true whereabouts were discovered she would be in a great deal of trouble. But she couldn't regret being here. She thought she could confess to Tristan what she'd never be able to tell Sebastian. "I always resented that I was left behind."

"Rafe resented being left at the workhouse. You two should talk sometime."

She glanced over at him. "Did you regret boarding a ship?"

"Thought it would be a fun adventure."

"Was it?"

"Sometimes."

She returned her attention to Sebastian's chest. It was broad and powerful. She imagined him wielding a fine-edged glistening sword in battle. Or perhaps he'd held a rifle and bayonet.

"Have you heard the rumors that he forced himself on me in the garden?" she asked, feeling the heat warm her face.

"I pay little heed to rumors."

She offered him a soft smile. "But you did hear them."

"Unfortunately."

"I wanted Sebastian to know that I was not the source. And neither was Fitzwilliam. I think perhaps it was your uncle, although I'm not certain what he hopes to accomplish."

"He just wants to make things difficult for us, I suspect. Sebastian cut off all his access to funds and has alerted everyone to whom Uncle owes money that he will only pay off what Uncle owes if he has their word they'll not extend credit to Lord David any longer. Makes it rather difficult for him to get along with life."

"Do you think whoever attacked Sebastian will try again?"

"I think Sebastian will be better prepared. He'll expect it now."

"It wasn't Fitzwilliam. I think you thought it was. But I saw no bruising when our paths recently crossed."

"Then I suppose we'll never know who it was. If you want that letter you sent him to be more than a delaying tactic for his learning the truth, you should let me take you home now."

She shook her head. "Not until his fever breaks." She peered over at Tristan. "But you may go on."

"And leave you without a chaperone? What sort of cad do you take me for?"

He made her smile when she thought she might never smile again. "He's hardly in a state to ravish me."

Tristan grinned, the familiar boyish grin. She was so glad he'd not lost it, wished Sebastian would reclaim his. "What do you know of ravishment, my lady?"

She giggled lightly. "Nary a thing. Only what I have read in novels."

He dropped his feet to the floor, bent down, and picked up his boots. "I'll be down the hallway if you need me." He grew incredibly somber. "I'm glad you're here, Mary. While my brother will probably not admit it, I suspect he will be as well when he awakens."

As long as he awakened. "Sleep well."

"If only I could."

She heard in his tone what he had not admitted. In sleep, like his brother, he too battled demons.

The room grew incredibly quiet after he left until all she heard was the ticking of the clock and Sebastian's labored breathing. She doused all the lamps until only the one beside her remained lit. It cast a pale glow over the unscarred portion of Sebastian's face. She was not repulsed by his scars, but she suspected upon waking that he would be grateful to know that she'd not sat there studying them.

"Pembrook."

She started at his unexpected outburst, fought not to panic at his sudden agitation. Again, he repeated the name of his estate, with a bit more force.

He gasped, opened his eye. "Pembrook."

Surely he was delirious. "No, you're in London," she told him, touching his brow.

He grabbed her wrist, jerked her near. Once the physician was finished with his task, they'd unbound Sebastian. Fire burned in his gaze. "Pembrook. All that matters. Must reclaim it."

"You have reclaimed it. It's yours again. No one will take it from you a second time."

He calmed, but continued to study her. "Mine."

"Yours."

He drifted back to sleep. Once again, she began to blot the dew from his throat. Until that moment she wasn't certain that she'd truly understood his obsession with Pembrook. It meant everything. Fevered, near death, he didn't call out for a woman or his brothers or even her as a friend. He called out for an estate, for land, for an ancient castle that had withstood the test of time.

It couldn't wrap its arms around him or comfort him or talk quietly with him during a long winter night. Yet it didn't seem to matter. He loved it. It was everything to him.

What was it about Pembrook that possessed men? To be owner of it, his uncle had done horrible things. To reclaim it, Sebastian had become a man obsessed so that he thought of nothing else. She'd set free a boy only to have him return with a heart that belonged solely to his heritage, to Pembrook.

Chapter 19

"**W**here is she?"

   "My lord," Tristan began, trying to calm the man who had burst into the foyer shortly after the clock chimed midnight. One of Rafe's men who was on watch outside had halted him until Tristan could be found. Fortunately he'd yet to retire, but instead had been enjoying whiskey in the library.

"Where is she?" Lord Winslow bellowed. "Mary!"

"Easy, my lord."

Winslow glared at him. "Do you know what you've done to her? You and your damned brother? You've ruined her."

"He had nothing to do with it," a soft voice called down.

Tristan glanced up the stairs to see Mary standing on the landing. When he looked back at Winslow, the man's face was so ruddy with anger that he feared he might have an apoplexy fit. "It's not what you think, my lord."

"She's dressed like a servant . . . coming from the bedchambers," he stammered.

She might be dressed like one, but she came down the stairs with such regal bearing that she'd never be confused for one. She'd pulled back her hair into a braid. It was a style familiar to him. She'd worn it often when she came to visit Pembrook but she certainly no longer looked like a child.

"You will come home with me this instant," her father ground out.

"No. Sebastian is fighting a fever. Until it is gone, I will remain here."

"You will defy me?"

"I have no choice."

"They can hire a nursemaid."

Slowly, regretfully, she shook her head. "No."

"Fitzwilliam will not tolerate this blemish on your character or this—all night in a bachelor's residence."

"How did you know where I was?"

"I was at the club. Fitzwilliam was there. Said he sent regrets to the Morelands. He wasn't of a mood to attend their affair with you at home nursing a headache. A headache. Of all things. You've never suffered so much as a sniffle. When I returned home and discovered you were not about, I confronted the carriage driver. He confessed to bringing you here. What sort of madness is this? Without your reputation, you have nothing."

She stepped forward and touched his cheek. "I saved Sebastian once before. I can do it again."

Winslow glared at Tristan. Tristan merely shrugged. "I tried to convince her to leave, my lord. She's rather set on staying. One of the female servants is with her. I can send them all up if it'll put your mind at ease. We owe her our lives. We would never take advantage of Mary."

"It doesn't matter if you do or not. The gossips will have a field day with this."

"I'll explain to Fitzwilliam," Mary offered. "He'll understand."

"Don't count on it, my girl. And then what? No other man will have you. Men do not fancy spoiled goods."

"She's not spoiled," Tristan ground out.

"In the eyes of Society she will be."

"Only if you say anything," Mary said quietly. "If you back my story that I was abed with a migraine, no one need know differently."

Tristan watched Lord Winslow struggle with his decision. He could only hope he never had any daughters. They appeared to be a great deal of bother.

Finally, Winslow nodded. "The matter of your presence here is to stay between us. I'll have your word on that, Lord Tristan."

"You have it."

"All right then. When you can return home, Mary, you do so by cover of night."

Instead of answering, she stepped forward, hugged her father, and whispered, "Thank you."

Then she was scampering back up the stairs to care for her patient.

"She's a brave girl, Winslow," Tristan said somberly.

"That will be little consolation, my lord, if word of her presence here does get out."

His arm was dead. Yet he would not move because to do so would be to awaken her.

She was in a precarious position much worse than a kiss in a garden. She was in his bed, her head nestled on his shoulder, and although he couldn't quite feel it, he knew his arm held her near. It didn't matter that she was fully clothed.

She was in his bed.

How long had she been here? How long had the fever raged? His side ached, was tender. He remembered fleeting images: the physician, Tristan. Rafe. Briefly. Once. *Don't you dare leave me again.* Or was that a dream? Mary. Cool water trickling down his throat. Cool cloth on his brow. Gentle reassurances, soft voice. Mary's voice. Always Mary. Tender touches. Mary. Encouragement. Mary. Awful-tasting broth. Mary. The fading scent of orchids. Mary.

Her hair had escaped the ribbon she'd been using to hold it back while she nursed him. So thick. So curly. However did she manage to pile it all on her head as she did? With the arm that still had feeling, he sifted his fingers through the strands that appeared to be coarse but felt like silk. Just like that night when he'd thrust his hand into her hair, thrust his tongue into her mouth. Barbarian. For a few moments, lost in her, he'd been able to leave behind the decisions that haunted him, the scars that marred—

With a jerk, he touched his face. Dammit! Where was the patch?

He twisted. On the far table. He couldn't reach it, pinned beneath her weight as he was.

She moaned, sighed, and he realized that his movements had disturbed her. Thank God, she was nestled on his good side. He could save her the grotesqueness. Although it was a bit late to spare her completely.

She lifted her head, squinted. "Relax. That side is in shadow."

Her voice was that of a woman roused from slumber, and something in his belly tightened as he imagined her rousing from slumber after a night of passionate lovemaking.

A night with Fitzwilliam.

If her reputation weren't completely tarnished. Again, he had to wonder how long she'd been here.

She stretched, a slow, sinuous movement that thrust out her breasts and challenged the buttons of her bodice to remain secured. Unfortunately they met the challenge splendidly.

Where had that thought come from? This was Mary. Friend, advisor, nurse. Woman. It was the last that unsettled him. Every time he saw her, he was reminded that she'd grown up, but here in his bedchamber he was well aware that they'd both grown up. The games they could play now were not innocent, would not result in giggles and laughter. Rather they would include long moans and deep groans—

The blood rushing into his arm caused painful pinpricks that brought his thoughts round to where they should have remained. "Your hair is a mess."

She laughed lightly, clearly not offended by his critical assessment. "I got caught in the rain coming here. I did little more than dry it which means it had its way. It takes much work to keep it tamed."

"I like it wild."

She stilled, her breathing shallow, her gaze on his as though he'd given her an uncommon compliment. She slid off the bed, and he could see her more clearly now. She wore a ghastly black dress that made her look like a crow.

"Anticipating going into mourning over my death?" he asked lightly.

She smiled again, although not as brightly. "I knew you wouldn't die. I wouldn't let you."

Just as she'd refused to stand by while his uncle plotted his death.

"You're feeling better. I was so relieved when your fever broke last night," she said.

"How long?"

"Three nights."

"You've been here the entire time?"

She nodded. "Father knows I'm here. He's not happy about it."

"I would think not."

She gave him a scowl. "But he'll do what he can to keep my whereabouts a secret. Tristan threatened the servants with dismissal if one of them spoke of anything that transpired within the residence. He can be quite intimidating."

"He should have intimidated you into leaving."

She grinned. "He tried." Her smile diminished. "I couldn't bear not being here while you suffered. I wish I'd been there for all your suffering."

She blinked rapidly, and he knew she was on the verge of weeping, bravely fighting it off because she knew he abhorred tears. He wanted to tell her that he was glad she hadn't been there. It would have only made things worse because he would have worried about her. Just as he worried now. Three nights. Her reputation would no doubt be in shreds.

"How will your father explain your absence?" What was wrong with his voice? Why did it sound accusing?

"Not to worry, Keswick. I'm not your responsibility. I shall send in your valet to tidy you up and have your cook send up a tray. Rest and regain your strength. I fear your uncle is not done with you yet."

She turned to leave.

He pushed himself up, swung his legs off the bed, and realized he wasn't dressed for company. He wasn't dressed at all. He clutched a sheet to his waist. "I don't know how to thank you."

She looked back at him as though he'd said the silliest thing she'd ever heard. "Remain my friend."

Did she think there was any way in hell that he wouldn't? That he couldn't? Besides his brothers, there was no one he cared for more. But even as he thought it, he realized that his feelings for her now were not what they'd once been. He wasn't quite sure what they were. He'd gone swimming with her as a child and not given much thought to her undergarments clinging to her body. Now he would give it a great deal of thought. Would notice the shadows that tempted a man, that tempted him.

"Always," he rasped so low that he wasn't even certain if she heard him.

"I'll see to your comforts. Then I must return home."

Don't go, hovered on the tip of his tongue but he bit it back. He would not show weakness, could not rely on anyone. That he already had far too much angered him. He needed to regain his strength and return to Pembrook.

In London he was doing little more than ruining Mary's reputation. He needed to distance himself from her. Maybe then he would stop hurting her.

Chapter 20

"**M**y father is most displeased with the gossip that is making the rounds. It seems things have moved from a kiss to your spending the night in Keswick's residence." Lord Fitzwilliam uttered the words as though unable to truly countenance them.

As soon as Mary had ensured that Lord Tristan would be aroused from slumber to watch over his brother, the valet was on his way to Sebastian's bedchamber, and a servant was preparing a tray for him, she asked for a carriage. After returning home, she fell into a sound sleep in her bed that lasted into the afternoon. She'd barely finished bathing when she was informed that Lord Fitzwilliam had come to call. In her father's library. Where he had proposed.

He stood implacably before her just as he had when he'd heard the gossip about the kiss. The gossip that had since reached his ears was much worse. So worse in fact that her father stood near the decanter table pouring amber liquid into a glass and downing it with such ferocious speed that she wondered why he even bothered with the glass.

"You were not to speak to Keswick—"

"I didn't. The entire time I was there, I spoke not a single word." Not precisely a lie. She had whispered, cajoled, soothed, reassured. And not once had she spoken only a solitary word. She'd always spoken at least two. She knew she was splitting hairs but she didn't like being chastised.

"You were in his residence for three nights."

She looked to her father. He merely shook his head. So he'd not told. Then how had Fitzwilliam learned—

"Someone saw you going in," he said as though she'd asked the question aloud. "Someone saw you leave."

"So Lord David has posted spies." She didn't want to contemplate that perhaps it was Fitzwilliam with the spies. "Keswick was ill. He couldn't take advantage of the situation. And even if he could have, he wouldn't have."

"No, he leaves taking advantage of you to moments in the garden."

"It was one moment and he didn't take advantage."

"So you welcomed his attentions."

Sighing, she studied her clasped hands. They were bare of jewels. She suspected they would never be adorned with a wedding band. "We've been over this. I see no reason to rehash."

"I fear I must withdraw my offer of marriage."

Her chest tightened and she squeezed her eyes shut. She'd known this could be a possible outcome to her actions. She swallowed hard, opened her eyes, and with all the fortitude she could muster, she met Fitzwilliam's gaze. "Of course, my lord. I had expected no less."

For a moment he looked uncomfortable, regretful even.

"I regret any pain or humiliation that my actions have caused you," she said. "I believe you to be a good man and that marriage to you would have been satisfying. But it is not in my nature to ignore someone in need, regardless of personal consequences. A quality which I believe would make me an exemplary wife, but a very challenging one."

As he studied his polished shoes, she almost thought she detected a smile on his face. "My father insists that I end this arrangement before any more damage can be done to my family's good name. While he cannot keep from me upon his death all that is entailed, he can keep funds from me until he dies. I have no source of income other than his generosity."

"My lord, if I may," her father said, stepping forward. "I could see my way clear to increase her dowry."

"Would it bring in five thousand a year?"

Her father bowed his head and she ached for him. "No, my lord. A thousand, perhaps two at best."

"Then regretfully it will not suffice. Besides, my father no longer believes Mary will make an exceptional marchioness. My family does not tolerate scandal. I do not wish to fall out of his favor."

"I can hardly blame you for that," she said.

"I wish you the best." With a perfunctory nod, he strode from the room.

She thought she should have felt bereft but all she felt was exhausted beyond belief.

"I should not have allowed you to stay," her father said.

"It doesn't matter. Someone was already watching. I need to let Sebastian know—"

"Mary."

"A letter. That's all. But he needs to know there may be a spy in their midst."

"Send your letter, then pack your things. We leave in two days."

"And then?" she asked.

"I've not yet decided."

"I don't wish to return to the nunnery."

"I don't wish to send you back." He poured brandy into his glass and downed it. "Mary, I know you considered the nunnery a punishment, but I didn't know how else to protect you. You were such an impulsive child and headstrong. I was afraid you'd confront Lord David."

She hadn't half-thought about it. "So you believed me?"

"I know as a lad he enjoyed pulling wings from flies. But you see I've never been good at confrontation. All we had were words that you might or might not have heard."

"I heard them."

"If he knew he might have seen you as a threat. The night you went to his ball . . . I didn't want you to go but Fitzwilliam insisted."

So he'd capitulated. It hurt to realize how weak he was. She had always loved him, thought him a giant among men. But he was so easily dwarfed.

"Were you going to leave me at the convent forever?"

"I don't know what I'd planned. I was too far into the drink by then. Didn't want you to see me. But your aunt, bless her, she took matters in hand. The drink calls to me so much, Mary. I was so pleased when Fitzwilliam showed an interest in you. You would be in Cornwall. Safe. I never thought to marry you off as a way to protect you. But your aunt had the right of it. But with the Pembrook lords back now, they can fight their own battles. Lord David will leave you be." He refilled his glass and downed the amber liquid. "You were deserving of a better father. I will talk to my nephew, make him understand that he must give you a yearly sum."

With her father's lack of forcefulness, she wasn't certain how well that would go.

"Perhaps when we return to Willow Hall, we can put our heads together and come up with something," she offered.

Nodding, he turned once more to his brandy. She had never before felt like such a burden. She rose gracefully and glided from the room, leaving him to his demons. She thought she would have made an excellent wife to Henry VIII, facing doom with her head held high.

"One of us has to marry her."

Settled in chairs in the sitting area within Sebastian's bedchamber, neither Sebastian nor Rafe blinked at Tristan's pronouncement. Tristan stood at the fireplace, his arm pressed to the mantel, his thumb rubbing on the marble as though he'd discovered a bit of dirt that simply wouldn't go away.

Sebastian had yet to leave his bedchamber. He was healing slowly and he exhausted easily. He'd asked Tristan to scout around and determine if Mary's reputation was safe.

Apparently it wasn't.

"Suppose we could play a round of cards," Rafe began. "Loser gets saddled with marriage."

"I wouldn't put it past you to cheat," Tristan said.

"Question is: would I cheat to win or cheat to lose?"

"We are not going to decide this with a game of cards," Sebastian growled. "Besides, the decision has been made."

"Oh?" Tristan arched a brow. "And who's it to be then?"

"You. You're the one who allowed her in here and then let her stay."

He'd expected his brother to protest. Instead, he simply gave a curt nod. "Right, then. I'd best go ask for her hand while she's still in London. Word is that her father is sending her away."

He'd taken but two steps before Sebastian ground out, "Damn you, Tristan. You know it will be me."

Sporting a mocking smile, his brother returned to the fireplace. "For a moment there, I thought you'd regained your teasing nature."

He'd forgotten how much he enjoyed initiating a good jest. "You're the one with the teasing nature. I was ever the more serious. That was how she told us apart."

"I suspect it went deeper than that."

Perhaps, but Sebastian was in no mood to explore what might have been. Instead he looked over at Rafe. "I assume you're not madly in love with her."

"Wouldn't matter if I was. Marriage is not for me."

He almost asked Rafe to explain, but the younger seemed intent on remaining a mystery. Sebastian shifted his attention to Tristan. "Would you give us a moment?"

"Without my feelings being hurt."

Tristan was making a point. Sebastian suspected his twin was growing weary of Rafe's moodiness.

"I'll have a carriage readied for you," Tristan continued as he strode from the room.

Now that Sebastian was alone with Rafe, he wasn't

sure what he wanted—needed—to say. "While I was fevered, I dreamed that you hovered over me and commanded me not to leave you."

Rafe lifted his broad shoulders in a careless shrug. He was only twenty-two but his eyes made him appear older, perhaps even older than Sebastian. "Tristan thought you might die. So I came."

"I would have taken you with me if I could, but if we remained together we had a better chance of discovery, and I feared that would lead to our deaths."

"You could have put us all on one ship."

"And if it sank in a storm, who would have been left to take back from Uncle what he stole? By separating there was a chance that at least one of us would survive to have retribution."

"Who would have cared? Land. Title. They're not flesh, they're not blood."

"They're our heritage."

"So is our blood." He averted his gaze. "We'll never agree on this. It's in the past. It's pointless to argue over what we cannot change."

"I won't ask for forgiveness because I don't believe I did anything that requires forgiveness. I did what I thought was best at the time. Perhaps with age or experience I would have made different choices."

Rafe shifted his gaze over, pinned Sebastian with it. "Will you be able to say the same about Mary?"

"No. From her, I do hope to one day earn forgiveness."

A corner of Rafe's mouth curled up. "I'm glad to hear that. I was beginning to think you considered yourself without fault."

"Hardly. I have many and can only pray that Mary will not suffer overmuch because of them."

And he could only hope that she would accept his

offer of marriage. He'd spoken true. He didn't think he owed Rafe an apology but that was not to say that guilt didn't gnaw at him on a daily basis. Now he would add Mary's ruination to his list of regrets. Mary.

A woman whose misfortune it was to serve as his savior.

"If Fitzwilliam truly loved you, he'd have stood up to his father. He'd have found a way to have you," Alicia said.

She'd arrived an hour earlier to assist Mary with her packing, but all she'd done so far was sit on the bed and watch.

"He never claimed to love me," Mary told her.

"But he asked for your hand in marriage."

"I suspect he loved the idea of my dowry. Besides, you're quite right. He should have stood up to his father. That bothers me more than his lack of love. To think that he would not have been his own man, that he would have been under his father's thumb"—she shivered thinking how easily her father capitulated on matters—"marrying him would have been a dreadful mistake."

She didn't want to contemplate that she felt this way because of Sebastian. He was his own man, made his own decisions, stood his own ground. Of course, his father was dead, but she couldn't imagine that he would have allowed his father to decide how he would live his life.

"I hate that you're leaving. The Season is not yet over," Alicia lamented.

"For me it is," Mary assured her. "You should have my gowns. They will require a bit of adjustment in the length, but I'll have no need of them."

She could see her cousin struggling with being both joyous at the additions to her wardrobe and sad because of what gaining them signified.

"It's just not fair," Alicia said.

"I knew what I was doing. I knew it was foolish. I knew it would have repercussions."

"Then why do it?"

How to explain? Mary stopped folding the nightdress. She should have had the maids packing for her, but she'd needed something to occupy her today lest she go insane with the waiting for tomorrow. Silly girl to spend her time here. She should go to the park and enjoy what she could of London while she was still here. "They're so alone here, Alicia, when they shouldn't be. They did nothing wrong, yet everyone looks at them with suspicion and doubt. Their uncle's word holds more weight than theirs. They are strangers in this world into which they were born. When I saw how ill Sebastian was, how much he suffered . . . I simply couldn't *not* be there. For all intents and purposes everyone else had abandoned them and I won't."

"That's what Fitzwilliam should have said to his father. Something along those lines."

"If he believed in me, then yes, I suppose he should have."

"Mama is striving to convince Uncle to let you stay with us."

"She'll have no luck there."

"Did you love him?"

"When I was a child, yes."

Alicia puckered her brow. "I thought you only met Fitzwilliam this Season, at the first ball."

Mary slammed her eyes closed. Why were her thoughts constantly turning to Sebastian? "Yes, you're quite right. I was fond of him. I don't know if I loved him. It seems to me that if I did, I'd be stretched across the bed weeping." She plopped down on that very bed beside Alicia. She adjusted the feather pillows behind her back. "I should be inconsolable, shouldn't I?"

"If you loved him, I should think so. May I be honest?"

"Are you implying that in the past you've been dishonest with me?"

Alicia gave her an impish grin. "Never on purpose, but this matter, well . . . I never thought Fitzwilliam was quite right for you. He is just so terribly . . . staid. He's rather like a boiled egg. Anytime you crack it open, you know exactly what you're getting."

"A boiled egg. How flattering. And what sort of *egg* should I marry?"

"I'm not certain you were meant for an egg at all. Christmas pudding, perhaps. You never know what you'll dish out."

Mary giggled, then leaned over, and hugged Alicia tightly. "I shall miss you and your wisdom."

"The boring balls will be frightfully more boring."

She drew back. "So few are left that it hardly signifies."

A brisk knock sounded on the door before her aunt waltzed in.

Alicia popped off the bed as though someone had pinched her bottom. "Did you have any luck?"

"I'm afraid not, no." Aunt Sophie glided up to Mary and took her hands. "Your father wishes to see you in his study. You will want to straighten up a bit as Keswick is there as well."

"What does he want?"

"I'm afraid he didn't confide in me."

To say good-bye perhaps? Had he heard that she was leaving? Or had he come to let her know he was well on the way to recovery and she would have to inform him that she would be returning to Willow Hall?

With Alicia's assistance, she prepared as quickly as possible to meet with her father and their guest. The pink dress she chose was unadorned with a high collar and long sleeves. Everything was left to the imagination. Rather than put up her hair, she simply pulled it back and tied it in place with a ribbon. She wanted to more closely reflect the girl of the moors rather than the lady of London. She wanted it to be a comfortable parting, so she felt no need to fancy herself up. She wasn't attempting to impress anyone.

When she strolled into her father's study, she realized the same couldn't be said of Sebastian as he turned from the window to greet her. He wore a dark blue jacket over a striking red waistcoat. She was so accustomed to him striving not to draw attention to himself that it seemed slightly out of character, but it was the perfect foil to his pristine white cravat. He was freshly shaven with no shadow across his jaw. His once unfashionably long hair had been expertly trimmed. He bowed his head slightly. "Lady Mary."

"Your Grace. I'm glad to see you so recovered."

"I still have a way to go I think, but at least I'm well on the right path, thanks in large part to your tender and generous ministrations."

Blushing, she turned to her father who stood near the fireplace, an amber-filled glass in hand. No fire burned, and yet his forehead was coated in dew. He took a quick swipe at it with his handkerchief before downing the liquid courage in his glass, and she wondered why he felt a need to shore himself up.

"His Grace has asked for your hand in marriage," her father said as though she'd spoken her musings aloud.

She jerked her gaze to Sebastian. He met her regard with a steady one of his own, although he looked far from happy.

"I'll leave you two to discuss things," her father said, setting his glass aside before striding toward her. He stopped just shy of her. "Under the circumstances I encourage you to accept."

He was offering her the illusion of choice, for she saw in his eyes that he would take the matter out of her hands if need be. He was worried about her future. And who would have her now?

The snick of the door closing vibrated through her almost like the ringing of a death knell. She thought back to the night she and Sebastian had kissed. When he had blanketed his mouth over hers, he'd caused her to lose all sense of propriety. She couldn't deny that she became lost in the sensations he elicited, but that was hardly enough to indicate that they were well suited to marriage.

"Your marriage at the end of the month can go on as planned, with just a different groom at the altar," he said quietly.

"You consider that a proposal?"

"I'm attempting to make right a wrong that was done to you."

"A wrong I brought upon myself."

"I kissed you in the garden."

"Which Fitzwilliam forgave. He forbade me to see you and I went to see you because of the awful rumors that you forced yourself on me."

"And stayed to nurse me back to health."

"My choice. You should not suffer because of it."

"How in God's name do you think I would suffer if you were my wife?"

"I bring with me scandal."

"You are no more notorious than I."

She bit her lip, gave a curt laugh. "I suppose our notoriety is tied together, isn't it?"

"Very much so."

"Do you love me, Sebastian?"

"Did Fitzwilliam?"

He sounded truly baffled as though the thought of someone being madly in love with her was beyond the pale. It irritated.

"He had a care for me." She strolled to the window and gazed out. "What are your plans?"

"To marry you."

His tone yielded no doubt. She might have laughed, relaxed, welcomed the notion of marriage to him if she heard even a hint of teasing. "I meant beyond that."

"Return to Pembrook with as much haste as possible." He removed something from his pocket, unfurled his fingers to reveal a disgustingly filthy bit of rag.

She wrinkled her nose, but then she paused in wonder at the frayed and faded ribbon that held everything together. It was nearly white but once it had been a bright yellow. "My ribbon."

"It holds the soil from Pembrook, soil I took that night. It is all that kept me alive, all that kept me going through the interminable years when I fought to find my way back. I could smell the richness of the dirt, the centuries that my ancestors had fought and died there." He closed his fist around it, clutching it tightly. "It's everything to me, Mary. It's all that mattered."

The daughter of an earl, she appreciated the value of

land and titles, but for Sebastian, it almost seemed to be an obsession. Family, flesh, blood, his brothers. Surely they mattered more.

As though reading her thoughts, he said, "All that my brothers and I endured was so that I would one day again have Pembrook in my hands. It is now mine, and I will let nothing—no one—deprive me of it. As my wife, you will share this with me."

"I don't know that I can love it as you do. It is a harsh foreboding place, and with your uncle's dealings, it has such a sordid history."

"It is my home."

Those few words, succinctly spoken, said it all.

"And what of us?" She shifted her gaze and found his on her. As always. But there was no warmth there, no yearning. He had erected a wall to his soul that she doubted she had the power to break through. "What do you envision for us?"

He looked away then. She watched as he tightened his jaw. "I know I am not your first choice for husband, and I rue the circumstances that forced you to have to choose me at all. But I will do all in my power to see that you never regret it."

Choice. Choose. Words that had no meaning. She was already considered on the shelf, and it would no doubt take years to put this incident behind her, for another gentleman to gaze on her and think her worthy. She would be far older, and perhaps wiser. Perhaps not.

She'd misjudged Fitzwilliam. What if she was wrong about Sebastian? They'd been friends once. Could they be more?

If not, would friendship be enough for her? For them both?

"I fear we know so little about each other anymore. What if we don't suit?"

"I should think the kiss in the garden indicated that we will be well suited to each other."

"That was only the physical. I need more. I need your heart."

His jaw clenched. "I can't promise you that."

She released a sad laugh. "At least you're honest. But what if one day you do meet a woman who steals your heart?"

"Do you honestly think a woman will look at what I've become and love me?"

She had to believe that, had to believe there was something in him worth loving. "Yes."

He laughed harshly. "You're blinder than I." He cupped her chin. "What choice do you truly have? Your reputation is in tatters. What sort of life will you have when you return to your father's estate? And when he dies, who will watch over you?"

"I can watch over myself. I could become a governess or a nurse. I could take my dowry and invest it. Find a small cottage." *Live out my life in loneliness, with no children, no love.*

"I owe you," he said quietly, "more than I can ever repay. I will be as good a husband to you as my father was to my mother. I will never stray. I will never beat you. I will give you a generous allowance."

They'd been friends once. She knew his childish heart had belonged to her. She refused to believe that she couldn't possess his adult heart as well. She took a deep breath, released it, and hoped she would not live to regret the words. "Yes, I'll marry you."

Once again he slipped his hand into his pocket, only this time he withdrew it to reveal the dangling emerald.

With a soft smile, she took it from him. "I hated sending it back to you, you know."

"Then why did you?"

"Because Fitzwilliam asked." Demanded. But he didn't need to know that. "Would you have returned it if I'd said no to your proposal?"

"Of course."

Licking her lips, she watched as his gaze dropped to her mouth. She wondered if he would kiss her.

Instead he said, "Well, I suppose I should see to getting a license."

"Yes, I suppose you should."

Chapter 21

❧❦

As Mary waited in a private room at St. George's, she wondered if she should be this calm. She almost felt nothing at all.

"I wish your mother were here to see you," Aunt Sophie said as she adjusted the veil one more time. She alternated between fiddling with the veil and the train, as though each time Mary moved didn't undo what had just been done. She wanted to tell her aunt to just leave everything alone until the last moment. Instead Mary tolerated her fluttering, drew reassurance from it.

Alicia came in through the door, her cheeks flushed, her eyes bright. "The church is packed to the rafters."

Mary had been a pariah, a woman shamed, a woman scorned. Now it appeared she was a romanticized figure. "Of course. Scandalous Lady Mary and the barbaric Duke of Keswick."

"This wedding shall polish your reputation, m'dear," her aunt predicted. "And his as well."

Not that their reputations would matter after today. They'd be holed away at Pembrook. A far cry from the parties and balls of London. She would miss them, but not the gossip. No, she could do without that for the remainder of her life.

A knock sounded on the door. Alicia opened it.

"It's time," her father announced in a tone Mary imagined a guard used when telling a condemned man the moment had arrived to pay for one's sins and head to the gallows.

Her aunt gave her a quick kiss on the cheek, adjusted her veil once more, and headed out the door after Alicia. She would take her place in a pew while Alicia would serve as Mary's maid of honor. She had no bridesmaids, even though Lady Hermione had offered to stand with her—to be closer to Lord Tristan no doubt. Mary had politely declined. Her cousin would serve her well enough.

Her father stood in the doorway, looking no more comfortable than he had any other time when Sebastian had called. She knew he was here not for her but for image. People would notice if he wasn't there, and who knew what speculation would follow.

She wanted him to say something. Tell her she was pretty or that he wished her happiness or that the Duke of Keswick was a good choice as a husband.

"Let's get this done," he said.

So much for wishes.

She squared her shoulders, lifted her chin, and tried not to be disappointed that all of this was a result of poor judgment. If only she'd held her silence on what she'd heard at Pembrook, she'd have not been sent to the nunnery; she would have had a Season when she was of a more marriageable age. If only she hadn't followed

Sebastian into the garden. If only she hadn't traipsed into his residence.

It should have been a day filled with joy and instead, it was simply an attempt to undo harm. Sebastian didn't love her. Perhaps he never would. Pembrook held his heart. She would always be second fiddle. But that didn't mean she was doomed to unhappiness. She wouldn't settle for anything less than contentment.

She placed her hand on her father's arm and allowed him to lead her into the vestry. She could hear music playing, could see Alicia. She didn't understand why Alicia had not been spoken for this Season. Perhaps next year without her troublesome cousin at her side, she'd have more luck. She deserved happiness.

Alicia smiled at her. "Ready?"

Mary nodded.

Alicia stepped into the church and the music changed, announcing the bride's arrival.

"Be happy for me, Papa," she pleaded.

"What is happiness, daughter? You will not want for anything, he promised me that. He said I was to have your dowry set aside. That it was yours to do with as you pleased. He has no need of it. It is a rare man who will take a woman to wife without a dowry."

"Yes, it is," she rasped.

"He has more spine than Fitzwilliam. I'll give him that."

"Thank you, Papa."

He nodded. "As I said earlier, let's get this done, shall we?"

Before she could even think of a response, he was leading her into the church. She was vaguely aware of the vast number of people standing as she strolled down the aisle. Hundreds crowded onto pews.

At the altar stood the man she was going to marry, facing her completely, because he had no choice if he wanted to watch her approach. His place put his scarred side toward her, toward everyone.

He, who strived so hard to keep his scars hidden, was revealing them now with the sunlight streaming through the stained glass windows. He had to have known that they would have a grand audience. Had to have known that he would be denied shadows.

They could have traveled to Pembrook and been married there in a small church in a quiet ceremony. But as she neared and could see him more clearly, she realized that they weren't being married here because it was convenient, because all the plans had already been made.

No. This was his gift to her. The wedding she'd been dreaming of for months. The gown she had selected, the ceremony she had envisioned. It was more. It was a public acknowledgment that regardless of how tattered her reputation, he would stand proudly beside her.

As she moved her hand from her father's arm to Sebastian's, she smiled brightly, fought back the tears. Perhaps theirs would not be a marriage filled with great love, but she realized that they would have moments such as this one when she was ever grateful that he was at her side.

Chapter 22

It seemed appropriate that it should be raining when they arrived at Pembrook, Mary thought. Gray skies unleashed a cold drizzle that threatened to turn the late afternoon into night. Mud worked up by the hooves and wheels slapped against the coach in an erratic rhythm, as it traveled along the drive toward the looming castle.

The wedding ceremony had provided a moment of unrealistic happiness and expectation. But as soon as the wedding breakfast had ended and they climbed into the coach, all pretense that theirs was to be a happily ever after vanished. Sitting across from her, Sebastian had become moody and sullen. They barely spoke. When they stopped at an inn for the night, they slept in separate rooms. Three inns, three nights of not knowing her husband's touch.

Where was the fire he'd unleashed in the garden?

Where was the tenderness he'd bestowed upon her in his bed when he was recovering from his wound? Had it all been pretense? Had he lost interest in the hunt?

"How do you know your uncle is not here now?" she asked.

"We have someone watching him in London, so we know where he is."

"But what if he slips away?"

"I know a few soldiers who didn't remain in the army. I hired them to keep watch, to ensure Uncle didn't strive to take up residence while I was in London. I should have hired more servants to set matters to rights. I fear there is a great deal of work to be done."

Two coaches carrying servants followed. Many were from the London residence. Some had been newly hired. Her father had given permission for Colleen to come with Mary. She was grateful to have a familiar servant within the ranks.

"It will give me something with which to occupy my time," she said.

"I don't wish it changed overmuch."

A reminder that it was his, not hers. She was an intruder.

"I don't wish to feel as though I'm a guest," she told him.

"I would prefer that you discuss with me any plans you might have before implementing them."

"Of course, Your Grace. We can discuss them now if it pleases you. I thought to have the floors scrubbed, the draperies taken outside, the dust beaten from them, the windows washed, the furniture polished—"

"You're angry," he interrupted.

"No." Hurt, more like, but she was not going to be a

whiny wife and admit such a thing. "I want it to be *our* home. I don't want to feel at Pembrook the way you felt in London—as though you didn't quite belong."

"You belong here, Mary. You're my wife."

She released a small laugh. "Am I, Sebastian? It's funny, but when we exchanged vows, I thought I would feel like a wife afterward, but I feel no different. Our relationship feels no different. Nothing has changed."

"Something has. We're no longer in London."

She forced a smile. He seemed to have missed the entire point of what she was saying. "No, we're not."

They were silent for several moments before he said, "I don't want you to feel like a guest here, Mary, but until you know what is of importance, don't do anything drastic."

"What of your uncle's things? He's bound to have left some behind."

"I intend to burn them."

The harshness in his voice unsettled her. It was ever-present when he spoke of his uncle, and it bothered her to know he still had so much hatred simmering inside him. While a part of her understood—he'd suffered immensely because of his uncle's machinations—another part of her worried that the bitterness would steal from their lives whatever happiness they might have been able to find.

"Perhaps coming here is not the best thing," she said softly, cautiously.

He tore his gaze from the window and she felt it land on her with a weightiness that demanded an answer even though he asked no question.

"So many bad memories are associated with Pembrook. You have other estates. Perhaps it would be better if we moved to one of those."

"Pembrook is the ducal estate. It has always been so. I am the duke."

"I'm not questioning your title, rather what will haunt us here."

"We will face it. Together."

She wondered how that would even be possible when they sat on opposite sides of the carriage, had during the entire journey. They were husband and wife now. They could sit beside each other. Yet they didn't. Even when she fell asleep it was the plush interior that provided a pillow for her head rather than her husband's shoulder. She'd not expected him to be so distant, so uncaring.

He didn't reach across to hold her hand or to even squeeze it in reassurance. For all the comfort he provided, she could be arriving here alone. It was too soon to have regrets, to consider that she'd made a huge error in judgment.

He'd told her that Pembrook was all that mattered. Yet somehow she had imagined that she did as well—if only a bit. Why else would he have been concerned about her reputation? Because he was a gentleman, because he took responsibility for his actions. His action, however, had only been to kiss her. She was the one who had prattled on about it.

He turned to look out the window, facing Pembrook as he seldom faced her—fully. She was not going to be jealous of stone and mortar. The moat had long since been filled in with dirt. The outer walls had been torn down. The looming castle keep with its turrets stood magnificently against the darkening skies. A flash of lightning silhouetted the tower that rose up behind it, made it seem more ominous, a building where murders were commonplace.

The ugly past, so much sorrow dwelled here. How could she possibly make it a joyous home? How could they find happiness when the memories of betrayal would always batter them?

Yet as she watched her husband, she saw peace settle into his features. Pride. Ownership. Satisfaction. He had usurped his uncle, reclaimed what was his, what had been in his family for generations.

He whispered, "Pembrook."

And she refused to acknowledge how dearly she wanted him to whisper her name.

The coach rattled to a jarring halt.

"It is all that has ever mattered," he said with conviction. "Welcome home, Duchess."

Mary watched as two men rushed out from the shadows, and her first terrifying thought was that Lord David had sent them to kill her husband. Then she remembered he'd mentioned hiring a couple of men to watch over things.

A footman opened the coach door, and Sebastian stepped out into the rain. She could hear it beating on his hat and greatcoat, but he ignored it. More important things were on his mind.

"Saunders," he greeted the first man to reach him. "How goes it here?"

"Everything is as quiet as men before battle."

"Good. See my duchess to the residence." He turned to her, where she hovered in the vehicle. Leaning in, he pressed something into her gloved hand. A key she realized. "I'll join you there in a moment."

Then he was gone, but she could hear him barking out orders. Someone produced an umbrella. The man he'd called Saunders handed her down and held the umbrella over her head as they made a mad dash through the rain to the portico. Her hem was soaked and the air chilled her by the time she arrived, but she turned and watched all the activity in the drive. A dozen servants brought from London scurried about. Most of the trunks were hers. They contained a trousseau that she had lovingly put together expecting a trip to Italy. She'd kept a couple of her favorite ball gowns—surely they would entertain here—and given the rest to Alicia.

The darkening skies had very nearly turned the late afternoon into night.

"Shall I unlock the door?" Saunders asked.

She shook her head. "I'll wait for my husband."

Neither as tall as nor as broad of shoulder as Sebastian, Saunders still had a soldier's bearing. She heard herself asking, "Did you serve with my husband in the Crimea?"

"Yes, ma'am. Didn't know he was a duke, though, until he sought me out and hired me to watch over things here. He just seemed regular. Never let on he was a lord."

She watched as Sebastian ordered servants about. How could anyone look at his commanding presence and not realize he was of the nobility? It was carved into every inch of him, in the way he presented himself, the way he addressed those around him. She pressed her lips together but in the end, she couldn't hold back what she wanted to say. She peered up at the man standing guard over her. "In London rumors surfaced that he was a coward in battle."

Saunders appeared horrified. "Never. Not even with three bullets in him. It was the cannon fire that brought him down. He'd have kept fighting otherwise."

"I never believed the rumors," she assured him. "The battle was an awful thing."

"We knew right quick that someone had mucked it up, but we followed our orders. Cowards we were not, but fools we might have been." He gave a brisk nod. "I should see what else I'm needed for."

"Saunders, I'm glad you're here to watch over him and the estate."

"Wouldn't be here to do either if not for him." Not waiting for her to respond, he trotted down the steps. She suspected their conversation had made him uncomfortable, but it had given her a bit of insight into her husband. She'd never thought for one moment that he was a coward, but neither had she considered that men were alive because of his actions. She'd never given much consideration to the specifics of war, only the general horror of it. Was it any wonder that Sebastian found parlor games to be silly nonsense?

He darted up the stairs. "I gave you the key so you wouldn't have to stand out here in the chill."

"I wanted us to go in together—husband and wife."

He seemed surprised, as though it hadn't truly dawned on him that they were married. She certainly didn't feel married. They could be merely friends considering all the passion that had passed between them since they exchanged vows. She wondered if he might at least kiss her before they went inside but he simply took the key from her, unlocked the door, and shoved it open.

He looked at her with impatience. "Go on."

"I believe a husband is supposed to carry his bride across the threshold."

"Why? You're perfectly capable of walking."

"Tradition. It's good luck. Oh, never mind. I know it's sill—"

She released a tiny screech as he swept her into his arms. Water dripped from his hat onto her. She studied the seriousness in his face, and wished she could believe that he'd married her because he wanted to, not because he felt an obligation.

"I suppose we can use all the luck we can get," he said.

She heard clapping, glanced over her shoulder, and saw the servants standing around giving applause. "I hadn't considered we had an audience."

"One that should be working."

"You're a romantic."

He shook his head. "No, but for you, I wish I was."

Tears burned her eyes, but she pushed them back as he stepped over the threshold. She was hit by the stale muskiness of someplace hardly ever used. Heavy shadows hovered. Sebastian set her feet on the stone floor and she felt colder than she had outside. He moved to a table and lit the candles in a candelabra. He held it aloft and the flickering flames chased back the darkness.

As she followed him into a front parlor, she heard the servants coming inside. Some no doubt would be carting in their trunks while others would see to unpacking them. But their duties did not interest her now. Rather it was her husband who occupied her attention as he strode through the room, dragging away the white cloths that covered the furniture, stirring up clouds of dust.

She sneezed. He glanced back at her. She smiled. "Apologies."

"No, I am to blame. I should have sent the servants ahead of time to see to matters, but I hadn't considered I'd arrive with a wife."

"But this way, it's rather like exploring, isn't it? We'll discover everything together."

"Such an optimist you are."

"I find no joy in being a pessimist." Walking through the room, she began tugging off her gloves. "At least he covered the furniture before he left. There seem to be bare spots on the wall." Rectangles of wallpaper that had yet to fade where something had protected them from the sun.

"As in London he removed all portraits of my father, myself, and my brothers. Oddly any portraits of my mother alone remained."

Turning, she studied him as he continued to yank off cloths with one hand, holding the candelabra high, uncovering treasures: sofas, plush chairs, small tables. "Why would he keep those on display but eliminate the others?"

"I don't know. I'm not sure I'll ever understand how his mind works. Not certain I want to."

"It is curious, though," she mused, glancing around, before sneezing again.

"Damnation."

"What?" She spun around. White sheets were still draped over half the furnishings in the room, but he was no longer tending to them. "Did you find something?"

"Yes, I discovered you have an inconsiderate lout for a husband. I was so anxious to reintroduce you to Pembrook that I didn't consider that you're no doubt damp and chilled from standing in the rain. Come, I sent the servants around to start fires. Your room should be warm by now. Cook is preparing dinner. It will be light fare, limited to what we brought from London, until she can get to the market."

He extended his arm, and she crossed over to him. "I'm not really that hungry anyway."

He led her into the massive foyer where stairs on

either side curved around to the landing on the next floor. As they ascended the steps, the light illuminated their path and the many portraits of all the dukes who had come before. But even here, some portraits were obviously missing.

At the top of the stairs, he guided her toward the left, past a closed door—

"My bedchamber," he said quietly as though she'd asked.

—and to a room beside it. He opened the door and she skirted around him. He must have sent several of the servants here first because nothing remained covered. A pleasant sitting area was arranged in front of the fireplace where a fire burned lazily. Lamps flickered on two tables. The drawn-back draperies revealed that night had fallen. The windows were ajar only enough to allow in the rain-scented air.

"Would you like a bath before dinner?" he asked.

"That would be lovely, yes."

"I'll have the servants see to it."

"Do the bellpulls work?"

"I don't know."

She crossed over to the bed and gave hers a yank. "I suppose we'll find out if Colleen comes up."

"Do you remember where the dining hall is to be found?"

"I believe so, yes."

"I'll meet you there in an hour." He left the room, closing the door behind him.

Mary sank onto the bed and wondered what the night might bring.

Their dinner was—as every dinner they'd shared since they'd wed—a rather quiet affair. It seemed to

Sebastian that he'd never mastered the art of conversation. He was, however, very skilled at ordering servants
about. He was pleased that they'd been able to ready the
main rooms quickly. More needed to be done: polishing, dusting, scrubbing, but at least they were uncovered and revealed the potential of what they might be.

Following dinner, as he and Mary strolled through
them, he wanted her to feel for Pembrook what he did.
To appreciate its magnificence, its history, its heritage.
Because now it belonged to her as much as it did to him.
It would pass down to their firstborn son.

Her laughter had once echoed through these hallways when she came to visit. A good many excellent
hiding places had awaited her then. But she had been
a child, without appreciation for what she scampered
through. With her hand resting on his arm, he escorted
her along the hallways and through the rooms. It was
not a drafty old castle.

His father had remodeled it. The inside was as grand
as the finest manor in England. For two years carpen-
ters had worked to turn great halls into several rooms.
Forty bedchambers, four libraries, several galleries, and
a good number of sitting rooms. It remained a maze,
but hardly cold. They stepped into one of two grand
salons.

"I'd forgotten how lovely it all was," she said.

"I'm surprised you noticed. You were too busy striving to find a place to hide."

She laughed softly, a musical sound filled with memories. "I was very good at hiding from you. You seldom
found me."

"Do not count on that happening now. You won't
escape me easily." He'd meant to keep it light, to tease
her, but it had come out harsh and stern.

"Would I want to?"

He glanced over at her. A mistake. Strong Mary appeared vulnerable, and he realized that his delaying their joining had given her cause for doubt, might even be responsible for this sudden awkwardness he sensed between them. But he wanted their first time together as true husband and wife to be here. At his estate. He walked these hallways because of her bravery. It was appropriate that they come together here.

"I hope not," he finally answered.

Chapter 23

He'd put it off for as long as he could—the bedding of his wife.

Sebastian tossed back another glass of whiskey. For courage. God, but he wasn't afraid of her. Rather he feared that she would be repelled if she saw what rose above her, if she opened her eyes—

He would take her in the dark. Complete darkness. With the canopied drapes drawn tightly around the bed. They could both pretend then that he was as devilishly handsome as Tristan.

She'd seen him before, of course, had even looked upon him kindly. But it would be far different when coupling with the beast, knowing it was his hands upon her. He was loath to admit now that all his previous partners had been beauties, that he'd never given the plain girls a glance. He suspected ladies fancied being with handsome gents just as men fantasized about being with beautiful women.

How he would like to see her in the light. Perhaps he would wake early, when dawn filtered into the room. She would be gorgeous. Of that he had no doubt. Yet she was burdened with him as a husband.

He should have made Tristan marry her. What did it matter which brother did? They all owed her. But only marriage to him would make her a duchess. Didn't she at least deserve the title and all the prestige that came with it?

He glanced over at the bundle resting on the table beside his chair, near the bottle of whiskey. Reaching out, he stroked the silken ribbon, smiling slightly as it wrapped around his finger. For as long as he could remember it had never remained straight. It had curled, just like Mary's hair. Tonight he might have silk ribbons to untie.

He pushed aside thoughts of the girl who had given him the ribbon. In the bedchamber beside his a woman waited. From the moment he'd first set eyes on her again, he'd tried to think of her as the scrawny, all-limbs girl who had raced over the fields of wildflowers with him. But she was far removed from that. She tempted him as no other woman ever had.

It wasn't fair to her that scandal had forced them into marriage, but he had promised her she'd not regret taking him as her husband.

It was time he made good on that promise.

Mary sat on the blue velvet chair near the window with her feet perched on the cushion and her toes curled around the edge. Her satin nightgown was drawn down over her legs, creating a tent over her limbs. Pressing her chin to her knees, she decided she was going to remove every damned clock from every damned room. She was already weary of the ticking serving as her only company.

Sebastian hadn't said good night when he escorted her to the door. He hadn't said anything at all. He simply opened it, and when she walked through, he drew it closed. But she had sensed the tension radiating through him during dinner and later when he'd walked her through many of the rooms. The residence was so large that she felt swallowed up inside it. It required a bold master, and Sebastian certainly seemed at home here. It also required a strong mistress, but she wasn't certain if she was up to the task. How could she manage this household if she couldn't manage her marriage?

Why did he touch her so infrequently? Where was the passion that had seared them in the garden?

She heard the click of a door opening and nearly shot up out of the chair. Instead she took a deep breath to calm her clamoring heart and watched as her husband prowled into the room. He glanced at the bed, seemed surprised by its appearance, and then his gaze found her.

He didn't appear happy, but he did seem relieved. Perhaps he thought she'd run off.

He'd removed his cravat, jacket, and waistcoat. A few buttons on his shirt were loosened. He wore the patch. She'd wondered if he would. It made her feel as though he were hiding from her. His large feet were bare, revealing his crooked toes. She'd first seen them when they decided to cross a small babbling brook as children. The sight of them reassured her. Something about him hadn't changed.

"Why are you smiling?" he asked suspiciously.

"Your toes. They're as funny looking now as they were when you were a boy. I didn't think you were going to come." The words had all run together, and she realized she was nervous. She shouldn't be. This was Sebastian, after all.

His progress into the room ended at the bed and he leaned against the post. She wondered if her words, pushed out while she still had the courage to say them, had halted his progress.

"Would you rather I hadn't?" he asked.

She shook her head. "No. I'm your wife. You're my husband. I want to be your wife." Could she sound any more idiotic?

He glanced down at his bent toes, wiggled them, then his gaze met and held hers. "I assume . . . you're chaste."

She nodded, swallowed, her mouth suddenly wretchedly dry.

He plowed a hand through his hair. "I've never—"

"Oh dear Lord. You're a virgin, too? I was hoping you'd have some experience. I haven't a clue where to begin. All Aunt Sophie advised me to do was drink two glasses of brandy."

A corner of his mouth twitched. Was it possible that here, at least, she would see his smile? She tilted her head, peered up at him. "Are you trying to smile? I'm not a virgin at smiling. I could teach you to do that."

She saw a flash of white that quickly disappeared.

"I'm not a virgin at all," he said. "I was going to explain that I've never taken an inexperienced woman to my bed. I understand that the first time can be painful. I wish it weren't so. I never want to hurt you, Mary."

She slid out of the chair and padded over to him. Reaching up, she cupped his face between her hands and turned it until she could see all of it. "Then share more than your profile with me."

She watched his throat muscles work as he swallowed. He placed his hand over hers, the one resting against his scars, turned it over, and pressed a kiss to her palm. She felt the heat from his mouth coating her skin with dew. She wondered how much of her might receive the same treatment.

"Perhaps in time," he said quietly, "but not tonight."

She thought about reminding him that she'd seen his scars, more than once, but she knew that he could excuse those moments as weakness when he'd been unable to prevent her from assisting him. Tonight they would share an intimacy that he no doubt thought would be marred if he revealed his true self. Or perhaps it was simply masculine pride. Whatever it was, she would forgive it. They would have many more nights together, and she would eventually gain what she wanted from him.

She touched her fingers to his mouth. "I want to see a real smile." She laid them against his throat. "And hear you laugh again."

"You don't ask for much."

"No, I don't. Not really."

"You've always been so feisty," he said. "I tell myself you'd have not been happy with Fitzwilliam. That perhaps what happened was for the best."

"Do you know I have not given him a moment's thought, not since he strode out of my father's residence? I regret that I may have caused him hurt or embarrassment. But I do not regret that he was not the man waiting for me at the altar. You must believe that, Sebastian. We can't spend our lives wondering, 'what if?' We must simply make the best of what we have."

"And did you have two glasses of brandy?"

She laughed lightly. "Three. But that was some time

ago. I fear the effects have worn off. I'm not feeling quite as warm as I was."

"You shall be soon enough." He cupped her jaw and tilted her face up to receive his kiss.

It was nothing at all like the kiss they shared in the garden. It lacked desperation. But it didn't lack passion. It was a nibbling, a slow exploration. His tongue waltzed with hers. She slid her hands up over his shoulders, into his hair, holding him near. His low feral groan vibrated through his chest, resounded against hers and she pressed herself closer.

She'd spoken honestly. She'd not given Fitzwilliam a thought since he walked out on her, but she thought of him now and realized she would not have been comfortable with him at a moment such as this. She would have feared his judging her actions. With Sebastian she experienced no fear of judgment.

He had always liked who she was. She'd never had to pretend with him. She could touch where she pleased, knowing he would not find fault. She could thrust her tongue into his mouth, and welcome his taking the kiss deeper. For his sake, she schooled her fingers not to seek out the scars, not to trace them, not to do anything to make him self-conscious about them.

Never separating his mouth from hers, he lifted her into his arms, carried her the short distance to the bed and laid her down, only then breaking off the kiss. He pressed one to her forehead, her chin. Then he leaned back, studying her as though he thought to memorize every line and curve, every slope and valley.

"You're going to douse the light, aren't you?" she asked.

"Yes."

"I wish you wouldn't."

Sadness touched his features. "For tonight. A woman's first time . . . ugliness should not be a part of it."

Tears clogged her throat, tears she refused to allow to rise to the surface. She could argue that he was not ugly, that she found everything about him beautiful, but she knew he was not of a mind to listen. It would build a strain between them, would dampen the joy they should find at this moment.

Lifting her hand, she cupped his unmarred side. "I'll leave tonight to your superior experience, but rest assured I'm a fast learner and some night you will have to leave it to mine."

"We shall see."

He moved away and she watched as he prowled through the room dousing the lamps. Almost desperately she memorized what she could see of him: the long limbs, the broad shoulders, the strong back. She wished he walked about without clothing, but that would come in time as well. What a wanton miss she was.

Only one lamp still cast its glow. The one beside the bed. Before going to it, he released the ties holding back the curtains that surrounded the bed as though he had no wish for even a star to peer through the window and gaze on them. One by one the heavy velvety curtains flowed together until only one remained tied back.

He approached the last lamp, the last sash. She wondered which he would see to first. She thought of whispering, "No," when he leaned over the lamp.

He took one last lingering look at her and blew it out.

Sebastian released the last sash, felt the air stir as the curtain fell into place. Even without the lamps providing light he could see shadows. He knew it was ludicrous to crave complete darkness for their first coming together, but he wanted to give her the illusion of having in her bed a man who was perfect in features if not perfect in heart.

He tossed aside his shirt and shed his trousers. He wanted tonight to be good for her. She tempted him to be better than he was. At least here, between the sheets, he could ensure that she was glad she married him. Finding the part in the curtains was more difficult than he'd expected but eventually he found it and slipped between them onto the bed. It dipped with his weight. He inhaled her scent, trapped within the cocoon he'd created, relishing the fragrance filling his nostrils.

"I thought perhaps you'd run off," she whispered.

He supposed the darkness required soft voices, murmurings. "Silly goose."

"I'm not silly."

"Are you nervous?"

"Should I be?"

"No. Just trust me to handle this."

"I do."

Reaching out, he felt silk, but not the silk of her nightdress. Silk of her skin. Her thigh. He slid his hand up—

Her hip.

"Your nightdress." His voice sounded rough, raw.

"I removed it."

"I see." Damned, but he wished she'd removed it before he doused the final flame.

"Are you disappointed?" she asked.

"God, no. I should have known you wouldn't be shy about this."

"It's not *this*, Sebastian. It's you. I've never been shy with you."

He felt her hand traveling up his arm, exploring. He closed his eye, imagining her exploring everything. She might be a novice at lovemaking, but he suspected she'd be a quick study.

He followed the curve of her hip, her side, until in his mind, he could see her clearly stretched out beside him. He rolled until he was half-covering her, until her luscious swells met the flat planes of his body. Heated velvet warmed his flesh.

Unerringly he plowed his fingers into her hair, cupped the back of her head, and blanketed her mouth with his. Inwardly he smiled at the flavor of brandy on her tongue. It added a dark richness to the kiss. But beneath it was the taste of Mary, and he sought it out like a man who had been denied drink for most of his life.

For that was how he felt. He'd been in a desert searching for an oasis and she was it. Her eyes were the green of lush vegetation, her hair the red of ripe fruit, her sighs the soft wind cooling his fevered skin.

He couldn't deny that he wished other circumstances had led to this moment, that she'd had a choice, that it was not scandal that had brought her to his arms. But neither could he deny that he was damned glad that she was here. And not because it had been so long that his body ached for want of a woman. But because the woman was Mary.

Lush Mary, whose hands trailed over him, tentatively exploring. Everywhere that she touched he felt as though a dead part of him was being brought back to life. He couldn't remember the last time that he had yearned for a woman's touch to this degree. It was as though he would die if she stopped touching him, if he were forced to stop touching her.

He trailed his mouth along the slope of her throat

and closed a hand around a pliant breast. He relished the weight of it against his palm. Easing down, he circled his tongue around her nipple.

Gasping, she dug her fingers into his scalp.

Closing his mouth over her areola, he wondered at the shade, cursed himself for insisting on darkness. What an utter fool he was. But he could no more leave her now to light lamps than he could cease to breathe.

If only there could be a way to shine the light on her without shining it on him.

She whispered his name, spurring him on to greater pleasures. The sole of her foot traveled along his leg.

He slid lower, bracketing his hands on either side of her ribs. How could she be so slender, yet so voluptuous? He moved down, dipping his tongue in her navel. Someday he would pour wine there and sip it. But for now it was enough to experience the saltiness of her skin against his tongue.

He slid down further, nestled himself between her thighs. The fragrance of her sex wafted around him. He blew at the curls. She sighed.

She did not question, she did not object. He lowered his face and kissed the very heart of her womanhood. He swirled his tongue over her, felt her quiver beneath him. So sensitive, so ready for his plunder.

He was aching with the need to plow into her, but not yet, not until he revealed what she could have. With mouth, tongue, and fingers, he taunted and teased, urged her toward greater heights. Her mewling cries echoed around them, trapped within their curtained confines. He heard her gasping, could feel her writhing.

Her fingers became entangled in his hair, tugged and soothed. His body was tense with need, but he fought it back. He would have her, but he would have her so slick and wet that he would slide in smoothly and save her discomfort.

He didn't want to hurt her, considered pleasuring her and denying himself, but she was a temptation he hadn't the strength to resist. He wanted to know how it felt to sink into her heated depths. He wanted to feel her pulsing around him, drawing out the last of his seed. He needed her to make himself complete.

He didn't know where that thought came from. Didn't want to acknowledge the truth of it. He had been too long on his own. He needed no one. Yet the declaration mocked him.

Unlike Mary, who never mocked him. Who accepted him faults and all.

Who was crying out and bucking beneath him, whose nails were scoring his shoulders.

Mary, Mary, Mary. Dear sweet glorious Mary, lost in the throes of passion.

Rising above her, he plunged into her and released a harsh curse when she screamed.

He stilled, but holding him as close as she was Mary could feel the tremors cascading through the entire length of his body. He had taken her on a journey of exquisite rapture. But it hadn't been enough to distract her from the pain of her maidenhead being breached.

Perhaps it wouldn't have been so bad if he hadn't been so large, but the fullness of him astounded her.

"Forgive me, Mary. Dear God." His face was buried in the curve of her shoulder.

"Shh. It's all right."

"I didn't want to hurt you."

"I know. The pain is easing. Give me a moment."

Their harsh breaths filled the air, echoed around

them. The musky scent of sex hung heavy around them. She didn't know why she'd never considered that love-making would come with a fragrance. Strange how it enhanced her desires, made her yearn even more for what could be between them.

"It was lovely, by the way," she murmured.

"Lovely?"

He sounded as though he choked on the word, but how could she describe what she'd felt? "Splendid, really. Spectacular." She released a self-conscious laugh, held him tighter.

He pressed his forehead to hers. "It can be like that when we're together."

"I might expire if I experience those sensations again."

"You won't."

"Is it like that for you, when you . . . reach that part."

"It's exceedingly . . . lovely." He chuckled low, a sound that vibrated through her heart.

"You're teasing me now. Is it all right to tease when we're doing this?"

"It's all right to do anything we want."

He shifted slightly, and she squeezed her eyes shut against the discomfort.

"Does it still hurt?" he asked, and she heard the worry in his voice. While he'd not been able to see her closing her eyes, he'd obviously been aware of her stiffening.

"Not so much. Move a little more. I think I'm getting used to it."

He took her mouth as though he owned it, and she supposed in some ways he did. There was a roughness to the kiss that had been lacking before. It more closely resembled the desperation she'd sensed in the garden. As though if he didn't have her, he would die.

Warmth swirled through her and her entire body responded by curling inward. It took her a moment to realize that he'd begun moving slowly, sliding out, then in, gently with no hurry, no rush. The kiss had initially distracted her, but now it became part of the sensations. His tongue swirling through her mouth, his hands knotting in her hair, his hips rocking against hers.

The discomfort receded, the pleasure returned. More intense, more encompassing than it had been before. This time she knew what to expect. Before she had fought it, feared it. Now she embraced it. Embraced him.

She caressed him, every inch that she could reach. She realized that he, too, had to be lost in the sensations because he didn't stiffen or object when her fingers encountered scars and continued to explore them. They were part of him, and as such, they were part of her.

Breaking off from the kiss, he rose above her and began pounding into her with a fierceness that called to the wildness in her. His grunts echoed around her. She felt the tenseness in his muscles, the quivering. Her own body reacted in kind: tightening, crying out for release.

When the climax hit her, she feared that he had lied, that she would die. How could anyone survive such intense pleasure? It rocked her to her core, left her with no bones, with the inability to move as Sebastian cried out with his final thrust.

Resting on one elbow, he buried his face in her hair. She could feel the hard pounding of his heart against her breast. She didn't know where she found the strength to skim her fingers over his slick back.

"That was even more lovely than before," she said breathlessly.

He laughed, a deep, rich sound, as he rolled off her.

He slid an arm around her, brought her in against his side.

It was strange but that one small act pleased her more than anything else that they'd done that evening. It gave her hope that one day he'd be glad that he married her.

Chapter 24

Awaking to the faint call of the lark, Mary remembered leaving a window open and realized it must be morning. Impossible to tell with the draperies around the bed pulled as tightly shut as they were. They locked in the warmth of body heat, the scent of lovemaking, and her husband's quiet snores. She wondered how late it was. It was the *only* reason that she leaned over and carefully parted the drapes—to try to determine the proper time, not to catch a glimpse of her husband. Or at least that had been her intention, but when enough faint light stole in to reveal him, she could not resist the temptation to make the most of it.

Sebastian was sprawled on his back. Long limbs tangled in the sheets, long limbs that had been tangled around her when she drifted off to sleep. His face was turned away from her slightly, but because she was to his left she was able to see the scars clearly. At some point during the night he had removed the patch. She'd seen the scars before, had refrained from studying them too closely when he was fighting the fever because it had felt like stealing something private from him without his knowledge.

Perhaps he would consider what she was doing now as the same, only now they were married and should have no secrets, no mysteries from each other. She could not say there was a beauty to the mottled flesh, but there was grace to it. He'd only returned to her life a short time ago, but she couldn't imagine him with Tristan's unmarred features. His face—scars and all—suited him. His temperament. His determination. All he'd endured to again walk these halls as lord and master. She wished he were more comfortable in his skin, that he would welcome the light touching upon it as they made love.

And they did make love. She could think of no other way to describe the tenderness with which he'd explored her body or the fiery passion with which he'd finally taken her.

She wanted to touch him now, comb back the hair from his brow, but she was loath to disturb him, to awaken him. The scars trailed down his shoulder front and back. His arm. How devastating the wounds must have been, how painful. Little wonder it had taken him so long to recover. Based upon when the battle occurred and when he returned to England, it must have been months. She wondered—

"Had your fill yet of staring?"

She gasped, startled with guilt. "How long have you been awake?"

"Long enough."

"I think you're beautiful."

"I think you're mad." He rolled onto his far elbow,

giving her a clear view of his back and the sinewy muscles that ebbed and flowed with his movements. He
reached through the opening on his side of the bed—for
his patch she was certain. "Let back in the darkness as
I've a mind to have you before breakfast."

She scowled, refusing to acknowledge the hurt at his
callous words. "Such flowery words, Your Grace. Defi-
nitely designed to make me swoon into your arms."

He stilled his movements. He didn't look back, but
she could see the tightness traveling through his shoulders, along his back. "You're my wife," he ground out.

"A wife still likes to be wooed."

"Then draw the drapes, and I'll woo you with my
body."

"No." She flung the curtain wider until the sunlight
poured in.

"Dammit, Mary!" He swung around—

Froze.

She fought not to cover herself, wondered if he could
follow the blush of her skin as the heat traveled over her.
She'd not put on her nightdress before falling asleep.
She was bared before him, the sheets pooled around her
hips. Without him even touching her, her nipples puckered at the heat in his gaze as it roamed slowly over her.
She watched his throat muscles work as he swallowed.

"You are so beautiful. Fitzwilliam obviously had
no clue regarding the treasures you hid beneath your
clothes or he'd have never let scandal keep you from
him."

"I told you I was chaste."

"Still, a man can imagine."

"You felt me last night. Is this what you imagined?"

Slowly he shook his head. "Only partially." Reaching out he trailed his thumb around one of her nipples.

"I imagined you dusky not pink." He skimmed a finger over a rounded swell. "And how the devil did you get a freckle there?"

"I don't know. Isn't seeing me better than not?"

"But to see you, you must see me."

"I told you I'm not repulsed by your scars."

"But to have them so near, to have them looming over you—"

"*You* loom over me. With strength and purpose. But my hands are small, so I can't know all of you. Only what I can touch. I want to know it all."

"All is hideous." His voice carried a distraction that pleased her, as he tugged on the sheet, slowly pulling it away from her hips.

She snatched it, held it in place. "Only if the light remains."

"Until I've seen you. Then it goes away."

"No. If it goes away, so do I."

"I'm your husband. You will do as I say."

"I'm your wife. Don't you wish to see me happy?"

He sighed deeply. "I'd forgotten what a trial you could be."

"Close your eye. Pretend you're in the dark."

"I will not even blink and miss a second of seeing you in the light."

She gave him a hopeful smile. "Can you not understand that I feel the same?"

"As I said: you are mad." He yanked hard on the sheet, revealing the alcove between her thighs. His breathing came harsh and heavy.

"The light?" she asked.

"Stays, damn you."

With a laugh she worked her way out of the sheet that remained then yanked away the linen covering him and simply stared, taking her fill. "No wonder it hurt when we joined last night."

"I wish it hadn't."

His voice held such regret that she could have wept.

"Aunt Sophie said it will only hurt in the beginning. I'm not sure what she considers the beginning. Will it hurt the next time, do you think?"

"I don't know."

"Doesn't matter." She straddled him before he could protest. Smiling brightly, she looked down on him and glided her hands over his chest.

"You're really not repulsed." His words were an astonished statement.

She lowered her face until their breaths mingled. "I'm really not."

Then she kissed him. She may have initiated it but he quickly took control. She would let him have this victory, because she'd won the major battle. Sunlight was warming her skin as much as he was. She loved the feel of his hands coasting over her body. His palms were rough, fingers callused. A soldier's hands. The hands of one who had toiled and fought. Not one who had done little more than study books and drink to excess. His lessons had come from life, living it, and very nearly being killed by it.

Was it any wonder that he showed impatience in ballrooms and thought trivial so many rituals of etiquette?

Drawing back from the kiss, she smiled at him, combed her fingers through his hair. She could see scars in his scalp that had been denied her before, and she realized he wore his hair long for a purpose. She could only hope that in time he would come to realize that none of it mattered. That when she looked at him, she saw beneath the scars to the man he was.

Brave. Caring—even if it was the land instead of her that called to him.

He cupped her cheek, tilted her face until she met his gaze.

"You are such a beauty," he said. "I was a fool to take you in the dark. I just thought it would be more pleasant for you not to see—"

She pressed a finger to his lips. "Don't try to read my mind. I suspect you will always guess wrong. Last night was wonderful. I don't regret it. The darkness added its own mystery to everything. Now the light will do the same."

She kissed him again, didn't object when he cradled her hips, lifted her up, and brought her down to envelop his shaft. She took him deep, felt satisfied, complete.

With his hands he guided her movements until she caught the rhythm. The sensations began building and she was in control of them. He glided his hands to her breasts, kneading them, scraping his thumbs over the taut nipples, sending desire coursing through her.

He knew so much and she knew so little, yet still she felt his equal in their lovemaking. His groans, his panting spoke volumes. Her pleasure increased as she watched his face. The strain to hold back, the clenched jaw.

Then she was the one panting as the pleasure spiraled. She rocked faster, harder. She dug her fingers into his chest, craned her head back, arched her spine—

And succumbed to a joyous awakening as they were both flung into the abyss together.

Chapter 25

As Sebastian guided his horse over the rain-drenched land, he cast a glance at Mary riding beside him. She looked magnificent in her dark green riding habit with her hat perched at a jaunty angle. He kept her to his right not because he wanted to spare her the sight of his scars, but because he wanted to be able to see her with as much ease as possible. Of course now it was difficult to look at her without seeing in his mind's eye her without a stitch of clothing. He'd been a fool to insist they make love in the dark, should have known that headstrong Mary would have her way. If she wanted light shining on them in the bed, light it would be.

He also should have realized that she would greet lovemaking with an eagerness to explore all facets of it. Fitzwilliam had been a bloody fool to walk away from her. But Sebastian couldn't regret that she was his duchess. Not after this morning. Hell, not after last night.

All the things he'd worried over, she turned into insignificance. Theirs might not have been a love match, but it was based on a deep and abiding friendship. More than some had.

"What did you do, all these years, while I was away?" he asked.

She gave him an impish smile, released a small laugh which echoed between them and lit upon him as lightly as a butterfly. Only it didn't stop there. It knocked at the edge of his soul, but he had learned that he needed to remain hardened to soft things so he forbade his soul from answering.

"What do you find so humorous?" he asked.

"Not humorous. Encouraging. It's the first time you've asked me about the life I led while you were gone. I've had a thousand questions, wanted to know what happened during every moment of your time away from here. I wasn't even certain that I warranted so much as an afterthought."

He furrowed his brow, clenched his jaw. Surely he'd asked after her welfare. Something. But nothing came to mind. Yet she'd married him anyway. Thank God for scandal. "I was occupied with thoughts of securing Pembrook and my titles."

She gazed up at the sky as though she was seeking rain. "Yes, I know."

"You say that as though you don't approve."

She pursed her lips, adjusted the reins.

"Mary?" he prodded.

With a long sigh and obvious reluctance, she said, "It's only that you seem not to allow much more in your life."

"Because nothing is more important. It has always served as my lodestar, given purpose to my life."

"Perhaps now that you've secured it you can expand your interests."

"I still have much work to do. I need to review ledgers, journals, and discover exactly what Uncle has done the past twelve years."

"Why can you not simply start with now and move forward?"

He shook his head, not certain why he was so bothered that she found fault with his methods. She was his wife. Her place was in his bed, not in his study. "As the daughter of an earl, you should realize that history is all-important. We must understand the past in order to meet with success in the future. Besides, there is a small chance that I will find something that will prove correct my suspicions about his murdering my father, or allow me the opportunity to ruin his life further."

She was quiet for several moments, and he wondered if he should apologize for his terse tone. If he did, he'd begin a habit that would no doubt leave him apologizing most of the day. He longed for the easy camaraderie they'd possessed as children. Only they were no longer children.

"I read," she finally said.

"Pardon?"

"What I did while I was at the nunnery. I read the Bible. I scrubbed floors. I stitched a thousand articles of clothing." Her laughter this time echoed sadness. "Or it seemed like a thousand anyway. I hate stitching, by the way. I have no intention of ever again threading a single needle."

"We have the means for you to hire servants to thread needles for you."

Finally, he had cajoled a smile from her.

"I'd rather hire them to rub my feet. I'm very fond of having my feet rubbed."

"I shall keep that in mind. Although I much prefer having other things rubbed."

"Sebastian, don't be naughty."

"I just thought you should know. You should also know that you were never an afterthought. I simply never thought of you as growing up."

"Just because I've grown up doesn't mean I can't still outride you." She urged her horse into a gallop.

He watched her go. A time had existed when he knew exactly how much of a lead to give her and how to pace his horse so that she would win. Always he had been able to deny her so little. Why did he feel that he was suddenly denying her far too much?

He spurred his own horse on. They were adjusting to new roles—husband and wife. And years of changing between them. She was no longer the young girl whose braid he'd liked to tug on. He was no longer the boy who had expected to step into his father's boots with barely a ripple in his life.

He had weathered numerous storms to get here. His brothers had suffered as well. He couldn't forget the price they'd all paid.

Mary was wrong. He couldn't begin with the present and move forward. He had to first conquer the past.

He'd let her win. Mary was fairly sure of it as she arrived at the blackened abbey ruins only a few gallops ahead of Sebastian. Time had taken its toll on the abbey. Weeds had reclaimed much of it. Two of the walls were so worn that one could easily step over them. She sus-

pected farmers or villagers had taken off with some of
the bricks and stone.

"I should have known you'd come here," Sebastian
said as he brought his horse up beside hers.

"I would like to walk around for a bit."

After dismounting, he assisted her from her horse
and tethered both beasts to a low-lying bush. He offered her his arm, and they strolled slowly around the
remains of the medieval structure. They stepped over
a low outer wall. Most of the ceiling and roof were
gone. It had been a tall structure, as though it had once
housed giants. "That first night at the ball, when you
made your grand entrance back into Society, you mentioned that Rafe knew the dark side of London. When
I was caring for you, it became quite obvious that he
doesn't live at Easton House. What does he do?"

Walking away from her, he skirted the edges of what
might have been the sanctuary and stopped at a window
that looked out over the hills. All that remained was
the frame. Above it was nothing except sky. He sighed
deeply. "You mustn't tell anyone."

"I'm not going to gossip about my family."

He glanced back at her, and she could tell he was
surprised by her words. She was astonished that he was.
"You're my family now," she said by way of explanation. "You, Rafe, Tristan."

"My apologies, Mary. Even if we were not married,
I know you'd not gossip about us." He removed his hat,
turned it in his hands as though he needed to concentrate on something besides the words he'd speak. "He
owns a den of vice."

She heard the displeasure in his voice. Not that she
blamed him. "You mean like gambling."

"Among other things."

"Well, surely now that you've reclaimed your title, he'll give it up."

"He says not."

"And you're not happy about that."

"Of course I'm not happy about it. But as I left him twelve years ago, he has decided it is a bit late for me to care about what he does with his life now."

"Where did you leave him?"

He crushed his hat, straightened it. "At a workhouse. I knew Uncle wouldn't look for him there."

"From a workhouse to a den of vice? Rather odd going. How did that come about?"

"I don't know. Somehow he ended up on the London streets. Maybe he ran away. He survived. I don't know the particulars. He won't talk to me about it."

"I'm sorry."

He released a brittle laugh. "It's not your fault. If not for you, we'd all be dead."

She crossed over to him, studied the strong lines of his face. She realized it was far more than the scars that had changed his features. It was remorse, regrets, burdens. She touched his jaw. "You did what you had to do. And what courage it took."

"There was nothing brave about it. I was terrified."

"Isn't that what courage is? Doing something even when you're frightened?"

He studied her for a moment. "I was frightened the day you kissed me here. Do you remember it?"

She welcomed the change of subject. She had hoped that coming here would remind him of better times. "My first kiss. I'm not likely to forget."

"Why did you do it?"

"Because I saw you kissing the silly milkmaid."

His eye widened and he laughed. It wasn't a large

laugh, but neither was it bitter or harsh. It filled her with hope that more laughter awaited them. He shook his head. "I never kissed a milkmaid."

"Yes, you did. I saw you."

"No, she was the egg girl."

She slapped his arm. He grabbed her wrist and yanked her close until she had to bend her head back to look up at him.

"Were you jealous?" he asked.

"No. I was angry. I was afraid you'd start playing with her. But then after we kissed, I thought, 'Well, that wasn't anything.' I stopped worrying about it."

He cradled her cheek. "It wasn't anything? I think it was the first time that I ever thought of you as a girl. Until then, you were just Mary, my friend. I was afraid my father would find out and I would have to marry you."

She laughed. "Oh, I was afraid of that, too. But I was afraid it would be *my* father who discovered what I'd done. And he would send me away. Only it wasn't very much of a kiss, not really."

He grew serious. "No, it wasn't very much of a kiss."

He lowered his mouth to hers, and this time the kiss they shared in the abbey was incredible, filled with warmth and passion.

As they entered the great manor, all the warmth from outside failed to come in with them. Mary shivered. She would love this place because he loved it, but she couldn't help but fear that they would never be truly happy here.

The butler, Thomas, approached. He'd come with them from London. She suspected he had no preference for where he worked as long as he was serving the young duke.

"Your Grace, one of the servants found a portrait of your father in the attic. I had it hung in the library."

"Excellent." But something in Sebastian's voice made Mary wonder if he rather wished they'd not had such luck.

"Also, a missive arrived from Lord Tristan. I placed it on the desk."

"Very good. We should like an early dinner."

"I shall see to it."

The butler retreated, and she couldn't help but feel that Sebastian was suddenly not nearly as relaxed as he'd been when they were out riding about. "I suppose I should prepare for dinner," she said.

"Perhaps you would take a moment to see if the portrait is to your liking."

"I would be delighted, but my father always told me that the library was the lord of the manor's domain, so what matters is if it is to your liking."

"I value your opinion on the matter."

"As you well know, I'm not one for mincing words."

"No, you're not." His smile was small, but at least it was there, and she saw affection in his gaze. He held out his arm and she placed her hand on it.

"You let me win today," she said, and felt his arm tighten beneath her fingers. "Did you always?"

"Not always. It's easier to win when one isn't riding sidesaddle."

"Ridden sidesaddle a lot have you?"

He chuckled. "No. Never. But I can't imagine it's very comfortable."

As they reached the library, the footman opened the door and they strolled in. She loved the masculinity of this room: the dark walls, the sturdy wood and leather furniture. The books. So many books. She adored reading. It introduced her to characters, took her to places where she was never lonely.

The portrait over the mantel was life-size and Sebastian's father had been a large man, rather like him. Perhaps not quite as broad, but then he'd had a slightly easier life.

"I'd forgotten how large he was," she said.

"I'm not certain I like it." Moving away from her, he went to the table in the corner. "Brandy?"

"No thank you. What is it about the portrait that you object to? It's an amazing likeness."

Sebastian took a long swallow of brandy, before refilling his glass. "It serves to remind me that I am a disappointment to him."

"However did you draw that ludicrous conclusion?"

He took another sip of brandy and leaned back against the bookcase, his gaze transfixed on the portrait. "I allowed us to be walked to the tower without a fight."

"And if your suspicions are correct, your father allowed himself to be whacked on the head. If he's disappointed in anyone I suspect it's in himself."

He barked out a laugh, a raspy sound that seemed as though it had been trapped somewhere rusting away and needed to be polished a bit. "You've always had such faith in me."

"Because I've always—" *Loved you.* But it had been a childish love, given so easily, without condition or expectation. Now she wasn't quite certain what she felt for him. She knew something in her chest tightened when she gazed on him. She wanted to ease his sorrows. "—known you would do what was right."

He laughed again, an edge of bitterness ringing out

this time. "Not always I fear." He glanced back at the portrait. "Think I shall have it moved to another room. I don't want him looking over my shoulder."

"I'll find a place for it."

"Thank you. Let's see what news Tristan has to impart."

Sebastian strode over to the desk, picked up the letter, broke the seal on the envelope, and withdrew the parchment. He unfolded the letter and read it. She couldn't tell if he was pleased or not.

"What does it say?" she asked moving nearer.

He folded the letter and placed it back in the envelope. "He's purchased for us some horses as a wedding gift."

"There seemed to be a lot of words there for so little news. What else?"

"Rafe is well. Tristan may return to the sea."

"There's something you're not telling me."

"I have no secrets."

"Then let me see what he wrote."

He studied her for a long moment, then handed her the letter. She scanned it quickly.

Brother,

I hope this letter finds you well and enjoying marital bliss. I found some excellent horseflesh in Hertfordshire that I purchased for you and your lovely bride as a wedding gift. It should arrive without much delay.

All is well at the estate in Shropshire. Tomorrow I head down to Wiltshire to check on things there. I am having difficulty comprehending why the Crown couldn't have given our ancestors all of their property in one place. While I've enjoyed not being in London, I miss the sea. Don't take offense if I raise anchor shortly after seeing to the tasks you asked me to.

The man watching and following Uncle reports that he rarely leaves the boarding house except to visit with his wife.

Rafe was well when I left London. He promised to watch over the residence. I'm not sure what to make of him. He seems to lead some sort of secretive life. Can only hope that in time he will trust us with it.

Give my best to Mary. Not a night goes by that I don't wish you'd have let me marry her.

Tristan

She turned and stared at him. "Tristan wanted to marry me?" she asked.

"If I wasn't willing."

"Why didn't you let him then?"

"Because I was willing."

"I thought you married me because you had no alternative."

"We should probably begin preparing for dinner," he said, completely avoiding addressing her inquiry.

Wasn't that interesting? He'd had a choice.

She could not imagine that Tristan had offered to marry her. Would she have been happier with him? Would he have taken her with him when he set sail or left her behind? Did it really matter? It was a bit of a revelation, though, to realize that Sebastian could have pawned her off on his brother. But he hadn't.

Of course, he hadn't, silly goose. If he was anything at all, he was a man who took responsibility for his actions. He kissed you in the garden. He felt obligated to marry you.

Only perhaps it was more.

Chapter 26

Following dinner, Mary sat curled in a chair in the library with her small rosewood secretary on her lap and jotted notes regarding tasks she needed to see to. The residence had a smaller library with a delicate desk in it that she assumed the former duchess had used, but she wanted to be near Sebastian. He worked at his desk, scouring through ledgers, making notations on a sheaf of paper beside him. So much needed to be done here that it was almost like starting over.

"Sebastian?"

"Hmmm?" He kept his attention on the books.

"I thought I might go to the village tomorrow and see about hiring some temporary help to assist the servants in readying the remainder of the manor. So much requires dusting, polishing, and scrubbing that I thought it would hurry things along."

"Splendid notion," he muttered distractedly.

"Then I thought I might go to Willow Hall. I know

Father was planning to leave London shortly after we did. I wanted to see about luring away some of his servants."

"Splendid notion."

"His gardener, for example, has been training his son in the trade. I thought we could offer the young man a position here as our gardener."

"Splendid notion."

"I think we would need more than one but it would be a start."

"Splendid notion."

"Then I thought I might very well scamper through the fields without my clothing."

"Splendid—"

He paused before giving her a pointed look. She smiled mischievously. "I wasn't certain you were listening."

He poured whiskey into a glass, then swirled it, watching her closely over the rim. "Feeling neglected?"

"A little."

"If I spend most of the morning in bed, and a good part of the afternoon riding, I must catch up with business in the evenings."

She drew a heart on her paper, blackened it in. "I know. It's just that many couples, after they marry, take a wedding trip."

"We did. We took a trip from London to here."

She scowled at him, then realized he was not being deliberately obtuse. "No, they go somewhere that they can be alone."

"We're alone here."

She bit back a growl. "Without responsibilities, so they can concentrate on each other."

He leaned back in his chair, one corner of his mouth

curving up ever so slightly. "Have an itch for me to take you again?"

She did, but not when he put it like that. She scoffed. "You're impossible."

He patted his thigh. "Come here. I can take you here."

She set aside her secretary and rose. "That's exactly what I desire. An uncomfortable tumble behind your desk."

"It won't be uncomfortable."

"I'm going to take a bath." She'd taken two steps—

"Mary?"

She stopped when everything inside her urged her to trudge on. His footsteps echoed toward her. They halted and his arms came around her, drawing her near. He kissed the back of her neck. "I need only a little while longer and I'll come to your bed."

"And *have* me?"

"Yes, unless you'd rather I not."

At least he was giving her the choice. There was something to be said for that, she supposed. Not all men would. "I'd rather you make love to me."

"All right," he said quietly and touched his lips to her nape again.

"Say it," she urged softly.

"I can't."

"Because you don't love me?"

"No, because it's too damned poetic and I loathe poetry."

She turned in his arms. "Do you love me?"

"Do you me?"

She studied him as understanding dawned. "You can't say the word. You can't say love."

"I care for you," he said irritably. "You must know that."

"Would you have asked for my hand in marriage if not for the scandal?"

"No, I'd have never subjected you to a life with me."

"Why do you think a life with you would be so horrid?"

Moving away from her, he began to pace. "Because I know what I am. Harsh. Determined. Focused on one thing: Pembrook. You want poetry, and gentle words, and softness. There is no softness in my life. Except for the bed. And you in it makes it softer." He stopped pacing and scowled at her. "Why the deuce are you smiling?"

"For someone who claims not to like poetry, you can be quite poetic. I'll be waiting for you to come *have* me."

She turned on her heel and marched from the room. For the life of her, she didn't know why her spirits were suddenly lifted. Perhaps because while he may not say it, she knew that she did mean a great deal to him.

Sebastian stepped into his wife's bedchamber to find her still bathing. She'd not seen him enter because she was hidden behind a screen, a fire blazing on the other side of her casting her in silhouette. She obviously hadn't heard the door because she was singing . . . no, humming . . . no, singing. She didn't know all the words, he realized. She sung the ones she did, hummed the ones she didn't.

" 'Be it ever so humble . . .' "

She had the voice of a lark at break of day. He glanced over to find her maid sitting in a nearby chair, staring at him, her embroidery abandoned on her lap. He placed his finger to his lips and, with a nod of his head toward the door, signaled for her to leave. She rose, dipped a quick curtsy, and quietly quit the room.

On bare feet, Sebastian padded over and carefully eased down to the edge of the foot of the bed. Mesmerized, he watched as Mary raised her arms. Through her humming, which was softer than her singing, he heard droplets dripping into the water, envisioned them rolling along her flesh, dampening it as they went. He'd considered having one of the rooms transformed into a bathing chamber, but he decided he much preferred the view offered by a bath before the fire. Strange how he found even her shadow alluring.

Perhaps part of it was because she didn't realize she was being watched. He'd never realized that a voyeur lurked inside him, but it was having a jolly good time, appreciating everything before him.

He hated the thought that he might have denied her—no matter how unintentional—something she wanted: a wedding trip. He'd spent so much time away from Pembrook, from England, that it had never occurred to him not to hasten here as soon as he could. Had Fitzwilliam planned to take her somewhere? He despised the thought of that man giving her something that Sebastian hadn't. He'd been so concerned with saving her reputation that he'd given no thoughts to her heart's desires. She had some. That he knew. After she'd left the library he'd glanced at the paper she'd left on her secretary. It was a boring list of tasks to be done but sprinkled throughout were small hearts. Whimsical. She wanted love and, regretfully, he didn't know if he could give it to her.

She lifted an elegant leg out of the water, pointed

her toes toward the ceiling, and his mouth went dry as all previous thoughts scattered. Good Lord, she was limber. He could take her with her legs braced on his shoulders. He watched the sensuous movements as she skimmed her hands from heel to thigh. Perhaps even to hip. Or maybe she stopped someplace in between, a haven he was anticipating visiting once again.

He became aware of her no longer singing, simply humming a soft provocative tune that caused his breath to come in labored pants. Did she go through these rituals every time she bathed?

She dropped back her head, released a deep sigh. "Colleen, I'm ready to leave the bath."

He swallowed hard. He was ready as well, but not to leave a bath—rather to leave his wife well and truly sated.

"Colleen? The towel? Don't tarry. My husband will be here any moment and I wish to be prepared."

If she were any more prepared, *he* might ignite. He came to his feet, wandered toward her, and snatched up a towel in passing. He came around the screen, and decided that in the flesh, she was exceedingly more delectable. With her eyes closed, she rested her head against the lip of the tub. All of her skin was dampened with dew. Her hair was piled in a haphazard manner on top of her head. Several strands had gained their freedom and they curled in wild abandon. Her limp hands draped over the sides. Her thighs were spread wide. The water lapped around her breasts, creating two lovely islands.

She moaned low, opened her eyes slowly—

Shrieking, she sank beneath the surface of the water until the islands were in danger of drowning. Pity.

"What are you doing here?" she demanded.

"Why the surprise? I told you that I was going to visit and I heard you tell your maid you were expecting me. At any moment."

She scowled. "How long have you been in here?"

"When I entered you knew the words to the song, then you seemed to forget them."

Horror crossed her features. "You heard me singing? Oh, dear God."

"You have a lovely voice."

"It's atrocious. I sound like a warbler."

"And here I likened you to a lark."

"Why did you not let me know you were here?"

"I was rather enjoying the shadow show."

She looked at the screen, then jerked her gaze to the fire, and he saw the reality of her situation dawn, as she muttered, "Entertaining silhouettes."

"Extremely entertaining."

She gave him an impish smile. "I think you're rather enjoying yourself now."

"I rather am, yes."

"I might have to teach you a lesson about spying on me and withhold my favors."

"I won't allow it."

She narrowed her eyes at him. "And how, Your Grace, do you expect to carry out that threat?"

"I will kiss every inch of your skin until you are as close to falling to your knees with aching need as I am now."

She grinned wickedly, and he thought he might burst. "I can see your aching need even with your trousers on. Hand me the towel that I might dry off and see to that need."

"I want to dry you and then I intend to make you wet again."

She gasped. "Such bawdy talk!"

"Bedchamber poetry."

"And here you claimed earlier not to like poetry." She studied him for a moment through half-lowered eyelids. Sultry wench made him feel as though he were the one unclothed. Her tongue appeared between her parted lips and captured an errant drop of water. Then she rose up out of the water like a brazen goddess, completely comfortable with her body, not a hint of shyness to be seen.

She would no doubt be the death of him.

She gave him a pouty look. "So carry out your promise, Your Grace. Dry me, then make me wet."

Mary wasn't certain where she found the courage to be so bold. She only knew that once he'd confessed to being close to dropping to his knees that she'd felt powerful, in control of the situation, regardless of his threat not to allow her to withhold her favors. She knew he'd not force her.

As it was he feared she'd not welcome his touch. Strange. She'd always assumed it was the man who made the woman feel comfortable with what passed between them, but it was her husband who required the reassurance that she was not put off by his scars. She loved it when passion overcame him, and he forgot they existed. She wanted them not to matter. She wanted the scandal that had forced them to marry not to matter.

She wanted love between them, so deep and abiding, that nothing mattered beyond them.

The chill of the air caused her nipples to pearl and pucker. His gaze dropped to her chest, smoldered. She watched his throat work as he swallowed. Indeed, she held the power.

"I'm growing chilled, Your Grace." She held out an arm and tried to present an innocent expression, a slight pouting of her lips.

She'd expected him to whip her out of the tub and dry her off quickly. Instead, he went down to one knee before her and draped the towel over his raised thigh. She lifted a foot and placed it on the perch he offered. He began at her toes and blotted the water slowly, gently, his attention focused on his task. Even though her hands were wet, she ran one through his hair. "I shall return the favor someday," she said quietly.

"What favor is that?" he asked distractedly.

"Intrude upon your bath."

"I did not intrude. I allowed you to enjoy it."

"You enjoyed it as well."

He lifted his gaze to her. "Immensely."

He finished patting her leg, then indicated the other. He dried her with touches as gentle as any she'd ever known, as though he feared the cotton in the weave would scratch her skin if he did not take care. When he finished with her leg, he set her foot on the floor and stood, looming over her. His size had never frightened her. While she was tall for a woman, he was taller than most men.

He patted dry her face, her neck, her shoulders, her breasts. Then he took one in his mouth, suckled. Moaning, she craned back her head, stared at the ceiling with its intricate scrollwork.

"Turn around," he ordered in a rough voice, and she realized that the task he'd set himself was as much torment for him as it was for her. Lovely torment.

She did as he bade, relished the cotton absorbing what little dampness remained. For a moment she did what she'd promised she'd never do: she thought of

Fitzwilliam and realized that she could have never envisioned allowing him to take such liberties. She would have welcomed darkness accompanying their encounters. She couldn't have been playful, teasing, or sensuous. What seemed so natural with Sebastian would not have seemed so with anyone else.

The towel skimmed along her skin as it cascaded to the floor and pooled at her feet. She felt a tug on her hair, heard the clink of a pin hitting the floor. Another tug, another clink. Three more followed before her hair tumbled around her shoulders.

Gathering it up with one hand he moved it aside and kissed her neck. "All dry," he whispered.

"Hardly." She was acutely aware of the dampness between her thighs.

He released a low laugh, slid his hand around her, and cupped her intimately. "Too easy."

She sighed. "I can't argue with the truth."

"I adore how responsive you are," he whispered, so low that she wondered if the words were more for him than her.

He swept her up into his arms and carried her to the bed. Only then did she realize that the light in the room came from the fireplace and much of it was blocked by the screen. The bed was mostly shadows as he laid her on it. He reached across her for the sash that held back the canopy drapes. She placed a hand on his shoulder. "No."

He stilled, looked down on her.

"We had the sunlight this morning," she reminded him.

He cradled her face, bent down, and kissed her forehead. "Tonight I need the dark, Mary."

It was such a heartfelt plea. How could she deny it?

He'd watched her bathe, teased her, and dried her. Anticipation had been building. She knew now was not the time to argue, not the time to try to convince him again that she was not put off by his scars. She pressed on his chest, pushing him back until she could sit up. Studying his face, she leaned in and gave him a quick kiss, before turning away and closing the draperies on her side of the bed.

She stayed as she was, waiting while she felt him leave the bed. The other draperies closed until she was encased in darkness. A sprig of light, the bed dipping, darkness again.

Turning back, she found him with unerring accuracy. She ran her hand up his chest, his throat, his jaw, his cheek until she felt the patch. He snatched her wrist.

"Let me remove it," she whispered softly. "You have the dark. You don't need this. If I'm completely bare, so should you be."

His fingers loosened their grasp. Ever so slowly she moved the eyepatch away. Before he could stop her, she pressed a kiss to the scarred flesh, not even certain he would be able to feel it.

"Mary," he rasped.

"I'm yours," she whispered.

Rolling her over, he proceeded to keep his promise. With hands, mouth, tongue he tormented her until she was certain steam rose from her flesh. She was ready for him long before he slid into her with a sureness that caused her to smile.

He was a masterful lover. She greedily felt for what she could not see: his muscles bunching with his efforts, his slick body moving in and out of hers, his tightened jaw, his damp hair. Pleasure spiraled through her as his grunts echoed around her.

When the cataclysm came, it hit them both at the same time. She held him close as his hot seed poured into her. His breathing harsh and heavy, he eased off her and brought her up against his side.

There she fell into a contented sleep.

Chapter 27

The days ambled along, each bringing a wealth of discoveries. Mary began to understand her husband's true devotion to Pembrook. He began each morning with a leisurely ride over his domain. She often joined him. He spoke with the tenants. He assessed the possibilities for future income. He noted areas where improvements were needed.

He was much more comfortable here than in London.

He'd even been relaxed when they'd visited her father. But more important, Sebastian had managed to put the earl at ease. Before they left, her father took her aside to inform her that she'd married a good man.

Of that, she had no doubt.

Mary stood in the garden, taking delight in the new gardener's efforts. Her father had been more than willing to let the young man go. He had also offered her half a dozen other servants, children to his longtime staff members who he'd simply never found the heart to relieve of their positions. But he had no need of them. She found a good deal of work for them to do here.

From her place near the hedgerow, she could see the stables, could see Sebastian talking with the head stableman and pointing out various horses. The recent arrivals—Tristan's gift—had come thundering in this morning. Sebastian had removed his jacket earlier and rolled up his sleeves to inspect each animal. He wasn't afraid to get his hands dirty. She'd give him that. She couldn't recall her father ever taking so much interest in the managing of his estate. He had overseers. They gave him reports. But Sebastian spoke with all the servants, issued orders, listened to their ideas. He wanted Pembrook returned to its former glory.

Not nearly as many tenants still worked the land but they provided the estate with a comfortable income. His other estates fared much better. Unlike Fitzwilliam, he did not need her dowry.

In spite of the tragic history that surrounded this place, he was at home here. She enjoyed watching him striding over his property. It was her true purpose in being outside when the gardener was perfectly capable of determining which type of flower should be planted in which spot. Sebastian loved Pembrook with all that he was, devoted himself to it. She tried not to resent that he wasn't as devoted to her. She truly had no cause for complaint.

He came to her every night. Usually he stayed with her until dawn. But some nights he was restless and would return to his bedchamber so as not to disturb her. Her assurances that she was not bothered did not sway him to stay. On those nights she would hear him call out. She wanted desperately to go to him, but she knew he wouldn't welcome her witnessing his nightmares.

"Your Grace."

She turned and smiled at the butler. "Thomas."

"The post has arrived. You and the duke each received a letter. I thought they might be important."

She took the envelopes he offered. He had already slit them open, but she didn't question if he'd read them. She knew he wouldn't dream of encroaching on his lord's and lady's privacy. "Thank you."

He glanced toward the stables. "It is good that His Grace is home."

"Yes, it is."

"If I may be of further service regarding the letters, let me know."

He strode back toward the manor. Mary smiled as she saw the letter addressed to her was from Alicia. She slid the paper from the envelope and began to read.

My dearest cousin,

I hope my letter finds you well and extremely happy in your marriage. I have a bit of news. Lord Fitzwilliam has asked for my hand in marriage. I have said yes.

I know this must come as a surprise to you, but I rather fancied him for some time and thought you the luckiest of girls to have snared him. I cannot tell you how happy I am since he began to court me. He has written me lovely poetry and sends flowers every morning. He has even managed to sneak in several kisses. He is quite talented in that regard.

Forgive me for carrying on so, but I am so happy that I wish to share it. I am terribly sorry for the scandal that forced your parting ways, and

you must believe that I took no role in the spread-
ing of the awful gossip. I took no glee from your
troubles, but I must confess that I was delighted
when he was placed back on the marriage mart. I
have prayed every day since that I would be for-
given for taking joy in your calamity.

I hope you will be happy for me, dearest Mary.
I have always fancied boiled eggs. I wish you only
the best and hope you are very happy with your
Christmas pudding.

My love always,
Your cousin Alicia

By the by, Mama sends you her love.

It was the stableman, Johnson, squinting at the distance that had Sebastian turning. Mary was trudging
toward him. He despised his limited vision. If she'd
been approaching from the other side, he'd have seen
her. But now having seen her, he knew something was
amiss.

"Finish up here," he ordered. He was grateful for his
long legs that ate up the distance between them. As he
neared, she smiled at him but something about it was
off.

"Walk with me," he said.

Mary fell into step beside him.

"Are you pleased with the gardener?" he asked.

"Yes. We shall have an abundance of color come
spring. We were discussing possibly building a green-
house so we could have flowers in residence all year."

"If it would please you, we shall do it."

"Do you not even wish to know the cost first?"

"I can fault my uncle with many things, but he was not a spendthrift."

"Then why kill those in line for the title?"

"Prestige, power. Maybe even love. Men do horrendous acts for all sorts of reasons."

They walked along in silence for several moments before he dared to ask, "What's troubling you?"

"Why would you think something is troubling me?"

"Mary, I know your moods." He put only the smallest bit of impatience and chiding in his tone.

She sighed, continued walking while the tall grass rustled against her skirts. "I received a letter from Alicia. Fitzwilliam asked for her hand in marriage and she agreed."

"This troubles you?"

She stopped but kept her gaze focused on the hills. He stepped in front of her, forced her to raise her eyes to his.

While his gut churned and he wasn't certain he wanted to know the answer, he asked, "Are you regretting that you're not married to him?"

A look of surprise crossed over her features and she released a light laugh. "Oh, no. That thought had never occurred to me. No, it's Alicia I'm worried for. I feel as though she's acquired a hand-me-down beau. She deserved to be the first person that someone asked to marry."

"By that reckoning I suppose you're a hand-me-down."

Her mouth dropped open. "Oh, dear Lord, I hadn't even considered that. Sebastian, do you doubt that I want to be your wife?"

"Should I?"

"No. Just because someone else asked first and I said

yes, doesn't mean that when you asked I wanted to say no."

"Perhaps it's the same with your cousin. She had a choice—if she didn't fancy him."

Which was more than you had, he thought. If Mary hadn't agreed to marry him, what sort of life would she have had?

She gave a brisk nod. "You've made a very keen observation there. It's quite possible that he has a care for her. She said he sneaks in kisses and that he's rather good at it."

"Sneaking or kissing?"

She laughed. He so loved her laughter and he'd heard so little of it since his return.

"I'm not sure. The kissing I suppose. I don't really know, because he never kissed me."

"Never?" What sort of jackanapes was he?

"No. Even when he had the opportunity, when we were alone—"

"When were you alone?" Dear God, was that jealousy he was experiencing? No, of course not. She was with Fitzwilliam. Now she was with him. He had no cause for jealousy.

"I went to see him, to question him about the awful rumors. Come to think of it, he was in his library and he appeared rather pensive. I wonder if he was beginning to have doubts about our marriage then." Her eyes widened. "Her dowry is not as large as mine and he told Father he wanted a large dowry. Do you suppose he welcomed the excuse to break it off? The cad!"

He heard a strange sound echoing around him, and realized it was him, laughing. With a smile as bright as the sun, she pressed her hand to his throat.

"I feared I'd never hear that sound again." Tears welled in her eyes.

"Don't you dare weep."

She swiped at them. "I just . . . I've missed it so much. What did I say to make you laugh? I'll say it again."

"You want your cousin to mean something to him and when you think perhaps she does, you consider him a scapegrace."

"I can't have it both ways, can I?"

"I wouldn't think so."

"I want her to be happy."

He cradled her face. "Are you, Mary?"

Instead of answering, she rose up on her toes and kissed him. He snaked an arm around her and drew her closer.

He remembered Rafe's question: would he cheat to lose or cheat to win?

Did she kiss him because she was happy or to distract him from the answer that she wasn't?

When she drew back she gave him a soft smile, then her eyes widened. "I forgot. You received a letter as well."

She handed it over to him. He removed the paper from the envelope and read it.

Sebastian,

Bad news I'm afraid. Upon my return to London, I discovered Rafe had been attacked by three ruffians near your residence. He is recovering nicely from a bullet he took to the leg. I discovered that our brother is a nasty bit of work. He apparently dispensed with two of the fellows rather quickly and coerced the other into describ-

*ing the man who had hired them before sending
that fellow to hell as well. If he isn't Uncle, he's
his twin.*

*Due to his injuries, Rafe was unable to con-
front Uncle straightaway. I immediately saw to
the task. Unfortunately Uncle has secreted away
from the boarding house. Rafe's man who was
keeping watch did not see him leave after Uncle
returned from a pub one night deep into his cups.
Or so the watchman thought. He did see an old
woman depart with a satchel later that night.
But when I questioned the young woman who
runs the house, she informed me that no elderly
people—save Uncle—resided there.*

*I know your first inclination will be to come
to London straightaway, but rest assured Rafe is
well on his way to recovery. You can accomplish
nothing here. See to your duties at Pembrook. I
will continue to search for Uncle until I can find
his trail.*

> *Watch your back, Brother.*
> *—Tristan*

Sebastian crumpled the letter. "Damnation!"

"What is it?" she asked, clutching his arm, worry
marring her features.

"Uncle tried to have Rafe killed. I've been wasting
the day away admiring horseflesh when I should be
searching for some evidence of what Uncle put into play
all those years ago. I must redouble my efforts. Focus
on proving him guilty of killing Father, of intending to
kill us."

Damn it! He had failed to protect Rafe once more.

He was almost to the house when he realized that Mary hadn't followed him. "Saunders!"

The man looked down at him from a parapet. "Yes, Your Grace?"

"My wife is not to be left alone on these grounds. Find her. Escort her to the residence."

He pushed through the door and headed to his study. Nothing was more important now than destroying his uncle. The man was determined not to give up. He was about to discover that his nephew could be equally determined.

Chapter 28

⁂

That night, after Sebastian made love to Mary, he was restless, tossing and turning, and with a kiss on her brow he told her he would sleep in his room so as not to disturb her. She didn't like seeing him leave. He'd been unusually quiet during dinner, and she suspected it had something to do with his worry over Rafe. While he hadn't said anything, she knew he felt guilty about his brother getting hurt.

There had been an almost desperation to their lovemaking as though he were striving to escape something, just like that night in the garden when he had told her that he wanted to forget—and then delivered a blistering kiss that *she* would never forget.

She didn't like the emptiness of the bed without him there. She considered joining him in his bedchamber, but it was obvious he wanted to be alone. So rather than do what she wanted, she did what she thought he needed: she remained where she was and drifted off to sleep.

Mary awoke to the arrival of hell. At least it sounded as though it had descended upon them. She could hear the thunder crashing around her. She scrambled out of bed and flew to the window. But gazing out, she could see no lightning streaking across the velvety black sky. But she did see light spilling out from the small window at the top of the northeast tower. The prisoners' tower. She could see shadows wavering before the light. She almost thought she could feel the building trembling.

Rushing across her room, she grabbed her wrap from the foot of the bed as she passed it, drew it around her shoulders, and hurried through the door that took her directly into Sebastian's bedchamber. A solitary lamp burned and revealed his empty disheveled bed. It looked as though he'd done battle there.

After grabbing the lamp, she scampered out of the room and down the stairs. As she raced past the clock in the entry hallway, it began to strike midnight. She'd never realized how haunting the sound was as it echoed through the hallways. With one hand, she clutched her wrap more tightly about her as though it could protect her from what she would find.

She was not frightened for herself, but for Sebastian. She could only pray that he had the strength to destroy the demons he faced. Holding the lamp as steady as possible, she skittered across the courtyard, ignoring the painful pricking of her feet. She had been a silly chit not to have slipped on her shoes, but then only one thought consumed her: doing whatever she could to ease his pain.

The heavy wooden door leading into the tower

creaked and moaned. After all these years, it still managed to send a chill of dread through her, just as it had that long-ago night when she had clutched a key so tightly in her hand that she'd broken skin. Going up the narrow winding stairs, her hand on the wall, she could feel the vibrations that came after each thunderclap.

At the top, standing ajar, was the door into which she'd once inserted a key into a lock. She had set the lads free. Or that had been her intent, but she feared that Sebastian was still trapped within those walls. She edged cautiously toward the opening and peered inside.

It was as sparsely furnished now as it had been then. A small table. Two tiny stools. And there was her husband, sledgehammer in hand, wielding it with a powerful force, slamming it into the wall. He was shirtless, his skin glistening with the sweat of his labors.

His damp hair flapped against his neck and face with his efforts. She could only see the side of his face, but it was view enough to see that it was contorted with his rage. Everything within her urged her to retreat, to leave him to his madness.

But she could no more leave him within the prison of his rage than she could have left him confined within these walls all those years ago. He had been her childhood friend, and perhaps had she been nearer to being a woman, he would have been more then.

He was more now.

She hated the way the intervening years had changed them all. Had made him angry and bitter. He frightened her now. The girl she had been had not hesitated to risk everything in order to take what she knew was the right action. Now she wavered, and in doing so, she left him in torment.

Swallowing hard, shoving her own fears aside,

knowing he could lash out at her, she took a step forward. "Sebastian?"

He brought the hammer back, then forward with
enough force that stone flew again—only this time he
broke through the wall. A small hole, but a hole nonetheless. Dragging in great draughts of air, he stared at
his accomplishment, the hammer immobile at his side.
He lifted it back up—

"Sebastian?"

He swung around. His skin glistened with the sweat
of his labors. She could see tiny gashes where flying
rock had struck him. But it was the torment in his face
that terrified her. So much pain, as though a thousand
daggers were being driven into his heart. A heart she
desperately wanted to reach. But he held her at bay. The
only time she felt a ray of hope that love could exist between them was when they were in bed together. There
her imagination would take flight. She imagined so
much: joy, laughter, smiles aplenty. She imagined greet-
ing the day with gladness instead of loneliness.

"Return to your bed, Mary."

"Let me help you."

His laughter echoed around them. A bitter laughter
that slammed into her as though he'd used the sledgehammer. "No one can help me."

Turning away from her, he arced the hammer in a
powerful swing and struck the edge of the opening he'd
created. Two stones catapulted into the night. Another
swing. Another brick. Again and again he swung. Little
by little the opening grew larger. His efforts dampened
the waist of his trousers, dampened his hair. His skin
grew so slick that she wondered how he could still hold
the massive tool.

Backing up, she sat on the tiny stool, felt it wobble

beneath her weight. She set the lamp on the table. Tears stung her eyes. He was in agony, fighting demons, and she didn't know how to help him. She only knew that she couldn't leave. But there was danger in approaching him. He was like a madman and if he struck her with that hammer, she had no doubt that she would die. Here in this sparse and lonely tower where three boys had waited for death.

Over the years, she had tried not to think about what it must have been like for them. It was too painful to bear. How frightened they must have been. How alone they must have felt. How betrayed. She pressed a hand to her mouth to stop herself from crying out to him, from distracting him. What damage he might do to himself if he didn't remain focused on his task.

The opening grew. His swings slowed, became less powerful. He stopped, dropped the hammer to the floor, bent his head back, and released a guttural howl that echoed around them and tore through her heart.

He fell to his knees.

She rushed over and dropped down beside him. His hands were curled in his lap, but she could see that his palms were ravaged and bloody. "Oh, Sebastian. My dear, dear Sebastian."

She tore a strip of muslin from her nightdress and began to wrap it around one of his hands.

"It started here," he said, breathing heavily. "I thought if I could tear it down, the nightmares might stop."

She cradled his cheek. "It must have been so frightening to be here, to be waiting, to not know—"

"I damned well knew. I forbid Tristan and Rafe to eat the food that was brought. I thought it would be poisoned. Rafe whined about how hungry he was, how thirsty, how cold. He was so young, so . . . weak. I knew eventually Uncle would send someone for us. Whoever it was would be kind to us. Would pretend to be our friend. Then he would take us out into the woods and kill us. I knew that's what would happen. I had a plan to attack him, but then you came."

She combed her fingers through his damp curls. "You escaped."

He shook his head. "I left Rafe at a workhouse. I can still hear him crying for me not to leave him. But that was why I had to. Because he wasn't strong enough. Tristan said not a word to me as we traveled to the docks. He said not a word when I sold him. I sold him, Mary, as though he were a bauble that I no longer favored."

She wanted him to stop. She didn't want to hear all this.

"He didn't say anything as I walked away, and in some ways that was so much harder than leaving Rafe crying for me to return."

"You had no choice," she assured him.

"Don't you think I know that? Every night when I sleep, I hear Rafe's cries and Tristan's silence and I am condemned by both. I just want the nightmares to stop. I want peace. I thought once I reclaimed Pembrook that I would have it. But there is no peace to be had. Not as long as Uncle breathes. I should have killed him when we were in London, only it would have made me as rancid as he."

She wrapped her arms around him, hugged him tightly, rocked him back and forth. "You could never be like your uncle. Tristan and Rafe understand why you had to do what you did. You just need to forgive yourself."

He shook his head.

"I know it's hard, but if you don't, you're going to become more bitter and angry until you are like him. Then he will have won." She held his face between her hands, forced him to meet her gaze. "I won't allow that to happen."

With his knuckles he touched her cheek. She could smell the coppery scent of blood that coated his palms.

"You've always been so strong, Mary."

"Not really. I just give a good imitation."

"I'm so glad you're here."

He leaned in and kissed her. It was a tentative kiss, a soft kiss. It lacked heat or fire, because he knew as she did that this was not a place for them to come together. This was a place that destroyed lives, and even their coming together would not be powerful enough to tear it down. No, it required the sledgehammer he'd been using, and laborers. He couldn't do the task alone.

"Take me to bed," she whispered.

With that he rose to his feet, pulled her up, and escorted her away from his hell.

Sebastian sank into the copper tub filled with hot water. It burned where the stone had cut into him, soothed where it had not. His muscles already ached from his efforts. He suspected they would be stiff and sore in the morning. He couldn't think of a time when he'd ever worked so hard, had put so much effort into any single task. Ah, but the reward . . .

When he knocked out enough stone so the moonlight could peer in, he'd never felt more victorious. He would tear down the tower. Every inch of it. The area would be converted into a courtyard where the moon and stars could always hold back the shadows. He would be freer then, but not completely. Not until he made his uncle's life more miserable, not until he found some proof of Lord David's crimes would he be content. He would find what he was looking for if it killed him.

He shouldn't linger here but it felt marvelous to simply soak. His baths were usually quick, while Mary seemed to take forever. Perhaps she had the right of it.

In spite of the late hour, she had awakened two footmen and had them heat the water and haul it to his bedchamber. He couldn't blame her for wanting the filth washed from him before he bedded her. He was covered in a thick layer of sweat and dust. He stank. That she had wrapped herself around him to kiss him astounded him.

She had the footmen place the screen from her room on one side of the tub. He never bothered with a screen, had thought modesty prompted her to use one, but she had insisted it would keep the fire's warmth contained, would hold the chill from his body. He couldn't deny that it created a cozy haven.

She had promised to come in to bathe him. He was growing weary of waiting. With his head resting back against the lip of the tub, he watched the shadows play across the ceiling and wondered what was keeping her. He despised that she'd seen the madness engulfing him, but he couldn't deny that he'd been glad to discover her standing there like an avenging angel. He'd have hammered at that wall all night if not for her bringing some sense back to him. She was always there in his darkest hour.

When his quest for retribution was completed, he would make everything up to her. He would take her on a wedding journey. He would purchase her a book of poetry. He would pluck flowers from the garden. He groaned. He was not a man who enticed a woman with poetry and flowers. She knew that about him. No, he would continue to use his kisses to sway her.

He wanted to kiss her now, to join his body to hers. So where the deuce was she? Maybe she'd fallen asleep. If so, he'd awaken her. Gently, raining kisses all over her. He'd begin with her toes and nibble his way up. But first he had to wash.

He shoved himself up—

"Hold still."

His wife's order came from the other side of the screen. He rolled his eye upward, toward the ceiling, toward the frolicking shadows. Damnation. "How long have you been there?"

"Long enough to know you don't sing when you bathe. Now don't move. I'm almost finished, and then I shall keep my promise to wash you."

"What are you doing?"

"It's a secret."

"I don't like secrets."

"Neither do I, but that doesn't stop you from keeping them from me."

"I don't keep secrets from you."

"How often do you awaken from nightmares?"

He gritted his teeth.

"Every night?" she asked quietly.

"Often enough. Tell me what you're doing or I shall climb out and ravish you."

"I want you to ravish me, but not just yet."

"What are you doing?" he asked again, with a bit more force behind the words.

"As I hate needlework, I recently took up the hobby of silhouetting. I rather enjoy it and all I need is a shadow."

He thought of how he'd watched her shadow movements and realized now that her insistence on his using the screen had nothing to do with keeping him warm. "You're creating a silhouette of me?"

"Yes. I want to show you what I see when I look at you."

"I know what you see."

"I don't think you do."

"I insist that you stop." He came up out of the water.

"I don't ask for much, Sebastian. Allow me to have this."

She didn't ask for *anything*, damn her. At least nothing of consequence. He dropped back into the water with such force that some of it splashed over the side. He glared at the fire, because he needed to show something his displeasure.

"Face forward as you were doing before you knew I was here."

With great reluctance, he did as she asked.

"Thank you."

"It will be hideous, all disfigured. I don't know why you would want it."

"Will we never have a portrait done?"

He had considered that. For posterity, it was important that a portrait of the eighth duke and his duchess hang in the portrait gallery. "I shall have Tristan pose with you for the portrait."

"But he is neither the duke nor my husband."

"He is what I would have looked like."

"How vain you are."

"I'm not vain. I simply see no need to subject future generations to this visage."

"I shan't pose with him."

"Then we shall have separate portraits done."

"We shall see."

Those words were a challenge if he ever heard one. But on this matter he would not relent. He sank further into the water and tried not to think of her staring at him, of her gaze traveling over his shadow. He had a strong urge to return to the tower and bang away.

He heard a whisper of movement, and she came around the screen. She held up her efforts: his profile in silhouette. It was all in black. There were no scars revealed. No ridges, no mountains or valleys where his flesh had been torn asunder and healed as best it could. No eye present, no eye missing. It gave the appearance that he was whole.

"This is what I see when I look at you," she said quietly. "A noble bearing. Your father's nose, I think. Your mother's chin. Strong lines. I see handsome features. I know you suffered, but I see resilience. I see the man I married. The man I'm glad to call husband. Tear down the tower. Tear down the whole damned castle." She knelt beside the tub and cupped his jaw, her fingers against his scars. "Just please stop hiding from me." She trailed her fingers down to his chest, pressed her palm against the spot where his heart pounded. "Tonight, in the tower, I caught a glimpse of what you've secreted away."

"You saw a madman."

"I saw a man who loves his brothers dearly, who had to make difficult decisions for all their sakes, a man tormented with guilt. When you look at yourself in the mirror all you see are the scars. When I look at you, I see this." She shook the paper. "I see a man I could very well come to love."

God help him, he didn't deserve her. He'd never deserve her. He thrust his hand into her hair, held her in place, leaned over, and planted a kiss on those lips that could say things that unmanned him. Where did she find her faith in him, when he had so little in himself? She accepted his faults, looked beneath the scars to the man he wanted to be. For her.

For tonight.

With her assistance, he quickly scrubbed away the remaining dirt and grime. He didn't bother to dry off. Simply stepped out of the bath and lifted her into his arms. With his foot, he knocked over the screen so the warmth from the fire could travel farther into the room. He carried her to his bed and realized that he'd never taken her here. He'd kept her from this room, considered it his place of solace. But she belonged here. She belonged in every room.

Setting her feet on the floor, he whipped her nightdress over her head before tumbling her onto the sheets. They were clean he realized, smelled of fresh air and sunshine. While he'd bathed she must have had a servant change them. A lamp burned on the bedside table. He wanted to douse it. Instead he left its light glowing— for her. He preferred the shadows, but she was meant for sunshine.

He would give her this. No more drawn curtains, no more extinguished flames.

Her hands roamed over him, eliciting pleasure wherever they traveled. Even the cuts and scrapes didn't bother him when she touched him. Nothing bothered him. Everything receded. The troubles, the guilt, the worries. Here, within his bed, she was all that mattered.

The lamps remained burning, the sashes remained tied. Without her asking for either. She felt as though something had changed, shifted inside him.

With his eagerness, Mary felt a renewed sense of hope that soon the past would be behind them. He was always enthusiastic in their lovemaking, but something was different tonight. She felt almost as though he were worshipping her. He left no place untouched, unkissed, unexplored.

She had so wanted him to understand that to her the scars were nothing. She had told him a hundred times—tonight she'd finally thought of a way to show him. She could not help but admire him.

She had spoken true: he had been forced to make difficult decisions. He'd only been a young lad then. There had been no right answers, yet each carried harsh consequences. He had done what he thought he needed to do. Now, she was doing the same.

Loving him, even knowing that he might never be able to love her. She would give him everything she could, give him a reason to let go of the past.

She pushed him onto his back and straddled him, taking her turn at kissing and touching and tormenting every inch of him. She was gentle when she came across the abrasions left by flying stone. She hated when anything hurt him, wished she had the power to protect him.

Rolling her over, he joined his body to hers with one sure thrust. He rose above her and she watched in wonder as he pumped his powerful body into hers. His face was set in concentration, in intensity. Reaching up, she trailed her fingers over his face.

With barely a loss of momentum, he took her wrists and locked them together in one hand above her head. He nuzzled her neck, nibbling the sensitive skin, causing her to writhe beneath him. She wound her legs around him as tightly as she could, felt him sink more deeply into her. Pleasure spiraled through her. He lifted himself up, and her enjoyment increased as she watched passion flow over his strong features. Silhouettes could capture the strength of his profile but not the beauty of the whole. She wished he could truly see himself as she saw him.

Chapter 29

$\sim\!\!\infty\!\!\sim$

Sebastian became relentless in his search for some proof that would condemn his uncle. Sitting in his library, Mary watched as he scoured through ledgers, journals, scraps of paper. Anything he could find. Why he would think the man would be silly enough to leave behind evidence was beyond her.

He had hired more men to patrol about. He'd forbidden her from riding, from leaving the residence. Even a walk in the garden was not to be tolerated. She'd become a prisoner here.

During the day he saw to matters of the estate but at night he was absorbed by his quest. When she was in need of a book, she would have to step over piles of papers and leather-bound journals. She wasn't allowed to touch anything. Some stacks stood for what he'd already sorted through. But the majority were for what remained.

Dark circles were emerging beneath his eye. He

shaved less often as though he couldn't spare the time. Just as he had so little time for her.

The only time they truly came together, the only time she really had his attention was when he came to her bed at night. Then she relished the moments, savored them, devoured them.

She was so lonely, so in want of attention that she felt rather pitiful about it. "Sebastian, what do you say to our having a picnic tomorrow?"

"I haven't time for such nonsense," he said gruffly.

She felt as though shards of glass assailed her. "Am I nonsense then?"

That seemed to get his attention. He looked up to study her. "I've never known you to be one to whine."

She didn't know why she'd bothered to ask for a picnic. Of late, food wasn't agreeing with her. She seemed to have little energy. Tears came with no provocation. So did irritation. "I'm not whining. I'm simply going out of my mind. For all the freedom you give me, I might as well be locked in the tower."

Not that a lock would do much good. He'd managed to knock out a good portion of the wall. He often hammered at it late at night which left them with weary servants during the day. Of late everything he did revolved around Pembrook. Even when they made love, she felt as though she didn't have his undivided attention. Afterward, he rolled off her and stared at the canopy, one hand shoved beneath his head. Eventually he would leave and several minutes later the crashing of stone would start.

"Tell me something that I can do to help you. Surely there are papers I can read or—"

"See to the affairs of the manor."

"I do, but even I need to do something fun from time to time."

"Fun? It's not a game here, Mary. He tried to have my brother killed. He wants Pembrook and he shan't have it. If it takes the remainder of my life, I shall see him ruined!"

And what of my life? she almost asked. *Our life?*

Sebastian wasn't certain what woke him. When he rolled his head to the side, he saw Mary standing at the window, wearing her nightdress, a lamp on a nearby table casting her in soft silhouette.

He swung his legs off the bed, snatched up his trousers, and jerked them on. He crossed the room to her, placed his arms around her, and drew her into the curve of his body. She didn't relax against him with a sigh as she once had. She remained stiff, unyielding. He lowered his head, pressed a kiss to the sensitive spot below her ear. "Come back to bed."

"I want us to leave Pembrook."

He stilled, studied her partial outline in the glass of the window where rain pattered. "Take a holiday?"

"Permanently. You have five other estates. We can make a home in one of those."

"My home is here."

She broke free of his hold and swung around to face him. "Did you hear what you said? *My* home. What of *our* home?"

"This is our home."

"No, Sebastian. It's not a home. Our life here is you reading through dusty old ledgers—"

"I'm striving to find proof of what he did."

"Do you honestly think he was stupid enough to write it down? What do you think you'll find there?"

"Perhaps someone he paid for very little work. Something that doesn't add up. The name of a friend.

Someplace he might go. I don't know. But there must be something."

She shook her head. "When you're not in your library, you're in the tower, hammering away at it. I understand why it must go, but hire someone to do it."

"*I* must do it. Every stone must feel the weight of my wrath."

"You're no different than your uncle."

Fury shot through him with a vengeance. He took a step toward her. He didn't know what his face showed, but she flinched before squaring her shoulders.

"I am nothing like him," he ground out.

"You are obsessed with this fortress."

"It is my heritage!"

"It encases your heart. Can you not see that?"

He swung away from her. "You know not of what you speak."

"I know that people have died to hold it."

He spun back around, seething. "For centuries. You're asking me to walk away from it."

"Yes. I can't live here. I can't make it warm."

All of this nonsense because she was cold, because of a few drafts? "We'll build more fires in the hearths. I'll purchase you heavier clothing."

She rolled her eyes toward the ceiling, looked at the rain slashing against the window. "It's not physical warmth I'm speaking of. It's . . . it's . . . it's love. There's no love here."

How could she not see it? He loved Pembrook with a fierceness that could not be denied. He owed it. It had kept him alive, had kept him surging forward when he'd wanted to retreat. She'd never know how often he'd considered taking an easier path, but always Pembrook beckoned.

As though she read his mind, she said sadly, "This is your mistress, your love. It takes everything from you and leaves nothing for me."

He wanted to deny her words. Instead they only served to inflame his anger. He didn't like that she found him lacking. "Then be gone. Move to one of the other estates that you think will provide you with this warmth you're seeking. Go live with your aunt. Return to your father. My place is here. Nothing will cause me to abandon it."

He spun on his heel and slammed the door on his way out. Stupid woman. How could she not understand what this estate meant to him?

It was everything. Without it, he was nothing.

Theirs had not been a love match. Mary knew she had no right to complain now that her marriage was not all that she'd hoped. After she changed into a simple dress, she pressed her hand to her stomach. She was fairly certain she was with child. If she told Sebastian, would he abandon this fruitless quest? Or would it further ignite his obsession?

She draped her cloak over her shoulders and brought up the hood. She was of a mood to ride. She didn't care that it was near midnight or that the storm was raging or that she would be alone. Because even if Sebastian was with her, she'd still be alone.

He would be thinking of Pembrook while she would be thinking of him.

It seemed improbable that she could love him, but she did. Ironically what caused her to love him were the very things that harped at her and promised an unsatisfactory marriage: his devotion to Pembrook. He was a man capable of enormous love, but only toward things: brick and mortar. Titles and estates. She self-ishly wanted the same level of devotion directed at her.

The servants were all abed. No one was to see her slipping out. She had planned to talk sweetly to any guards who might try to halt her, but she saw no one.

She had a momentary spark of guilt, considered telling Sebastian her plans, but his fury, his parting words had lashed at her. Had proven to her that between them there would never be love.

With the rain pelting her, she walked across the grounds toward the stable. She thought she heard a movement. A cat, a mouse. Night creatures seeking shelter from the storm.

But she feared that for her there was no shelter.

Footsteps sounded, rushing toward her. Sebastian—

He grabbed her, hooked his arm around her throat, cutting off air. She couldn't breathe, couldn't scream. A cloth covered her nose. She recognized the pungent smell from when the physician had tended Sebastian's festering wound: ether. The darkness hovered at the edge of her vision.

"Sleep, Duchess," Lord David murmured. "For a little while at least."

She fought harder to escape his clutches, but she only managed to fall into oblivion.

Sitting at his desk, Sebastian poured more brandy into the glass, downed it, relished the burn. He glanced over to the chair where Mary usually sat, watching him. When his frustration level grew because of lack of success in finding anything that would prove his uncle's machinations, he would look at her and find solace, the strength to carry on. He couldn't imagine her not being there.

He didn't want her to leave, dammit. He shouldn't have challenged her. She was no doubt packing her things now. Perhaps she would only go as far as her father's estate. Then he could ride over to visit with her from time to time. He could share his progress.

He downed more brandy. What did she care of his progress? Had she not made that clear enough?

Were you not listening? he chastised.

He'd been too angry to give credence to her words. How could he make her understand?

He withdrew the pouch from a pocket in his trousers. From the moment he'd poured soil into it and closed it off with Mary's ribbon, it was never far from him. The ribbon curled around his finger. He unfurled it, drew comfort from its tenacity as it wound once more around him. It had faded with time, become worn and frayed, but still it remained steadfast. Like its owner.

Like Mary.

He brought the bundle to his nose, inhaled the rich scent of—

Mary.

It was not the fragrance of rich soil that filled his nostrils, that brought solace. It was a fainter fragrance. A hint of orchid, but more the essence of Mary, trapped in the ribbon that still clung unyieldingly to his fingers.

All these years, she'd been with him. During his darkest moments. During his worst despair. During the long days and nights when death hovered.

Always he had clung to this. A handkerchief given to him by his father. Soil gathered by his own hand. And a ribbon given to him by Mary. Without hesitation. Without question.

He'd fought, battled, schemed. He'd always thought it was Pembrook to which he so desperately wished to return. Pembrook. He'd thought it everything. Only now did he realize—

The crash of breaking glass shattered his thoughts. Glancing over, he saw a stone resting on the carpet. Around it was tied a ribbon. Mary's ribbon. The one she wore when she was of a mind not to take the time to pin up her hair.

His gut clenched with foreboding. He rose with such force that the chair tumbled backward. He snatched up the rock. Paper was wedged between the stone and ribbon. The knotted ribbon would not give way to his clumsy fingers.

Fingers he realized that were trembling.

He rushed to the desk, grabbed the letter opener, and used it to slice free the ribbon. The paper fluttered down. He grabbed it, unfolded it, and stared at the familiar penmanship.

> *Admire the work you've done on the tower. Shall make it so much easier for your wife to fling herself off of it.*
> *Tell no one or she will fall to her death.*
> *Come alone or she will fall to her death.*
> *Bring no weapon or she will fall to her death.*
> *You have ten minutes to join me here or she will fall to her death.*
>
> *Your beloved uncle*

Sebastian took little time to prepare. He grabbed his greatcoat and slipped it on as he charged through the door into the courtyard.

He looked up at the tower. He'd managed to knock

down a portion of the wall, but not all of it. Through the opening he'd created—an opening large enough for a person to stand in—he saw Mary at its edge, her skirt billowing in the wind. Lightning flashed, and he saw her more clearly. Saw that she was not there by choice, that a man held her.

Dread slammed into Sebastian. He'd hoped to see something different, even knowing that he wouldn't. Was that not the purpose of hope? To give a person a reason to carry on, even when all was lost?

How she would chastise him if she thought for a moment that he had given up. All his life—even when he'd thought her absent—she'd been there urging him on. And now he was in danger of losing her.

Unmercifully the rain pelted the stone, slashed sideways, drenched her, no doubt soaked the stone floor, making it slick. How easy it would be for her to slip out.

To fall an incredible distance and to land in a crumpled heap. Broken. Dead. Gone from his life when she'd only just truly returned to it. They had been strangers, cautiously waltzing around each other, until the night he'd begun destroying the tower. Something had happened that night. Something had shifted within him. She, with so little force, had knocked down the walls to his heart.

He'd just failed to let her know it. That was the reason she'd lashed out at him tonight. Because she didn't know what he felt.

He would not survive losing her. He knew that now. He could give up Pembrook. He could give up his titles. But he couldn't give up her. Never her.

He bounded across the green to the looming tower, through its door, and up the stairs. At fourteen, he'd been terrified of what might happen when he reached the top but he'd carried on because he was the duke.

He was more terrified now, but he raced up them because of what might happen to Mary if he didn't.

At the top, the door was ajar in dark invitation, awaiting him. It seemed only appropriate that what had begun here, should end here. In that room, he'd learned there were more things to fear than the dark. At this moment, the terror of what he might lose sent shudders through him. But he couldn't let his vulnerabilities show. For Mary's sake, he had to be stronger and more courageous than he'd ever been in his entire life. Considering the challenges he'd faced, that was saying a lot.

Taking a deep shuddering breath, he marched into the room. He should have accomplished more here. Should have hired men to help him tear it down, brick by brick. Just as Mary had suggested. She was so wise, so thoughtful. He relied on her counsel, yet had seemed to ignore it of late. Whatever had possessed him to discount her?

The lantern set on the table provided enough light for him to see that his uncle held Mary close, the end of a pistol's barrel tucked up against her chin, causing her head to tilt back at an awkward angle. He knew the direction the ball would travel through her, knew she would be dead before it finished its journey.

She looked limp and appeared to be struggling to keep her eyes open. "Don't give into his demands," she slurred. "Don't let him have Pembrook. He doesn't deserve it."

"Shut up, girl," his uncle warned, shoving the barrel in deeper, forcing her head even further back.

"What did you do to her?" he asked.

"Bit of ether to subdue her."

He needed to stall for a bit of time so she could

regain her wits in case his plan didn't work and she needed to make a run for it. "Interesting scar on your cheek, Uncle."

His face twitched and Sebastian thought he wanted to rub it but in order to do that he'd have to release his hold on Mary. "Damned signet ring," he muttered.

"You were the one who attacked me at the Weatherlys'. Do you intend to murder us all?" he asked.

"Accidents. I cannot control accidents. Or a distraught soldier wanting to kill a coward. Or ruffians who have a score to settle with someone from the darker parts of London."

"You hired the men who attacked Rafe?"

"Of course I did. Fools. Not as skilled as they advertised."

You underestimated Rafe, he thought, and wondered exactly how Rafe had acquired his talents.

"Do you not think suspicions will be aroused when we all meet untimely ends?" he asked.

"Suspicion is not proof of evil deeds done. If it were, half the men I know would be sitting in Newgate."

If they were his acquaintances, they probably should be.

"But your death will be the most dramatic," his uncle said. "Your wife went completely mad, shot you, and in her grief over killing you, threw herself from the tower."

"You do have an imagination. The makings of a macabre novel. But you don't have to kill Mary. You only need to kill me."

"And leave her as a witness to tell the world what I did?"

"She was a witness before and she kept it all to herself."

It was difficult to tell in the dim light but he thought his uncle paled. Lightning flashed, eerily illuminating him.

"What did she witness?"

"She overheard you tell someone to kill the lads in the tower."

He laughed, a mad sort of sound that echoed between the stone walls. "She's the one who knocked out the guard, unlocked the door. I should have known. I thought it was the stable boy. He even confessed before he died in the dungeon."

Sebastian's stomach roiled. "You tortured him?"

"The guard said it was someone small. The lad was small."

"And no one noticed that you killed him?"

"He was a stable boy. I told the servants that my nephews must have inspired him because he ran off. Why would they think I lied?"

"And the man who was to kill us?"

"I sent him to find you. He failed. Hanged himself."

"I suppose you helped him along."

He smiled cunningly. "I did. Big fellow. Hurt my back hauling him around. It's still bothersome."

"And did you help Father along as well?"

He chuckled darkly. "Do you want a confession?"

"I want to die knowing the truth."

"The truth. I loved her. You should have been my son."

Her? His son? Sebastian thought of his mother's portraits still hanging in the manor. Mary had thought it odd. "You loved my mother."

"I loved her with all my heart. Your father was duke by then. Keswick wanted to approve her before I asked for her hand in marriage. So she and her family came here for a country party in the fall. Your father strode into the room and conquered her with little more than a smile. They were married by Christmas. He only took her because I wanted her."

Sebastian had been only four when she died. Yet he knew without doubt that his father loved her. With all his heart. He always spoke of her with reverence and adoration.

"I left. For years I lost myself in wine and women. Then I came to my senses. I knew if I ever wanted to find love again, I needed to be a duke. So I killed your father easily enough. But then you and your brothers ran off. And I had to *wait* to make a bid for the title so suspicions would be few. Then I met Lucretia. She wanted a duke. She wanted me! But then you came back. I can only have her if I have the title."

"I understand the power of love, Uncle. What it will make men do. Take me, but let Mary and my brothers live."

"Sebastian, no," she pleaded.

"Mary," he ground out, glaring at her, wishing he had time to tell her everything. All that he felt, all that he realized too late. "You will do as I say. As I desire."

"Your brothers will seek revenge," Lord David said derisively.

"No. Neither of them cares about the titles or the estates. They've made lives for themselves apart from all this. I've written them a letter. It's on my desk. Mary will take it to them. It instructs Tristan to set sail with Mary and Rafe. They'll get word back to England that the ship sank, and that they're dead."

His uncle laughed. "You truly believe they'll do this, give all this up?"

"Neither of them wants it. They never have. It's

always been only me. I am all that stands between you and the title."

"Sebastian, no!" Mary shouted.

His uncle shook her, and Sebastian held his breath. If the pistol went off, all this would be for nothing. All the pain he'd endured, all the suffering . . . for nothing.

"Who'd have thought you'd be so clever?" his uncle asked.

"But you release Mary now."

His uncle studied him, and he saw the pistol lower a small fraction. "You must think me a fool to believe such a poppycock scheme."

"I swear it on my father's grave. And do you know why I will do this?" His hand was in the pocket of his greatcoat, his fingers curled around the handkerchief, the ribbon wound around his finger. He removed the bundle—

"What the hell?" his uncle shouted, pointed the pistol at him—

Mary screamed and shoved at his arm—

Using the only weapon he had, Sebastian slung the linen bundle toward his uncle to distract him as he lunged—

An explosion ripped through the night. Something scalded his arm.

He saw his uncle duck to avoid the soaring object, lose his balance, his feet slipping out from beneath him—

"Mary!" Sebastian yelled.

She was in the path of his flailing uncle, caught in the maelstrom, her arms windmilling—

Sebastian reached out, snaked an arm around her, jerked her into the curve of his body as he flung himself to the side, and crashed into the wall, plummeted to the floor, Mary sprawled over him. He heard his uncle's high-pitched shriek, saw the look of terror on his face as he disappeared over the ledge.

It seemed as though everything had happened within the space of an eternity, but he knew it could not have been more than a few seconds. There had been no time for thought or planning. Only reaction. Only instinct.

He was shaking badly, as though he'd been dunked in a river of ice. Mary was trembling as well and weeping.

"You fool! You shouldn't have come here," she cried.

"I couldn't leave you to him."

She lifted herself up and stared down on him. He could see her tear-stained face. "Did you really think he'd believe that hogwash about a letter to your brothers?"

He threaded his fingers through her hair. "I spoke true, Mary. I was going to explain to him why . . . show him the soil that I had carried with me for so long." He swallowed hard. She deserved to know what he only just realized, sitting in his library, when he knew he had a true chance of losing her. "The bundle of Pembrook soil that I took with me, held secure with your ribbon . . . during the worst times, whenever I doubted what I endured would be worth it, I would take it out, hold it to my nose, and smell home. Always, always the richness of Pembrook filled my nostrils. But I only just realized that it wasn't the dirt that spurred me on. It was your scent, trapped in the ribbon, the ribbon that always curled around my finger. You were always with me, Mary."

More tears welled in her eyes, but they were not the tears of anger or fear. But tears of wonder.

"I kissed you that night in the garden, knowing what it might cost you, but fearing more what I would lose if

I didn't. Forgive me, Mary, for the selfish bastard I am. I didn't recognize why I couldn't let you go. I only knew that I couldn't."

"Do you know now?" she rasped.

He nodded. "It was never the soil, it was never Pembrook."

"What wasn't?"

"What I so desperately wanted to return to. It was you. It was always you. I love you, Mary. With all my heart. I'll tear down the castle. I'll build you a proper manor. We'll move to one of the other estates. I don't care. Just don't leave me. Please don't leave me. My life is nothing without you."

She wept all the harder, burying her face against his throat. He felt her tears scalding his skin.

"I'll never leave you," she rasped. "I've loved you for so long. The boy you were. The man you are. We've lost so much time. I don't want to lose any more."

He threaded his fingers into her hair, lifted her slightly so he could gaze into her eyes.

"No more moments lost, Mary. Not between us."

Chapter 30

It was a beautiful day. Sebastian couldn't remember a day when the sun had been so warm. The breeze toyed with the leaves in the trees. The sky had never been a brighter blue. It was as though all of nature celebrated the demise of Lord David Easton.

Tristan and Rafe had arrived the evening before. They agreed with his decision not to lay their uncle to rest in the family crypt. Instead he was to be buried in a churchyard in a nearby village. It was a peaceful, quiet place, too good for him. But Sebastian was weary of dealing with guilt. He could show mercy in this one regard.

He had informed Lady Lucretia of his uncle's passing. She sent a lock of hair to be buried with him, but indicated no other desire to mourn him.

His brothers stood with him at the graveside. Although ladies generally didn't attend funerals, Mary was there to hold his hand and lend him strength.

The vicar's words were short and concise. "May God have mercy on his soul."

The plain wooden coffin was lowered into the ground. As two custodians began to shovel dirt into the grave, Sebastian and the others turned and began walking toward the waiting carriage.

"What of his wife?" Tristan asked.

"I've made arrangements for her," Sebastian said. "A monthly stipend. She shouldn't be punished for youthful bad judgment."

As they neared the open carriage, Sebastian said, "I need a moment with Rafe alone."

He knew he could possibly find a time alone with him back at Pembrook. But he wanted neutral ground. And calm filled his soul here.

Mary gave him a soft smile and a peck on the cheek before walking off with Tristan.

"Trust her with a man that none of the mothers in London would trust their daughters with?" Rafe asked. Other than a slight limp when he walked with the aid of a cane, he showed no outward evidence that he'd had an encounter with his uncle's villainy. Sebastian's arm was in a sling as it recovered from the bullet that had passed through his muscle.

"I'd trust him with my life. Just as I do you."

Rafe seemed taken aback. He glanced down at his polished boots.

"Rafe, I know I should have taken you with me. I would ask you to forgive me for leaving you behind," Sebastian said quietly.

Rafe lifted his head, studying him for a moment as though judging his sincerity, then nodded. "Consider it done."

"That easily?" Sebastian asked, unconvinced.

"I blamed you when I should have been blaming Uncle. He's dead. Let the past be buried with him."

"I do hope someday you'll tell me what happened with you during all those years we were away."

"Someday, perhaps. Although I wouldn't hold your breath waiting for it."

Sebastian nodded. He'd have to be content with that.

As he and Rafe began walking toward the carriage to join the others, Rafe said, "Something seems different about Pembrook."

"It's once again a place of love."

"Love Mary do you then?"

"I always have."

"This evening, dress in your finest evening gown," her husband had told her an hour earlier. "I am of a mind to have a very formal dinner."

No company he assured her. Only the two of them. His plans coincided well with hers, because she was of a mind to tell him that she was with child. It chilled her to the bone when she realized that if Lord David had killed her, he'd have killed her child as well.

It had been two weeks since that awful night when Lord David had dragged her up to the tower. She awoke often with nightmares, the sound of the gun's report echoing between the stone, the look of desperation on Sebastian's face when he reached for her, his cry, "Noooo!"

He remembered screaming her name, but little beyond that. She recalled it all, every horrifying second, when she thought she would plummet to her death, when his arm snared her from the opening, when he threw them back, twisting his body so he was beneath her, cushioning her landing.

His blood, her tears, his heartfelt words. How they held each other in bed that night and every night since. The one thing they'd not done was make love. It was enough to hold each other near, to listen to each other breathing. To awaken in the throes of a nightmare and to feel his lips brush across her brow as he whispered soothing words.

"It's all right. Everything's all right now."

His arm was healing. Today was the first that he'd been able to manage without the sling. She'd caught him a couple of times testing it, extending it, nodding as though satisfied with his efforts. She'd been so afraid he'd lose the arm, when he'd lost so much.

She gazed at her reflection in the cheval glass. She wore her pale pink gown with the dark green velvet trim. At her throat was the emerald the lords of Pembrook had given her.

A light knock sounded on the door and Colleen opened it.

"Is she ready?" an impatient voice asked in a low whisper.

"Yes, Your Grace."

Mary walked across the room, stepped into the hallway, and smiled. "You must be hungry."

"For the sight of you."

Poetry from her nonpoetic husband. Oh, and he did look handsome, although she knew he wouldn't believe her if she said the words. He was freshly shaven, his hair styled to perfection. He faced her squarely, his eyepatch giving him a rakishness that set her heart to fluttering. He wore an unbuttoned black swallow-tailed jacket with black trousers and a pristine white shirt. His vest and cravat were gray. Where a pocket watch would be housed was a small lump that she knew was the soil he'd carried with him, wrapped in her ribbon.

"You're so beautiful," he said with appreciation.

"You must not believe these are merely words, because they carry the weight of my heart," she said. "To me, you are truly handsome."

He smiled, a true smile that touched his gaze, and although only one side of his face curved up, the other too burdened by scars, it was enough. "As I have said before, you are mad."

His tone was light and teasing and it lifted her spirits.

He extended his arm. "Shall we?"

She wound her arm through his. "Your arm has healed?"

"Almost completely," he said as they descended the stairs. "A few twinges here and there."

"I thought we might have your brothers here for Christmas."

"I would like that. Perhaps while they are here we shall have a portrait done."

"I am not having a portrait done with Tristan."

"I want one of you and me," he said quietly. "And one of my brothers. They will not be us as boys. Those portraits are gone forever I fear, but Tristan has heard of a rather good artist who goes by the name of Leo. Word is that he has a talent for capturing on canvas a person's heart. Perhaps he can portray me with kindness."

"If he is half as good as claimed, and he sees what I see, I believe you will be most pleased."

They reached the foyer and he escorted her down a hallway.

"This is not the way to the dining room," she pointed out.

"I'm quite familiar with the layout of the residence."

"Then why would you take a wrong turn?"

"Not a wrong turn. I have something in mind before dinner."

He approached a set of double doors guarded by two liveried footmen. It led into the largest salon in the residence, where grand balls had once been held.

"Sebastian—"

"Shh."

The footman opened the doors. When Mary and Sebastian stepped through, music began to play. Her eyes widened at the sight. A small orchestra sat in the balcony. A half dozen chandeliers hung from the ceiling. Every candle in every one was flickering. There had to have been over a hundred. The room was alight as no other in the residence had ever been. A mirrored wall reflected the polished floor and the flowers arranged around the outer edges. Nothing else was in the room. No furniture.

"Will you honor me with a dance, Mary Easton, Duchess of Keswick?"

Tears stung her eyes, but before she could answer he was sweeping her over the dance floor.

"However did you manage this?"

"With a good deal of help from my brothers and your father. The orchestra traveled from London and stayed with him until I was ready for them."

"I love waltzing with you," she told him. He was a marvelous dancer when he had the room in which to move.

"I thought if we practiced, by next Season I might not make such a mess of it."

"We don't have to go to London. We can stay here if you prefer."

"I will have a seat in the House of Lords. I cannot shirk my responsibilities. Besides, my wife once told me that she loves the glitz and glitter that is London."

He swirled her from one side of the room to the other. She caught their reflection and thought she'd never seen a happier couple.

"And the timing will work out well," he continued. "I'm having this residence razed come spring."

He had mentioned doing so before but she'd thought it was only the emotion of the moment. "I told you it's not necessary."

The final strains of the melody faded and another began before they could even take a breath.

"I think it is. This house is . . . cold. You were right about that."

"But it's your legacy. You were correct about that."

He smiled, and she thought she'd never tire of seeing his mouth curve up. When they were aged and glancing at each other across a room, still he would have the ability to cause her heart to soar. "I want something here that is not tarnished by hatred or jealousy or murder. We'll hire an architect and he'll design whatever you wish: small or large. I care not. The land holds the history of Pembrook, not the brick and stone. We'll build a new legacy for my heir."

She released a quiet breath. "He may be here sooner than you think."

He stopped as though he'd rammed into a wall. His gaze dropped to her stomach. "Are you?"

With tears in her eyes she nodded. "Yes."

He knelt before her and pressed a kiss to her waist. "It will be a boy."

"I feel that way as well, but if it's not—"

"No matter. She will ride across the dales as though she was born to them. And a brother will someday follow in her wake."

He brought himself to his feet and lifted her into his arms. The orchestra continued to play as he strode from the room.

"Are you carrying me to dinner?" she asked.

"To bed. Tonight, Mary, I'm going to make love to you."

"You always did. I don't need the words."

"But I want you to have them. Every day, for as long as we breathe."

Epilogue

He waited for the dark of the moon. Call him superstitious, but it seemed important that what he wanted to do should take place on an eve when there was no moon. Just as there had been no moon on that fateful night so many years before.

Mary rode beside him, as she had so long ago. Only he held the lantern. What an unchivalrous cad he was to have not thought to take it from her before.

He had hired architects to design the new manor house. It would be built on top of a rise and look out over all the land where the Dukes of Keswick had once ridden. Where the present duke now rode beside the lady he loved. The one he *had* always loved. The one he *would* always love.

"Are you lost?" she asked.

He laughed. God, but it felt good to laugh. "Not anymore. Not with you at my side."

With the light from the lantern, he could see her

smile. She knew what he was saying. She gave him purpose. She was his lodestar, his compass, his true north.

"Be that as it may, we have been traveling in circles for almost an hour now."

"I can't find it," he admitted, disappointed with the truth. He'd thought he'd never forget a single moment of that night. Perhaps it was a good thing that some of the memories were fading away, to make room for better ones.

"Find what?" she asked.

"Do you remember that night when I asked you to stop, and I gathered up the soil?" He didn't wait for her to answer. It was a rhetorical question. Of course she remembered. "I was looking for that spot."

"I think we've gone too far south."

"I was thinking we hadn't gone far enough."

"Is it important?"

"I thought it was. But now I realize it's not. This place will do just as well." He extended the lantern. "Will you hold the light?"

She took it from him. He dismounted and knelt between their horses.

"What are you doing?" she asked.

"Returning the soil to the land."

"Are you sure you should do this? You kept it with you for so long."

"I'll keep the ribbon. I intend to thread it through my watch chain."

"Help me down so I can be there with you."

He did as she asked. Then crouching, he very gingerly untied the ribbon and unfolded the handkerchief. She knelt beside him and watched as he sprinkled the soil over the grass.

"I'm not certain you should have done that."

"I am." He took the lantern from her and set it on the ground. Then he brought her to her feet and splayed his fingers over her stomach, where their child grew, one who would one day gallop his horse over the soil as his ancestors had. "It's where it always belonged. Just as I am where I belong: with you. I love you so much, Mary."

Reaching up, she cradled his face. "I love you, Sebastian. With all my heart, with all I am."

Taking her into his arms, he lowered his mouth to hers and kissed her deeply.

The ghosts from the past no longer whispered to him. All he heard was her sweet sigh.

All he knew was that when he was with her, he was as whole as any man had ever been.

*If you loved SHE TEMPTS THE DUKE
and want to read another passionate,
heartrending story about a devilish Lord
prepared to fight for his title,
turn the page for a sneak peek at*
New York Times *bestselling author
Sarah MacLean's*
A ROGUE BY ANY OTHER NAME

*On Sale March 2012
Avon Books*

BOURNE

London
Winter 1822

The eight of diamonds ruined him.

If it had been the six, he might have saved himself. If it had been the seven, he would have walked away with triple his holdings.

But it was the eight.

The young Marquess of Bourne watched the card fly across the lush green baize and slide into place next to the seven of clubs that lay face up on the table, teasing him. His eyes were already closing, the air was already leaving the room in a single, unbearable rush.

Vingt et deux.

One more than the *vingt et un* on which he had wagered.

On which he had wagered everything.

There was a collective gasp in the room as he stayed

the movement of the card with the tip of one finger—as bystanders watched the horror unfold with the keen pleasure of those who had narrowly escaped their own demise.

The chatter started then.

"He wagered it all?"

"Everything that wasn't entailed."

"Too young to know better."

"Old enough now; nothing makes a man faster than this."

"He's really lost all of it?"

"Everything."

His eyes opened, focusing on the man across the table, meeting the cold grey gaze he had known his whole life. Viscount Langford had been a friend and neighbor to his father, handpicked by the former Marquess of Bourne as guardian to his only son and heir. After Bourne's parents' death, it had been Langford who had protected the Marquessate of Bourne, who had increased its holdings tenfold, ensured its prosperity.

And then taken it.

Neighbor, perhaps. Never friend.

Betrayal scorched through the young marquess. "You did this on purpose." For the first time in his twenty-one years, he heard the youth in his voice. Hated it.

There was no emotion on his opponent's face as he lifted the mark from the center of the table. Bourne resisted the urge to wince at the dark scrawl of his signature across the white page—proof that he'd lost everything.

"It was your choice. Your choice to wager more than you were willing to lose."

He'd been fleeced. Langford had pressed him again and again, pushing him farther and farther, letting him win until he couldn't imagine losing. It was an age-old play, and he'd been too young to see it. Bourne lifted his gaze, anger and frustration nearly choking the words. "And your choice to win it."

"Without me, there would have been nothing to win," the older man said.

"Father." Thomas Alles, the viscount's son and Bourne's closest friend, stepped forward, his voice shaking in indignation. "Don't do this."

Langford took his time folding the mark and rising from the table, ignoring his son. Instead, he leveled Bourne with a cool look. "You should thank me for teaching you such a valuable lesson at such a young age. Unfortunately, now you've nothing but the clothes on your back and a manor house empty of its contents."

The viscount cast a glance at the pile of coins on the table—the remainder of his winnings from the evening. "I shall leave you the money, how's that? A parting gift, if you will. After all, what would your father say if I left you with nothing?"

Bourne shot up from his chair, knocking it back from the table. "You aren't fit to speak of my father."

Langford raised an eyebrow at the uncontrolled display, and he let silence reign for a long moment. "You know, I believe I shall take the money after all. And your membership to this club. It is time for you to leave."

Bourne's cheeks flamed as the words washed over him. His club membership. His land, servants, horses, clothes, everything. Everything but a house, a few acres of land, and a title.

A title now in disgrace.

The viscount lifted one side of his mouth in a mocking smile and flipped a guinea through the air toward Bourne who instinctively reached out, catching the gold coin as it glinted in the bright lights of White's card room. "Spend it wisely, boy. It's the last you'll have from me."

"Father," Tommy tried again.

Langford turned on him. "Not another word. I won't have you begging for him."

Bourne's oldest friend turned sad eyes on him, lifting his hands in a sign of helplessness. Tommy needed his father. Needed his money. His support.

Things Bourne no longer had himself.

Hatred flared hot and bright for the briefest of moments, before it was gone, extinguished by cold resolve, and Bourne placed the coin in his pocket and turned his back on his peers, his club, his world, and the life he had always known.

Vowing revenge.

Early January 1831

He did not move when he heard the door to the private room open and close quietly behind him.

He stood in the darkness, silhouetted by the painted window overlooking the main room of London's most exclusive gaming hell. From the club floor, the window appeared as nothing but a stunning work of art—a massive piece of stained glass depicting the fall of Lucifer. In brilliant hues, the enormous angel—six times the size of the average man—tumbled toward the pit floor, cast into London's dark corners by Heaven's Army.

The Fallen Angel.

A reminder, not simply of the name of the club, but of the risk that those who entered took as they set their marks to the plush baize, as they lifted the ivory dice, as they watched the roulette wheel turn in a blur of color and temptation.

And when The Angel won, as it always did, the glass reminded those who lost of how far they had fallen.

Bourne's gaze flickered to a piquet table at the far end of the pit. "Croix wants his line increased."

The pit manager did not move from his place just inside the door to the owners' suite. "Yes."

"He owes more than he will ever be able to repay."

"Yes."

Bourne turned his head, meeting the shadowed gaze of his most trusted employee. "What is he willing to place against an extended line?"

"Two hundred acres in Wales."

Bourne watched the lord in question, who was sweating and twitching nervously as he waited for judgment to be passed.

"Extend the line. When he loses, see him out. His membership is revoked."

His decisions were rarely questioned, and never by the staff of The Angel. The other man headed for the door as quietly as he had entered. Before he could leave, Bourne said, "Justin."

Silence.

"The land first."

The soft click of door meeting jamb was the only indication that the pit manager had been there at all.

Moments later, he came into view on the floor below and Bourne watched the signal travel from boss to dealer. He watched as the hand was dealt, as the earl lost. Again.

And again.

And once more.

There were those who did not understand.

Those who had not gambled—who had not felt the thrill of winning—who had not negotiated with themselves for one more round, one more hand, one more shot—*just until he hit one hundred, one thousand, ten thousand* . . .

Those who had not known the luscious, euphoric, unparalleled feeling of knowing that a table was hot, that a night was theirs, that with a single card, everything could change.

They would never understand what kept the Earl of Croix in his chair, betting over and over and over again, fast as lightning, until he'd lost everything. Again. As though nothing he had wagered had ever been his to begin with.

Bourne understood.

Justin approached Croix and spoke discreetly into the ruined man's ear. The peer shot to his unsteady feet, outrage furrowing his brow as anger and embarrassment propelled him toward the pit managers.

A mistake.

Bourne could not hear what was said. He did not need to. He'd heard it hundreds of times before— watched as a long list of men had lost first their money, then their temper with The Angel. With him.

He watched Justin step forward, hands raised in the universal sign of caution. Watched as the pit manager's lips moved, attempting—and failing—to settle and calm. Watched as other players took note of the commotion and as Temple, Bourne's massive partner, took notice as well and headed into the fray, eager for a fight.

Bourne moved then, reaching toward the wall and pulling a switch, activating a complex combination of pulleys and levers, triggering a small bell beneath the piquet table and drawing the attention of the dealer.

Notifying him that Temple would not have his fight that evening.

Bourne would have it instead.

The dealer stayed Temple's impossible strength with a word and a nod toward the wall where Bourne and Lucifer watched, each willing to face whatever came next.

Temple's black gaze fell on the glass, and he nodded once before leading Croix through the throngs of people below.

Bourne descended from the owners' suite to meet them in a small antechamber set apart from the main floor of the club. Croix was cursing like a dockside sailor when Bourne opened the door and stepped inside. He rounded on Bourne, gaze narrowed with hatred.

"You bastard. You can't do this to me. Can't take what is mine."

Bourne leaned back against the thick oak door, crossing his arms. "You dug your grave, Croix. Go home. Be thankful I don't take more than my due."

Croix lunged across the small room before he had a chance to reconsider, and Bourne moved with an agility that few ever expected, clasping one of the earl's arms and twisting them both until Croix's face was pressed firmly against the door. Bourne shook the lean man once, twice before saying, "Think very carefully about your next action. I find I am not feeling so magnanimous as I was mere moments ago."

"I want to see Chase." The words were slurred against the oak.

"Instead, you'll see us."

"I've been a member of The Angel since the beginning. You owe me. *He* owes me."

"On the contrary, it is *you* who owes *us*."

"I've given enough money to this place . . ."

"How generous of you. Shall we call for the book

and see how much you still owe?" Croix went still. "Ah. I see you are beginning to understand. The land is ours now. You send your solicitor round in the morning with the deed, or I come looking for you myself. Is that clear?" Bourne did not wait for an answer, instead stepping back and releasing the earl. "Get out."

Croix turned to face them, panic in his gaze. "Keep the land, Bourne. But not the membership . . . don't take the membership. I'm a half a tick away from marrying. Her dowry will cover all my losses and more. Don't take the membership."

Bourne hated the keening plea, the undercurrent of anxiety in the words. He knew that Croix couldn't resist the urge to wager. The temptation to win.

If Bourne had an ounce of compassion in him, he'd feel sorry for the unsuspecting girl.

But compassion was not a trait Bourne claimed.

Croix turned wide eyes on Temple. "Temple. Please."

One of Temple's black brows rose as he crossed his massive arms across his wide chest. "With such a generous dowry, I'm sure one of the lower hells will welcome you."

Of course they would. The lower hells—filled with murderers and cheats—would welcome this insect of a man and his terrible luck with open arms.

"Bollocks the lower hells," Croix spat. "What will people think? What will it take? I'll pay double . . . triple. She's plenty of money."

Bourne was nothing if not a businessman. "You marry the girl and pay your debts, with interest, and we shall reinstate your membership."

"What do I do until then?" The sound of the earl's whine was unpleasant.

"You might try temperance," Temple offered, casually.

Relief made Croix stupid. "You're one to talk. Everyone knows what you did."

Temple stilled, his voice filled with menace. "And what was that?"

Terror removed the minimal intelligence from the earl's instincts, and he threw a punch at Temple, who caught the blow in one enormous fist and pulled the smaller man toward him with wicked intent.

"What was that?" he repeated.

The earl began to mewl like a babe. "N-nothing. I'm sorry. I didn't mean it. Please don't hurt me. Please don't kill me. I'll leave. Now. I swear. Please . . . d-don't hurt me."

Temple sighed. "You're a not worth my energy." He released the earl.

"Get out," Bourne said, "before I decide that you *are* worth mine."

The earl fled the room.

Bourne watched him go before adjusting the line of his waistcoat and straightening his frock coat. "I thought he might soil himself when you took hold of him."

"He would not be the first." Temple sat in a low chair and stretched his legs out in front of him, crossing one booted ankle over the other. "I wondered how long it would take you."

Bourne brushed a hand across the half-inch linen cuff that peeked out from underneath his coat, making certain the swath of white fabric was even before returning his attention to Temple and pretending not to understand the question. "To do what?"

"To restore your clothing to perfection." One side of Temple's mouth curled in a mocking smile. "You're like a woman."

Bourne leveled the enormous man with a look. "A woman with an extraordinary right hook."

The smile became a grin, the expression showing off Temple's nose, broken and healed in three places. "You aren't honestly suggesting that you could beat me in battle, are you?"

Bourne was assessing the condition of his cravat in a nearby mirror. "I'm suggesting precisely that."

"May I invite you into the ring?"

"Anytime."

"No one is getting into the ring. Certainly not with Temple." Bourne and Temple turned toward the words, spoken from a hidden door at the far end of the room, where Chase, the third partner in The Fallen Angel, watched them.

Temple laughed at the words and turned to face Bourne. "You see? Chase knows enough to admit that you're no match for me."

Chase poured a glass of scotch from a decanter on a nearby sideboard. "It has nothing to do with Bourne. You're built like a stone fortress. No one is a match for you." The words turned wry. "No one but me, that is."

Temple leaned back in his chair. "Anytime you'd like to meet me in the ring, Chase, I shall clear my schedule."

Chase turned to Bourne. "You've paupered Croix."

He stalked the perimeter of the room. "Like sweets from a babe."

"Five years in business, and I remain surprised by these men and their weakness."

"Not weakness. Illness. The desire to win is a fever."

Chase's brows rose at the metaphor. "Temple is right. You are a woman."

Temple barked in laughter and stood, all six and a half feet of him. "I have to get back to the floor."

Chase watched Temple cross the room, headed for the door. "Haven't had your brawl tonight?"

He shook his head. "Bourne snatched it out from under me."

"There's still time."

"A man can hope." Temple left the room, the door closing firmly behind him, and Chase moved to pour another glass of scotch, walking it to where Bourne stood staring intently into the fireplace. He accepted the offering, taking a large swallow of the golden liquor, enjoying the way it burned his throat.

"I have news for you." Bourne turned his head, waiting. "News of Langford."

The words washed over him. For nine years, he'd been waiting for this precise moment, for whatever it was that would come spilling from Chase's mouth next. For nine years, he'd been waiting for news of this man who had stripped him of his past, his birthright.

His history.

Everything.

Langford had taken it all that night, all the lands, the funds, everything but an empty manor house and a handful of acres of land at the center of a larger estate—Falconwell. As he'd watched it all slip away, Bourne hadn't understood the older man's motives— hadn't known the pleasure of turning an estate into a living, thriving thing. Hadn't understood how much it would smart to turn it over to a mere boy.

Now, a decade later, he did not care.

He wanted his revenge.

The revenge he'd been waiting for.

It had taken nine years, but Bourne had rebuilt his fortune—doubled it. The money from the partnership in The Angel, along with several lucrative investments, had given him the opportunity to build an estate that rivaled the most extravagant in England.

But he'd never been able to reclaim what he'd lost. Langford had kept it all in a tight grip, unwilling to sell it, no matter how much he was offered, no matter how powerful the man who offered. And very powerful men had offered.

Until now.

"Tell me."

"It is complicated."

Bourne turned back to the fire. "It always is." But he hadn't worked every day to build his fortune for land in Wales and Scotland and Devonshire and London.

He'd done it for Falconwell.

One thousand acres of lush green land that had once been the pride of the Marquessate of Bourne. The land that his father and grandfather and great-grandfather had amassed around the manor house, which had been passed down from marquess to marquess.

"What?" He saw the answer in Chase's eyes before the words came, and he swore once, long and wicked. "What has he done with it?"

Chase hesitated.

"If he's made it impossible, I'll kill him."

As I should have done years ago.

"Bourne . . ."

"No." He slashed one hand through the air. "I've waited for this for *nine years*. He took everything from me. *Everything.* You have no idea."

Chase's gaze found his. "I have every idea."

Bourne stopped at that, at the understanding in the words. At the truth in them. It had been Chase who had pulled him from his lowest moment. Chase who had taken him in, cleaned him up, given him work. Chase who had rescued him.

Or, who had at least tried to rescue him.

"Bourne," Chase began, the words laced with caution. "He didn't keep it."

A cold dread settled deep within. "What do you mean, he didn't keep it?"

"Langford no longer owns the land in Surrey."

He shook his head, as though he could force understanding. "Who owns it?"

"The Marquess of Needham and Dolby."

A decades-old memory flashed at the name—a portly man, rifle in hand, marching across a muddy field in Surrey, trailed by a gaggle of girls sized small to smallest, the leader of whom had the most serious blue gaze Bourne had ever met.

His childhood neighbors, the third family in the holy trinity of the Surrey peerage.

"Needham has my land? How did he get it?"

"Ironically, in a game of cards."

Bourne could not find the humor in the fact. Indeed, the idea that Falconwell had been casually wagered and lost in a card came—again—set him on edge.

"Get him here. Needham's game is *écarté*. Falconwell will be mine."

Chase leaned back, surprised. "You would wager for it?"

Bourne's reply was instant. "I will do whatever is required for it."

"*Whatever* is required?"

Bourne was instantly suspicious. "What do you know that I do not?"

Chase's brows shot up. "Why would you think that?"

"You always know more than I know. You enjoy it."

"I merely pay closer attention."

Bourne's teeth clenched. "Be that as it may . . ."

The founder of The Fallen Angel feigned interest in a spot on one sleeve. "The land that was once a part of Falconwell—"

"*My* land."

Chase ignored the interruption. "You cannot simply retrieve it."

"Why not?"

Chase hesitated. "It has been attached to . . . something else."

Cold hatred coursed through Bourne. He'd waited a decade for this—for the moment when he would finally reconnect Falconwell Manor with its lands. "Attached to what?"

"To *whom*, more like."

"I am in no mood for your riddles."

"Needham has announced that the former lands of Falconwell are to be included in the dowry of his eldest daughter."

Shock rocked Bourne back on his heels. "Penelope?"

"You know the lady?"

"It's been years since I saw her last—nearly twenty of them."

Sixteen. She had been there on the day he'd left Surrey for the last time, after his parents' burial, fifteen years old and shipped back to a new world with no family. She'd watched him climb into his carriage, and her serious blue gaze had not wavered in tracking his coach down the long drive away from Falconwell.

She hadn't looked away until he had turned onto the main road.

He knew because he'd watched her, too.

She'd been his friend.

When he had still believed in friends.

She'd also been the eldest daughter of a double marquess with more money than one man could spend in a lifetime. There was no reason for her to have remained a spinster for so long. She should be married with a brood of young aristocrats to care for.

"Why does Penelope need Falconwell for a dowry?" He paused. "Why isn't she married already?"

Chase sighed. "It would serve me well if any one of you would take an interest in Society at large rather than our meager membership."

"Our *meager membership* is more than five hundred men. Every one of them with a file thick as my thumb, filled with information, thanks to your partners."

"Nevertheless, I have better things to do with my evenings than educating you on the world into which you were born."

Bourne's gaze narrowed. He'd never known Chase to spend evenings in any way other than entirely alone. "What things?"

Chase ignored the question and took another pull of scotch. "Lady Penelope made the match of the season years ago."

"And?"

"The engagement was overshadowed by her fiancé's love match."

It was an old tale, one he'd heard countless times, and still Bourne felt an unfamiliar emotion at the idea that the girl he remembered might have been hurt by her broken engagement. "Love match," he scoffed. "A prettier or wealthier prospect more like. And that was it?"

"I am told she has been pursued by several suitors

USA TODAY BESTSELLING AUTHOR

LORRAINE HEATH

She Tempts the Duke

978-0-06-202246-2

Sebastion Easton always vowed he would avenge his stolen youth and title. Now back in London, the rightful Duke of Keswick, he cannot forget the brave girl who once rescued him and his brothers from certain death. But Lady Mary Wynne-Jones is betrothed to another.

Waking Up With the Duke

978-0-06-202245-5

Ransom Seymour, the Duke of Ainsley, owes a debt to a friend. But the payment expected is most shocking, even to an unrepentant rake like him—for he's being asked to provide his friend's exquisite wife with what she most dearly covets: a child.

Pleasures of a Notorious Gentleman

978-0-06-192295-4

A shameless rogue, Stephen Lyons gained a notorious reputation that forced him to leave for the army. Upon his return he is given the opportunity to redeem himself, and Mercy Dawson will risk everything to protect the dashing soldier from the truth that threatens to destroy their growing love.

in the years since. And yet, she remains unmarried."
Chase appeared to be losing interest in the tale, continuing on a bored sigh. "Though I imagine not for
long, with Falconwell to sweeten the honey pot. The
temptation will have suitors swarming."

"They'll want a chance to lord it over me."

"Probably. You are not high on the list of favorite
peers."

"I'm nowhere on the list of favorite peers. Nevertheless, I shall have the land."

"And you are prepared to do what it takes to get it?"
Chase looked amused.

Bourne did not miss his partner's meaning.

A vision flashed of a young, kind Penelope, the opposite of what he was. Of what he'd become.

He pushed it aside. For nine years, he'd been waiting
for this moment. For the chance to restore that which
had been built for him.

That which had been left to him.

That which he had lost.

It was the closest he would ever get to redemption.
And nothing would stand in his way.

"Anything." Bourne stood and carefully straightened his coat. "If a wife comes with it, so be it."

The door slammed shut after him.

Chase toasted the sound and spoke to the empty
room. "Felicitations."